The
Broken
Shield

by

Timothy Reynolds

Second Edition

Cover Art & Design by Timothy Reynolds
Author photo: Cometcatcher Media

First Edition: 2014
Second Edition: 2017
Library and Archives Canada Cataloguing in Publication

Reynolds, Timothy G. M. 1960-
The Broken Shield / Timothy G.M. Reynolds

ISBN: 978-0-9939631-3-1

1. Urban Fantasy.2. Science Fiction. I. Title. II.
Title: The Broken Shield

Cometcatcher Press
Calgary, Alberta. Canada.

**In Memory of Phoenix,
who was very real**
2004-2014

For:

Sue Campbell… without you in my life, this story would never
have been told with as much heart;

For Liam and Teagan Venables.
Happy always-belated birthdays!

~

This book is dedicated to:

The Lost Shields in my life:
Ken Reynolds, George Goodrich, Tracy Gauvreau, Paul Richardson,
Randy Golby, and Maurice 'Skosche' Scott;

and to Craig Venables, best friend and Shield of Light.

~

Special thanks to:

Jennifer Rahn, my primary reader who sliced, diced,
and encouraged this project from Day One;

David B. Coe, who saw something special even in the early drafts;

Danita Maslankowski and Celeste Peters, each for painstakingly going
through the manuscript and giving it much-needed fine-tunings;

Katherine Salter for proofing and critiquing;

Brent Nichols for the line-by-line;

Adrienne Kerr for invaluable guidance;

and the members of the *Imaginative Fiction Writers Association* for
critiques, encouragement, and the write-offs.

~

Table of Contents

On Being a Shield of Light

Here are the words of Shield Master Wei recorded at various times over the centuries by Brother Abiel Lovejoy, and published by **Bone Arrow Press**, behind the Shield Master's back.

"There are certain objects, animate and inanimate, which have been imbued with Light Extraordinaire. They are called Loci, or Locus in the singular. Dark would possess these objets de lumière to keep their Light from the populace and upset the Balance in favour of Chaos. It is the very simple duty of the Shields of Light to keep their Loci safe."
~Shield Master Wei (322 BCE. Circa: breakfast.)

"Shields of Light: they live, they die, they are reborn old souls in new bodies. They are ignorant to their purpose for the first eighteen years of their new lives and then they 'awaken' and know what is required. From time to time over their centuries of lives they may doubt themselves and they may doubt that Light can hold back Dark and maintain Balance, but they are Shields and they know that their purpose is simple—protect the Loci, serve the Light."
~circa 528 CE. While feeding the survivors of the Antioch earthquake.

"Pattern: found in the paths we travel, the associations we make, the actions we take, the communications we produce. Pattern is Life but it is the enemy of the Shields of Light, for it is through Pattern that the Dark finds the Shields and the Balance is upset."
~1886 CE, while soaking in the Banff Hot Springs Reserve.

"Anyone given a dozen lifetimes can learn to be a great leader, but to learn to be a good Shield takes a dozen times a dozen lifetimes because with each lifetime it gets more and more difficult to find the Balance, to avoid habit and comfort, to live a life unique from the previous ones."
~417 CE while hanging laundry out to dry.

Chapter One: Skateboards & Brimstone

Deep sleep, then a small bark.

...a dog?

Harff.

Liam cracked one eye open, the other maintaining a tenuous hold on sleep. A short-legged, tubby, scruffy Yorkshire terrier stood on his chest and grunted softly at him. Liam closed his eye again. His ragged breathing smoothed out so the Yorkie settled down over his heartbeat, with her butt nestled under his grey-and-red whiskered chin. Liam sighed.

"If you actually want me to get up and take you out, sitting on me probably isn't the best move." She didn't move. "All right... five minutes—then you're *off* and I'm *up*. Whatever made me think I'd be allowed to sleep in on my own birthday?" The dog grunted in reply and Liam smiled. It was nearly impossible for him to get angry at Phoenix when all she wanted to do was be close to him. Neither one of them really had anyone else, at least no one else who knew the truth about who they were.

Liam dozed off, reminiscing about the day the two of them had met but voices in the dark nudged him off track. Voices that sounded far off in both space and time. One was shouting and one was obedient, but strong. Both spoke a form of Gaelic rarely heard outside of Faerie, but Liam understood.

"Find them, Dax! Shatter the Shield once and *done*, then bring me the pixie!"

"Yes, m'Lord."

Oberon, King of Faerie? Liam thought so. And the other was probably a bounty hunter. He was sure they were talking about him, but he was too exhausted to care. He drifted deeper into sleep and the voices faded.

oOo

Phoenix actually let Liam have another thirty minutes sleep before she couldn't wait any longer and woke him again, this time with a warm lick on the end of his nose. He shook the sleep off quickly and she scrambled off his chest to let him up. He grabbed his cane with his good right hand and shuffled his way to the apartment's bathroom in silence. Twenty minutes later they were out in the prairie sunshine that warmed the city of Calgary all around them.

Liam tugged a plastic grocery bag out of his pants pocket and stepped off the asphalt path onto the freshly cut grass. He looked down at Phoenix then at the small pile of warm excrement she had just squatted and deposited. "You couldn't have waited until we got closer to home, could you?"

She barked a hoarse little reply at the Shield.

"It's just that next to the bike path—I could get smoked by some Lycra-stretching Yuppy on skinny tires."

Harff.

"Fine. Then just stay put while I figure this out."

Phoenix sat down on the grass, more than happy to rest her short legs. With the plastic bag and the retractable leash in his right hand, Liam tightened his unsteady grip on the wooden cane with his left and began a slow-motion drop to one knee. With a few inches to go, his left arm couldn't take the weight anymore at that angle and he dropped to the grass with a soft thump.

Harff.

"Yah, I'm okay, thanks. At least I didn't land in your little 'deposit', missy." He lay the cane down and went about picking up the crap, using the bag as a glove.

Soft growl.

Liam grabbed the cane near the rubber-tipped end. "How many?"

Harff, Harff.

Locking the leash retractor with his thumb, he left it on the grass so he could brace himself. "Left or right?"

Harff. Harff. Growl.

"Gotcha—one each. No, no magic. Keep out of this, but stay close. I can handle it, I think." Liam could now hear the approaching footsteps as two pairs of rubber-soled shoes scuffed from the grass onto the path behind him. There was a rattle of skateboard wheels against a thigh and then he noticed the sounds of traffic, the river flowing past, and an approaching in-line skater he could see out of the corner of his eye.

"Hey, old man." The voice was young—late-teens, early twenties at most—coming from Liam's left.

"I'm not old," Liam muttered.

"What you say, old man?" From the right. The left was closer, the right was younger, smaller, and fidgety. Probably high. Both males, which would make this both harder and easier.

"Your damned fat rat just crapped where we were gonna sit, dude."

"Our spot, dude. *Our* spot. I ain't sittin' in dog crap or rat crap. Ain't sittin' in *crap*, old man."

Liam started a slow turn to his left. The attack would come from the right, from the more stoned of the two, and he had to find an edge before it happened. "Fifty isn't old, *dude*. And I've already picked up the crap."

"Not good enough, dude."

"Yah, not enough. *Lick* it clean, dude!"

The kid moved in fast to shove Liam down onto the grass but, even 'crippled', Liam was faster. He pivoted left-to-right on his knee, backhanding the cane hard into a teenaged shin, then pulled back and made a fast, solid, upward tap to the kid's temple as the stoned little dumb-ass reached for his shin. The skateboard clattered to the pathway and the amateur predator went down but Liam didn't wait to confirm that he stayed put; instead he dropped forward, facedown on the grass, just as the second skateboard swung at his back. It passed right over top of him and its wielder, caught off balance, stepped closer to Liam to steady himself. Liam rolled over and swung the cane. It caught a wrist and there was a muffled snap. He swung his good foot and hit the kid's knee laterally. He pulled his kick just a bit so as to not ruin the knee for life but the kid still screamed like a six-year-old as he collapsed. Liam thwacked him once in the back of the head and the screaming stopped.

Phoenix scooted out of the way, dragging the blue retractable leash with her as the attacker came down on the bag of fresh, warm, soft crap with a thump. Liam sat up slowly, awkwardly. With effort, he dragged himself up the cane until he was back on one knee. Two older male cyclists pulled up hard, coming to the rescue a bit late.

"You okay, buddy? What the hell happened?"

"I'm good, thanks. They refused to pay for their first lesson in respect so I gave them the second lesson free."

One of the cyclists helped Liam to his feet while the second pulled out a phone and dialled 9-1-1. "Get these little pricks arrested so they won't hurt anyone else. You sure you're okay? It happened so fast I didn't exactly see what happened."

Liam shook his head. "No cops. I'm fine." He whistled softly and Phoenix waddled over, dragging the leash. Liam used his good hand and the crook of the cane to scoop up the retractable leash. "I'm not pressing charges so I'll be on my way. Thanks for the help, fellas." A siren approached, still a long way off, and Liam knew the Samaritan had ignored his request not to call. Damnation. The two men turned back to the downed skateboarders so Liam quit the scene as quickly as he could, Phoenix trotting along beside him.

"How about we cut the walk a bit short, grab the car and go get the grocery shopping out of the way?"

Harff.

"Yes, I'm fine to drive. You just worry about navigating and leave the piloting to me, thank you very much."

oOo

Wallace Tabak winked at Luta, Tau Drake's receptionist, as he strode past her and into her boss' office without knocking. She was twenty-three to his fifty-five, but he knew age was nothing to women who were attracted to power. He also knew from Drake that Luta was one of those women, but when she didn't return his smile, Tabak didn't have time to wonder at her lack of enthusiasm before he was through the portal and into the second most important office in the DökktEfniTækni—DET—complex. The most important, of course, was his own. Or at least it *was* until he saw who was sitting behind Drake's desk. He dropped to one knee and forced his eyes to stare at the floor.

"My Lord!" Out of the corner of his eyes he could see Drake's polished shoes standing off to the side. His second-in-command had known their master was here and had failed to warn him!

"Get up, Wallace."

He knew the deep, resonant voice came from behind the desk but seemed to emanate from the very air around him, vibrating him right down to his bones. He stood up as commanded and forced himself to look at the massive silhouette framed by the bright Santiago sun.

"I have your soul, I don't need obsequious grovelling as well. Now pour yourself a drink and relax. If I'd wanted you dead I certainly wouldn't have called you into a meeting to do it."

Tabak glared at Drake on his way past him to the silver tray of decanters and crystal rocks glasses on the credenza, but his second-in-command simply raised an eyebrow and shrugged.

"Don't blame Tau, Wallace. He has no more idea why I'm here than you do. I could just as easily have chosen *your* office, but there's something intoxicating about the scent of fear that wafts up from Luta whenever she sees me. It energizes me. Now, sit."

Drake and Tabak both took up seats facing Drake's desk, drinks in hand.

"I'm here because of that team of Reapers we lost, right here in Chile."

"But that was years ago," Drake pointed out.

"2010. It was just after Wallace convinced me of the importance of technology in the hunt for Shields and proposed the construction of this facility. I agreed with you then and I still do, but I need to start seeing greater returns on our various fiscal investments and DET is currently at the top of the list. Every time we kill a Shield and get possession of a Locus, our aid and rebuilding efforts following the resulting disaster bring financial gain to our earthly endeavours but, more importantly, it allows my Reapers to harvest souls to feed my legions.

"I lost more than the twenty demons who were sent back below when their bodies died in that bus accident; I lost every soul those twenty would have harvested in the century they have to remain below before I can bring them back up. I want... no, I *need* a serious shift in the Balance. I need Loci taken out of circulation faster so that Despair can get a stronger foothold, and I need Shield deaths coming with greater frequency so we can Reap and feed. There's a whole ecology at work here, gentlemen, and DET technology can make it happen."

"What about—?" Drake asked.

"Magic? Please, Tau. The spell-casters are still using the same spells they were during the Inquisition. Except for the occurrence of an adept or two every century, nothing new has been developed in eons. They're 'maintaining' and that's all. I know Wallace's pet team is almost ready to launch so I'm going to apply the pressure to you so that you can in turn make it felt amongst the rank-and-defiled. Your staff may have freely given themselves to me in exchange for their insignificant, petty desires being granted, but that doesn't mean I'll wait forever for them to prove their worth. I don't care that more than half of them didn't take the pact seriously, *I* do." He waved his hand and Luta entered from the outer office to stand just inside the door, trembling, awaiting his command.

"Gentlemen, I want the Shields dead, I want all one-hundred-and-forty-four Loci out of circulation, and I want Master Wei on his bleeding knees begging for a fucking truce." He nodded at Luta and the young woman stepped to the center of the office, between the two leather chairs and their occupants.

"Feel my need, gentlemen. Feel my *wrath*." The Lucifer clapped his hands together and pointed his interlocked fingers at young Luta's chest. Before either Drake or Tabak could react, the woman grabbed each of them hard by the hair. Raw, dark power flowed out of their master's hands, between Luta's breasts, through her arms and down into the top two men of DökktEfniTækni.

Wallace felt the burn of pure evil as magnified by the lens of Luta's fear. He felt every stitch of her dread, every iota of her terror... and then it all stopped and he was back in his office, staring at the news feed on his wall screen.

"You have served me well in the past, Wallace. Don't falter now." The voice was in his head and then it was gone, and with it, all but an echo of the pain.

oOo

Takeko didn't miss Luxor in the least. She'd found the Egyptian people beautiful and the culture fascinating, but she'd never found her comfort zone there as a woman. She was forty-seven when the Dark finally tracked her, cut her down and took her Locus while she coughed up blood and let out her last breath. She never would have said this to Master Wei, but it was almost a relief when the Dark found her there—twenty-nine years was a long single run for a Shield, even with a Locus as small and innocuous as daVinci's Quill, the swan feather he used to tickle his model to get the smile he wanted for the Mona Lisa. Twenty-nine years with a Locus wasn't a record, but it was close. Markus had Shielded a Locus for thirty-one, and Juliette had made it to nearly thirty-five, but twenty-nine was Takeko's personal best. At the time she probably should have appreciated more the small size and convenience of the Quill, because the forever-moving karmic circle never failed to come around and balance things out. Now was one of those times.

The three-foot-long sword of Carolus Magnus was not just the usual emotional burden to bear, but a physical one as well. At over three-and-a-half pounds, it was the most awkward of the Loci she'd ever been blessed to Shield. No, that wasn't true, and she knew it. The Last Egg of Loch Ness took that prize. There were many days during *those* ten years when she wondered why on earth Nessie couldn't have been a chicken or even an alligator, rather than the darling behemoth she was. Good grief, it was no wonder that the Egg had the highest turnover rate of all of the Loci—it was just so damned hard to Shield. But that's also why it was so easy for Light to retrieve it before it got squirreled away or destroyed or whatever the Dark did with the Loci when they got them. Of course, hers was not to reason why, but rather to just do and die, or something like that.

Cape Town was much more to her liking. The summer-in-December, winter-in-July turnabout had never bothered her like it did the tourists who flooded the city. Luxor had one season and that was *bloody hot and bone dry*, so Cape Town was a nice change after thirty years of the Middle East. Besides, after centuries of Shield work, and eighteen years in hectic Tokyo, Takeko found Cape Town to be just the vacation her soul needed.

At twenty-four she'd only been a Shield for six years so far this time around, but six years Shielding the sword of Carolus Magnus was beginning to wear thin. The last time she'd Shielded the sword, it had been perfectly acceptable to wear a blade on one's hip, but in 21st century Cape Town the push for a firearm-free South Africa put a damper on carrying a three-foot-long sword through the streets. Thank the stars above that she had the Internet and her sculpting. She wasn't stupid—she knew that Patterns were easily found in Internet use, so she kept her online time to a minimum. She logged on just long enough to update the online catalogue of her artwork and to print off the orders. Oh, and long enough to harvest her 'crops' on Farmville, the cyber farm game she played through a totally bogus Facebook profile.

Takeko also knew all of Master Wei's admonitions regarding Shields and Art, but each and every piece she created was completely different from the one before it. She even went so far as to list her work under fourteen different names in the catalogue. The Dark were resourceful and determined, but she'd been at this long enough to deserve *some* credit for being able to Shield herself and her Locus.

Being a cautious one, though, Takeko flashed a quick glance in the mirror over her monitor to confirm that the four-foot-long abstract painting behind her still hung where it belonged. A cheap acrylic jumble of colors on a three-inch-deep stretch frame she'd picked up in the market a couple years ago, it was the perfect size to hide the sword, which hung, wrapped in silk, on the wall behind it. French officials were certain that the original sword of Carolus Magnus—or Charlemagne, as some historians referred to him—hung in the Louvre in Paris. Takeko was well aware that there was much controversy over whether or not the sword ever even belonged to the ninth-century King of the Franks and Emperor of the Romans but the fact still remained that it had been used to crown many French monarchs over the centuries, and it was imbued with the Light like no other sword in history.

The morning sun snuck past the sheer window coverings and a trio of shafts found the painting, punching up the colors and giving the lines a sharp edge, seemingly reflecting the nature of that which it hid. The open French doors leading to the balcony let in a refreshing tangy breeze from Table Bay, and the sounds of crashing waves intermingled with traffic on nearby Regent Street. As soon as she'd finished uploading the current image and inputting the bowl's specifications into the catalogue, she would put in an hour on the treadmill to chase away the cobwebs and get her blood flowing for the day.

A knock at the door snapped her head around. Who...?

"Courier pick-up," came the answer through the door to her unvoiced question. It was the familiar voice of her usual courier, Demetri. A tanned, shaved-bald, super-fit, long-distance runner, Demetri had even managed to occasionally find time in his schedule to make a much more personal delivery behind the closed doors of her flat. Takeko had lived too many years to be a prude about casual sexual hook-ups and Dem was more than happy to oblige, especially when his tiny, fit, Japanese customer answered her door hot and sweaty from a session on the treadmill. She'd hoped for a repeat this morning, but Dem was an hour earlier than she'd expected so his schedule was most likely jam-packed. She called up the security camera over the door on her computer monitor and the crisp color image showed Demetri smiling up at her, his uniform shirt and shorts crisp, clean and professional. Takeko clicked on the camera icon next to the image to capture his marvellous smile then reached around the side of her flatscreen monitor and turned it off. She didn't see any need for Dem to know about her secret little photo obsession.

Moistening her lips with her tongue, she pushed her wheeled desk chair back and stood up. At that very moment, her coffee maker beeped, but the usual six beeps were cut off at three. The sounds of the street and the surf stopped in mid dull roar. Without a second thought for Demetri, Takeko whipped off her thin, steel-mesh-reinforced belt and spun the buckle until it clicked and formed a razor sharp snake's head. The preternatural silence from the street was all the warning she needed that the Dark Hunters had found her, so she turned to face the French doors leading to the tiny balcony. That's where they were coming from, and they were the only noises she would hear until the attack was over. She pushed down on the button of her Shield Emergency Transmitter until it locked in with a click and hoped it would be received in time.

Quickly, she moved to her windbreaker on the coat tree and without taking her eyes off the balcony doors, she deftly snagged her gun from the holster hanging under the coat. It was locked, loaded and the safety was always off. She was ready for the Dark. This is what she was made for, who she was. Her snakehead belt spun a lazy figure eight in the air and the gun was pointed up at the ceiling, ready to acquire a target and take out the enemy.

The knuckle knocking on the door behind her startled her and nearly made her fire off a round. "Crap. Dem." She took a step backward toward the door and raised her voice just enough for him to hear her calm, steady voice. "Dem, can you come back a little later. This really isn't a good time. I'm, um, on the phone with my da'. Mum's sick. I should have the package ready after lunch."

The silence around her continued. The only guaranteed warning Shields ever got was when everything went silent except the sounds of the agents of the Dark approaching. Everything except the Dark...

"Crap! Crap! Crap!" She spun to face the front door, to face the Dark agent who had just knocked a second time, but it was too late. Before she could bring the gun into position, Dem kicked the door into Takeko's face and charged through the doorway onto the downed door with his own weapon raised. The tiny Shield went down under the weight, pinned from the collarbone down, her nose broken, the snakehead belt limp and useless. Demetri stood, looking down at his trapped prey, blood all over her face. He pointed the gun at her forehead.

"I want the sword. Tell me where it is and I'll make this quick. Make me look for it and I'll make you suffer a *very* long time. I'll carve you up and turn your beautiful smile inside out, just for fun."

Takeko gathered her strength and tried to lift the door. Demetri was too heavy for her to get it more than a few inches off of her chest, but a few inches was all she wanted. Her pinned right hand still held the gun and now it was more or less aimed as best she could under the circumstances. "Are you sure that's what you want to do, Dem? Hurt me? I could give you the sword and then we could…" she lowered her voice to a soft whisper. Demetri leaned down to hear her whisper and that's when she pulled the trigger six times. The first two slugs slowed as they tore through the thick door, but rounds three through six found their marks in rapid succession and Demetri was punched up and off the door. Takeko shoved the door off of her and stood up, slowly.

The slugs should have simply gone in one side of the Hunter and out the other, but because their force had tossed him, she was certain he was wearing armour under his shirt. Sure enough, she could see the dark grey Kevlar through the fresh holes in his uniform. His gun hand twitched and Takeko's snakehead belt flashed once, twice, slicing the tendons in his wrist. Demetri screamed through clenched teeth.

"Are you alone?" Another ground-down scream was the only answer she got.

"How many of you bastards are there?" She raised her own gun and centred the sights on his forehead. She pulled the hammer back, Demetri's eyes widened with fear and Takeko finally got an answer to her question, except that it came from behind her, from the balcony.

"More than enough." The single word was punctuated with a sizzling sound just before the Taser hit her in the back. "Runestone, hurry up and find the damned Locus! She had plenty of time to send out an alarm." His headset squawked.

"LIGHT WARRIORS! Coming in through the street door on the run!"

"Dammit! Forget the Locus. Theta, grab Delivery Boy there and clear out. I've got the Shield. Runestone, cover our exit. Back the way we came. Move! Move! Move!"

In the aftermath of the Tasing, Takeko barely felt the sting of the hypodermic needle enter her hip before she blacked out and was thrown over a broad shoulder like a side of lamb.

oOo

At 1:22 AM on Liam's eighteenth birthday, he woke out of a deep, dreamless sleep more than two thousand years older than when he'd gone to bed. He also woke up with a purpose greater than following in his father's footsteps as a real estate magnate in the sleepy city of London, Ontario.

It was a hot, August Tuesday and Liam wasn't expected at work at the movie theatre until four so he sat in the kitchen with his habitual toasted raisin bread and bowl of Cheerios, waiting for the call or knock that he knew was coming. In the past two thousand or so years he'd received horsemen, foot soldiers, scullery maids, noblewomen, priests, hunters, farmers, milliners, and special delivery mail on his Awakening. In the latter fifth of the 20th century, he had to expect any of the above plus Canada Post or Purolator to deliver the message telling him where and when to meet his Shield Liaison to receive his next Locus.

At twelve minutes after noon, the angular, red plastic Contempra phone on the kitchen wall rang. The birthday boy reached over and plucked it off of the cradle.

"Hello."

"Happy Birthday, Liam!" It was a cheery young woman. A stranger with a warm, sexy, Irish lilt. "My name is Kathy Lee."

"Hi, Kathy Lee."

"I hope I'm not calling too early, Liam. I didn't wake you, did I?"

"Thanks for asking, Kathy Lee, but I was very much awake when you called."

She laughed lightly. "Yes, I suppose you would be. Have you got time for a cuppa tea this afternoon? I've got a present for you, and someone I'd like you to meet."

"Someone to meet?" Liam's hackles rose at the change of procedure. It was always a one-on-one, with the Locus passed on as a 'gift'. It was almost always in a public place, strangers meeting for the first and probably only time, but behaving like long lost friends or relatives for watching eyes. Kathy Lee or Ingrid or Atsuko would appear to be alone but Liam knew there were always at least three Warriors in the area covering the Liaison's back and watching for any hint of Dark. Sometimes Liam spotted the Warriors but more often than not he gave his attention over to the Liaison and the 'birthday present'.

"This is a special treat, Liam. Just take a seat on the northern-most bench on the east side of Victoria Park and we'll find you. Is an hour enough time?"

"Lots of time, thanks." It was actually just enough time for him to get cleaned up and get there early enough to scope out the three-block by two-block park in London's core.

Half-an-hour later he parked his old Camaro a block east of Victoria Park on Waterloo Street and retrieved his bat and ball from the car's trunk. He walked casually through the neighbourhood of fine, stately homes and into the park near its southeast corner. He checked his watch and saw that he still had plenty of time to circle the perimeter of the park to get a feeling for the situation. His newly reawakened instincts were strong and he quickly found a Warrior of Light sitting on the edge of the amphitheatre's stage reading a thick paperback. Liam also knew that he was meant to see the man because while Liam was watching that Warrior, others would be watching Liam.

It was a beautiful day and foot traffic meandered along the

pathways of the lightly wooded park, but quick, experienced observation told Liam that most of them were stroller-pushing mothers and urban dog-walkers—hardly a threat to a trained Shield armed with a maple Louisville Slugger.

With three minutes to spare, he took a seat on a bench down the pathway from the one he was told to sit at. He closed his eyes and listened to and felt the world around him in a depth that had been impossible yesterday, before his Awakening. Snippets of conversations drifted his way, as did tiny giggles and laughs from strollers and carriages. Dogs passed dogs and he heard soft barks or the tell-tale snuffle of the standard canine sniffed greeting. Then Irish Kathy Lee's voice rose slightly above the others and Liam opened his eyes slowly, looking in her direction as if he was simply curious.

"Get back here, you silly dog! Stop right there. I said 'STOP'!"

A silver-grey puppy so small as to be easily mistaken for one of the park's dozens of squirrels charged across the grass toward Liam. Two or three yards behind the pup, trying to grab hold of the trailing leather leash, was the dog's owner, Kathy Lee. From Liam's perspective as an ancient Shield, she was very young, no more than twenty-five; but from his perspective as an eighteen-year-old girl-chaser, he saw a hot, older chick with short, light-brown hair, glasses and a slender, athletic maturity lacking in most of the girls his own age. He was so intent on trying to read the words on her tight t-shirt that he didn't notice the pup reach his feet until two little paws bumped his leg.

"Harff". The bark was little more than a cough, soft and slightly hoarse, almost as if it was an imitation of a bark by someone who wasn't sure they wanted the world to notice them. Liam couldn't resist and picked up the pup.

"Hey, aren't you a little cutie." Although he said it to the dog, he sort of hoped the Irishwoman thought he meant her.

"Aye, that she is. Her name is Phoenix." Kathy Lee took hold of the loop end of the leash and handed Liam a small piece of paper. It was Master Wei's clean and precise handwriting, with his characteristic Chinese economy. *Liam I present to you Princess Teagan Wayfellow, heir to the Pixie Meadows of Compton Down. She is wanted by Oberon himself in payment of a debt owed to His Majesty by her father. Her family have long been friends of the Shields and so I have agreed to keep her hidden away here in our world while we negotiate with Oberon. Also, as expected, Kathy Lee has your Locus, Noah's Olive Pit. What this means, my son, is that for a time, you will have both Dark and Faerie trying to catch your scent.* The pup licked Liam's hand and settled onto his lap. Scratching her affectionately behind an ear seemed like the most natural thing in the world for him to do.

"A Pixie? *That's* a first."

Kathy Lee smiled and sat down next to him, close enough to hint at an intimate familiarity to any watchers. Liam soaked up the smile and luxuriated in her proximity. "I've been told we've helped out the Wee Folk on more than one occasion over the centuries, but this situation is unique. I'm serious, Liam, when I say that she is to be *Phoenix*. She chose the name herself as well as the form she is going to take in our world. Never speak her real name out loud—from *your* lips it will draw attention like you've never had before. Master Wei selected you personally for this assignment." She reached into her pocket and gently, reverently extracted a small leather pouch with a red ribbon tied around it for show. She placed it on Liam's open hand, covering it warmly with her own. "Will you accept both duties?" She held up a disposable Bic lighter and he stopped petting the dog to take it.

Curled up and content on his lap, Phoenix looked like she'd never belonged anywhere else. "Of course. I accept the honour and acknowledge the responsibilities." He bowed his head for a moment, then lit the note on fire and held it until it burned away to almost nothing. He let the last nub of paper float down to the dirt at his feet, ground it down, and handed the lighter back to his enchanting Liaison. Phoenix licked his hand and broke the very human spell. Liam smiled down at her. "She's a Yorkie, isn't she?"

"Yes. And despite her size, she's not a puppy. She'll be this size and age for as long as she's here. I've only looked after her for three days, but I've already fallen in love. I won't insult you by telling you how important she is to her world and ours, but will add that she now has a big part of my heart so watch over her, please."

"Of course. You're always welcome to visit, Kathy Lee."

"That would be marvellous, but we both know you'll be leaving London soon and I have to return home to Dublin. We'll not cross paths again, Liam."

"Then let me say that it was indeed a pleasure to meet you. Phoenix, Kathy Lee has to leave now. Did you want to say 'good-bye'?"

Teagan/Phoenix's head popped up and she quickly scrambled from the Shield's lap to Kathy Lee's where she looked deeply into the Liaison's eyes. Kathy Lee misted up. "You be well, lass. Stay out of trouble, will you?" She picked up the dog-that-was-a-pixie-princess and kissed the top of her head. Phoenix looked up and licked Kathy Lee's nose in return. They sat in silence for a moment, then the moment passed and they knew it was time to split up and follow their own paths. Kathy Lee passed Phoenix gently back to Liam and handed him the leash, signalling to her team that the hand-off was official and complete. Without another word she kissed him softly on the cheek, stood and walked away. Liam couldn't help but notice that she had the cutest wiggle.

He put Phoenix on the ground and started off along the path. "Home again, home again, jiggedy jig, eh?"

Harff.

"That's what I just said, Your Majes... little miss."

Chapter Two: Magic & Motorcycles

"For a Shield, an excess of Pattern is a beacon. An absence of Pattern is a beacon. The perfect Balance must be found between Pattern and No Pattern."

~Shield Master Wei (1175 CE while admiring the leaning Capanile of Pisa.)

oOo

Déshèng hung up his Smartphone and jammed it back in the pocket of his red leather motorcycle jacket. Hunter Team *Delta Nueve Cinq* didn't need some stupid cow from Head Office to tell them who their target Shield was. Their Regional researchers were the best in the firm and they had not just the highest kill-and-acquire rate in China, but also the highest in the entire hemisphere.

The target Shield went into Café Nanook over an hour ago, probably for their outstanding shrimp pork soup. From where the four Hunters sat across the street on their Suzuki and Yamaha motorcycles they could still see him in the booth at the back with his girlfriend and two hangers-on that seemed to be with him whenever he went out in public. If they weren't such fawning simpletons, the two could be mistaken for bodyguards. The fifth and sixth members of *Delta Nueve Cinq* watched the back alley, just in case Jùnrén—who went by Jeremy to please his Hong Kong girlfriend—went out that way.

"If Head Office wants to start second-guessing us, they can come out here and do the job themselves." Déshèng spit on his helmet's visor then wiped it down and polished it with the bandana he kept in his back pocket. He hated bugs on his visor almost as much as he hated interference from management.

"I checked Regional's data myself. It doesn't get any more solid. I've even *seen* the Loci myself, when he got drunk and brought them out at a party. There's *no doubt* he has the Bracers of Atlantis. He's cocky and proud." Baojia was cocky and proud, too, but Déshèng knew his man had ten years of Shield-Hunting success to back up his ego.

"He's also a Shield," Zongxiàn reminded them. "He's been in this form for only twenty years, but his mind and memories and experiences are of a thousand or more years. We *cannot* underestimate him." At thirty-eight, Zongxiàn was the oldest member of the team and the best spell-caster in Asia.

"Then take him now. If he catches wind of us he'll be gone *with* the wind."

"Not in there, Baojia."

"Why not? It's just him, his bitch, the leeches, and one or two staff.”

Déshèng turned away from his vigil of the café, and squinted at Baojia. “How do you think we knew he would be *here*, *now*? The waitress is my cousin. We wait. Two bikes, two blades. Third man gets the Loci, fourth covers the other three.”

“Who does what?”

“Rock-paper-scissors for choice.”

“I prefer dice.”

“You cheat at dice, Baojia. And cards. Rock-paper-scissors is fair.”

oOo

Jùnrén/Jeremy was riding an adrenalin high. He’d just played the best jai alai match of his life and beaten the club champion with a perfectly thrown cortada that had angled low and caught Ping completely off guard. There was no trophy involved but the dozen witnesses would ensure that it was a legendary match that would take Ping many years to live down.

“A cortada like that shows where the skill on the court truly lies. It’s my favourite kill shot.”

“It was the best I’ve ever seen you play, Jeremy. You *ruled* the court.”

“Of course I did, Xue, the stars foretold that today I would be king.”

“Really!?”

“Nah. My fortune cookie at lunch actually said ‘Try to keep your head down and watch where you step’. But I want to be King of the Day, so I’m King of the Day.”

“And that makes me Queen?” His eighteen-year-old girlfriend leaned in, squeezed his arm with one hand and his thigh with the other under the table.

“Of course it does. Britney, Queen of the Day.” Jeremy pulled the sleeve of his jacket up to check his watch, and the light caught the hammered silver of the bracer he wore on that arm. He slipped the sleeve down to cover it up. “We have twenty minutes to get to the theatre.” He checked the bill sitting on the table and dropped a handful of Macanese patacas on top of it to cover the cost of the meal with a healthy tip for the shy waitress who couldn’t take her sad eyes off him.

oOo

Because their CMRs—camera-and-mic-rigs—were mounted on their helmets, all Déshèng needed to do was press the switch under his own rig to start the live feeds from his entire team. The feeds were recorded and relayed to the satellite by the laptop in Wang’s pack, and

Wang was in the position of least risk at the rear door.

"Feeds *on*. Broadcasting far and wide. Shield in question is Jùnrén 'Jeremy' Tat. Locus is the pair of Royal Atlantian Wedding Bracers. Take down will occur momentarily."

The Shield chatted briefly with the café staff and started moving to the front door. Baojia, Chéng and Déshèng loosened the hilt straps on their swords and as soon as the Shield turned his back to walk down the wide brick sidewalk, the bikes roared into action. Chéng and Baojia hopped the curb, dodged the trees, scattered other pedestrians, drew their katanas and 'charged', with Déshèng behind Baojia, tucked low.

oOo

The world went silent. Jeremy pressed his alarm and had his Colt out of the holster before he realized that the silence was actually being filled by the roar of approaching motorcycles. He saw the glint of steel blades drawn and fired off six fast rounds—three left and three right. The Hunter on the left took two rounds in the chest and one in the throat, which nearly decapitated him. His helmeted head hung to one side as his corpse crashed the bike into a granite pillar, narrowly missing Britney.

His second grouping of three shots caught the other Hunter in the chest and kicked him up and off his bike. Jeremy easily sidestepped the bike as it sped past only to crash into what sounded like a tree behind him. Before he could acquire the next target, a third Hunter roared up in the wake of the second runaway bike and a blade briefly reflected the light from a nearby neon sign before it flashed in.

oOo

"I've got the kill, you get the bracers!"

"Done!"

Déshèng almost ran Baojia over when he moved in for the kill. The veteran Hunter had flown back off his bike, hit the brick walk, bounced and rolled out of the way while his bike had continued on.

The Hunter Team leader had to admit that the Shield was faster than he expected, but he wasn't fast enough to dodge the steel of a katana in the hands of a master. If he'd dropped to one knee to shoot like a truly seasoned soldier would have, then the Shield might have ducked the twenty-six-inch blade, but he took a solid stance like he was at a practice range and it cost him his arrogant life. The cut was clean and his severed head hit the sidewalk before the body knew it was gone.

Déshèng sheathed his sword and slammed on his brakes.

Momentum carried him fifty feet past the Shield so by the time he was stopped and twisted around in his seat, Zongxiàn had sliced off both of the Shield's arms just below the shoulder and jammed the bloody, severed limbs into his saddle bags after confirming that both Bracers were attached. Baojia was back on his feet and picking up his bike by the time Zongxiàn was back on the road and racing past Déshèng. Déshèng waited a moment to make sure Baojia's bike was operable and as soon as it roared to life he was off after Zongxiàn.

"Split up. Rendezvous Number Three. Go two blocks and match speed of traffic. Blend if possible, elude if necessary. We lost Chéng but no time to mourn. Warriors will be en route. Good work. Shield terminated and Loci recovered. How you doing back there?"

Baojia grunted.

"*That* good? If you can ride we'll tend to it at the rendezvous."

"I can ride."

"Perfect. Live feed off." He tapped the switch under his CMR and sped off into traffic.

oOo

The soft-yet-insistent alarm and flashing sun icon on his computer monitor startled Maurizio from his Italian translation of *The Time Machine* on his tablet, but since it was actually his primary job to listen for the alarm and react as he'd been trained to do, he recovered quickly and went into action. With his left hand he tapped the icon on the touchscreen to acknowledge the alert while his right hand tapped the microphone switch on his headset. His voice was calm and clear even though his heart pounded, as it did every single time the Pending Disaster Alarm sounded.

"Duty Team to stations." His voice sounded throughout the two-story complex hidden in the hills above Lake Como in northern Italy. He touched the icon a second time and the personnel brief of the Shield in question popped up. The left half of the screen was a photo and the right was the relevant data. By the time he'd read it through, the first of his three fellow Duty Team members charged through the archway and plopped herself at her station behind him. Teresa—the newest member of the team—was logged in and ready before her butt even started warming the chair.

"Theta online. Monitoring Seismic."

Maurizio heard two pairs of footsteps on the hardwood floor and then twin squeaks of chairs taking modest weight. He tapped a corner of his monitor and five rows of twenty screens each lit up the entire south wall.

A throat cleared. "Beta on station, monitoring media and initializing air-traffic-control scanning." Bartolommeo unwrapped a

Toblerone bar and settled in.

Pierrette took a sip of her fresh cappuccino and placed her spill-proof mug to one side of her desk. "Delta in place and monitoring weather. Narrow it down for us, boss."

"Macau, Macau, China. Alarm received minus fifty-two seconds. Shield link severed..." he looked back at his monitor and the countdown timer in the bottom right corner. "... minus forty-five seconds."

"A quick one," Pierrette remarked. "Weather is clear of storm fronts for... three hundred kilometres all around Macau."

"Seismic is holding st—". There was a triple beep from Teresa's system. "We've got post-kill seismic. Building *fast*. Epicentre is..." she leaned in toward her monitor and typed on her keyboard. "... Mainland China. Putting the coordinates up on the wall now." The latitude, longitude and depth below ground level of the epicentre of the quake appeared on the wall above them in foot-high numbers overlaid on a satellite photo of China's lower mainland.

"Noted and logged, Theta. Beta, notify Warrior Network and the Locators. Let's get this Locus back and see if we can minimize the damage."

"How much time have we got?" This was Teresa's first 'event' since she'd joined the team last week.

Maurizio answered her while he hammered away on his keyboard and kept the process flowing smoothly. "The stats show that when we can reclaim a Locus within twenty-four hours, the death toll from the related disaster is half what it could have been."

"That doesn't make sense. How can they know what's half of something that hasn't happened, yet."

Maurizio smiled. This girl was quick—she'd probably get fast-tracked out and up. "I have no idea. It has to do with statistical probabilities and actuarial science. The whole thing was designed by former math geeks from the insurance industry. All I know for sure is that when we *don't* get a Locus back within twenty-four hours, the death toll goes way up, and that's why we're here. Didn't they cover this in Training?"

"I was sick on Tuesday."

"Not a problem, but I need you to get the notes for that day from someone because you also missed the lecture on *Patterns & Shield Life*."

"Will do." Her computer beeped again and she looked back at the new pop-up. "Oh no. It's bad. Seven-point-eight."

Bartolommeo leaned back in his chair and interrupted. "Warriors and Locators confirmed into the loop." He checked his monitor again. "Nothing on mainstream media, yet, but multiple seismic monitoring stations are confirming the incident."

"Copy that. With the Warriors and Locators up to speed we can take a moment. Pierrette, would you please light the incense for the lost Shield, Jùnrén, whose first born name was..." he checked the brief still on his monitor. "Whose first born name was Chakor. Teresa, did they cover the ringing of the bell in Training?"

The rookie half-smiled. "They did. I'd be honoured to ring it for Jùnrén who was first born as Chakor." She and Pierrette got up and went over to a small, linen-covered table under the wall of monitors where Pierrette lit a small incense cone. Jasmine smoke quickly scented the room, spread by the slow-turning ceiling fan. Pierrette returned to her desk and Teresa picked up the tiny mallet on the table. She turned to her three teammates and they all crossed themselves as a sign of respect in faith rather than an enforcement of religion. Very gently, Teresa rang the Tibetan prayer bell three times, waiting each time for the ring of the previous strike to fade away. When the third ring faded she reverently placed the mallet back on the table and spoke in a clear but emotion-filled voice.

"Sleep well, Chakor, for you are a Shield and you are loved. What you do you do for all mankind, and though at this moment there is sadness in our hearts, there is joy, too, for we know that you will be back and you will join the corps of Shields to once again give us hope, once again protect the Light and to keep Darkness at bay. Sleep well, Chakor, for you are loved."

The room was silent for one minute, and then erupted in activity once again as Maurizio's team got back to work.

oOo

The slow, deep claxon sounded not only in the century-old farmhouse but also throughout the five-building dairy farm. The seven people working on the farm turned off, dropped, and abandoned whatever they were working on and sped to the smaller of the two barns.

Even from only a dozen yards away the little barn was nothing but a barn, with peeling brown paint, a rusty crowing rooster wind vane, and a muddy track leading up to double tractor-wide doors that never seemed to close that last half-foot. A small, engineless Massey-Ferguson tractor rusted beyond salvation in a patch of long timothy grass and the small corral adjacent to the barn held a couple of happy-to-graze-all-day goats.

But once a person passed through the second set of worn doors, the illusion was dispelled completely. Other than a small stall for the two goats, the accoutrements of a barn were completely absent. A circular, twenty-foot-diameter section of the floor was raised up two steps and what occupied the dais was more an odd Tibetan temple than a

Minnesota dairy farm.

The spell-spinner was already in the barn when the rest of the team arrived singly and in pairs. Liv was usually the one to sound the gong in the first place so she'd had a head start. The Warriors—Ansfrid, Baldur and Eilif—nodded to her as they rushed to grab their gear and suit up.

"The Bracers of Atlantis. Macau, Macau, China. 82 degrees. Street clothes," was all Liv said, but it was enough to tell them where they were headed and what to dress for, though they always hoped not to be there long enough to worry about the weather.

Liv picked up a piece of natural chalk and printed the destination's longitude on a piece of two-inch-square slate and placed it next to an eight-inch-wide brass Tibetan singing bowl. She double-checked the text message on her phone and chalked the second set of coordinates: the latitude. She placed that slate next to a somewhat smaller polished bowl and worn mallet. The third bowl, the smallest one, she left alone. Once the bowls were prepped she stripped out of her dirty coveralls, down to her faded khaki t-shirt and shorts. She pulled her shoulder-length red hair out of its pony-tail and finger-combed it out, then rinsed her hands and face with water in the ever-present bowl on the milk stand next to the goat stalls. Barefoot, she climbed up the two steps and walked to the centre of the spell-spinning configuration, careful to walk on the stone edges of the tiny canal carrying the spring water around and through the winding, seven-point, symmetrical configuration.

Each of the three bowl singers—Peder, Jorunn and Vidor—stripped down to their own basics, picked up their bowls, mallets and, for two of them, slates, then took up their own positions. The diagram hanging on the wall quite clearly showed who was supposed to go where, but the team had been working together long enough to know exactly what was required of them.

Former competitive kick-boxer Liv lowered herself gracefully down into the exact centre of the two-foot-wide circle of fine coral pink sand that was her domain. Peder, Jorunn, and Vidor each sat within their own water-surrounded sand circle at the vertices of a large equilateral triangle within the outer ring. All three quickly found their own comfortable positions facing Liv in the centre.

The Warriors about to be sent halfway around the world moved quickly and silently onto their own yard-wide crystalline circles not much more than an arm's-reach from Liv, at the vertices of their own smaller triangle within the triangle within the circle. Ansfrid, Baldur and Eilif each went down on one knee with the other tucked to their chest and their palms pressed down on the polished agate circles beneath them.

Of all the weapons, tools, and implements carried by the three

Warriors beneath their loose-fitting street clothes, arguably the most important for each of them was the vial of charmed water and sand taken from the source within this very barn. When the mission was complete, for good or bad, a Warrior simply had to smash the vial at their feet, releasing Earth, Water, and Charm and they would be pulled back to the base by the spell-spinning team who maintained a link until the mission was completed.

Peder placed the longitude slate in his bowl and began rubbing the outside rim of the bowl slowly and steadily with the pestle-like mallet. The tone was a perfect *G*. It was the Home note. Jorunn placed the latitude slate in her bowl and started the bowl singing with a practised touch, adding her perfect *C* to Peder's *G*. Vidor picked up his mallet and soon joined a pure *D* to the two tones filling the barn.

The three-part bowl-song charged the air and at the same time purified it as if scrubbing it with pure Light. Whatever any members of the team had been fretting over or thinking about just drifted away without weight or consequence. The pure three-tone electrified each of them, and then Vidor on the third bowl took a deep breath and blew hard into his bowl. The last vestige of daily trivia in each of the team member's minds was blasted away, a mystical sirocco giving the three-tone substance, the power to touch and interact.

The wind was her cue so Liv began spinning. She spun with her heart and soul because the lives of her three warriors plus the Shield-in-distress all relied on her abilities. With her left hand on top and her right hand on the bottom, she circled them in opposite directions over her root chakra. She felt the power build, felt the pull at her root by the three pure songs become one.

She spoke the long-lost word for Earth and a small amount of sand around her spiralled up to spin above her moving arms. She stabilized the spin then spoke to Water and the spring around her fed a half-gallon of pureness to her task. A bit louder she said Air's name and Vidor blew another long, strong breath into his bowl, which Liv's power magnified. Finally, she whispered an invitation to Fire and two bright points of pure Light rose up out of Peder and Jorunn's bowls, joining the elemental helix rotating quickly above Liv's root.

One...two...three full rotations and she reached into the helix with her far-sight. She urged her mind forward, surging toward the coordinates and after a moment she could see the scene clearly.

It was an urban street and a small crowd was gathered around two fallen men. The far-sight let her not only visualize the scene, but determine who was Dark, who was Light and the layout within a fifty-yard radius circle.

She spoke calmly to her Warriors: "Shield down. One Hunter down. Urban street. Small crowd. No living Dark. Putting you in an alley sixty feet east." Then she whispered a word only her root heard and a tight, controlled stream of fire shot straight up and out of the top of the helix. It split into three branches and each writhing branch leapt at the nearest Warrior.

The fire streams spun around the Warriors in tight spirals defined by the disks of agate each knelt on. Liv pulled from her root, drew from the sand, water and bowl-song and willed the power into the golden fire. For a brief moment, cylinders of power hid Ansfrid, Baldur and Eilif, and then with three flashes they were gone and the fires pulled back into the helix.

Liv slowed the spinning helix so that it only rotated once every two seconds. Peder, Vidor and Jorunn slowed their bowl-songs until the rotation of their mallets around the outside of the bowls matched the rotation of the helix. This was their holding pattern and they could maintain it for up to an hour, although they'd never gone beyond forty minutes in the three years they'd been spinning together.

While the bowls sang, Liv kept a watchful eye on her Warrior Team through the link. She watched while they sprinted from the alley and split up. Ignoring a screaming young woman, Baldur went straight to the dead Hunter, searched for but didn't find a wallet, pulled up the man's visor and photographed his face. He placed a remotely-operated flash-bang grenade next to the corpse and then joined Ansfrid and Eilif at Jùnrén's body. There was a lot of blood on the sidewalk but Liv had seen blood before—probably too often—so she didn't flinch.

Baldur triggered the grenade and the thunderous bang and blinding flash near the Hunter's body stunned the onlookers standing over Jùnrén's remains. Those who weren't numbed ducked for cover and that's when the three Warriors made their move. Ansfrid respectfully scooped up Jùnrén's head while Eilif hefted the torso over his shoulder and Ansfrid stood guard. The three of them smashed their vials nearly simultaneously and Liv increased the power feeding the link.

"They're coming home!"

In response to her shout, the bowl singers dropped out of their holding pattern and went back to full singing power. Liv pulled her energies together, drew on her root once again and began spinning her team home. The distance was incredible but she was up to the task. She felt the link grasp the Warriors and their burden and then she willed it back to her root. If she'd had to compare it to a mundane task, she probably would have gone with a hand-over-hand retrieval of fishing net using slow, strong, steady pulls.

The silence in the barn was deafening when Eilif materialized with Jùnrén's body in his arms. Tears flowed freely down the big man's tanned cheeks. Baldur materialized then stood up from his agate pad and walked over to Eilif where he gently, caringly reunited Jùnrén's head and torso. Ansfrid moved immediately off the spell dais and over to a simple high table where he lit three candles for the lost Shield.

Liv stopped spinning and the bowl-songs were stilled. The silence lasted a respectful minute before the team continued on with the clean-up. Baldur approached Liv where she stood at the edge of the dais and gently brushed the sand off of herself with a horsehair brush. "No Loci, Liv. They took the Bracers by removing his arms. Best to let the Search Team know so they can try to retrieve the rest of him, too."

Liv swiped at a tear. "Will do. Good work, Bal. Thank you. I'll also let HR know so they can work it into the cover story when they return him to his family." She wiped another pair of tears.

Baldur put his hand on her arm in comfort. "Are you okay?"

Even though she was standing two steps up on the dais she still only looked Baldur in the eye. "He was so *young*." She stepped down and into his offered hug.

"Maybe, but his soul was so much older."

"I know, I know, but just because they Awaken at eighteen and get back a million memories doesn't mean that inside there isn't still some of the cocky eighteen-year-old thinking he's invincible."

"HRs been working on dealing with that dichotomy for a few years now, but in the meantime I guess we cross our fingers and do our best to get to them when they call, before it's too late."

"True enough. Maybe there's something we can do better there. Can you bring this up at the staff meeting after dinner?"

"Of course, Liv." He kissed the top of her head and released her from the hug. She turned to face the rest of the team.

"Reports on my desk within the hour, please. And the staff meeting is still a 'go' after dinner. Good work today, everyone. We may not have been there in time to save the Shield or his Locus, but we sent and retrieved without further losses."

"Thanks, Liv."

"Back atcha, boss. It was a good spin."

"Thanks, Boss-Lady. Yah, it was a solid spin."

Liv picked up the sand rake and lovingly restored the spell dais to a state of readiness, allowing tears to fall for the lost Shield and Locus.

oOo

Hiwa slowly, steadily rubbed the well-worn wooden cylindrical mallet around the outer rim of her brass singing bowl, producing a steady, clear tone that filled the high-ceilinged cavern, muffled a bit by the sandy floor then amplified back down by the amethyst crystal-studded rock walls. On a thin, unrolled wool rug beside her lay one-hundred-and-forty-four semi-precious stones in a precise grid. Each stone vibrated a little with the bowl-song.

Coriander closed her eyes and lowered herself into a lotus position on her small hand-woven wool rug, facing Hiwa. The bowl-song reached out to Coriander and at first only the fine brown hairs on her arm stood up, then, as the charge worked its way down to the follicles, her skin warmed. The warmth moved from the surface down through her epidermal layers into the muscles, tendons and ligaments, which relaxed at the ephemeral touch.

Her blood warmed and soon she felt like the heat of a small sun sat in her chest, radiating out and warming the whole world around her; when in fact she was drawing all of the energy in and cradling it close. The energy born of the bowl-song was blood in her veins and arteries, pumped out to her extremities and then back again to her core. She cleared her mind, slowed her breathing and her power pulsed at sixty beats per minute. She concentrated and slowed it further. At fifty beats of sanguine bowl-song per minute, she was ready.

Coriander spoke the spell softly and quickly in a language most scholars discounted as long dead and in a dialect no scholar even suspected had ever existed, but which the Spell-Spinners of Light had been fluent in for well over two thousand years. To accompany her words, Coriander's hands moved quickly over her Root Chakra as though she were finger-painting circles on an invisible canvas. Sparks of power followed her left hand clockwise and her right hand counter-clockwise. Her eyes were still closed but she knew that the power was building without having to see the visible manifestation of the two sparkling, green and gold rings of pure light.

She opened her eyes at the exact moment her hands ceased spinning and although *she* was motionless, the two rings of light still spun counterpoint to each other. They spun so fast and furious that when she slapped the two of them together they bucked and twisted and resisted for a split second before they grabbed hold of each other and melded into one ring now motionless, suspended over her root.

Quickly and deftly, Coriander tilted the new ring into a vertical position perpendicular to her centre, inserted her index fingers into the opposite sides of the ring and started slowly spinning the new structure in at the bottom and away at the top. When it made exactly eleven rotations she cupped her hands abruptly and pulled them to the left and right, drawing the power out of the centre of the spinning ring and into an orb eight inches across.

She held her hands steadily in place and gradually the ring shrank and was absorbed by the orb. The orb grew more opaque and while she could see a hint that the centre still spun, the shell became stationary. She concentrated on that shell, that crust, and soon movement began across the surface. Shapes and lines slid across the surface of the orb, and, fed by the bowl-song, they slipped into a pattern familiar to any third-grade school child.

When she was sure it was ready, Coriander placed both hands palm-up under the manifestation of her power and without actually touching it she lifted it up to eye-level where she could clearly see that it was now a fully-formed model of the Earth as seen from space. She spoke a single word in that odd dialect of the not-so-dead language and a pinpoint of light spiralled lazily up from Hiwa's bowl to drift slowly but directly to hover over the globe.

"Show me... the Bracers of Atlantis."

There was a moment of hesitation as if the tracker light was thinking, mulling over the request and trying to decide what to do; then it dropped down to a finger-width above the globe and circumnavigated it twice before settling on a spot in the South China Sea. Coriander twisted her hands as if adjusting large dials and her view of the globe zoomed in. She 'dialled' the globe quickly, fine-tuning the zoom, increasing the detail around the locator. Eventually she had it 'dialled' down so tightly that she could see twin glows moving along a coastline.

She whispered a word and numbers popped into her head. Without moving her gaze from the globe she said the numbers loud enough for the microphone in the corner to pick up her voice. "Plus twenty-two degrees, eight minutes, twenty-five-point-six-nine seconds by plus one-hundred-thirteen-degrees, forty-two minutes, forty-seven-point-five-seven seconds. Just off Sanjiaoshan Island."

A clear, French-accented older female voice answered her from a speaker in the shadows. "Copy that. Speed and heading?"

Coriander tuned a bit more. "Four-hundred-eighty knots at a heading of fifty-two degrees north east."

"D'accord. Merci. Now, the Shield: Chakor, most recently living as Jùnrén. Reincarn location, s'il-vous-plaits." Stopping the bowl-song for only a moment, Hiwa picked up a tiger's-eye gem from the rug and placed it in the exact centre of her bowl. She returned to rubbing the mallet around the bowl and the tone she produced was a new one, one specific to the Shield, Chakor, who had been Jùnrén. Coriander noticed the difference in the tone and nodded to Hiwa.

"Affirmative, Control. Proceeding. Stand by, please." Coriander snapped her fingers and the locator shot up off the globe and hovered in the air, awaiting her command. It vibrated slightly, almost eager to please, like a loving pet, and Coriander smiled as she dialled the globe back to its full view. "Good boy. Now, show me Chakor."

This was a much harder to task than finding Jùnrén's lost Locus. As it circled the globe, the locator shifted from pure white to a dark gold matching the tiger's eye in Hiwa's bowl. It circled slowly around the globe, seeking, changing its path as it sought out the reincarnated Shield.

In response to Hiwa's new bowl-song, the naturally occurring crystals in the cave began to resonate harmonically and the resulting pastel purple and pink glow added another layer to Coriander's spell-spinning. The locator picked up speed, seeking, searching then it abruptly stopped, frozen. Coriander tilted her head in thought.

"Sunspot report, please."

"Heavy and sporadic. Solar winds are steady and holding. Overall interference is within tolerance," was the answer from the speaker.

"Merci." Coriander waited, maintaining the spinning patiently. Patience and Perseverance were the Two Key Ps to being a successful Spell-Spinner and, according to Spell Master Ba'al, Coriander had an abundance of both, putting her on the fast track to getting her own Spin-Search Team.

Hiwa played and Coriander spun, waiting. Neither wavered in her task and they were rewarded after only ten minutes when the tracker light started moving again. Seventeen minutes later the light hit the globe and stuck. Coriander rapidly expanded the globe until new coordinates entered her head. "Minus twenty-nine degrees, fifty-seven minutes, fourteen-point-three-five-six-two seconds by thirty degrees, fifty-six minutes, point-eight-zero-one seconds." She continued to spin, waiting, knowing there was more information to come yet. After another minute she found what she sought. "Born at 12:52PM. The family name is Mabuza and the name they are leaning toward is... Zigmund — *Ziggy*."

"Acknowledged." There was a pause while the dispatcher monitoring their spinning made a series of computer entries. "Monitor assigned. Spinning complete."

"10-4. Spinning terminated." Coriander placed her hands palms-up and open on her knees and emptied her mind. The tracker light returned to Hiwa's bowl and the globe dissipated and drifted back into Coriander's root. The glow on the crystals of the cave faded when Hiwa stopped her spinning and returned Chakor's tiger's eye to the rug containing the selection of Shield link-stones.

Five minutes later Coriander and Hiwa walked into the facility refectory together and were waved over to a table by Hussein, one of its two occupants.

He smiled. "Did you hear? Rumour is that there's some new tech Dark is using to find Shields."

Hiwa joined Hussein and her own sister, Ifwa, at the table while Coriander headed straight for the juice machine where she dispensed grapefruit juice for herself and Hiwa.

"What do you mean 'new tech'?" Hiwa was always sceptical of Hussein's rumours. He was infamous for taking facts and filling in the blanks with pure fantasy.

"I mean someone got word out that they're working on a Smartphone app that's supposed to help speed up their search or something.

"Great. Will they ever give up?"

Ifwa put a hand on Coriander's arm. "Our predecessors never had to worry about iPhones or Androids or Blackberries. The Dark *cast* their spells and Grandma *spun* better ones. The Balance has always been in our favour."

Hiwa corrected her sister. "Not always. The Inquisition stands out as a particularly Dark chapter in history."

"No pun intended?" Hussein smiled. He loved to play with words, especially when it drove the rest of them to distraction.

"Oh no — pun *fully* intended, dude."

Hussein nodded. "Murder for the sake of organized religion."

Ifwa shook her head. "Dude, I prefer to think of it as Politicized Spirituality."

"Nice one! Nails it on the head."

"Just remember to give me credit for it when you steal it, Huss."

News of the new app worried Coriander. "What do we do about this Smartphone thing? Does it work? Is there anything we can do to counteract it?"

"Just chill, Cor. There's no tech that can match our spinning. Relax. Our jobs are safe."

"'Relax'? 'Chill'?" Coriander's face reddened but Ifwa cut her off. "Insensitive much, Hussein?"

Coriander stood up so fast that her chair flipped over with a loud crash. "You think this is about *jobs*? I think you need to be scheduled for a Loyalty Check, Hussein. Doing this for the money is something a Dark-monger would do."

"I'm *not* Dark, dammit!" But Coriander didn't care. She stormed away and Hussein's words fell on her retreating back.

Hiwa stood, shook her head at Hussein and followed her partner out of the refectory. Ifwa picked up her sister's abandoned half-full juice and took a sip. "H, sometimes you're an idiot and the rest of the time you're a *stupid* idiot."

"What did I say?"

"She's descended from two Shields, you moron."

"*Two* Shields? That's so forbidden that it's..."

"'Forbidden'?"

"Yah. It's *wrong*. Two Shields in the same place is suicide."

"We can't control who we love and Shields have even less control over their lives than the rest of us."

"You *approve* of two Shields...?"

"I approve of *Love*. It's what we're all fighting and working for. Without love, there's no Light, just Dark."

"Yah, but..."

"No. No 'buts'. You either agree or, like Cori said, you're on the wrong side. Choose, Hussein. *Before* you and I spin again."

Ifwa picked up the juice and left Hussein wondering how news of the Dark using tech had suddenly turned around and bitten *him* in the ass.

Chapter Three: The Patterns of Death

"In art are found the Patterns of the artist. The soul of the artist is in the subtle strokes of the brush, the turn of a favourite phrase, a joy-giving familiar progression of notes. They are all Signatures, all Patterns, all Beacons to be seen, traced back to their source by the Dark."
~Shield Master Wei (1735 CE while sipping tea.)

oOo

Liam leaned heavily on the grocery cart, his Locus—the Olive Pit—secure in a vial of olive oil in a pouch hanging around his neck, inside his shirt. His cane was wedged in the cart between the groceries but leaning on the wobbly-wheeled cart was the easiest way to get around the store. Phoenix slept, unseen on a towel at the bottom of the small, worn, canvas pack on Liam's back. Even though she hadn't been to this particular Safeway in nearly a year, they all looked alike and offered little in the way of excitement. Besides, the No-Dogs Rule at all grocery stores made it prudent for her to stay hidden. If they got caught, there could be a report and if there was a report, there could be email and if there was email there could be tracking by the Dark. Making the Six-o'clock News would attract the Hunters faster than creating a deadly Pattern.

Patterns could kill. Of all the cities in the world Liam could have chosen to retreat with Phoenix, Calgary was the one place where Patterns and no Patterns walked hand-in-hand. With serious westernized settlement not starting until the late 1800s, Calgary was so young that Faerie had no foothold here, and that was what got Liam's attention in the first place. The confluence of the Bow and Elbow Rivers created a natural rhythm, which helped blanket other Patterns. As the ears found it difficult to hear over the roar of a nearby river, so the Dark found it difficult to distinguish traceable Patterns where rivers converged, especially when one of the rivers was a River of Light.

The Bow River was glacial and nearly pure. Although it picked up some of the detritus of mankind in its travels through or past five communities, even after the devastating flood of 2013, the Light was still strong in the waters when the Bow cut through Calgary on its way from the Bow Glacier to Hudson Bay. Liam found the trout fishing to be superb and the Light to be both refreshing and renewing. Lately, however, even the proximity of the Bow couldn't brighten his heart when his mood darkened.

His weak left hand slipped on the handlebar of the shopping cart and the cart veered between the shelves of pasta-mixes-for-the-lazy-and-incompetent and a stand-up display of toilet paper, jolting him back to the simple job at hand. "Dammit." He limped backward two steps and then moved around the obstacles. The bottle of pickles clinked into the jar of tomato sauce at the bottom of the cart. Only two more aisles to get through, he reassured himself. He wasn't using a list this time because he'd used a list last time and two in a row was a Pattern. He couldn't let his body fall into any rhythms. Creatures of habit fell back on their ingrained Patterns and while that made it possible for other people to multi-task like they did, for him it would send out a tiny Beacon. A Beacon the Dark could see if they happened to glance his way at that moment. All it took was suspicion and he was found. Of course, stressing over Patterns in grocery shopping was probably a little over the top, but lately Liam couldn't help but worry of the niggly little things. The small stuff of life was his bane these days.

In the past the Dark had caught his scent more than a few times, but he'd been able to run, take his Locus and flee, but this time there could be no running. Hobbling, maybe. Limping, definitely. Wheeling even, in the near future. But nothing with any kind of run-from-the-predator speed he'd once had and would always need. He looked at his left hand, weak and unable to maintain a serious grip for any length of time. A week ago it had been fine. A week ago he'd had a few problems with his vision and a minor control problem with his left leg but on Tuesday he fell while jay-walking downtown and the screaming horn of the approaching Light Rail C-Train nearly scared the actual crap out of him. He'd managed to get up and get to the curb, then the sidewalk before the train rolled past, but the scare was enough. The next day he picked up the cane at Value Village.

The second-hand cane was a far cry from the beautiful mother-of-pearl-inlay, ivory-handled, ash-shaft sword cane he'd once swaggered around St. Petersburg with. If he were completely honest with himself, though, that sword cane had never really been much more than an affectation, while this Value Village prop was going to be more and more important to his survival as the days, weeks and years went by. Damn his failing body anyway. He grabbed a jar of bread machine yeast from a shelf and steered the rattling cart down the last aisle to the cashier.

He paid cash, turned down Molly-the-chipper-cashier's kind offer to get a Safeway savings card and wheeled his bagged groceries out the front doors. The breeze felt great. Liam took a moment to place the backpack in the cart and open it up so Phoenix could poke her head out and play navigator to get back to the car. Still leaning on the cart, Liam stopped at the sidewalk's bicycle-stroller-wheelchair slope and waited for a lone BMW to pass. He half-expected the Bimmer to race by, ignoring him or daring the 'cripple' to try and cross, but the grinning driver stopped, reminding Liam of yet another reason he liked this city—just when Calgarians seemed ready to move in for a kill-stroke, kindness shone through. The lie was put to the stereotype. Patterns were broken.

By most standards, the drive back to the apartment was uneventful, but for Liam it was pure hell. He was down to one-and-a-half hands for steering and his reflexes seemed to be lagging as well, so the dodge-car-like stream of traffic in Calgary's core both frustrated and terrified him. By the time he pulled the old Corolla into his building's underground garage, he was shaking badly and nearly in tears. Over the centuries he'd been stabbed, hung, shot, beheaded, drowned, and burned to death, but right at that moment he'd take any one of those again over having to go back out on the streets in the car.

He tilted his seat back and closed his eyes. Phoenix climbed on his lap, feeling her protector's frustration. Liam stroked her head, relaxing more and more with each touch of her silky hair. He couldn't remember a time that he'd been so dragged down.

"Fifty shouldn't be that bad, P, but for some reason this time it is. Is it the being alone? Is that it? The *last* time I made it to the half-century mark I was with Lynette and we had kids and grandkids. The two of us snuck away and danced in the meadow until moonrise and then made love until sunrise, steaming as our body heat warmed the dew trying to settle on us. Of course, back then I *could* make love at fifty. The time before that was during a famine and there was no Lynette, but seven of us found a watered-down jug of wine and sang our hearts out in celebration of that fifty. So what's happening this time?"

"After more than two thousand years, am I finished as a Shield?" Phoenix nuzzled his hand. For so long his whole *raison d'être* had been simply avoid the Dark, at all costs, even his life. Keep his Locus away from the Dark. Keep the disasters at bay. He'd lost count of the times he'd done this. Or maybe he couldn't remember for the same reason that he couldn't walk without support, see without squinting, or carry a case of beer in two hands. "And I don't even *drink* beer. I gave that up long ago, right after I drank myself into a stupor with Eric Bloodaxe in Stromness on Orkney. The Dark found me just before dawn and beat me into the arms of Death while I made a drunken last stand in order to protect the Last Egg of Loch Ness. No beer. The occasional shot of rye, but no beer."

oOo

Wearing latex gloves, Shield Brother Jacqueson lifted the cheap painting off the wall to reveal the wrapped Sword of Carolus Magnus. Behind him, his aide, Brother Abiel, was searching the flat for any signs that Takeko had been anything other than a simple artist abducted from her home. Judging by the scarcity of fingerprint powder on everything, the local Crime Scene team had come and gone without doing much more than a cursory examination of the apartment. The police had tossed a few drawers and flung a few sofa cushions in what appeared to be a half-hearted search for a reason for the crime but there was still some semblance of order left in what had been Takeko's home. The painting even hung askew on the wall from when one of the various myopic klutzes had bumped it on his or her way past.

"Have we found Takeko, yet, Brother?"

"No, sir." Abiel tapped his Bluetooth headset. "She lives. We think she's been taken to…"

"Don't say it. Say nothing. We can't trust this space and have to be out in two minutes."

"Yes, sir."

"Did you learn this over the phone?"

"They called while you were making the blessing."

"Tech isn't our friend, Brother. We don't need them knowing how much we know, if that makes any sense."

"It does, sir. The call was scrambled."

"If you say so. I trust you know what you're doing. My concern is that they're learning to use the new technologies faster than the Shields can counter them."

"War chests fund most technological advances, sir, and they do have their fingers in every war chest."

"But we're not without our own resources, though, are we Brother?" He looked at his watch. "Time's almost up. We have to go. Why on earth would they leave the Locus behind?"

"I'm told the Warriors were on scene quite quickly."

"Maybe so, but the Hunters have never avoided a fight before now. Why have they taken the Shield and not the Locus?"

"I'll ask them when I see them, Brother."

Brother Jacqueson smiled at the sarcasm. "See that you do. Before then, though, I want to know why the Warrior Team didn't recover this Locus. It's their job. We shouldn't be here at all."

"The initial report suggested that they had only just gained the stairway up when the police arrived. They managed to sprint to the apartment and confirm that the Hunters had taken Takeko but had to return to base empty-handed or open fire on the local law enforcement."

"Do we have any Shields near Awakening to take on this Locus?" He headed for the makeshift plywood door criss-crossed with Police tape. Abiel closed the last drawer of Takeko's desk and followed

Brother Jacqueson out of the flat. "No sir. Not for another three weeks."

"Marvellous. Now, where is the guitar case we brought with us?"

"In the boot of the sedan, sir."

Brother Jacqueson shook his head. "Not much good it does us in there, Brother." He handed his aide the silk-wrapped sword. "Hide this under your coat then until we get to the sedan while I consider who can Shield it in addition to their regular Locus."

oOo

LIAM'S JOURNAL:

Written old school style—pen on paper. Black ink in a spiral notebook. Have tried this before, 20 or 30 times with mixed success. But I can't NOT put something down. Screw the rules. I'll snap if I just keep holding it in. I've had journals before and there's never been a problem. No art here, so no Pattern. No Pattern, no risk. But NOT creating is killing me, literally. I swear the degeneration of my body is a result of centuries of not being allowed to create, not being permitted to paint or sculpt, or play my banjo or even write dirty haiku.

The human soul was not meant to go without art, without creation on a personal level. Those who think they have no art are wrong. There is art in everything, but only the enlightened can see it. I see it. I need it. But this journal will have to suffice because Master Wei was right—there are Patterns to art.

I learned that lesson the hard way when they tracked me to Jacopo Bassano's Venetian studio back in 1548. I remember it with such precision because it was only days after my 18th birthday. I had just had my Awakening so even though my Shield memories were intact, I was physically not quite an adult. I was apprenticing to Master Jacopo, mixing pigments, when we heard them pounding at the door. Jacopo ushered me out the canal-view window and I swam for it, my recently-earned Locus wrapped in an oilcloth and jammed in my jerkin. It was my second time Shielding Buddha's Pebble and, as it turned out, my shortest time ever as a Shield. I swam in that foul water, then sprinted across the Piazza San Marco and into the alleys, home. I was sure I'd lost them. I knew Venetia better than anyone—I'd lived there three lifetimes already and was cocky and so sure that I could easily outsmart a handful of one-life Dark Hunters.

Some lessons take more than a few lifetimes to learn, though. I didn't think that maybe they'd found me at the studio because they'd already been to my home. I found my mother and father lying together; crossbow bolts feathering their bodies and Father's short sword gripped tight in his calloused fisherman's fist. My older sister, Aniela, died almost as quickly, with a sword thrust through her chest, probably defending her baby, year-old Donata, our family's little gift from God. I heard Donata's weak cry from her basinet in the next room and when I rushed through the curtains to grab her and take her away, I was stopped by a Dark Hunter's sword through my belly.

"You could have been a gifted painter, Lucio. But then, it is *because* you paint that we found you so soon. Tsk tsk."

I would have taken a long time to die if the Hunter Captain hadn't withdrawn his blade from my gut at that moment and beheaded me. I suppose I should be thankful he was a proud soldier and kept his blade sharp, because I felt only the smallest sting under my left ear before I died.

Painting, drawing, writing, *art* is in my soul... and it's the bane of my soul.

Just so you know, I found Donata years later. She was nearly forty, with children and grandchildren of her own. Sometimes the Dark show mercy. More often, not.

o0o

Arvinder rushed out of the Pimlico Tube Station, down the four steps and across Rampayne Street toward Lupus Street, completely unaware that the skies over London were clear and more than a few stars were visible in spite of the glow from the British capitol. Nor did he notice the cheerful little smiles on the faces of his fellow Tube passengers when they passed close by and their souls sensed the presence of Light.

"Bloody hell!"

The bus Arvinder wanted had just turned the corner and there was no way he could catch up in his new Berlutis. He was going to be late for his doubles rematch and Heatley was going to be furious. He hated scheduling games, but this was a fun grudge match he'd fallen into at St. Dorothy's Badminton Club once they found out he'd played on the British National under-18 team. Schedules created Patterns, and Arvinder knew only too well what damage a Pattern could wreak once the Dark caught your scent.

He was still dressed in what Heatley called his Hugo Boss-Me-Around suit—his whites, court shoes, and a pair of Carlton racquets were in the bag clutched tight under his right arm as he half-walked, half-jogged west on Lupus Street toward the comfy little church which housed the gay badminton club. When Heatley had first suggested to Arvinder that he drop by St. Dot's and lob the shuttle around for an hour or so before they headed off to the local pub for a pint, he'd expected to have a casual game or two, maybe work up a bit of a glow, and then toss back a Courvoisier or two with Heatley and his chums.

What he'd discovered was a level of play that stretched his old game to its max, and he'd loved it! He'd tried two of the other gay clubs in town, but St. Dot's was the first one that actually challenged him to pick up his socks and work up a sweat. It was also one of the few places in London where he didn't feel the oppressive presence of the Dark around every corner.

At the bottom of his sports bag, in a padded box, wrapped in a towel, was his Locus—a hand-carved wooden representation of Aten, the disk of the sun in ancient Egyptian mythology. Carvings of Aten abound in the world, but this particular carving had been a gift from Panhsj, a male slave, to Queen Nefertiti herself in 1330 BCE. Panhsj carved it in secret for the woman and queen he loved and although he knew the beautiful Queen of Pharaoh Akhenaten could never return the love of a slave, Panhsj risked his life to place it at her bedside when he thought no one watched.

But Panhsj was caught and executed without the knowledge of his Queen and, not long after, Nefertiti herself vanished. It has been suggested that the queen had indeed loved Panhsj back and for that she was poisoned by one of the old priests who still had not forgiven her and the Pharaoh for their radical religious reforms. But before priests of the old gods could desecrate her remains, the queen's body and the carving vanished into the night, in the care of her own faithful priests. Her tomb was so well hidden that it has remained untouched, but the little carving of love and wood never made it into the tomb. Nefertiti's senior priest wanted to hold on to something to keep his queen's memory alive and so he'd slipped it into his robes and kept it safe. Now it was Arvinder's task to keep it safe and out of the hands of zealous collectors, Egyptian nationalists who believed all Egyptian relics should remain in Egypt and, of course, The Dark.

The carving and its hermetically-sealed box were actually quite light and although he'd had one or two curious eyes spot the box over the years, he deflected interest by simply telling people that it contained the ashes of his first love, who'd been claimed by AIDS. No one ever asked about it a second time nor did they show any interest in examining the contents. His first love, Reid, *did* die of AIDS-related complications, but he was buried in a family plot near Reading.

Nefertiti's Aten had been his Locus for almost fifteen years and Arvinder knew that the odds were slim he'd get another fifteen if he stayed in London—this ancient city was thick with the Dark. He checked his Rolex again and picked up his pace. He crossed over Lupus Street to the south side and cupped the tiny, high-powered, 4G-connected emergency transmitter on the chain around his neck, out of reflex. Even though he had two razor-sharp, twenty-six-inch Filipino talibong blades secreted in the bottom of his ADIDAS sports bag, the transmitter gave him peace of mind with regard to the wellbeing of his Locus.

His disposable phone rang and he just *knew* it was Heatley, wondering where the hell he was. Bloody impatient queen! That Eton old boy needed a serious unknotting of his knickers. He dodged a smiling old bloke shuffling from the shoe repair across the walk to the bus shelter, then Arvinder jogged past the Pimlico Toy Library and zipped around the corner into Glasgow Terrace. Only a few yards to go. His phone rang again but stopped in mid chime. A blanket of silence crushed the air around him, except for the sound of his leather-soled Berlutis on the asphalt. Then there were other noises, but Arvinder was already down on one knee, reaching for a talibong.

In his rush to flip over his bag and get at his weapons, he forgot all about the transmitter hanging inside his Calvin Klein shirt. Multiple boot scuffings from the street behind him brought his head up, but too late. A cricket bat swung around and only a last-second reflexive twist let him take it on his shoulder rather than his head.

Arvinder was knocked away from the bag and quickly surrounded. There were at least four, maybe five, black-booted skinhead punks, and under the washed-out light of the street lamp none looked like they were out of their teens.

"Grab th' Paki poof an' his fag bag an' drag 'im over be'ind the 'edge! Quick, ya bast'rds!"

His attackers did just as they were ordered and that was fine with Arvinder because he preferred fewer witnesses. He struggled a bit, to make it look good, then they dumped his bag with him on top of it.

"Fine th' fing wot we got paid t' fine and then do this Chutney Farmer good. Make it look like nuffin' more'n a poof beatin', but make it permanent-like."

"Git offa th' bag, poof! We gonna mess you up right!"

At least two strong hands grabbed the back of his jacket and hauled Arvinder upright so that they could get at the bag. Expecting a terrified 'Paki poof' in a suit, the thugs froze when he came up silent and swinging sharp steel. Two went down fast and silent with blurred stabs and thrusts before the remaining four—he confirmed there were only six in total—could move. He could see now that of the four standing, three were only street hooligans being paid to be muscle, but there was something about the fourth one that made Arvinder keep one eye on him while he made quick work of the three.

The little one with the cricket bat shouted a considerate warning as he raised the bat and stepped in for what would have been a killing stroke even in the hands of a child, but Arvinder dropped low, spun on the damp grass and sliced the Andrew Strauss-wannabe clean across the abdomen. Black t-shirt, leather vest and flesh all parted soundlessly and the scruff went down. Arvinder knew a kill when he felt one so he didn't even confirm it, just kept his body turning and his blades moving. A set of chains rattled to his right so he raised a blind blocking arm and brought an underhand blow around and up into the crotch of the next assailant. A hard upward thrust-and-pull and it was done.

The fourth man was circling around, trying to get to the bag, but Arvinder moved to stand over it and defend it with his life. The third teen looked at the butterfly knife he'd just flicked out of his pocket but was smart enough to realize it was useless against the talibongs. He pried the cricket bat out of the owner's still-twitching hand and stepped up to Arvinder.

"You jus' killed me mates, poof! W'en Shawn-o's done wif you, they'll need to wipe off th' blood jus' to find out you're *brown*." His forearms flexed and his tattoos popped as his grip tightened on the bat. Arvinder dropped the tips of the blades a little and blew Shawn-o a kiss. Shawn-o blinked and did exactly what the Shield expected him to do—he took the bait. The fast, rage-backed swing nearly caught Arvinder in the chin, but he leaned back and it whizzed past without making contact. Arvinder stepped into the long follow-up of the bat, blew Shawn-o another kiss and shoved both blades deep into the young thug's chest.

The Shield heard a clanking sound behind him and ducked, his blades still embedded in flesh. The length of chain caught poor, dead Shawn-o in the forehead and knocked the corpse away so that Arvinder was able to easily pull the talibongs free. He lashed out with his foot but the last man standing was quick, and not without some training. The man was also scared, though, and scared men make mistakes. He swung the chain again, to keep Arvinder at bay, and then he ducked in to retrieve the now blood-splattered ADIDAS bag. "We're everywhere, Shield. Y'can't stop us but we c'n stop you. I'll just tike this li'l treasure from you and leave you t' wonder when we're going to come in the night and gut you f'good."

His mistake came when he glanced down to find the straps of the bag after a blind attempt to grab at them came up empty. Arvinder didn't wait for a second chance and threw his left-hand talibong to force the Dark Hunter to move right. With bag in hand, he went exactly to where Arvinder needed him to be and the Shield dove straight over a corpse and sank his second blade into the back of the worn leather jacket. The scruffy leader in the jacket collapsed like a punctured hot water bottle and Arvinder rolled off, taking the blade with him. The sounds of the neighbourhood returned.

There was no time to search the bodies or even to see if any of them still lived, which he doubted. The Shield retrieved the thrown blade, wiped both off on the grass, sheathed the pair back into the bottom of the bag, peeled off his blood-soaked jacket and wrapped it inside out around the bag. A quick look left, right and above showed two geriatric heads watching in curious silence from a balcony four floors up, but neither one of the old birds appeared to have any kind of recording device in hand so he turned and walked briskly back out to Lupus Street.

His phone started ringing again and he laughed without answering it. "Sorry, Heatley old boy, you'll not be getting any joy from Arvinder tonight, or *any* night for that matter. It's time Arvi-boy tried the Isle of Wight, or maybe Munich."

Chapter Four: Liam's Widow

"Two Shields in the same place at the same time draw the Dark like ants to honey. A Shield operates in complete isolation. It can be no other way."
~Shield Master Wei (1939 CE to Ernest Hemingway at Hotel Ambos Mundos.)

oOo

Brother Paul looked at the satellite phone Housyar had just handed him. Larger than a cell phone, with a big, pivoting aerial, it really was his only option and he knew it. "There's no question that the Bracers are there?"

"None, sir. They'll only be in Chinese airspace for another thirty minutes, but they'll be within ten nautical miles of the Chinese Carrier *Guan Yu* in five minutes. An intercept could force them to land at *this* airport." He tapped the printout he had brought with him to Paul's office.

"We're cutting it close."

"Too close, but it's our only choice at this time. Can our contact make it happen this fast?"

"There's only one way to find out, isn't there?" Paul dialled the number from memory, not because he used it often but because his memory held onto numbers in a mutant way that he liked to think wasn't as freaky as it really was. The phone was answered immediately.

"Brother Ying, it's Brother Paul. May I impose upon you for a favour? Thank, you, Brother. Here is what I need..." In less than a minute he summarized the plan and the urgency and disconnected the call.

"He will make it happen." He returned the phone to Housyar. "Now, you'd better scramble a Warrior Team to that airport. This will be fast and furious and the Hunters will be suspicious and prepared. We must simply be better prepared."

Housyar dialled a number of his own, speaking to Paul as he did. "Let's get those Bracers back."

oOo

Simon Mayhew knocked once on the dark-stained oak door and entered the massive, high-ceilinged office without waiting for a reply. Mick Crowley sat behind his room-dominating solid walnut desk, leaning back in his leather chair, looking at the monitor of his seventeen-inch laptop. It was a book-shelf-lined, dark-wood-panelled, velvet-draped, Hollywood-cliché of the office of the 'evil financial emperor' and Mayhew loved it. He was a huge fan of American cinema and had helped his cousin set up the office when they'd first acquired the building. But this was not a good time to be admiring Mick's office décor. He spoke into the deadly silence.

"Did you see it? Did you watch them bollocks it up worse than a celebrity marriage?" Mayhew tried to keep the whine out of his voice.

Crowley leaned forward, gently closed the laptop with a click and tilted his head as an animal would before deciding whether it was facing an ally or a meal. He made his decision and leaned back again, left fingers spinning the platinum ring on his right ring finger. "What did you expect, Simon? I mean, really. I hand you the intel on this Shield, point you in his direction, show you his *Pattern* and ask you— nicely, mind you—to bring me Nefertiti's Aten. A simple, priceless, wooden carving made by a slave for his true love. Nothing too complicated. Nothing I would even think of as *strenuous*. Kill the Shield, take the prize, return home, pop open a nice, cheap Merlot to mourn another loss for Light and another win for Dark, then get on with the evening." He gestured at the bottle of California merlot next to two crystal wine glasses on the silver tray on the sideboard to his left. "I ask again, Simon, *what did you expect*? What did you expect the result to be when you hired six street wankers to take down a trained Shield and then sent them off willy-nilly to do the job while you sat in your bloody office watching it on a live video feed? I let you recruit your first very own Hunter Team and you let me down."

"He's a raving poof. It shouldn't have been a difficult job."

"*I'm* a 'poof' you stupid prat! Does it make me any less capable of gutting you and eating your spleen? I certainly hope not, because I will, you know. I most certainly will, if you lose this Shield and we have to start the hunt all over again. Now, go back to your little hidey-hole and contact your goddamned network, use all the bloody technology Tabak in Santiago has loaned us and *find... that... Shield!*"

Simon shut his mouth, his reflexive retort lost in mid-thought. He turned quietly and started for the door. He heard a whisper of cloth and the muscles between his shoulder blades tensed in anticipation a deathblow. It didn't happen. When he reached the door he looked over his shoulder and Mick was leaning back once more, his eyes closed, his headphones in his ears and probably some sort of pulse-pounding Death Metal drowning out the world around him. As Simon closed the door behind him he heard Mick singing softly to himself "Ain't no mountain high enough, ain't no valley low enough..." As soon as the door clicked shut, Simon whipped out his Blackberry and initiated a call while striding down the hall to his office. It was late, but as he bragged to the office staff, the Dark never slept.

oOo

Takeko woke up blind and vomiting up her eggs-over-easy breakfast, but she didn't care about either because she was in excruciating pain. Someone had torn her shoulders out of their sockets and then driven steel bolts through her thighs—at least that's what the synapses were telling her brain. She tried to sit up and discovered that she was hog-tied with her hands and feet zip-tied together, behind her back. The steel bolts in her legs were cramps, Charlie horses; and the dislocated shoulders... well, they might just be dislocated shoulders. She arched her back a bit to relieve some of the pressure but she couldn't hold the position for long.

She'd been in messes before, but this was feeling like the mess-of-all-messes. She finally lay as still as she could and listened. She wanted to scream out loud—curse and bellow and scream to relieve the pain, but she listened. She heard the whine of turbine jet engines and the gentle motion from side to side and up and down—like a laid-back roller coaster run by a stoner afraid of speed. The engines were close, though and not big ones. The pitch of their whine told her it was a small jet, probably one of a fleet owned by the Dark. The cavalry was going to have a bloody tough time finding her up here. Rough wood scratched her cheek and she could discern sunlight leaking through a yard-long corner seam of what she assumed was a shipping crate.

That was the bad news. The good news was that she was still alive. Of course that meant she was in for long sessions of torture and pain and misery—but as long as she lived there was hope.

Takeko would rather endure torture at the hands of someone she could look in the eye than the pain she was in, alone in the crate next to her own vomit. She was trying to get up the courage to take a deep breath of the fumes around her so she could scream for someone's attention when she heard a soft cough. She had company. "Anyone who wants to open the box and let me out—even in chains with a dog collar—will be my new best friend."

"I would if I could, señorita, but I can't so I won't." The Spanish-accented mature man's voice came from up and to her left.

"Then can I put in a formal request..." The pain in her shoulders threatened to derail her resolve and burn up her false calm. "...A formal request for someone who can, please?"

"They already know. Try to relax. Want me to sing you a song or tell you a story?"

"A *what?*"

"A song or a story. To help pass the time since neither one of us is going anywhere and has nothing else to do."

Anything was better than listening to her own ragged breathing and elevated heart beat. "Can you hum?"

"I can hum with the best of them, señorita, but I sing best of all." He proceeded to softly sing a few bars of La Bamba.

In spite of her situation, Takeko was impressed. Her captor had a beautiful tenor voice. "That was magnífico. You can sing to me any time."

"¡Muchas gracias! señorita. I sing in the town choir. My father was lead tenor with the National Opera, so I am coming by it naturally. I..." he stopped mid sentence as if interrupted. Takeko suspected he was listening to instructions on some sort of headset or earpiece. After a moment he answered with a simple 'sí'. She could hear a hinge squeak as her captor moved in his seat.

"Señorita, I must go. There will be no more songs."

Damn. She'd hoped to win him over to her side, at least enough to get her restraints loosened. "Please don't. I love your voice. It warms my heart and makes me forget the pain." She was answered by the whine of the turbines. "Please. Please!" Nothing. She was alone again, though she suspected that he was still listening and watching, while Takeko waited. "It's okay, señor. Te perdono el error de sus caminos." *I forgive you the error of your ways.*

oOo

Only seven seconds before the flashing hand warned him not to cross the intersection! Seven bloody seconds in morning rush hour! How the hell was a cripple expected to make it across in that time? Oh, sure, Liam grumbled to himself, there were still nine more seconds before the light actually changed, but *sixteen seconds* for a gimp with a cane and a short-legged mutt to get across a busy intersection?! Bull! He only wanted to walk to Prince's Island to give Phoenix some exercise, but he couldn't just walk the five blocks directly from the apartment because he'd done that once last week. He had to pick another route, a seemingly random route, a route that wouldn't form a Pattern with previous routes they had taken. It was such a simple walk to take, too. A year ago he was running it at top speed, with Phoenix tucked under his arm or in a large-wheeled push-stroller, but his fiftieth year hadn't been kind to him at all. His wonky vision had first slowed him down—if he couldn't see the traffic clearly he couldn't avoid the bike messengers who careened up and down the streets and sidewalks of downtown, heedless of vehicles and pedestrians alike. Then it was his leg. At first it just tingled but it slowed him to a walk because he suspected it was a pinched nerve brought on by the jarring motion of his running. Three months ago his left knee had given out while he was in line at a Tim Horton's trying whatever was new to the donut and coffee chain's menu. The knee he knew was a problem with his patella he'd had since he was a teen, but in conjunction with his vision and his leg-tinglings, he wondered if maybe he should just suck it up and go see a doctor.

But he didn't. He hobbled along, pushing himself to the new limits that his body was imposing on him. He tried to walk everywhere; both for fresh air and for the flexibility being on foot gave him when the inevitable attack came. With the Dark bearing down on you was no time to be stuck in traffic in either the Corolla or a city bus. On foot he'd been able to dodge and duck in and out, using all of the paths and alleys and escape routes he had long ago mapped out in his head. Then he'd slipped on black ice and he'd gone down *hard*. To keep from landing on Phoenix walking beside him he had twisted in mid-fall. The chiropractor he finally went to see said that it was a noble gesture, but he was paying the price now. Two of his rib heads had popped out, which explained the excruciating pain he'd been in, lying there by the front steps of the red granite office tower.

Pretty, petite, *deceptively strong,* Dr. Lindsay had popped the ribs back in, adjusted his hip, and fixed the alignment in his neck, easing the pain considerably. At least for a few days. Then one day he'd turned his head to the side, sneezed hard, and popped at least one of the ribs out again. What this all added up to as he walked with Phoenix was that every step took effort and every step hurt like hell, even with the cane.

"This is getting ridiculous, P. I mean, the knees have been a problem on and off since I was in junior high, but the rest of it... I just can't figure out." Phoenix licked his hand. "Yah, I know. Go see a doctor. That means leaving you in the car or leaving you at home, you know. I think someone might catch on if we put you in the pack, cuz at some point you'd have to go to the bathroom and those clinics have a *minimum* three-hour wait."

Phoenix climbed off Liam's lap and onto the bench. "Ready to walk?" She snorted like a miniature pig after truffles. "Me too." He clipped the leash onto her harness and lowered her to the grass. "I hate making you wear this, but there are too many big dogs that'll make a meal out of you before I could bend down to rescue you. At least with this thing I can snap you back up into my arms before I slay the beast with my razor-sharp wit and lightning reflexes."

The two of them started off down the path, Liam staying tight to the right side while Phoenix walked on the grass, leaving plenty of room on their left for runners and cyclists alike. Liam kept an especially wary eye open for skateboarding punks.

The cool, dry air of the foothills of the Rocky Mountains blew strong and true along the riverside path scrubbing Liam's soul clean and making his mysterious symptoms fade just a little as the two of them sauntered without plan through the trees on the island just north of downtown. Frisbees flew, Hacky Sacks were kicked aloft and people of all shapes and sizes strolled, jogged, skateboarded, Rollerbladed and cycled along the pathways, showing more consideration and awareness for others than did the always-in-a-hurry drivers on the city streets beyond the tiny island. Music came in from at least three different directions to serenade them and Liam could pick out a guitar, drums—possibly bongos, accompanied by the voice of a poet who fancied himself possessed of the Beat—and what had to be an Irish flute.

"We haven't heard a tin flute in awhile, Miss P. Wanna go find it?" Phoenix stopped and sat, her eyes wide. Liam shuffled along another step or two before the retractable leash went taut. He looked back, surprised. "What? Suddenly you're a music critic? Since when do you *not* want to dance to the flute? Since when do you..." Phoenix grunted and pulled the leash in the opposite direction. Liam suddenly understood. "Damn. I didn't think of that." He listened to the flute for a moment. "It does sound almost too good, too much like a Faerie pipe." He let Phoenix lead them off on a course perpendicular to the music—away, but not obviously so.

"Could they know we're here in Calgary? They couldn't *possibly* know we're here. Dammit, they know we're here. That was quick, by Faerie time. Better wander home and pack, I suppose." He looked down at his weak hand and fumbling leg. "Great timing—just when we need to run, I can't." Phoenix barked softly and dropped back beside the Shield, giving him her complete trust and confidence. She added a growl and Liam laughed. "So *you'll* protect *me*? I love the gesture, but it'll be a short battle—no pun intended—when they do catch up to us. They won't be sending a couple of mental lightweights who give the skateboard community a bad name."

The two regained the asphalt pathway and slowly, almost casually, crossed over the bridge. Liam led them south, aiming for the LRT platform leading to the northeast. They lived downtown but they still needed to avoid creating a Pattern of walking home from the park.

oOo

Becca pulled the road-dust-covered white Jeep Compass into the Tower Parkade, found a parking stall on a middle floor and backed in, careful to leave enough room to open the rear hatch and retrieve her bike. She shifted into Park, leaned over the centre console and opened the glove compartment. She pulled out a worn multi-head screwdriver, rifled through the few pieces of paper to make sure there was nothing of hers stuck in with the previous owner's detritus. Nothing. She climbed out of the vehicle and crouched down to check under the seats and between the seat cushions. More nothing.

She stood up, gently closed the door and looked around the garage. No one in sight, no obvious cameras pointed in her direction. Moving to the front of the Jeep, she quickly removed the British Columbia license plate. A second look around assured her that no one had suddenly stepped out from behind one of the two-dozen cars nearby. Slipping between the Compass and the red Sunfire in the next stall, Becca moved around back, popped the hatch and took out a pair of worn, green nylon pannier bags and a scuffed, two-foot-long black plastic drafting document tube. She put them to the side and went back in for her Kuwahara mountain bike. The Jeep, panniers, tube and bike were everything she owned, and technically, she didn't even own the car.

Leaning the bike against the concrete wall behind the Sunfire, hanging the tube over the handlebars and the panniers over the bike's cross bar, Becca ducked down and made quick work of the two screws holding the rear licence plate in place. The Province of Alberta didn't require its residents to have front license plates so it could be days or weeks before someone thought to look at the rear plate of the soon-to-be-abandoned vehicle. By then she'd be unavailable to answer questions about how a car from Richmond, British Columbia got all the way through the mountains to a commercial parking structure in Calgary. Of course the plates didn't even match the vehicle so when she dropped them into a garbage can somewhere outside the garage, the connection would be one more step removed.

The screwdriver went into one of the panniers then she closed the rear hatch and she returned to the driver's seat. She switched on the four-wheel drive and slowly, gently, backed the car up until there was a metal-on-concrete grinding sound and the rear of the Compass lifted as the exhaust pipe and muffler were forced over the abutment that was meant to keep drivers from backing into the wall. Becca ignored the grinding and kept going until the rear bumper was tight against that wall. No one would see that the plate was missing until they moved the vehicle forward at least a foot, and for that they'd need a tow truck or the key, which she pocketed after shifting into park and turning the engine off. The key would find a completely different garbage can and she would buy herself a bit more time, which, as Master Wei had reminded her repeatedly over the centuries, is really all she could ask for.

It took only a moment to slip the plates into a pannier, clip both bags onto the bike's carrier, check the document tube to ensure that her Locus was still inside, then slip the tube's carrying strap over her shoulder and wheel the bike out from behind the Sunfire and mount up. She pressed the remote lock in her pocket and the car's horn honked and lights flashed as it was secured and the alarm set. A quick look back to let her subconscious brain click through her mental inventory to see if she'd forgotten to do anything... and then she was off down the parkade's spiral ramp and out past the exit barrier to the street. It was urban air, but it was a cool breeze on her face and Becca felt good to be on the move with her Locus but without the stolen car.

oOo

The drizzle started when Liam and Phoenix were two blocks from the train platform and not having much luck moving against the crowd. The Saddletown train they needed went past on 7th Avenue while they waited in the rain to cross at the light. Liam cursed to himself, as did two or three others at the light.

The second North-East-bound train pulled up to the platform, dropped a few off, loaded a lot more and departed, all while Liam was struggling to get the change out of his pocket and into the ticket dispenser. "God-dammit...! Stupid fu..." He dropped a two-dollar coin and watched as it managed to roll past every shoe, boot and sandal between him and the edge of the platform where it rolled off and out of reach. "Screw it. We'll take a chance on a single ticket, Wetdog." Phoenix 'Harffed' softly and Liam awkwardly scooped her up and cleared away from the ticket dispenser so the person behind him could demonstrate how simple the task was when you didn't have rebellious muscles and nerves fighting you every step of the way. Liam didn't bother to watch, but instead limped behind the big curved concrete pillar where he leaned and watched for the next train.

He liked Calgary's northeast—it was an area heavy with hard-working immigrants from all parts of the world, many of them refugees from persecution and famine and slaughter who came to Canada, freedom and a world of conspicuous consumption and mass consumerism. More often than not the new Canadians kept to themselves on the buses and trains, though occasionally shy eye contact was made by someone just trying to make an honest human connection that they might not have been able to safely make back in their homeland.

Liam preferred transit in the northeast—no one cared who he was—unlike routes which led to neighbourhoods where not looking like an oil and gas industry grunt or civil servant set off the alarm bells in the commuters' heads and they watched you closely, surreptitiously, while texting spouses, children, lovers or co-workers.

A Somerset-Bridlewood train pulled into the station and the passengers heading to the south end of the city boarded, leaving Liam and a dozen or so others to wait for the northeast train sitting a block back, waiting for its turn at the platform. Liam made a mental note where the doors opened on the train currently loading and shuffled to get opposite where the next set would be.

Lately it took him long enough to board the train without having to start between doors and try to hobble-run to get in before the umpteen seconds were up. The train schedule was tight and the operators were given no flexibility to wait for passengers who weren't prepared to rush. They even had signs on the trains requesting passengers not to hold the doors for others as it delayed departure. Welcome to the western world where the Almighty Schedule overruled human decency and consideration.

Some days Liam was amazed that Light hadn't already succumbed to Dark, sending him and all the other Shields to whatever unemployment line serviced recycled mortals. While the approaching train waited at the traffic light—Liam always got a kick out of the fact that Calgary's Light Rail Transit had to wait at traffic lights like everyone else—he wondered what would happen to himself and the other Shields if the Dark ever did win. Would it be a life of torture and despair here in this realm or would he finally be killed outright, once and for all, to go on wherever he was destined to end up?

By the time the train pulled up to the platform the crowd heading to the northeast had grown again and Liam had to jostle his way in so that there'd be a slim hope of getting a seat, even with the ones nearest the doors designated as priority seating for the "mobility impaired". In Calgary, as with anywhere else, he'd found it was a crapshoot whether or not a fellow traveller would stand so that the elderly, pregnant or infirm might sit. Sometimes he gave his own seat up and sometimes he didn't—always trying to avoid creating a Pattern. Of course, when he ignored another person's need he felt like crap and that was the one Pattern he couldn't avoid.

This time he got lucky and got a window seat.

oOo

When the rain started, Becca stopped briefly to make sure the lid was tight on the document tube before pulling up her hood and continuing to walk the bike along pedestrians-only Stephen's Avenue. After crossing over 1st Street she hopped back on the bike and cut through the one-block-square Olympic Plaza, determined to put some distance between herself and the Jeep in spite of the rain. She reached the sidewalk on 7th Avenue just as a commuter train pulled up beside her, held up at the traffic signal ahead. Without knowing exactly why, she stopped the bike, and looked up at the train, half-expecting to see it full of Dark Hunters, or cops looking for cyclists who abandon cars in parkades, or both. She scanned the faces in the windows but they were just the usual mix, heading out of downtown for one reason or another.

Then she saw one face she knew, or *thought* she knew. He was at least forty, sporting a goatee, dressed in what looked like a hoody and an oilskin slicker. He was holding a small scruffy dog up to the window so it could see the world as it went by, although the train was standing still. He was looking up at the sky—probably wondering when the damned rain would stop—when he suddenly looked right at her as if she'd called his name, which she couldn't have because she didn't know it. As soon as their eyes met, though, she *did* know it. Skosche.

Chapter Five: Code Red

"A Shield has eighteen years of innocence before his or her Awakening. Eighteen years to experience a true life, free of the responsibilities of a Shield. Eighteen years to be reminded what Light is all about and why the worlds need Shields."

~ Shield Master Wei (1301 CE while watching the Jongleurs perform in Paris.)

oOo

The rain was thinning outside but Liam was still glad to be inside the train. If he could, he'd have ridden the rails all day, back and forth across the city, staying dry and watching people. He'd never really minded the rain before, but his fifty-year-old joints weren't so fond of the ache when the weather changed and it went from dry to wet or vice versa. The train only went half-a-block before it stopped for the traffic light. Phoenix grunted on his lap and put her paws on the window so she could look out. He picked her up so she could see better.

"There's not a helluva lot to see out there, P. Just trees in Olympic Plaza and people getting wetter than us." He pointed upward and squinted. "See, the rain isn't as heavy but there's no sign of the sun shining through, so be glad we're out of it at least for awhile. Wouldn't want to be that bike messenger—she's getting *soaked*. She's..." The young woman stood astride her bike, looking into the train at the dry faces and then she looked at Liam and smiled as only an old friend could smile. Liam smiled back, confused at first because he'd never seen her before, but then she laughed like all of the time and space separating this moment from their last together was gone, vanished, and he knew her better than he knew himself. For in this single moment his vision was perfect again. Crystal clear. She was Kirabo and Sarah and Yindi. But Lynette was who she would always be to him, because Lynette was who she was when he had loved her, married her, had a family with her, and broke almost all of the Shield rules for her. His heart, his soul, his centre, his Light.

She smiled up at him and waved a tiny finger wave, knowing that he knew that she knew and that's all either of them needed to know. The traffic light changed and the train moved forward, on to the next stop. Frantic, desperate, Liam twisted in his seat and watched her ride away into the rainy park. Then she was gone and his vision went back to less-than-perfect and he was lost again. But he wasn't. Lynette was *here*, though she didn't look at all like Lynette. She looked more like she had when she'd been Sarah, but with shorter hair and a few more freckles.

He struggled to his feet because, despite the closeness of the Dark or Faerie in the city and despite the fact that the synergy produced by two active Shields in the same place at the same time was almost palpable to anyone nearby, *especially* the Dark, Liam had to find Lynette. He had to hold her close and tell her that... tell her... dammit! He just had to find her!

"Excuse me. Sorry. Got on the wrong train. Sorry. Excuse me..." he apologized as he shoved his way out to the aisle with Phoenix clutched tight to his chest and his cane hanging over his arm where it banged into his shins but wouldn't smack into anyone else. He didn't have much time. As soon as the train cleared the intersection it would be slowing on approach to the City Hall platform and Liam needed off—Lynette was out there!

Passengers parted and one even grabbed Liam's elbow when the train lurched and it looked like he was going to fall.

"Thanks."

"Bin there, my bredda. All fruits ripe."

Liam looked closer at his benefactor just as the train came to a stop and saw that the young black man was missing his right leg from just below the knee. The prosthetic leg was painted with a large flag of Jamaica and his face was one, big, peaceful smile. Liam smiled back. "Yer a bashy one, bredda. Stay cris."

The door opened, Liam tightened his grip on the cane and made his way out onto the platform. He limped to the railing over the sidewalk and leaned against it, looking back west. "Where did she go, P? Originally she was coming this way, on the sidewalk, but it looked like she changed her mind and headed into the park. She could be blocks away by now."

The dog-that-was-really-a-pixie-princess struggled in Liam's arms. "You want down? Think you can find her in the rain?" She harffed back at him. "You got it, missy. A-hunting we will go." Foot traffic on the platform thinned a bit with the train's departure so Liam put Phoenix down, locked her retractable leash short so she wouldn't trip anyone up, and let her lead him down the steps and south on the sidewalk. So intently was Liam scanning Olympic Plaza west across the street that he didn't notice the rain stop nor did he hear the distant sound of a tin flute moving closer.

oOo

"Have you got something to show me, Ghazar? Something I was maybe expecting six weeks ago?"

"Yessir, and I think you'll agree that it was worth the wait."

"I doubt that very much, young feller, but you might as well make your pitch."

The geek in the khakis, sandals and the *"There's No Such Thing as Gravity, the Earth Sucks"* t-shirt plucked the lab's Smartphone up out of its charging cradle and handed it to the 'suit' standing beside his desk. The 'suit' never actually wore a suit, and instead was more comfortable in jeans, cowboy boots and plaid shirts, but he was the CEO of the Dark's corporate face, DökktEfniTækni, and that made him *the* 'suit'. Ghazar didn't mind 'suits'—he planned to be one himself, someday—but Wallace Tabak was a 'suit' with a honed stainless steel edge to his management style, and that made Ghazar run everything through his mental filters at least once before he said it out loud in Tabak's presence.

Ghazar's predecessor—his best friend, Mundhir—had overestimated his importance to DET and not only failed to complete two *major* projects on time, he'd also lied about it and tried to hide his failures from Tabak and the executive team. Mundhir was terminated without notice and the only severance he got was when the VP of InHuman Resources severed his head from his body in the courtyard during the last corporate Town Hall meeting. DET ran things a little differently than anyone else in the Chilean alternative to Silicon Valley, and Ghazar had no problem with that. Great rewards required great sacrifices—followers of the Dark knew that, and Ghazar had been an enthusiastic member of the fold since he'd killed his first neighbourhood cat and discovered a taste for causing pain in others.

Ghazar overestimated neither his importance nor his abilities, though he knew he was almost the genius his parents had touted him as and he knew that if there was anyone here in Santiago who could create the app that Tabak et al wanted on all the Hunter Teams' Smartphones by month-end, it was him, Ghazar ben David, PhD, Fulbright alumnus, Dark coven member, and master of the staff skateboarding half-pipe.

"Ghazar, young fella, what the hell am I lookin' at here?"

The Smartphone's screen had gone dark. Ghazar stood up quickly and extended his hand to get the device back. Tabak just shook his head and held onto the phone.

"Just tell me what to do, son. If you can't explain it to me right here and now, then it's not gonna do much good in the field. Treat me like the idiot your predecessor was and explain it."

"Um, yessir." Ghazar turned his mental filters on full power and took his boss through it one step at a time. "Press the button on the bottom of the face to turn it on, then swipe your finger across the slider to access the menu." Tabak followed Ghazar's simple directions. Ghazar leaned in a bit to make sure the screen looked like it was supposed to. "Press the company logo and give the app a moment to start up."

"I sure as brimstone hope there's more to it than this, because

Mundhir showed me this much a month ago... and we all know how that went."

Ghazar swallowed and nodded. He looked at the Smartphone in Tabak's hand and saw that the app was loaded. "It should all look about the same up to this point, sir, but this is where it gets fun."

"'Fun', Ghazar? You think I've invested a billion dollars into this company so we can have *fun* with Smartphones? Maybe I should have hired that Warren Gray fella away from RIM and gone in that direction. Don't give me 'fun', give me *results*."

"A poor choice of words, sir." Ghazar took a deep breath. "Look at your screen, please. Press the smaller company logo up in the left corner. That will use the GPS feature to find the user's location within two metres. I know that's nothing special, yet, but it's the necessary initial step when you first open the app." Tabak pressed the button, unimpressed but showing patience. "Now, sir, press the Green Spiral in the upper right corner." Tabak did so. "That will make the uplink with the server here in Santiago, scrambled and routed six-ways-to-Saturday."

Tabak smiled. "That's 'six-ways-to-Sunday', young fella."

Ghazar tried to smile back. "I was raised as a Jew, sir, so my father always said 'Saturday'."

"Point taken. Go on, son."

"The real work is being done by our own systems here. I won't get too technical, but our own little DETNADEUX can process almost twelve petaflops of data per second. That's twelve *quadrillion* operations per second—the fastest private supercomputer on the planet. But she needs to be for the algorithms we have her running. Through our government, military, and law-enforcement contracts we've gained access to most of the world's connected surveillance data. Everything including traffic cams, private security systems which upload to off-site servers, Google, Facebook, and the various national agencies, including—but by no means limited to—America's NSA and Homeland Security, Greece's NIS, Egypt's Jihaz Amn al Daoula and Australia's ASIS. DETNADEUX is pulling everything in and checking for Patterns. She's..."

Tabak held up his hand and interrupted Ghazar's stream. "Son, we already got Pattern-analysis software. The best there is. And an automated text message from DETNA-ONE to any phone can pass along the information almost instantaneously. You're not impressing me, here, Ghazar."

Ghazar dared a small smile. "DETNA-ONE is capable of crunching data with the best of them, but we have to feed her the data ourselves. She can only use what we give her. Someone has to decide what to feed DETNA-ONE. DETNADEUX doesn't have to be fed, nor does a decision have to be made. She grabs at each and every open data feed *on the planet* and analyzes what she sees. Everything from emails to Tweets to retail store security cameras. She's not intelligent by any means, she's just the biggest, fastest data-cruncher ever built. Big Sister *is* watching."

"And what can she do with that data? What's the point of all this?"

"DETNADEUX has been fed every bit of data we have on every Shield over the last two-thousand years. Fact, fiction, legend, it's *all* in there. Were they left-handed? Did they prefer sword to bow, soup to salad, boys to girls, dogs to cats, coke to heroin. *Everything* we know about every Shield." He took a slurp from the mug of cooling Chilean tea on his desk.

"So she's got a long reach and a big memory. Not yet impressed, Ghazar."

The programmer swallowed the tea and dared to take another sip before going on. "This is where we ramped it up a bit. It was Rhianna's idea and it's a brilliant one." Tall, lanky, tattooed, shaggy-coifed Rhianna waved shyly from the crowd of twenty now gathered around Ghazar's workstation. Ghazar nodded at her and continued. "DETNADEUX takes all of the data we know about Shields in general, and adds that to the mix. The never-written-down-by-Shields rules of Master Wei, their operational methods at the management level... everything we know from their communiqués to the facts gleaned from Shield tortures over the centuries. There are Patterns there, too. They're only human, so they're as prone to habits and Patterns as the rest of us. Try as they might, they can't get away from their human nature."

Tabak retrieved a pack of gum out of his shirt pocket, pulled a piece out, unwrapped it, popped it in his mouth, and returned both the pack and the empty wrapper to his pocket. He didn't offer anyone else a piece. "You've got my attention. You've thought outside the box I gave you. Of course, Rhianna isn't the first one to think of looking at the big picture, but she *is* the first one to do it with regard to this application of the data. Go on, Ghazar."

"DETNADEUX crunches a planet's-worth of data at light speed and finds the Patterns, applies all the math and fuzzy logic we've taught her and plays a game of 'Where's the Shield?'. We know that when a Shield is killed they're reborn within the hour somewhere on the planet. We know that for eighteen years they're invisible, untraceable. At their Awakening on their eighteenth birthday, when all of their previous memories come flooding back in, they become a Shield and someone shows up, usually the next day, with a Locus. At that Awakening, their behaviour changes. They're no longer the innocent they were, and it's almost impossible to hide the change completely. DETNADEUX searches for data like that, too. School records, police records, emails, texts and PMs between family members and lovers and BFFs… searching for sudden changes which occur with twenty-four hours of a person's eighteenth birthday."

He took the last sip of tea and put the mug back on his desk. "What this all boils down to, sir, is that we've assigned a registry number of our own to each and every known Shield and when you call up that number on your Smartphone, DETNADEUX gets your message, and sends you the latest most-likely data, real time. We are tweaking the details, trying to eliminate false alarms, but I expect we'll have the operational Beta version ready to present to the Board of Directors by the end of the week. We can upload to all four-hundred field units in an hour once we're given the go ahead."

"Ghazar," Tabak smiled a big Texas smile, "I think you and your team have got a future with DET. Crunch time, though. Has it been field-tested? I'm more than happy to have my son-in-law's team up in Canada give it a go."

"Thank you, sir, but we have a team leader in Tasmania that's closing in on a Shield and is more than happy to give ShieldBreaker a try. The sooner the better, he says."

"'ShieldBreaker' hmm? I like it. At least for the Beta version. It lacks subtlety so we may have to tone it down when we do the wide release. Get it done yesterday, Ghazar, and keep me in the loop." He looked at the crowd around them and simply raised an eyebrow. They parted like the Red Sea to let him pass, then crowded back around Ghazar again once the CEO was gone. One member of the team drifted off to women's toilet, to fire off an email from her personal phone.

oOo

Tracy shifted the pillow under her brace-wrapped knee and tried to get more comfortable on the sofa but didn't have much luck. A knuckle pounding on the unit's door startled her and everything went silent in an instant. The Shield swung her leg off the ottoman and rolled over, one hand reaching for the gun holster under the sofa and the second for the knife tucked into her knee brace. She forgot all about the alarm transmitter hanging around her neck.

"Relax, Trace. Stay put. I've got it." Beside her on the sofa, Tracy's cousin, Kimbra, put the universal remote on the coffee table next to their breakfast dishes and got up to answer the door. Tracy saw "MUTE" on the flatscreen on the wall and relaxed. The Dark weren't here, yet.

Before Kimbra could reach the door there was a second knock and a familiar voice called out. "Oi, Trace, it's Em." Kimbra stretched a kink out of her back, unlocked and opened the door, letting in Emily from the unit down the hall. "G'day, Kimbra. I thought you lot were headed up to Maui to chase surfies."

Kimbra stepped aside to let Emily in. "Gordo leaves this arvo, after lunch, but Deb 'n I fly out Sunday."

"Good on ya. Wish I could tag along. Been here all my life and I'm still not one for Tasmanian winters." She glanced at the frozen image on the screen and sighed. "Ooh. '*Inception*' with my true love, Leo. I absolutely *adore* him. Strange bloody movie, but who cares when it's Leo?" A tinny, distant baby's giggle came from the pocket of Emily's jumper and she whipped out the listening end of a baby monitor. "Crap! Trace, can I steal you away from Leo for twenty? I have to run down to the milk bar for bread and whatnot and Loverboy himself is doing overtime and won't be home until late. Twenty, tops. Kyle is still sleeping and Caya is tearing it up in the Jolly Bouncer. You haven't had a seizure in ages now, so twenty should be aces, right?"

Tracy laughed. She didn't get to see the twins nearly often enough and it was a perfect, cold day for it. Her 'epilepsy' was just a way she got out of babysitting—no one leaves carpet grubs with an epileptic for more than a few minutes, and no Shield wants children around when the Dark drop by unannounced. "No worries, Em. I've got it covered. No seizures in weeks." Or *ever*, for that matter, she added in her head. She grabbed her crutches and looked wistfully at the screen. "Leo will just have to wait for me. Sorry Kimbra." She stole a glance at the old steamer trunk stacked high with books. It wasn't the subtlest place to hide her Locus, but the Last Egg of Loch Ness didn't exactly fit in a desk drawer or on a string around her neck.

Emily added kindly, "Yah, sorry Kimbra. Twenty, tops. You're welcome to come over, too."

"Thanks, Em, but I'd better get a start on my laundry—it's why I'm over this early in the first place." She walked over to the giant orange nylon laundry bag near the kitchen island and gave it a kick.

"You mean it's not to drool over Leo?" Emily winked wickedly at Kimbra.

"It would take Leo in person to get me out again in this bloody weather. Him and the idea of meeting young, nubile, Maui surfies while I'm wearing rank grundies."

"Ew, 'nuff said. You need anything? My shout."

"No, I'm good, thanks, Em."

"No worries." She stepped aside so Tracy could get out into the hallway. "Later, then, Kimmy."

"Later, Em."

The door latched and locked when Emily pulled it shut and she caught up to Tracy as she crutch-hopped down the hall toward the twins. "How's the knee doing, Trace? Surgery go alright? What did they do, exactly?"

"They did an arthroscopy on my ACL, which is just a fancy way of saying they fixed my knee but I'm off the skis for the season."

"Better you than me. I hate needles and such." More giggles came from the baby monitor but they were at Em's door so she opened it, reached in, grabbed her jacket and purse. She handed Tracy the baby monitor. "I've got my iPhone, but I'll be gone twenty tops, I promise."

Tracy kissed her friend on the cheek and shuffled past her and into the unit. "Go, Em. It's all ace." Emily hugged her back and ducked into the fire stairs leading down to the street. Tracy took a look up and down the hallway, thinking she heard something, but only the usual sounds of dish-clankings, conversations and talk shows drifted out of the half-dozen units. She touched the sheathed knife tucked under her University of Wollongong hoody in the small of her back, then moved inside and bolted the door.

oOo

Liam scanned the half-block-square Olympic Plaza as he shuffled along the rain-soaked pedestrian walk, but although there were a dozen or so people and a few of them were on bicycles, there was no sign of Lynette. He hadn't seen her in over a hundred-and-fifty years and yet here she was, in a Canadian prairie city, riding by on her bike like she didn't have a care in the world. Even in that brief eon-encompassing glance he could see that she was in her twenties and obviously past her Awakening but she looked like she was living a normal life. Except that she'd recognized him, known him for who and what he was. Where the hell had she *gone*?

Resigned to having her pass through his life again in an instant, he didn't argue when Phoenix pulled him over to the grass next to the ticket kiosk. While Phoenix relieved herself shyly next to a shrub, Liam plopped himself down on a bench.

"You look like you need a good laugh or ten."

Liam looked for the source of the voice, thinking—*hoping*—that Lynette had snuck up on him. The voice was young and female, with a bright, happy, infectious tone and... *not* Lynette. She was stationed in the kiosk under a strange, bright poster for the local Fringe Festival. "Laughs come few and far-between these days," he replied as he turned to face her. She smiled the biggest, whitest smile he'd ever seen on a woman and his heart jumped. "You've got the second-most *enchanting* smile I've ever seen."

"It runs in the family. And what do you mean, 'the second-most'? That's no way to get a girl's attention, even an engaged one." She held up her left hand to show the blood-red-ruby-on-platinum band.

Liam got up from the bench and worked his way over to the kiosk, not comfortable raising his voice even to carry across a few yards. "I've seen some of the most beautiful smiles in history and when I say second-most, that's not shorting you at all. It's also a tip of my hat to your absent fiancé because he gets to see that glow every morning over the kitchen table."

"Wow. A flatterer of *serious* proportion. The owner of the *most* enchanting smile must have stolen your heart completely."

"You have no idea." He could read her nametag now that he was closer. "Actually, Carissa, you might. She just went through here, I think, on her bike." Phoenix finally finished sniffing around the bush and wandered over to join Liam, the leash retracting as she waddled over. Carissa noticed the dog for the first time.

"Oh! It's *you*. She said to watch for a man with a little dog but I didn't see the little dog so I assumed it wasn't you."

"So you've seen her?"

"Seen and spoken to. She even left a message for you, I think. She didn't leave her name or yours."

"We don't know each other's names, yet."

"That's so romantic, I think. Well, the message is a weird one, but kinda cool."

She handed over a folded receipt and, leaning on the counter, Liam pinned it down with his weak left hand and unfolded it with his right. It was just a drawing, but it was exactly what he needed to see—an alchemical symbol.

Carissa leaned over to get a closer look. "I love it! Can I copy it and make it my next tat?"

"Knock yourself out, Carissa. It's the alchemists' Spirit of Mercury. Did she say anything?"

"She said for me to watch for the older guy with the chin fuzz and the scruffy little dog and to tell him—you—'Hi. Not right now'." She copied the Spirit of Mercury down on the back of a Fringe Festival flyer.

"'Hi. Not right now'?"

"That's it, that's all."

"The 'older guy'? She had the nerve to call me 'the older guy'?"

"Older than me, I guess she meant."

"Okay, *that* I'll accept. But I am not that much older than her."

"Sorry, but you sure look it. She's gotta be about my age, twenty-five at most, but you're looking old, maybe forty-five or fifty."

"Good guess. I'm fifty. I'm an old man." He smiled.

"Downright ancient." She smiled and winked at him.

"Girl, if you only *knew*."

"Then you definitely need a laugh or two. Come hang out at the Fringe Festival."

"The schedule is a bit full right now, kiddo."

"Well, it's going on all next week, too. Just check us out on-line to see the full schedule."

"Sorry, I'm not on-line. No computer. I go to the library when I need one."

"No...? Wow. Stone Age, dude. Okay." She handed him a Festival brochure. "Old school it is, then. The whole Festival's listed here. Hey, if I see her again, I can text you if you want."

Liam chuckled sadly. "No texting, either."

"Voice call?"

"No phone."

"A message on your Facebook Wall?"

"No Facebook, either. No MySpace, no Twitter, no eBay, no bill-payments online."

"How do you survive off-grid like that?"

"I've survived this long *because* I'm off the grid. That grid is the home of the Patterns that kill, and they never go away. Post it yesterday, delete it today, see it online somewhere tomorrow."

"Just don't post anything that could bite you in the ass."

"In my line of work, it *all* bites you in the ass, one day or the next." He carefully folded the brochure and placed it in his pocket. "Like you said—Stone Age. I appreciate you wanting to help, though." He looked around the Plaza for inspiration and saw a tall, round, event pillar plastered with posters for every conceivable rock band, stage show and live DJ event in town. "Tell you what. If you see her again, tell her to draw that symbol on whatever poster is on the bottom of the south side, facing the Epcor Centre."

"What if someone tears off the poster or staples one over it? You could miss her."

"Then I guess it isn't meant to be, this time." He and Lynette had been as ships passing in the night for centuries, so he was used to just missing her. London, 1579. Rotterdam, 1835. Auckland, 1923. At least, that's what he remembered. He had no idea these days if any of his memories were close to the reality he lived. None of that mattered, though, because as his body, mind, and spirit betrayed him, right here and now in Calgary, he really needed to hold her close. Really needed her to kiss the tender spot on his neck and tell him it'll all be okay. He sighed, holding back tears. At least he knew where in the world she was, and that would have to do.

"Wow, a romantic."

"I guess. More likely a pragmatist. We've been missing each other on and off for a long, long time." The whistling of a tin flute bounced off of the concrete and glass buildings around them and Phoenix whimpered. Liam heard it, too.

"Carissa, it's been a pleasure. I hope to see some of the events, but even if I don't get those laughs you've so astutely pointed out that I need, you've helped me beyond measure. For you and your very fortunate fiancé, may love and laughter light your days, and warm your heart and home. May good and faithful friends be yours, wherever you may roam. May peace and plenty bless your world with joy that long endures. May all life's passing seasons bring the best to you and yours!"

The bright-eyed young woman smiled the smile that nearly captured Liam's heart only moments before. "That's so sweet! You didn't just make that up, though."

"Of course not. It's an old Irish blessing."

"I *know*. I first heard it in Dublin. Thank you! *Go n-eírí an bóthar leat.* May the road rise with you."

"That's all I've ever asked for, sweet lady. Now, as my tiny friend here reminds me, we gotta go. Do us a favour, though and turn your back for two minutes; that way if anyone asks which way we went, you can honestly say that you have no idea."

"Will do." She turned away.

"Be safe, youngster," he whispered and then he picked up Phoenix and shuffled off through the Plaza. It was time to get the hell out of town for a while.

oOo

"Master Wei, may I have a moment of your time, please. It's urgent.

"A 'Code Red', DW?" The Shield Master smiled kindly.

"I suppose so, sir."

"I am all ears, my son. Please, sit." He motioned to the small, leather Egyptian camel saddle that passed for guest seating in his office-cum-sanctuary. DW sat and the tiny brass bell suspended beneath the arched seat rang pleasantly.

"Sir, I have a Facebook friend who works for our... 'competition'."

"Yes, I remember you mentioning her before."

"Well, sir, she's just sent me a message hinting that they have developed a Smartphone app that could devastate us when it goes live."

"I have heard rumours of this myself. Was she able to give you any details?"

"Not exactly, but she did give me a link to what she claims is a summary of its capabilities."

"And what did you find there?"

"Well, sir, I haven't clicked on it, yet. I wanted to clear it with you first, plus I don't think I should do it here, on campus."

"You're worried about leaks?"

"Yes sir. Also, it could be a trap. Then again, if this is what she says it is and we have a chance to get ahead of it, I don't want to lose the advantage we might gain."

"DW, my son, you are thinking more and more like a team leader every day. I think this would be an excellent time for you to take your lunch break. As a matter of fact, would you mind picking up an egg salad on croissant from the little patisserie in town?" He pulled a clip of bills out of his robe and peeled one off the top.

"You mean the one near the power lines where spells can't get a fix?" DW smiled and took the bill from the master. "It would be my pleasure, sir."

"Take your time, DW—I believe Systems is next on the schedule for fire sprinkler maintenance so there won't even be a desk for you to come back to until an alternative space is prepared."

"Yes sir." The young programmer departed, leaving the Shield Master to his own thoughts, which, over the centuries, Wei had found to occasionally be a most disturbing place to be.

"Tea," he said to the sound-dampened sanctuary. "All will find Balance within a cup of tea," and he set about fixing himself a pot of his custom blend, anticipating the warmth that would clear his head and let him focus on the issues on his plate.

oOo

Rhianna's dancing Sailor Moon avatar popped up on Ghazar's monitor, speaking with Rhianna's voice. "I've got the Australian Team standing by, Ghaz."

"Which one?"

"*Gamma Ocho Neuf* in Tasmania. Devonport. And they're ready for the ShieldBreaker upload whenever we are."

"How close are they to the Shield they're tracking?"

"They say it would be a week before they're certain enough to move, so if ShieldBreaker can speed that up, they're happy to give it a try. They're worried that this one suspects they're nearby and she may run."

"She probably does and will. That's what makes a Shield a Shield. All right, then. I'll upload it to their Smartphones while you get everything new they have on this Shield input into DETNADEUX so she can factor it all in."

"Will do.

oOo

Phoenix was more than happy to get into her backpack so that Liam could concentrate on eluding the suspected pursuit. It was getting late and they still needed to get home, pack some supplies and hit the road to Bankhead before the sun was completely down.

oOo

Rhianna's voice once again interrupted Ghazar's thoughts but this time it came from beside his chair rather than from his monitor.

"The Team's got ShieldBreaker and I've uploaded the data they've been collecting for the last couple of years."

Ghazar spun his chair around and leaned back so he could see her clearly. She kept her long arms folded and stood just out of arm's reach.

"Cool. Let's get this stupid test over and done with so we can present it to the Board and rock this company."

"There's a problem."

"What do you mean, 'a problem'? ShieldBreaker is ready for this field test. DETNADEUX is ready for this damned test."

"Yes and no. When I ran all of the numbers I only come up with a seventy-two-point-six percent probability."

"Just seventy-two-six? Run the numbers again."

"This is DETNADEUX, Ghaz—seventy-two-six is what the data gives us."

"Then you input the data wrong!" He stood, but still only came up to her nostrils.

"I didn't *input* it at all. It's their own data and it was a direct upload."

"Then check the damned file to make sure it's not corrupted!" His raised voice started drawing a small crowd from around the lab. Rhianna kept her voice calm and steady.

"Done and done. *Twice*. The data is solid. Seventy-two-six is what we've got to work with. Or we can let them track, follow, and compile for another couple of days and see if that improves our numbers." She knew pushing the test ahead was a mistake and decided that if she didn't take a stand now, she'd face her own 'termination'.

"Damn! Damn! Damn! In two days we could be following Mundhir. ShieldBreaker has to be tested *now*." He looked around at the faces of his gathered team. "Do we know what the problem is?"

They all remained silent, content to let Rhianna continue to carry the ball on this one. She was okay with that. "They had four possibles on the ground before they applied ShieldBreaker, which got them down to two, leaning more to one than the other."

"Then tell them to pick one and get it *done*."

"*Pick one?* Twelve petaflops and a billion or so dollars and you want to screw it all up by having them 'pick one'?"

"Exactly. *You* know and *I* know that two more days of data will just bump the seventy-two-six to a hundred-even, so we move now and look brilliant instead of just smart."

"And if they're wrong?"

"Then *their data* is wrong and it's on *their* heads."

Rhianna took a step back, making the distance even more obvious. "Ghaz, are you high or just having a Stupid Day?" Ghazar ignored the question and that made Rhianna wonder if maybe she'd hit the nail on the head. He wasn't a heavy user but he'd been known to 'enhance' his mental abilities periodically with chemical additives.

"Tell them to follow their instincts and pick one."

"No. *You* tell them. You're ShieldBreaker Team Lead so *you* make the call. I'm taking my coffee break. Let me know how it goes. The number is on a sticky note on my desk." She walked away, shaking her head at Ghazar's folly and hoping she could stay clear of the backlash when it hit. She could have simply pushed the bar of the exit door and slipped out to the landscaped quad they used for their breaks in good weather, but Rhianna wasn't naive about how things worked at DökktEfniTækni. She used her key card to exit out of the lab and then went down the hall to the refectory where she again used her card to gain entry. The security logs would show exactly where she was when the field test went to hell, no matter what Ghazar's coerced witnesses might say.

Chapter Six: Brother Paul & Ozzy

"The walking man is a beacon amongst the runners, the weeping man a beacon amongst celebrants and the man of peace a beacon amongst combatants. A Shield of Light must not be a beacon to the Dark."

~Shield Master Wei (while remaining in the pack of the 1975 Boston Marathon.)

oOo

Ghazar charged down the aisle between the cubicles to Rhianna's desk, with half of his team right behind him. The number was right where she said it would be. "Everyone get back to your workstations. Even when this test succeeds we'll have tweaking to do so be ready." One or two of the newbies did as they were told but the others stayed put. "Let me put this another way..." he looked each and every one of them in the eyes as he spoke. "Anyone not at their desk monitoring the data stream and live feed when this *vital* Beta test gets run, can go hand in their resignation right now. Expect the usual severance."

It took a moment and no small amount of grumbling, but eventually he was alone at Rhianna's desk. He took out his Smartphone texted the message he'd ordered her to do herself. If she didn't want to step up to the plate, then he'd take all the damned credit for himself.

oOo

Emily took only five minutes more than 'twenty tops' and relieved Tracy with much love and thanks. "No seizures then, Trace?"

"Just a little one, but the kids didn't seem to notice. Once I stopped thrashing about it was all aces." She winked at Emily who smiled back.

"Funny girl, Trace. Thanks heaps for watching the little carpet grubs. Other than your seizure, they didn't give you any trouble?"

"Just giggles and farts from Caya and snores from Kyle."

"Ripper. I owe you one." Tracy reached for her crutches. "Need a hand, luv?"

"No worries, Em. It's feeling ace. Might even hobble down the hill for a Sprite."

"Good onya. We still on for pasta on Saturday?" She moved to the kitchen and started emptying her sacks.

"Wouldn't miss it. I'm bringing my special sauce." Once again she thought she heard something out in the hall. "I'd better get back and make sure Kimbra hasn't messed up her whites and colors. She was whinging that I had the wrong soap but I don't think she knows laundry from dish soap." With her crutches clutched in one hand, Tracy unlatched the door quickly and hopped out into the hall, ready. It was empty. "Later, Em. Lock up behind me."

"Later luv.

oOo

Liam had long-ago decided that *not* taking the elevator up eight floors would raise more eyebrows and red flags than would setting the Pattern of *taking* the elevator every time he came or went from home, so the elevator it was. In a lazy world, it's best to just follow the herd. Of course, now that even walking on shag carpet gave him difficulties, the elevator was the only common sense choice. Some of his neighbours weren't so keen on dogs in the building so he carried Phoenix in his arms as he rode the elevator up alone.

"You know, P, we should probably go back to using that front carrier we got you a few years back." Phoenix grunted, not happy. "Yah, I know the little art-deco girly-girls on it are a bit too cutesy for either one of us, but it lets me keep you safer when that's getting harder and harder to do every day." A small whimper was his only reply as they got off the elevator and started what used to be a short walk down the hall to the apartment.

"Are you ready for a road trip, P?"

"Where are you going, Liam?" The disembodied voice came from ahead of them, from the open door Liam hadn't noticed across the hall from their own. Norinne.

"Camping for a couple days, Nor." She didn't like to camp, so Liam knew the thought of tents and bugs and outhouses would dissuade her from trying to invite herself.

She stayed in her vestibule until Liam drew even with their doors, and then took a half step into the hall. She was a slender, fortyish woman who kept her dark hair short, sometimes hiding it under one of her many silk scarves. Her somewhat darker complexion would have been pretty if she hadn't always looked so sad, like someone had hurt her badly when she was young and she'd never really recovered. This was a woman who had been a victim for so long she didn't know how to be anyone else. "Do you have to?"

"Yah, we do. We're... expected."

"Where?"

"That's what I'm waiting to hear. I have to get in and check the answering machine. Our friends are supposed to call and leave a message." Century after century as a Shield made him an accomplished liar. He transferred the keys he'd been holding in his left hand over to the right while Phoenix tried to balance on his arm.

"I'm bored, Liam."

"Go for a walk, Nor. It rained for a while but stopped just before we came in. The city is washed clean and smells fresh. Perfect to banish boredom." She got bored easily and often came to Liam to have him 'fix it' with a cup of coffee or directionless conversation.

"I have to go to Safeway for groceries."

Liam was thankful they'd already done their shopping because he really didn't want the complications of taking No-Decision Nor with him. A trip that took *him* ten minutes—maybe twenty in his current condition—would be thirty or forty-five with Norinne because she wouldn't put a single item in her cart without asking for his opinion. She was a sweet lady, but a complete lack of self-confidence kept her from taking even the minor risk of choosing Coke over Pepsi, or vice versa.

"Sorry, Nor. We're leaving shortly." He struggled with the door and Norinne noticed the cane for the first time.

"Why do you have a cane, Liam?"

He put Phoenix down and she shook off the last of the rain and sat at his feet. "I've been having a little trouble walking and stuff. This helps."

"Are you sure you should be camping? Maybe you should stay in the city." She now noticed his semi-curled left hand. "You've had a stroke! Stick your tongue out." She crossed the hall to get a better look in the flickering fluorescent light.

"It's *not* a stroke, Nor."

"Stick your tongue out." Her tone was unexpectedly strong and insistent.

He did as he was told and his tongue went out straight, no listing to one side or the other. He wiggled it and then stuck it straight out at her. "See, no stroke."

"Smile."

"I don't feel like smiling, I'm tired."

"Liam, please smile. This is serious." She smiled, to encourage him and he realized that she really was a pretty woman who should smile a lot more.

He smiled back. "See still straight." He frowned, wondering. "It *is* still straight, isn't it?"

"It's *perfect*. Like you. Now repeat after me: 'Don't cry over spilled milk.'"

"Don't cry over spilled milk?"

"Yes. Say it. It's another stroke test, to see if you have slurred speech. Say it."

"I just did."

"Oh. Yes, you did. Sounded good. Now close your eyes and raise both arms as high as you can." She held out her hand. "Here. I'll hold your cane."

Liam was exhausted and not in the mood for this, but he also felt better having someone else know what he was going through and to confirm that it wasn't a stroke. He shifted his back to the hall wall, handed Norinne his cane, closed his eyes and raised his arms as high as he could get them. Norinne's sharp intake of breath made him open his eyes, alert for danger.

"Oh, Liam."

His right arm was straight up, pointing at the ceiling. His left was only at shoulder height and not particularly straight. Damn.

"I still don't think it's a stroke, Nor."

She handed him back his cane and gave him a gentle hug. "Maybe, maybe not. It could be MS."

"MS?" Not something he'd considered, but he was sure he was too old to just be developing symptoms.

"Multiple Sclerosis. I saw a *Healthy Body, Healthy Mind* special about it on PBS. Or it could be diabetes, but I think MS is more likely."

"Really? MS or diabetes are my choices?"

"Or a stroke, but I think MS. I'll Google it and print off some information for you. Don't go camping, Liam. You shouldn't even be driving."

He saw where this was going and he had to nip it in the bud. "I can drive just fine, thanks, Nor. There's not a lot of call for me to raise my hand above my head when I'm on the highway and the old girl is an automatic so I don't have to worry about a clutch."

"Liam…"

"Nor… it's only for a few days. I'll be fine." Phoenix waddled off into their apartment.

"I was hoping you'd watch TV with me. I've got the new season of *Dexter* on DVD."

It was a well-produced show, as far as Liam was concerned, but he'd seen so much death over the years—and even been murdered himself too many times to count—that sitting through Hollywood's version of it held no appeal at all. "Going camping, Nor. *Dexter*'s not my style. But thanks."

Phoenix charged back out into the hallway, barking her hoarse, short, bark three times. She climbed up on Liam's shoe and butted his leg with her head. Norinne took a step back.

"Your dog doesn't like me."

"Nonsense. Phoenix likes *everybody*. She's just trying to tell me something. She's probably hungry since it's been a few hours since either of us has eaten."

"She still doesn't like me."

It was time to go. "Nor, Phoenix likes you, but you think what you want because we have to go."

"You don't want to come to Safeway with me?"

"I'm sorry, no. As soon as we find out where we're camping for the weekend, we're gone." Good grief!

"Okay. I'm sure you'll have fun without me. Maybe I'll see you in a few days." She turned and walked back into her apartment, dragging her feet on the carpet and seeming to collapse in on herself a little bit with each step.

Liam shook his head in disbelief and followed Phoenix into the apartment where he closed and double-bolted the door. "Thanks for the rescue, P, but I wonder if that was your intent at all." Phoenix barked happily from the living room but Liam sat on the small hallway stool, taking the time to hang up his damp jacket and take off his shoes before going to see what the ruckus was about. The little Yorkie ran back and forth between the slow-moving Shield and whatever it was that had her attention in the other room, out of sight from the stool.

"Damnation, P, just relax, would you *please*. Either help me with my laces or at least wait quietly."

A too-familiar human voice answered him from the living room. "I have been called many things by you, but 'Damnation' is not one of them. And if you were cursing the Princess, then I had expected better manners from such a venerable Shield."

Liam gave up on the laces of the second shoe and yanked it off impatiently, taking the sock with it. He hobbled into the living room with one sock on, one sock off and wearing the genuine smile Nor had only too-recently tried to draw out of him. Tears rose in his eyes and he nearly fell into Brother Paul's open arms. Affectionately exchanging dog greetings with Phoenix was Paul's own, ever-present, much bigger, canine companion, Ozzy.

"Brother..."

"Liam."

They hugged a long time, Liam's tears coursing down his cheeks and soaking into Brother Paul's green fleece. After a moment, Phoenix curled up silently on Liam's bare foot, knowing she was needed. Eventually Liam found the strength to loosen his grip and release the Senior Shield Liaison who had been as much a brother to him as any of the dozens of blood brothers he'd had over the centuries. Paul led Liam to the couch and made him sit, then he reached down and every so affectionately lifted Phoenix up to join them. Ozzy sat at Paul's feet and placed his furry head on his master's lap.

"Your Highness, it is an honour to see you again." Phoenix licked his hand and curled up in his lap. Paul looked closely at Liam, sadness evident in every faint wrinkle and laugh line. "You, my brother, do not look well."

"I'm not. Don't know what's up, but I'll admit to you and only you that I'm scared."

"Then it saddens me even more to have to add to your burden." He gently handed Phoenix to Liam then reached under the couch and slid out the guitar case containing the silk-wrapped sword of *Carolus Magnus*. Ozzy moved over next to Liam's end of the couch, out of the way. "We need you to Shield two Loci for a short time." He lifted the case onto his lap, opened it and unwrapped the beautiful Loci.

"*Two?*"

"Yes, brother. One of your sisters was taken captive in Cape Town yesterday but we were able to make a rare recovery. There's no one else available. No Awakenings for weeks."

"No one else?"

"You are the best, our first and only choice. I had them teleport me here, and you *know* how I hate to teleport. There is something big happening with the Dark, and Master Wei needs me elsewhere and unencumbered, so not even *I* can Shield this Locus. I can't stay long, because two of us in one place…"

"You don't know the half of it. Lynette's here, too, so there's *three* of us. And Faerie is bloody close. Here in the city. We're only home long enough to pack up the camping gear and get out to Bankhead for a few days."

"The ghost town near Banff, in the Park?"

"Exactly. It turns out that the coal from the old mine allows Her Highness in your lap there to change back to her true form without being sensed by the Dark or Faerie. It's a trick the pixies have used for eons to outwit elves and brownies and Bankhead is the perfect spot because it's a ghost town and not far from the banks of a River of Light, the Bow."

"I know the place well. I also know that the mines themselves are deep and a place of great danger for you. Should anything find a way up out of them, you won't last long and Oberon will have his pixie princess." Phoenix whimpered in his lap. "But I *do* understand your need and hers and I agree that it is the most likely the safest place for you both, for now." He shook his head. "*Three* of us, here and now in Calgary?"

"Three."

"Then we *must* leave. I had hoped we could share a meal, but we can't risk it."

"Can I offer you a ride somewhere?"

"A kind offer, but even *that* would be pushing our luck. Go camping. I will move away from your home before I have them teleport me back. We'll meet again. Either Abiel or myself will find you when we have an Awakened One who can Shield this Locus. Be safe. See a doctor when you get back. I'm worried about you, brother."

"Me, too. I'll go see the local 'shaman' when I get back."

The Dark were near and they both knew it. They hugged quickly and released. Brother Paul picked up and gently cradled Phoenix in his arms. "You, dear lady, please keep him safe, and make sure he sees that doctor. He has many lifetimes of stubborn in his bones. If you need us, Your Highness, remember the transmitter he wears around his neck. If Liam cannot press it, *you* must." Phoenix looked the Shield Master in the eyes and nodded, and then she licked his hand affectionately before he placed her on the floor where she and Ozzy could say their farewells. And then they were gone. Liam closed the door and bolted it behind them.

He wiped a sleeve at his tear-damp eyes. "We gotta go, little one. Right bloody *now*." As quickly as he could, Liam dragged the tent, sleeping bag and his always-ready internally-framed camp pack out of the bottom of the bedroom closet. It was a slower process than he would have liked but he got it done. He grabbed clean underwear and socks from the laundry basket just inside the door and stuffed them into the side-pockets of the pack. Then he reached under the bed and pulled out a leather case wider and shorter than a tennis racquet case and fumbled with the zipper. When he finally got it open he checked the mini-crossbow's string for wear, confirmed that the simple trigger mechanism was oiled and that there was a supply of short-but-deadly bolts.

It had a thirty-pound pull and was silent and deadly within twenty feet. Reloading was slow, but could be done with just one good arm and one good foot, so it was the perfect weapon for Liam under the circumstances. Of course he prayed he didn't even have to take it out of the Toyota's trunk because where they were headed had a serious ban on all weapons of a hunting nature. The Park Wardens in Banff National Park confiscated everything from slingshots on up and if there were any problems, the area was policed by the R.C.M.P.— Canada's federal law enforcers—and they were never far away. All of which still wasn't going to keep Liam from taking in a crossbow, a three-foot-long sword, an arm-sheath of four throwing knives and, of course, a silenced Springfield .45 with three full clips of ammunition and a box of subsonic rounds. It sounded more like camping Texas-style, but such was the life of a Shield, he thought—even a crippled one.

oOo

Carissa straightened the Fringe Festival brochures in the stand on the kiosk's window counter and added another half-dozen or so to fill it up. There were only fifteen minutes left in her shift and she liked to have everything stocked up and ready for whoever opened up in the morning. The enchanting notes from a well-played flute drifted through the wet Plaza and she stopped to listen. She and Rogan had spent two years in Ireland and never heard quite the purity of tone that this musician was master of. The song came closer until it seemed to stop right behind her kiosk. She listened and a giggle rose from her heart. *It was beautiful,* like she'd fallen into Faerie and was being serenaded by none other than Puck himself, or whoever played the flute in Faerie. She just had to see who it was so she reached for the bolt securing the door of the kiosk. A pure, strong, soft male voice just beyond the door spoke as clearly as if he were whispering in her ear.

"No need to look. Just relax and think back for me, lass. Éist le mo bhriathra. Éist ach dom." *Listen to my words. Listen only to me.* "An raibh a fear agus an mhadra teacht ar an mbealach seo?" *Did a man and his dog come this way?*

Carissa nodded to no one in particular. "Is ea. Ní fada ó shin." *Yes. Not long ago.*

"Cén treo an ndeachaigh siad, a mhuirnín óg álainn?" *Which direction did they go, my beautiful young darling?*

"North nó ó dheas nó soir nó siar . Ní fhaca mé i gcás, a dhuine uasail maith." *North or south or east or west. I did not see where, good sir.*

The flute played again, this time a slower, deeper, more resonant tune. It was as if the whole orchestra of Oberon's Royal Court were playing behind the little pipe. Carissa's eyes drooped and she fell deeper into the music. The voice continued.

"Arís iarr mé, a ndeachaigh siad treoir, a ghrá, mo shaoil, mo chailín stór?" *Once again I ask, which direction did they go, my love, my life, my darling girl?*

Carissa smiled and warmed at the love and desire she felt for the flutist. "Ingach macántacht, Ní fhaca mé iad imeacht, mo ghrá amháin." *In all honesty, I did not see them depart, my one true love.*

A hint of impatience crept into the voice beyond the door. "A tríú huair iarr mé, agus ní mór duit a fhreagairt fíor... treoir taistil ina raibh siad, dá?" *A third time I ask, and you must answer true... which direction did they travel, these two?*

"Fhírinne labhairt liom, le haghaidh tú mo chroí, Ní fhaca mé an dhá imeacht." *Truth I speak, for you my heart, I did not see the two depart.*

The flutist fired out three sharp, angry discordant notes and pretty little Carissa collapsed to the floor of the kiosk, deep asleep.

oOo

After Becca left the message and the sigil for Skosche with the girl at the booth she rode south, away from the park and the abandoned

Jeep and out of downtown. The rain didn't last much longer so she worked her way back up the Elbow River Pathway and then back west through the East Village to the youth hostel. She looked around. It was both isolated and had a lot of ways out of the area, but it was hemmed in by two nearby rivers, which limited her escape options considerably. She locked her bike in the iron rack and stood for a moment in the post-rain peace, feeling the ionized air all around her.

Closing her eyes she could feel a River of Light close by and it gave her comfort. She could also feel the Dark in the city... and the presence of *strong* Light. There was an unusually powerful Shield presence in Calgary right now and that was more than enough reason to just stay the night and run at dawn. She wondered, too, if getting rid of the car was such a good idea after all—the police didn't scare her nearly as much as the Dark did.

The hostel's lobby was quiet but there were only a few beds available and they were in the women's dorm. She needed sleep and a dorm was better than under a bridge so Becca was soon checked in, changed into dry clothes and lying back on her assigned cot. Her panniers fit easily into the locker under the bed and the tube containing her Locus fit just fine under the covers with her. This wasn't her first time in a group sleeping arrangement, but at least this time there was no sea water leaking in or rats fighting with her for the dry corner she had managed to claim in a rank, disgusting ship's hold. Music drifted over from another traveller's headphones and it was so much more comforting than the snap of sails and the creak of timber off the coast of Massachusetts. Ironically it sounded like Celtic-flavoured Great Big Sea and that was just fine with her.

She wanted to take her Locus out and make sure it was okay, but that was her OCD speaking, not the Shield instincts and training. She'd wrapped Bunjil's Pipe perfectly: silk, linen, canvas and bubble wrap, but she loved to hold it and feel the delicate carvings in the baobab shaft. So far she had been able to pick out platypus, koala, Huntsman spider, kangaroo, brush-tailed possum, numbat, wallaby, saltwater crocodile, bandicoot, and fin whale—all intricately worked into the wood, intertwined with each other, distinctly individual but part of a beautiful, enmeshed whole.

Legend had it that smoke from the pipe would reach Bellin-bellin the musk crow, Keeper of the Winds, and he would get the invitation to Bunjil and invite him down from the stars to share a meal. Bunjil was the supreme god in aboriginal Australian mythology and to have him share a meal was the greatest honour. Becca also figured that with Bunjil around, the Dark could just kiss her butt and leave her alone.

oOo

It took two trips and four painkillers, even with the collapsible luggage cart he kept in the front closet, but Liam and Phoenix finally got on the road. He'd sensed Norinne across the hall, watching through her peephole, but she didn't try to dissuade him again from camping so it was all good. He was sure he'd have to have plenty of details of the fun and carousing he had with his 'other friends' when he got back, but he'd worry about that when the time came.

Once on the highway, Liam was surprised at how easy it was to drive even with the wonky arm and leg. The relatively straight line of the Trans-Canada was almost relaxing compared to the craziness of the city. He still had enough control and strength in his left arm and hand that he could use the turn signals without much trouble, and his left leg really had nothing to do but keep the right one company. He did lean a bit to the left and he didn't have quite the range of motion when checking his left blind spot, but overall, he felt more comfortable behind the wheel of the Corolla than he had in weeks. It also helped that they were driving into the mountains and Liam found that no matter how crappy he felt when he started out, the closer he got to the eastern face of the Rockies, the lighter his spirit got. This was a good decision, he acknowledged.

He turned on the radio and found a classic rock station to accompany them into the sunset. Phoenix lay sleeping on her fleece blanket on the passenger seat, content to snore along with the music and the hum of the tires on the asphalt. Liam looked at the layer of dust on the dashboard and wondered how a car parked in a rented garage with the windows rolled up could get so dirty on the inside.

Forty minutes after leaving Calgary behind, Liam pulled off the highway into the peaceful mountain community of Canmore and into the drive-thru of the local Tim Horton's coffee & donut haven—he really needed a little caffeine and sugar right now. He'd brought buns, corned beef, fresh fruit, cheese, and a few other odds and ends from home to get them through the next couple of days but he preferred his coffee fresh. Phoenix dozed on her blanket in the co-pilot seat and they were soon back out on the highway.

"Almost there, DogDog." Phoenix barked softly and there seemed to be a sparkle to her eyes, as they got closer to the former coal-mining town of Bankhead.

oOo

Hunter Team *Gamma Ocho Neuf* in Devonport received the go-ahead message from Head Office so the team leader, Bob, ordered the driver to pull the beat-up Chevy van over. The six ex-military, former mixed-martial-arts competitors were dressed like everyone else on the Tasmanian city's streets, but there was no disguising their seething anger with their frustration with Head Office.

"They agree with the seventy-two-six we got but say we should proceed based on best estimate."

"Crikey!" The driver, Joff, turned to Bob in the passenger seat. "All this crap about new technology replacing years of solid groundwork by us and Regional and they want a bloody *guess*?!"

"*Estimate*. An educated one."

"Call it what you bloody want, Bob, seventy-two-six is still a lot less than we go on when we *don't* have Head Office poking their bloody noses in."

"I'm with Bruce. Can we appeal this to Regional?"

"It came from Santiago, so there's no appeal. Regional might agree with us, but they won't countermand a direct DET order."

"Squid nuts!"

"Squid nuts?"

"Just shut up, Bruce." Bob looked at the lone man in the jump seat at the back of the van. "What have you got for us, Tone?"

Tony looked up from his computer tablet. "She's been one of our top two choices all along, so it's not that much of a stretch. The numbers back it up. She's been a bit slow on her feet lately, so it shouldn't even be too tough. The cameras I installed have her not too far from her unit. I saw her leave a short time ago."

A previously silenced voice cut in. Leon. "I've never been happy with this one, Bobbo. Too much out of sorts for me. She could be a Shield or she could just be a wingnut."

"I'm with Leon on this."

"Dammit! The bloody mega-monster-computer can't give me one-hundred-percent and my own bloody team can't even agree." He went silent for a moment and the team knew that his wheels were spinning so they let them. "Tough wallabies, mates. DET says we go so we go. We're a team so we go together. Anyone wanting out, raise your hand and, well, you know how that'll go—your Kevlar won't stop a head-shot." No hands were raised but five of them rested lightly on their holstered weapons and three reached surreptitiously for door handles. "Fine. The good news is that she's got the Last Egg so it won't be hard to find it. Bruce..." he looked straight at Bruce in the seat behind him. "I want you to have that spell *ready* this time. We know how fast the Light Warriors come when called so no buggering around this time wondering when to get started. Cast the spell before the blood hits the floor and find us that Egg."

Bruce simply nodded.

"Good on ya. Now let's review what we know about this Sheila and get this done."

oOo

Liam put a hand-written note on the dashboard of the car that read "Broken down. AMA coming in the morning. We're staying at The Ptarmigan Inn". Then he locked everything in the trunk that wasn't vital or valuable and started the long, arduous, shuffling, limping trek down the hundred-or-so steps from the parking lot to Lower Bankhead and then the hundred yards along the coal-strewn path. Except for starlight, it was as dead black and moonless as the bottom of the nearby coal mines Brother Paul had warned him about. Once upon a time Liam would have been terrified of stumbling on these steps as encumbered as he was and in the condition he was in, but tonight he slipped on a pair of Russian Night Owl night-vision goggles and they let him see every detail of both the steps and the terrain around them. If the Dark came hunting tonight, he'd see them first.

The rain that hit Calgary that afternoon had missed Bankhead completely and so Liam was able to find a dry spot in the ruined foundations of the old town for them to bed down in. He spent twenty minutes hauling grocery bag after grocery bag of brittle anthracite coal from a nearby slack pile into the overgrown skeleton of the briquette-making building and when he was done he had what looked like a rough bulls-eye, eight feet across, with a wobbly ring surrounding a three-foot-wide bull in the centre. Once all of their gear was within the outer ring Liam lifted Phoenix out of the carrier, unhooked her harness, and gently placing her on the bulls-eye. He pulled out a clean child-sized t-shirt and pair of tights from the pack pocket and placed them beside her. Then he snapped the goggles up out of the way, lowered himself with a thump down onto the bedroll and waited.

Phoenix sniffed the air, then walked around the outer ring of coal, carefully examining every inch. In a couple spots she pawed coal from a thicker part of the circle to a thinner part. When she was done and seemed satisfied, she trotted over to Liam and licked his hand affectionately before returning to the bulls-eye and curling up as though to sleep. The air around her began to glow gold and warm, like a miniature sunrise, subdued by thin cloud cover. The glow didn't extend further than the bulls-eye, even as it intensified. After the dark of the night, the golden glow forced Liam to look away for a moment, to let his eyes adjust. When he looked back, the transformation had started.

The light solidified in places, creating sparkles, which began circling the tiny dog. The sparkling light spun faster and faster and grew thicker and thicker until Liam couldn't look directly at it. He looked away again and saw that the light, as bright as it was, now didn't go past the outer ring of coal. Not a mite of it reached even the walls of the small stone structure around them.

Soon he couldn't see Phoenix at all through the luminous tornado and that's when it seemed to grow, stretching and bulging and twisting until it was exactly as wide as the bulls-eye and about three-feet-tall. Liam was sure there was more to the enchantment than just the transformation because no matter how hard he tried, once they left Bankhead and returned to the city, he could never remember the details of any of the hundreds of changes he had witnessed. Every time he saw Phoenix once again become Princess Teagan, he wept like it was the first and only time he would witness the miracle. It was like watching the birth of a very special, magical sibling.

An hour went by, or was it a minute? Possibly a second had flitted past in the blink of a giant's eye. Liam was unsure and, if he was honest with himself, uncaring. He was a witness to beauty and that was enough. A pale, slender, sparkling arm came out of the light and snatched up the t-shirt and tights and pulled them back inside the luminous maelstrom. A moment or a thousand passed and the light changed. When the spinning slowed and the sparkles faded away, Princess Teagan—Heir to the Royal Pixie Meadows at Compton Down—straightened her back and stood up to her full two-foot-nine height, dressed in a slightly-too-big t-shirt and fitted tights. She stretched her arms out as wide as she could, shook her waist-long copper tresses free, and twisted her neck to one side until Liam heard vertebrae pop. She then wiggled her long, pointed ears to make sure they still worked, wiggled her slightly longish, pointed pixie nose, and finally wiggled her little bum before leaping straight off the bulls-eye and into Liam's lap, throwing her slender arms around him. She whistled a melody in his ear and he laughed as loud as he dared. Pixie lights popped into being and danced in the air all around her.

"I've missed you, too, Teagan."

Whistle.

"Sorry... *Great Princess Phoenix, Scourge of the Dark and Shield Protector.*"

She giggled uproariously and kissed him on the cheek.

"Hungry, P?"

Whistle.

"Me, too. We sort of left Cowtown in a hurry and the cream from the coffee is rumbling in my belly." He shifted off the bedroll and reached for the pack but tipped over on his weak arm and flopped shoulder-first into the dirt and coal. "Son of a...!" The princess was there in a flash and lifted him up with supernatural strength, whistling her concern.

"*Fine*. It's *your* turn to cook. I'll just sit my useless butt here and watch."

Whistle.

"Not watch *your* butt, sit on my own and watch you *cook*. For crying out loud, you're like my little sister—your butt is just a butt."

Whistle.

"Oh, you were teasing. Well, it's hard to get the nuance of tone and pitch when I haven't heard a whistling pixie in a couple months. My ear is a little rusty."

Whistle.

"No thank you, I don't want you to *oil* my ear. It was an expression."

Giggle. Whistle.

"Still teasing? Fine, you tease the poor human while he dies of starvation."

Whistle.

"A couple of corned beef sandwiches for me and whatever you want for yourself in that limited portable pantry."

Whistle.

"I'm sure there's enough beef for both of us." He shook his head. "I must be in the company of the worlds' only carnivorous pixie. I suppose that's what I get after thirty-two years of feeding steak to your dog-form. There's also some cream in there somewhere."

She started rummaging for dinner and let out a casual whistle.

"What? Run that by me again."

She stopped pulling supplies out of the pack and came to stand in front of the Shield. She spoke again, in a longer, slower series of whistles.

"You can do that? Heal me? Fix me?"

Whistle.

"Through homeopathy or magic?"

Whistle.

"I was afraid of that, P. No-go on the magic-o. It would leave a permanent trace on me that would be easier for the Dark to see and follow than a flare gun at sea. My duties as your protector would end abruptly and you'd be taken back to Faerie and probable death." He reached out and squeezed her tiny hands with his good one. "I adore you for suggesting it, but we're just going to have to muddle through as best as we can."

Whistle.

"Yes, magic lets you take the dog shape, but the shape-shift is a part of you, your nature. A spell cast on me would be like gold plate with a scratch—so easy to spot when the base metal underneath is exposed. A scratch to your solid-gold nature would reveal nothing but more gold. Does that make sense?"

Whistle.

"Just a little? Well, it's late and I'm starved and we both need some sleep."

Phoenix whistled brightly, executed a perfect back flip to land on her feet next to the pack. Two minutes later she laid sandwiches and cold Cokes on the ground between them. They were so hungry that they ate in silence, serenaded by the sounds of the night, which in the middle of the Bow Valley in the Rocky Mountains included everything from porcupine snuffling to coyote howls, and the occasional soft, leathery flap of bat wings as they hunted in the starlight. Liam felt completely at home—and completely incapable of protecting the sweet little pixie princess sitting opposite him or Shielding his two Loci. But he ate, knowing that if nothing else, he wouldn't fail because he was weak from hunger.

oOo

Even though the coal-circle in the ruins contained and shielded the pixie magic from the Dark and Faerie, not everything that hunted at night in the Rocky Mountains needed to sense magic to find its prey.

Chapter Seven: The Last Egg of Loch Ness

*"Death can and will come to a Shield in a hundred different ways.
It can be neither resisted nor denied. A Shield can fight Dark but not
Death. In that last moment before Death comes a Shield can feel loss,
shame & the sting of failure, but if a Shield has been the best Shield
possible under the conditions at hand, then there is no loss, no shame
and no failure. Dark battles Light and Light battles Dark... forever.
The Shield always comes back to play its part, and for that, a Shield
can stand tall and straight."*
~ Shield Master Wei (1605 CE at the funeral of Mughal Emperor
Abu'l-Fath Jalal ud-din Muhammed
Akbar I.)

oOo

It was nearly lunchtime in Devonport when the lads of *Gamma
Ocho Neuf* were able to locate the Shield with the Last Egg of Loch
Ness. They'd been a team for nearly five years with a perfect record of
ten-out-of-ten for taking out Shields and taking possession of Loci of
Light. In that five years they'd replaced only one team member and it
had been a simple I-left-my-Kevlar-at-home-but-I'll-be-okay incident.
He wasn't. They were fighters and killers and they loved what they
did. The fact that they got paid very well for it and had a great health
package from DökktEfniTækni made life all that sweeter.

"There she is." Tony pointed from the middle seat where he'd
moved so he could see out the windscreen. "Just limping across Best
Street and making for Coles for groceries. Dark green windbreaker
over a blue jumper. Blue rucksack—that'll be where the Egg is—and
the black Brisbane Lions cap."

"The *Lions*? For that alone we should put an end to her misery."

"You're an idiot, Bruce. The Lions are a young team building to
the championship." Leon was a life-long, dyed-in-the-wool Brisbane
fan.

"They got their balls handed to them by Adelaide last week."

"And Adelaide got their balls handed to them by the Eagles the
week before. The season's not over."

"Are you two bloody finished? Do you think maybe we can get
this done?"

"Sorry, Bob. Let's do it."

"Oh, thanks heaps for your permission, you drongo. Now, check
your weapons one last time. And just so you know, the Bulldogs are
the only team worth putting money on." His wide kiss-my-ass smile
was greeted with groans and the clicks and snaps of clips being

removed, checked and replaced, safeties thumbed on and rounds being chambered. Bob believed that many an ambush was blown because someone chambered a round within hearing distance of the enemy.

"Turn in at Wooly's then cruise on back west to Coles. Back us up to the shrubs in the middle of the lot there, and then we'll cover the lot. Tone, stay with the van. Joff, we'll tail her into the store and split up— observe but do not approach. Bruce, take your spells over by Kmart on the west side of the lot. Leon, hike around back and check for exits. If you find any at all, even locked ones, cover them and we'll pick you up on the way out. Nate, you're rover, staying out of sight but ready to back up any action. Try to stay between her and Best Street because if she gets past us, across Best and up on the hill, it becomes a footrace we'll never win, even if she looks a bit gimpy.

"Bob?"

"Yah, Joff?"

"Tell me again why we can't wait until she gets home and take her there. Less exposure, more control… just saying."

"Point taken. Tone?"

"Her building is a secure one with more cameras than this parking lot, which isn't saying much because this lot is primitive. The last camera through here was probably on the Google Streetview van last year. Out here she's limited to the weapons she can carry. Her defences are restricted. She can run and scream for help, but back at her unit who the hell knows what she can bring to bear on us. Our estimated casualty rate there is fifty-percent, *minimum*. Out here, with *this* Shield, it's zero. This should be a quick and easy take-down."

Leon holstered his weapon and pulled his sleeves down to cover the sheathed blades on his forearms. Then he slipped his CMR over his left ear and clicked it on. Everything he said was now being recorded by Tony's gear. Once the action started Tony would open the live feed for management to follow along. "This one stinks, Bob."

"You said that, Leon. Opinion noted. You want out?"

"Not a chance. I'm just going on the record one final time because the numbers and video on this Shield don't feel right. I've got an aunt they locked up nine, ten years ago. Extreme case of paranoid schizophrenia. That's what this looks like. That damned ShieldBreaker app can't tell the difference. This woman follows no Pattern other than she stays clear of Patterns because she thinks Big Brother is watching. Well, we are. Every step she takes and every move she makes isn't to avoid us, the Dark, it's to deal with the demons in her head, the fear of a lifetime of poorly-treated illness."

The entire team was silent. A few mouths hung open. Bob popped his own earpiece in. "Well… point made. Believe it or not, mate, I actually agree that there's something not right about this."

"Then let's move on to the other choice. She's a much better fit.

She's the Shield, I'll wager my life on it."

"You work for DökktEfniTækni, Leon, you already bet your life." Bob sat silent for a moment, then shook off the thoughts and took a deep breath. "Sound on. Testing them in 3...2...1." The rest of his team scrambled to get their CMRs in place and turned on. "Beta?"

"Check." Tony.

"Delta?"

"Check." Joff.

"Gamma?"

"Check." Nate.

"Kappa?"

"Check." Leon.

"Runestone?"

"Check." Bruce, and his spells.

"Beta, are all eyes up?"

Tony looked at the seven-way split screen on his laptop, six of which showed what the lads of *Gamma Ocho Neuf* were seeing. "All aces, Bobbo."

"Good stuff. Now, we have orders from Santiago—from *Corporate*—to take down a Shield *today*. We will follow those orders, but we will follow them *our* way. Same configuration, but we treat this as more research, not a takedown. If we can confirm she's a Shield, we do what we came here to do. If we confirm she's a false alarm, we rendezvous back here and get set up for the other target. Beta, start the live feed the second our boots hit the ground. Then I want you running and re-running everything we know about our second choice. The moment you can confirm she's our better gamble, you call us off and we take it. I want that Last Egg of Loch Ness in my hands by tea time."

"Tea time?"

"Tea. With my mum, Bruce. Four o'clock."

"*Tea*, with your mum?"

"She's the Weapons Master at Regional, you drongo."

"*She's* your mum?"

Bob clenched his teeth and took a long, slow, breath. "We'll finish this conversation later, Runestone. In the meantime, have the spell ready or you'll be talking directly to Mum when this is done." He opened his door and stepped out into the parking lot, ending the conversation. The team followed, spreading out to casually take their positions in the half-filled parking lot.

Tony started crunching the numbers as fast as he could.

oOo

With her *cafe con leche*—espresso and scalded milk with a pinch of salt—in hand, Rhianna stopped at Ghazar's workstation. "All done?"

He smiled, kindly. "All done. The team has been activated and we should get news within the hour. I emailed Tabak directly to let him know where we stand."

She hoped for Ghazar's sake that it went well. "Then I'll get back at it. The app is only translating seamlessly into ten languages so I want to see where the problem is. It seems to be the Pacific Rim languages that're giving us trouble so I may borrow JJ for a bit."

"Brilliant. Thanks. The live feed just went up if you want to keep an eye on the team."

"Ooh. Now *that's* entertainment." She smiled her awkward, crooked smile.

"Don't we know it?"

Rhianna tipped her cup to him and wandered back to her own workstation. Ghazar opened a drawer and took out a little blue bottle of a little mental-enhancement elixir he'd cobbled together for himself. It was meant to be mixed with water and have a calming effect on the mind and body while letting him stay alert, but Ghazar unscrewed the bottle and held the dropper directly over his tongue. He squeezed the bulb and squirted the raspberry-flavoured juice in, then licked his lips and put the bottle away. He only hoped it acted fast and settled his racing mind before the operation got rolling full steam ahead.

oOo

Liam lay on his back, looking up at the somewhat blurry Milky Way directly above the ruins, his head cushioned by his still-rolled-up sleeping bag. Princess Phoenix-Teagan danced in the darkness, the white headphones of Liam's iPod barely visible in the black of the night. She spun and twirled and flipped and rejoiced in the music and the freedom, even if she was stuck in the coal circle. Liam closed his exhausted eyes and listened to the night, his good hand loosely holding the Springfield .45. There was something out there in the meadow. Something big. It was nearly silent, but Liam had been a hunter and Shield in enough lifetimes to recognize the tell-tale twig snaps, the difference between the brushing of a leaf against fur and that of leaf against leaf and branch against branch.

He sniffed the air, but there was nothing out of place. Something was downwind, though. It moved slowly, confidently, circling around until it was upwind, and then the smell hit Liam. As caught up in the music as she was, even Teagan caught the earthy, old, musty, musky odour. She stopped mid-pirouette and somersaulted over to Liam where she quickly propped him up into a sitting position. Liam handed Teagan the crossbow and he held the pistol at the ready. They waited.

There was a subtle crunch of a great, soft weight on nearby coal scraps and the shadows in the shattered doorway of the briquette-making building got three shades darker.

Liam grinned. "Hi, Beauty. We've been waiting, hoping."

The shadow moved into the ruin and stepped over the ring of coal, careful not to disturb it. She knew how important it was. She lowered her tallness down into a cross-legged sitting position on the bulls-eye. Teagan handed the little crossbow back to Liam and clapped twice, softly. Pixie dust rose from her hands and spun quickly into a globe that illuminated everything within her coal circle with a soft green light. She placed it on the ground next to Liam where it continued to spin and illuminate. The last Sasquatch east of Revelstoke reached out and poked it with her finger, making it rock in place. When she was satisfied it was just a pixie light, she opened her arms and Teagan leaped into them.

oOo

Bob and the *Gamma Ocho Neuf* team were just a group of blokes between footie matches off to pick up a few necessities. At least that's what Bob hoped the world around them saw. He let Joff follow the Shield into the store first and then drifted in after him, picking up a basket from the stack inside the door and going left while Joff went right. He scanned the store and thought he caught sight of the Shield's Brisbane Lions cap limping towards the frozen goods aisle. He strode to the other end of the store and down through the produce section, aiming for the back.

"Delta, have you got her?"

"Next aisle over. Kitchen Tools aisle. Wonder if she'll be picking up any eggs today."

"Funny. Drift past. Tell me what you see. And make sure you're carrying something so you look like you're shopping. You don't have a basket or a cart so she's going to think..."

Joff interrupted him. "Oy, lady, what do you think you're doing?"

Bob spoke quietly and quickly. "Delta, whatever it is, back off, leave now. Walk away. I'll take over."

"She's grabbed a..."

An angry female voice snapped at Joff and Bob could hear her clearly through the CMR link. "Who're you talking to? You won't take me alive, mate!"

"Oh crap! Alpha, she's got a cleaver! I'm running out of bloody options here!" Bob ran from the other end of the store, down the back aisle, dodging carts and kids, doing his best not to bowl anyone over and make this worse than he was afraid it was about to get.

"Run, Delta! Run! Clear out! Now!"

"Lady, you're nuts! Alpha, I'm cornered!" Two aisles away Bob heard the crash of a cart and a woman's scream, then Joff came skidding around the end of the aisle, straight for him. Hot on his heels was the woman the numbers said was likely the Shield. Judging by the crazed off-meds look in her eyes and heavy limp, though, Bob was now pretty sure she was more rabid dog than Shield. Joff was past him and down another aisle when Bob got an idea. He stepped out of her way, behind the short toothpaste section. "Slow down a bit Delta, you're losing her." He walked as quickly as he dared down a parallel aisle, hoping to reach the front doors right behind the alleged Shield.

"Slow down?! Are you as bloody drongo as *she* is?"

"Not by half. Runestone, get ready with the spell. Beta, start up the van. Gamma, get round the front. Kappa, she's coming out, right behind Delta. She's armed, so do *not* engage directly. Delta, lead her toward the van. Let her get close. Kappa, tranquilizer dart only. I'm agreeing this crazy Sheila probably isn't a Shield, but the crazy act is a bloody brilliant one and I'm not losing the Egg because she plays a good wingnut. Everyone keep an eye out for her backup. Nothing says she can't have her own support. Watch for Warriors."

Bob cleared the doors four paces behind the woman and a store clerk was right behind him. "She didn't pay for that knife! Oy, stop! You didn't pay for the knife, you old dog!" Bob slowed and just as the clerk passed him, he kicked the youngster's back foot into his leading foot and the clerk took a nosedive head-on into the side of a parked car. Bob let him lie, stunned and bleeding.

"Runestone, cast the spell!" He saw Bruce coming at the woman from the side, his fingers working madly to shape the spell.

"Ostendo lumen!" Nothing happened. "Alpha, I don't think she's got..."

Bob watched as the woman took notice of Bruce and threw the cleaver straight at his face. Bruce didn't have a chance. The spell-casting slowed his reflexes just enough that instead of ducking away from the spinning blade he dodged a just a little and took it in the neck, his left arm too slow to block it. From less than ten yards away Bob drew his sidearm and fired three quick, silenced shots into the woman's legs. He couldn't risk a headshot from that distance for fear of hitting the pack and the Egg.

"I've got her and the pack! Kappa, get Bruce! Delta, open the side door! Gamma, we're coming to you and out the back exit of the lot. Stay put. Cover our asses if we need it, mate." Bob ran full out, slowing only to put a close-in fourth and final shot into the head of the screaming woman before holstering his weapon, grabbing the body by the arm and dragging her up and through the open door of the van. Leon was right behind him with Bruce and as soon as Joff slammed the door, they drove away. Twenty seconds later Nate jumped in the passenger door as the van rolled past him.

Bob grabbed the bloody pack and ripped it open. It only took a quick look to prove that seventy-two-six wasn't a good enough probability. "Beta! Feed off, now!"

oOo

After the operation went live, Ghazar relayed the live feed to his tablet, grabbed his leather jacket, slipped out the side door to the courtyard and paced in the corner under the tall, evergreen Mayten tree watching the test of ShieldBreaker go down in Tasmania. As soon as the *Gamma Ocho Neuf* team leader opened the Shield's bag, Ghazar *knew* he was a dead man, knew that ShieldBreaker's failed field test had just killed him outright. He wanted to puke, to just vomit up all the Darkness he'd been force-fed since he was a kid and then reinforced since he'd been recruited, but he could do that later. Right now he had to *run*.

He tossed the company's trackable tablet in the wire mesh garbage can and re-entered the building through the Accounting wing. A minute later he slipped out through a fire door and quick-stepped across the floodlit parking lot to his Harley Nightster. He estimated he had about two minutes before they noticed he was missing, and this late at night it would be at least another two minutes before they noticed his bike was missing.

A slow, steady, deep-throated bell suddenly sounded behind him and Ghazar realized that this just wasn't his day for breaks. He popped the clutch and raced to the lot exit where the night cleaning staff were just coming through the gate. He zipped out past the security guard's booth before the barrier could drop and blasted out along Las Catalpas to Camino El Cerro. Although he had fully expected tonight's field test to be a success, the app designer was prepared for failure, as he had been since Mundhir's 'termination'. Sewn into his jacket were two false passports, fifty thousand American dollars and an open ticket on Lan Chile under one of the phony names. He hadn't been to America since graduation so he planned to fly from Santiago to Los Angeles, through La Paz, Bolivia, Quito, Ecuador and possibly one or two other changes of direction he would decide on once he got airborne. His only hope was to stay ahead of Tabak and the Hunter Teams of DökktEfniTækni until he could hit the ground Stateside and disappear.

oOo

Wallace Tabak regretted not watching the live feed right at the desk of Ghazar ben David because if he had, he could have reached out and snapped the stupid little app designer's neck when the

Tasmanian operation went south in such an ugly way. But he'd been watching it in his office and instead had to be satisfied with throwing his two-pound *ciudad de Santiago* marble paperweight through his Sony HDTV. Then he slapped a button on the communications board flush-mounted into his monstrous desk and barked commands.

"Get Ghazar ben David in here, *now*! If he resists, Taser him but don't kill him—I want that distinct pleasure for myself. If his assistant, Rhianna What's-her-name is still in the building, bring her, too, but play nice with her—she's not in any trouble, yet."

oOo

Princess Teagan whistled up an old Pixie tale for her hirsute friend, Beauty, replete with jigs and flips and trilling songs worthy of an epic. The lonely Sasquatch clapped and laughed quietly but earnestly as the tale unfolded while Liam drifted in and out of sleep. When the princess was done with the tale, she skipped over and kissed him on the forehead, but he didn't stir. Beauty reached over and slapped the sole of his boot, which snapped him awake in a big hurry.

"What? I've heard that story a dozen times, and as funny as it is, I'm exhausted. I'm sorry. I wasn't trying to be rude."

Beauty slapped Liam's boot again and pointed a long finger at his chest. The story telling between the three of them was a tradition of sorts and Liam knew that it was his turn to tell. As soothing as Teagan's whistling was to his soul, so his smooth, mellow human voice was to Beauty. A caring, intelligent creature forced to live alone by encroaching humanity and scarcity of mates, she hungered for their visits every month or so. Liam understood very little of what she said but she seemed to understand *him* quite well and Teagan had no trouble at all comprehending Sasquatchian or whatever Beauty's native tongue was.

"Are you sure? I can't take a pass on this one?"

Beauty shook her head and Teagan whistled her own objection.

"Fine, but it'll be a short one." He sat up as best as he could and leaned on the bedroll. "It was 1956. I was in Mexico with an expedition for the ROM—the Royal Ontario Museum in Toronto—looking for Mayan ruins in the cenotes, the underwater sinkholes and caves of the Yucatán peninsula. This was before National Geographic came in and made their big discovery so we were the first to go diving in this area. Back then I was Frank and I was the SCUBA expert on the exploration team. My Locus at the time was the Star Stone, which I was able to wear in a leather bag around my neck. Some things are easier to guard than others." He scowled at Teagan and she stuck her tongue out at him.

"We were on our way to Chichen Itza, where we were to meet two local guides. Craig, the driver, and I were sitting in a cantina in Merida, about twenty miles inland from the Gulf of Mexico. Craig got up to go find himself an outhouse when this Hispanic fella about sixty years old sat down in Craig's chair. He was dressed in the drab olive green of militaries around the world and sported the bushiest black moustache I'd ever seen. His English was excellent and his accent said he'd spent some time in the U.S. He had a manila folder with him and got straight down to business.

"'Señor Munro, please allow me to welcome you to Mexico. I am Alberto. I know who you are because your expedition has filed much paperwork with my government so that you may come and help us recover some of our lost heritage. In that paperwork is your complete resume, including your skills with boats, aircraft, firearms, and something called SCUBA.'"

"'I am originally from a beautiful island nation not so far from here, and it is for my homeland that I have sought you out today.' Our cute little waitress appeared and Alberto ordered three more of whatever beer it was I'd been convinced would help me deal with the sun and the heat. He went on and I listened, curious and clueless.

"'Señor Munro, a great tragedy takes place in my motherland. El Presidente has become a lazy and corrupt leader, exploiting my stunning island for American corporate and criminal profits. But a great man wishes to take back our homeland and restore her to her full glory. He is my dear friend and he has asked of me to gather skilled, trustworthy men to help us with this sacred duty. You are a pilot, a sailor, and a marksman and I am asking if you could be persuaded to pilot one of our seaplanes, to help a great man save his people.'"

"Right about this time, the waitress dropped off the beers and Craig came back to the table. Not being one of too many words himself, Craig simply pulled up a chair, swung it around backwards and sat, leaning his folded arms on the back. Alberto nodded to him with respect and handed him one of the beers, but his next words were directed back at me.

"'Please think about my request. There truly is no pressure. Your answer can even come after your work here is done, but before you leave lovely Mexico, if you please. We will, of course, pay you with American dollars, in part because it would be ironic and in all of this we must maintain some sense of humour to survive. Enjoy your visit and be certain you visit el Castillo in Chichen Itza—a truly awe-inspiring sight. When you need to speak to me, simply ask any local for General Bayo. They will get word to me and I will come to you. We are very informal here, but very efficient.' He chugged his beer, dropped a handful of pesos on the table and left the cantina. The sound of his old Jeep starting up was easily heard over the clanking of the pair of ceiling fans over the bar and the tables.

"Craig took another swig of beer and raised one eyebrow, sort of to ask what that was all about.

"'They need a pilot for a little coup they're planning. He wouldn't say where, but I'm guessing Cuba."

"'You going to take them up on it?'

"'This little adventure is enough risk for me, buddy. No one's attempted what we're doing by diving into these caves looking for artifacts, so the good General can make do without me, I think."

"'Smart decision.'

"And that, Beauty and the Phoenix, is how I almost helped Fidel Castro take back Cuba."

Beauty grunted and Teagan whistled a translation.

"What do you mean, 'What's a *Cuba*?'" He laughed. "Okay, I guess a story of human political drama wouldn't be too interesting to you. Did I tell you about the time I met Nessie at Loch Ness?"

Grunt and whistle were both accompanied by head-nods.

"Fine. Then I'm out of stories for the night. Besides, I need some sleep. You two can stay up all night and chat, but I'm going to shut down and reset, so to speak." He struggled to unroll the sleeping bag but the stuff-sack gave him trouble. Beauty noticed Liam's curled left hand and grunted a question. Teagan whistled an answer but Liam was too frustrated to be paying much attention. The next thing he knew Beauty took the bedroll from him, and gently pulled the sleeping bag out of the sack. Then she and Teagan laid it out flat and Teagan undid the zipper with her tiny, much-more-dexterous fingers.

By the time his bed was ready, Liam's tears of frustration were commingled with tears of joy that he was cared for by two such unique ladies. He curled up and was asleep in short order. Beauty slipped out quietly but returned minutes later with her arms full of fresh pine boughs, which she covered her human friend with, careful not to disturb the ring of coal.

She and Teagan sat and chatted softly for a few minutes, with the whistling Pixie explaining all of Liam's symptoms and how he wouldn't let her use magic to help him. Beauty snorted, whispered something about 'eating the earth' and slipped away into the dark. Teagan unrolled her own tiny sleeping bag and curled up next to Liam.

oOo

Tabak's desk phone rang and he slapped the speaker button. "Give me good news, *now*."

"He's running, sir. I'm in the Security Office right now and we can see Dr. ben David on the cameras heading for Exit 14. It leads to

Parking Lot 'C'."

"Stop him! Sound the damned alarm! Alert the gate, dammit!" A long, slow alarm started chiming throughout the building. He looked for something else he could throw at the shattered Sony but all he had was his coffee mug and it was a gift made by his granddaughter so it was safe. Instead he just slammed his fist down on the desk. Hard. "Where's his side-kick? Did we lose her, too?!"

"Not at all, sir. She's on her way over to your office now."

"Good. Catch ben David. Leave enough men to keep the facility secure, but *go get him back.* How are we tracking him?"

"We know that he's already dumped his tablet, because it still shows up as being in the complex, not far from his office. We have tracking bugs in his phone, his watch and one under the gas tank of his motorcycle. All standard. We'll get him back very shortly, sir."

"See that you do." He disconnected the call and dialled another.

A soft, feminine, Spanish-accented voice answered. "Tech Support. Esperanza speaking."

"Esperanza, do you have Call Display?"

"Yes sir, Señor Tabak."

"Good, you know how to use it and you know who's calling. I need someone over to my office to remove my flatscreen and install a new one. It was the fifty-two-inch Sony, I think."

"I've got your file up sir, and it was the fifty-six-inch. I will have someone up shortly with a new one and to take the old one away. Are you sure it's not something one of our team can fix right there for you?"

"No, Esperanza, I'm pretty sure this one needs to be recycled."

"Yes sir. I've just entered the work order and they will be up as soon as they get your new Sony out of inventory."

"Very good." He disconnected the call. He firmly believed that true leaders attract more bees with honey than with vinegar, but being nice was exhausting when he really wanted to tear ben David's arms off and beat him to death with them. A knock at the door broke his chain of thought. "In!"

The massive, tempered, frosted glass door swung open and Dr. ben David's assistant, Rhianna What's-her-name came in. She was pale and shaking, but trying to hide it. Her eyes darted around the office and settled on the three Japanese swords in the stand on the credenza. She nearly fainted.

"Come on in, Miss…"

"Sokolowski. Dr. Rhianna Sokolowski."

"Rhianna, I'm going to assume that you saw that mess in Tasmania. I got your email and checked all of the security footage so I know that you weren't even in the wing when it was sent. I also reviewed the numbers you suggested and, in hindsight, now agree completely. I suppose I was like Ghazar, hoping that the odds were in our favour, but now I know we should have trusted the petaflops of data DETNADEUX crunched to get the results she did." He sipped his coffee.

"I want you to rerun the numbers and let me know how we look with this latest 'development'."

"It's already done, sir." She shifted from foot to foot, still nervous knowing that the swords were even in the same room. "DETNADEUX is programmed to give us an alert when any of the ShieldBreaker results hit one hundred percent. When I factored in the woman that was killed in Australia, the results came back one-hundred-percent on the second choice. I know that sounds like something any idiot could come up with on their own, sir..."

"My thoughts exactly. We can't afford this kind of mess, missy. If we can't speed up the tracking of Shields then all Hell is going to pay. Rhianna, do you remember the presentation on Balance Shift from the Town Hall meeting in June?"

"Of course, sir. It's why we're all here."

"That it is, young lady, that it is. Of course there's also the entire industry we've created around the resultant disasters. We take a Locus, kill a Shield, then step in and help the survivors of the disasters—for a fee. But until we can start cutting down their Shields faster than they can replace them, it'll all balance and the money won't matter. We need it to swing *our* way. Tip the scales in our favour so we can start reaping what we've been sowing for millennia. The people of this little blue marble may not know what's happening behind the curtain, but without real Chaos, we're just thugs with an agenda."

"Sir, she's one-hundred percent. I'll give the *Gamma Ocho Neuf* team the order right now, from right here if you want—that's how sure I am."

"Good. You have bigger balls than Ghazar, although without risks there're no rewards. He just shouldn't have taken risks which made us look stupid and put us in the public eye more than usual." He waved at the pair of chairs facing his desk. "Please, sit. I've got them hunting down young Ghazar right now. Have any suggestions? Any idea where he might be headed?"

She sat. "The airport. Block it. He's probably heading to Los Angeles, either on his own passport or under the name of 'Bernie Walmstein'."

Tabak raised an eyebrow in genuine surprise. "And you know this *how*?"

"We both got, um, drunk after a long night working on ShieldBreaker a month or so ago and we, um, we..."

"You ended up naked and sweaty together and he couldn't keep his mouth shut? Does that about sum it up, young lady ?"

Rhianna blushed deeply and ducked her head. "Yes sir."

"Nothing to be ashamed of, Rhianna. Many a man of power has been brought down by a woman of allure. You did well. Now, prove to me that ShieldBreaker works and fix what went wrong tonight and his job is yours. In fact, find him and kill him yourself and bring me *conclusive* proof, and I'll give you his company condo as a bonus. One way or another he won't be needing it anyway, so prove to me you have what it takes to do some major damage for us, Rhianna. Show me what you can *really* do for DökktEfniTækni."

Rhianna finally smiled, though not without a hint of fear that Damocles' sword hung by horsehair over her head. One small misstep and she would have to run a lot farther and faster than Ghazar was going to. "Sir, I'm certain of ShieldBreaker's results. I'd like to give the order to the Hunter Team to proceed to the correct target and then I want to go after Ghazar. I have some ideas where he might be going if we don't catch him at the airport."

"Good girl! That's what I like—initiative! Send it, and then go get him. Do you need anything from the armoury?"

"No thank you, sir." She stood quickly.

"Excellent. Go to it, while I get the word to our people at the airport."

Rhianna left without another word and Tabak reached for the phone, determined to salvage something from this night. While he was on the phone the tech crew arrived with his new HDTV.

oOo

Bob was furious. The dead woman's pack had contained a huge plastic jar containing the foetus of a pig pickled in formaldehyde. *A damned pig!* And then Leon found the paper-plastic hospital outpatient bracelet on the woman's wrist and Bob's sudden scream of rage nearly shocked Tony into driving the van into a post.

"Crazy! She was just goddamned *crazy!* We lost our spell-caster to a bloody crazy Sheila! Tone, find us a back alley dumpster for this mess! You others strip Bruce of everything that can identify him or us. Don't forget the tracking chip in his left arm. I think his is under the hawk tattoo. Try not to get any more blood on you than you already have. Bloody *Hell!*" He yanked his Smartphone out of his pocket and turned it on. As soon as the screen came up he jabbed the ShieldBreaker app with his thumb. The app came up and he jabbed at 'Refresh Data'. It only took ten seconds, but that was too long for him.

Two nearly simultaneous chimes got his attention. One was ShieldBreaker showing him that the new results were a solid one-hundred and the other chime was an incoming call. He answered the call.

"Alpha. Go."

"Proceed with Secondary Target." It was a female voice instead of a text message. "Authorization *Gamma-Ocho-Neuf-Two-Two-Niner-Foxtrot-Soko-Romeo*. Repeat it back."

"Confirming Secondary Target, authorization *Gamma-Ocho-Neuf-Two-Two-Niner-Foxtrot-Soko-Romeo*. Proceeding ASAP."

"Confirmed. ASAP. Condolences to your Team for their loss. A new spell-caster will be enroute, but you'll have to clean this up without him."

"Confirmed. Out."

"Out."

"Tony, find me that Shield!"

"Already done. Corner of Henry and Hiller."

"Then let's go get this done because we've just worn out our bloody welcome in this town."

Chapter Eight: Bigfoot

"The higher standard Shields are held to is enforced by no one but each Shield for him or her self."
~Shield Master Wei (1963 CE to a total stranger on a grassy knoll in Dallas.)

oOo

Liam slept fitfully and so woke up when Beauty hunched her huge frame through the doorway and stepped carefully back across the coal ring. She handed Teagan a rough-hewn wooden bowl containing what looked like crushed roots and herbs in a paste.

"What have you two ladies been up to while I slept?" Beauty snorted and grunted and Teagan translated once more.

Liam laughed. "She says I have to 'eat the earth'? Is that anything like 'Bite me'?"

Impatient grunts and frustrated whistles followed.

"I have to eat what's in the bowl and it's all of the earth? Ah, gotcha." With three tiny fingers Teagan spooned up some of the beige paste and held them out for Liam to taste. Reluctantly, he did. "Okay, the taste and texture are fine—nutty and earthy, but refreshing." Teagan held out more but Liam shook his head and worked himself up into a sitting position. "I'll feed myself, thanks. I've always believed that when a woman feeds a man by hand it should be sensual and romantic, not like licking my sister's fingers." Teagan gasped and whistled an off-key trill, wiped her fingers on the rim of the bowl and dropped it in Liam's lap.

"Old fashioned? I'm *old fashioned*?"

Whistles.

"*And* I'm a sex-obsessed *human*? That is so..." He stopped and licked his lips, moving his tongue around in his mouth, over his teeth. "Why is my mouth tingling? This isn't magic is it? What did I tell you about magic, P?"

Whistles from Teagan and an insulted grunt from Beauty answered him.

"No, I don't think you're stupid, but this doesn't feel natural in my mouth."

A series of grunts and a whistled translation.

"I've been eating processed human crap for so long that my mouth is in shock from real, healthy, earth food?" He spooned a mouthful himself, carefully getting every drop. "Should I ask what's in it?"

A negative grunt.

"No translation needed. Do I eat it all now? I'm pretty full from the sandwiches, and the Coke bubbles are giving me serious gas."

Grunt. Whistled reply. Grunt. Whistle to Liam.

"A spoonful of this a day until it runs out? What does it do, besides make my tongue tingle?"

Whistle, without a grunt.

"Okay, fine, I'll eat it. You sound like every one of my mothers: *Stop asking questions and eat it, it's good for you.* Once again the present and my own history outnumber me. Fine. I'll shut up and eat a spoonful of this every day until it's all gone bye-bye."

Simultaneous whistle and snort.

"Yes, I can even do it without being sarcastic, but where's the fun in that?"

Beauty suddenly sniffed the air and grunted softly. She gathered up tiny Princess Teagan Wayfellow in her arms and licked her cheek, and then she picked Liam up very carefully and far too easily and held him close.

"Time to go, eh, Beauty? Miles to go before you sleep?"

Beauty snuffed and Liam almost thought he saw a tear on her ape-hairy face.

"You travel safe, okay. Don't get spotted. Everyone carries a camera these days and two seconds of footage of you running through the woods like your father did in Bluff Creek in '67 would not be good. I know he eventually convinced them to tell the world it was a hoax, but video quality has improved considerably since then and every moron with a camera phone would be hunting high and low for you. You'd never get another night's sleep." Beauty licked his check, placed him back down on his sleeping bag and slipped out of the circle and beyond the Pixie light. A single twig snap was the only sound Liam heard of her as she slipped away, and he was sure that she made it on purpose, just for him.

oOo

Mick Crowley logged off the Internet and pressed a button on his office comm panel. A list of numbers appeared on the screen but he couldn't focus on it yet. He was furious that the field test of this 'ShieldBreaker' the people in Santiago had run with one of the Australian teams was so completely ballsed-up. They all knew it was one thing to kill an occasional innocent during a Locus takedown, but it was least expected that the Shield get killed and the Locus get taken. Dark teams couldn't just tap innocents in the back of the head and toss their bodies away like trash. Maybe in the distant past, but video surveillance and tough-to-corrupt judges had made that nearly impossible in the civilized world. He clicked on the last number called and waited for his idiot cousin to pick up.

"Mick."

"Simon. Forget the tech that Santiago was on about. Use legwork to find that Shield and get that Locus. I'm leaving for Head Office in three hours."

"Done, Mick."

Something sounded odd in the background of Simon's end of the call. "Where are you?"

"I'm in my office."

"Is that my assistant I hear there with you?"

"Um, yes."

"At seven in the bloody morning?! Zip it up and get out onto the streets looking for this Shield. Use every Hunter Team we've got, if you have to. You've got until this time tomorrow to find him because when I land in Santiago I want to check my email and see two pictures: one of the Shield's bloody, beheaded remains, and the second of Nefertiti's Aten on my desk, showing the view of London out the window behind my chair." He could hear Simon mumbling to Marguerite in the background. "Can I make this any clearer for you, Simon? Bollocks this up again and there's nothing your mother can say to my father that will help you with Head Office. Not a damned thing."

"Yah, sure Mick. Done. Consider it done. Finished. Complete."

"Really? Then why hasn't Marguerite already landed her slut's bum at her desk outside my door?"

"On her way, Mick, on her way. Just, um, cleaning up."

"Much appreciated. Tell her to come straight in when she's all zipped up and tucked in."

"Of course." Mick could hear him mumble again to Marguerite, his hand not completely over the mouthpiece of the phone. He came back on the phone. "She'll be right there."

Mick hung up and had to restrain himself from throwing the phone across the room. Instead he called down to the concierge and ordered a car to be ready in fifteen minutes. Then he deliberately, gently slipped his cell phone into the inside pocket of his blazer and poured himself a double shot of the forty-year-old Highland Park 1958 single malt whiskey from the crystal decanter on his sideboard. Swirling it around, letting it breathe, Mick raised the tumbler to his nose to rejoice in what was rumoured to be the world's most expensive scotch. His pulse slowed, his head cleared, his tension drained. Then he knocked the liquid amber fire back and it lit him up all the way down to his groin. He was now ready to conquer Light single-handedly.

oOo

Throughout the entire night Becca regretted the decision to stay at the Hostel. It was a great place to stay for regular people, but for a Shield, there was too much exposure in the dorm room. Any one or three or six of the women around her could be Hunters. She knew that their information showed that ninety-four-percent of the Hunters the Shields had encountered were men, but those were the Teams of the past. If *she* were running the Hunter Teams, she'd have more than a few all-women Teams and at least fifty-percent mixed Teams. For all she knew, the Dark already thought like that and the Team seeking her was capable of infiltrating a women-only dorm.

She really needed to calm down. Seeing Skosche here-and-now was unsettling her more than it should, but she knew that two Shields in one locale would draw the Dark and she was ill prepared to run right now. For the nth time, Becca kicked herself for getting rid of the Jeep. The bicycle would have been great in a city the size of Calgary if she could settle and disappear into the madding crowd, but not with Skosche here, too. Dammit! Her right hand tightened on the case containing the Pipe while the left held tight to the butterfly knife she usually kept in her back pocket. She slowed and deepened her breathing and willed her body to relax, one muscle at a time, starting at her toes, working her way up. By the time she'd flexed and released her abs it seemed to be working. She could sense the tension sloughing off like a shed snakeskin. A light sleep finally came to the Shield protecting Bunjil's Pipe.

oOo

No one noticed the quiet, grey-bearded, turbaned Sikh as he walked into the Food Court of the *Pride of Burgundy* ferry bound for Calais, across the English Channel from Dover. Not the crying baby in the stroller ahead of him, not the purser in the gangway, and not the twenty-ish Dark Hunter with spiked blond hair and black leather long-coat in the corner absorbing every word of a dog-eared paperback copy of Robert J. Sawyer's *The Terminal Experiment*. But Arvinder noticed each and every one of them, especially the reader. He'd seen the reader before, coming out of the London office of DökktEfniTækni. Most Shields disappeared into the woodwork, trying to stay under the Dark 'radar', and although Arvinder didn't exactly draw attention to himself, he did like to know whom he was up against. He'd done a little research of his own and the Dutch firm of DökktEfniTækni — Dark Matters Technology — stood out front and centre. He watched them so he'd know when they were watching him. At over six feet tall, Spikey-Blond over in the corner stood out in any crowd and Arvinder never forgot a good-looking lad.

But Arvinder the Sikh was here to disappear, not draw more attention to himself by flirting. He found his own little corner of the

Food Court between two Indian Sikh families, and he let them absorb him into their scene. The fact that he was really a Goan Catholic didn't stop him from blending into other cultures when necessary. Arvinder wasn't even his birth name this time out. Blending in was what Shields did best. Of course it didn't hurt that he'd spent two lifetimes as a Sikh, and even met the Guru briefly just before his death in 1538. Arvinder, like most Shields, had been raised in nearly every religion in the world over their many lifetimes, so no matter what his current body was raised to worship, his soul was entitled to follow whatever faith it needed to in order to survive and protect his Locus.

oOo

Tony rebooted his laptop and was waiting for the login screen.

"Well?" Bob was not a happy leader. They were a block from the Shield's building but Tony couldn't confirm the location of the Shield herself.

"Thirty seconds, max." He couldn't get a picture on any of the wireless cameras he'd set up in the area so he'd rebooted, hoping that would solve the problem.

"When's the last time you saw her, live or on camera?"

"The *last* time?"

"The... last... time, Tone."

"Probably yesterday afternoon."

"Then get the damned system back up and get me something *fresh*."

oOo

It wasn't just that the old van didn't quite fit in the neighbourhood, or that it had tinted windows and was sitting with its engine running, but Tracy had a Shield-strength hunch that something was *very* wrong and something bad was going to happen here on Hiller Street. She was armed and ready, as always, but just this one time, she'd left the Egg behind because she was just getting some fresh air. She intended to be back home in the shake of a lamb's tail, but that meant that she was a Shield without her Locus and hobbling on a pair of crutches.

She pressed down hard on her Shield emergency transmitter on the end of the chain and as quickly as she could, she crutch-sprinted around the block and came up on her building from the rear. She'd been a Shield too long to fumble with her keys or get all wigged out by the presence of the Dark. She was up the stairs to the second floor in record time and burst into the unlocked unit.

"Kimbra!"

"In the crapper, Trace."

Tracy talked while she retrieved her weapons hidden around the unit. "Finish up fast and get out here."

"Easier said than done, Cuz."

"Do you remember when I told you that a day would come when I would give you orders and expect them to be followed without question?"

Kimbra laughed. "Yah, right, like you could order someone around."

Tracy heard the toilet flush and the tap water running. She slipped into the Kevlar vest that looked like a heavy leather biker's vest to the casual observer. Kimbra came out of the bathroom wearing a smile that vanished when she saw Tracy's armament laid out on the coffee table. "That time is now. You promised. Swore a solemn oath."

"That was *ten* years ago. We weren't much more than kids. What the hell are you on about, Trace, and where did you pick up the boys toys? Is this a paintballer?" She reached for the loaded H&K MP7 submachine gun.

"Kimbra! Stop!" Tracy hopped over on her good foot and grabbed her cousin's wrist. "*Get out*, now! Go get Emily and the twins and get them the hell out of the building. You've got less than a minute. No questions, luv, just go! Out the back door and north up Henry Street. If you see any mean-looking blokes, don't flirt, don't even make eye contact. Just look casual and walk slow!"

"But..."

"Kimbra, this is *not* open for debate! Get those kids out, *please*. People are going to die here and I don't want you to be one of them!" She screwed a suppressor onto the MP7, muttering to herself. "I should never have let people in. Never never never. A Shield knows better. *I* know better."

Kimbra stopped at the open door. "Trace, I can help. Tell me what to do..."

Tracy looked up and remembered why she was a Shield of Light. "I love you, Kimbra. Give Mum and Da' my love, and no matter what anybody says, I'm one of the *good* guys. NOW GET THE HELL OUT! And close the door behind you, please."

The tears flowing down Tracy's cheeks nearly made Kimbra stop and come back into the unit but the weapons and the thought of the babies down the hall being in danger forced her to follow the orders as she'd once promised.

Tracy didn't even see the door close; she was too busy hopping on one foot, shoving furniture around, and setting up a barricade she could defend.

o0o

"I'm back in. I've got the feed. If she goes in or out of the building, we'll see her. What do you th... wait! There's someone leaving the building. Got two Sheila's and one of them double strollers."

"Could it be her?"

"Negative. One's too tall and one's too young."

"Leon, go take a casual walk around the block, pass them face on and come back. Carry your CMR if something comes up, but don't wear it so they don't get spooked. No visible weapons. Go."

oOo

Tracy decided to make her last stand in the kitchen, using the island as her final defence. She lay all of her spare clips and a sheath of blades on the floor back there for easy access. She dragged the steamer trunk containing the Egg into the bedroom to the foot of the bed where she tossed some dirty clothes out of the hamper onto it and then she returned to the living room. She brought her laptop up off of stand-by and clicked on the camera icon tucked in the top left corner. She now had a full 360-degree view of the building and the block as well as the interior public spaces of the structure. She had a total of a dozen cameras giving her coverage. She saw Kimbra and Emily strolling the kids up Henry Street and then she saw one man exit the van and start around the block in the opposite direction.

"Damn damn damn!" She grabbed the sniper rifle, her crutches and her keys and moved as quickly as she could over to Emily's unit. Letting herself in, she hopped out to the balcony, hoping she could still see Kimbra and Em. She could. She ducked down behind the solid wood balcony wall and watched. After a moment the Hunter came jogging out from between two houses and walked straight at the women. Tracy watched him through the rifle's scope, seeing the strength of his walk, the way he scanned the street around him without looking like he was doing it, and the way both hands were tucked into his jacket pockets. No, they *weren't*. He had one hand behind his back. Tracy sighted on his chest but noticed the outline of body armour like her own and moved her sight up to his throat. It would be a harder shot, but a guaranteed kill. She waited, finger on the trigger.

He smiled at Kimbra who had probably smiled back, unable to resist a well-muscled, clean-cut man. They passed each other and he turned to watch them walk away, probably admiring the sway of the hips of her two best friends. For that alone she should have at least shot him in the back of the knee, but she could now see what he had in the hand behind his back—a communication headset of some sort. He lifted it to his head and spoke as he continued toward Tracy and the second-floor balcony. She ducked back behind the barrier and could hear him as he passed by, ten metres away.

"No worries, Alpha. Not the target. A couple of cute Sheilas with two brats. I think the one was giving me 'the look'." There was a pause as he listened to 'Alpha'. "I'll be there in one. Just..." and he walked out of hearing range from Tracy. She hopped back into the unit, back down the hall and into her own semi-fortified home. She watched on her laptop as the Hunter strode past the front of the building and re-entered the van. The camera didn't have a great angle, but she thought she saw at least three others in the vehicle. None of the other cameras showed any other vehicles capable of carrying Hunters. She clicked on the feed she was getting from the camera on the corner of the balcony and confirmed what she feared most—she didn't have a clear view of the van from there.

She had hoped to be able to pick them off with the rifle as they exited the van, but there was a damned tree in the way. She considered going up to the roof, but there was no way her knee brace would let her climb the ladder. She looked at her watch. Where were the Warriors of Light when you needed them?

o0o

The Hunters of *Gamma Ocho Neuf* Team weren't going to get any readier. Bob wondered to himself if they should wait two days for the new spell-caster to arrive and just keep an eye on this Shield until then, but he also knew that once the media got ahold of the story of the shooting in the Coles lot this morning and discovery of the bodies in the dumpster, the Shield would be fore-warned, fore-armed and on the run.

"Right then, mates, let's get this done. No room for cock-ups this time. No spell-caster, no easy time finding the Egg. The good news is that the Egg is bloody hard to hide and it won't be far from her, so shouldn't take us long at all, once we eliminate the Shield. CMRs on. Again, Tone, live feed once our feet hit the ground. Turn us around and pull up in front. Standard Formation for a two-entry building assault. If I have to explain that, then eat your bullet now. Bruce was usually with me so I'll fill the gap myself. Tasers only on all civilians."

Tony waited until a moving truck drove past and turned up Henry Street before making his U-turn.

o0o

Tracy's cellphone vibrated in her pocket and she nearly peed herself from surprise. She pulled it out and checked the caller ID. It read "Service de Lumiere" but the number was blocked. She answered it.

"This had better be the bloody cavalry."

"Who else would it be? You've moved around since you called for us so we need a Situation report."

"Sit-Rep? Um, Three to six Hunters in a white van down a block to the west. They've already done a walk-around so I'm expecting the Silent treatment any second. I'm in 203, facing the front. I have a balcony and am barricaded as best as I can be. One stairway in the front, one in back. They match the two access points. I've cleared out some civilians but not all. I'm armed to the teeth but in a bloody leg brace so mobility is severely limited."

"Roger that. We just drove past the van. Its brake lights were lit up so we concur that they're about to move in. We're parked two houses north and will take them out from behind. We'll try to eliminate them before they reach you, but there are only three of us, not including you."

Tracy heard a vehicle pull up in front of the building and doors open and close. "They're here. Hope to see you soon. Out."

"Out." Except for the voice on the phone, she was suddenly covered in a blanket of silence. The Dark were coming.

"One way or another, let's make this quick, 'cuz I'm starved," she said to no one in particular. She thumbed the MP7's safety off and braced herself for the assault. She was protected from attacks from both the balcony and the front door, but not for long—she had only one set of eyes and two hands to shoot and reload with.

She didn't hear any glass breaking and a quick look at the screen showed that the Hunters had managed to pick the lock without any trouble. She watched as three Hunters came in the front entrance and moved up the stairs. They didn't even hesitate so she knew that they knew where she lived. She picked them up on camera again when they reached her floor and started toward her door.

There were two more at the back door but they were having trouble with the lock. Finally one of them raised his rifle to break the glass with the butt stock but he suddenly folded like a puppet with cut strings. The second Hunter turned and dove away from the door but wasn't fast enough and Tracy could see his body take two shots to the ribs and one to the head. Two Warriors of Light dressed in SWAT gear cat-footed quickly into view and dragged the bodies away from the back door. One of them looked up at the camera and flashed Tracy a thumbs up while the other one ripped the CMR from one of the corpses and held it to his own ear. Using a digital auto-pick on the lock they were inside quickly and moving up the back stairs at a run.

Tracy saw that the three Hunters who had come in the front were at her door. Two stood back-to-back, watching the exits from the stairwells as well as the doors of the other units, while the third one lifted his leg and kicked her door in. At least, that's what was supposed to happen. The week she moved in, Tracy had replaced the cheap wooden door with a steel one and then painted it to look like old wood. She'd also had the doorframe reinforced and two extra deadbolts put in. Her door wasn't being kicked in any time soon.

Of course it wouldn't stop explosives and she watched the door-kicker stick a long strip of grey putty along the next to the locks. Semtex, she assumed. Possibly C-4. Either way, she had company and they were tired of waiting out in the hallway. A triple muzzle flash from each end of the hallway put down the two Hunters standing sentinel but one managed to get off a couple shots of his own. One of the Warriors took the hits in the shoulder and spun around on his way down to the floor. Tracy was watching him writhe in pain so she missed it when the Hunter with the explosives dropped down behind the corpse of one of his teammates and returned fire. He was pinned down from two sides and he knew it.

Tracy heard the sounds of his suppressed shots through the door and decided that it was time to end this before more Warriors fell or one of her neighbours stepped out to investigate the commotion. She slid her finger along the touch pad on her laptop's keyboard until the little arrow was over the door icon on the right side of the camera views. She double-clicked the door. There was a loud 'clank' sound in her ceiling and on the screen she watched the suspended ceiling outside her door swing away and a weighted steel mesh net drop on the Hunter. She clicked on the lightning bolt next to the door icon and a charge equal to that of a TASER X3 surged through the mesh, incapacitating the Hunter. By the time she killed the current to the net, hopped over to the door, flipped the bolts and opened it, the Warriors had disarmed and handcuffed the Hunter and removed the Semtex from the door.

"Perfect timing, boys. Just drag everyone in here and we'll see to our own injured." She hopped aside and held the door for them while the two still mobile Warriors moved quickly to clear the hall. They couldn't do anything about the blood, but that wasn't going to matter soon, anyway.

"Get your Locus, your weapons and your travel kit, please, miss— we have three minutes to be out back."

"Roger that." She hopped into the bedroom to the trunk and retrieved the Egg. Since it was always in its protective travel case, she only needed to grab her prepared travel bag from the closet and her crutches. When she returned to the living room the two bodies were dumped in a corner, her weapons and laptop computer had all been collected up in a duffel bag and the prisoner was back on his feet, though clearly not in complete command of his motor functions. The injured Warrior held his good hand out for her travel kit.

"Allow me, miss."

"But you just got shot. You're bleeding. Aren't you?"

"Not at all. The armour prevented penetration. My shoulder is dislocated and possibly broken, but I'll live. I still have one good shoulder and you need both of yours for the crutches, so please give me your bag."

Tracy handed him the bag, slung the Egg case on her back like a packsack and tucked her crutches under her armpits. "Lead the way."

It was almost exactly three minutes before the four of them were inside the moving truck and ready to leave. Tracy wanted to call Kimbra and Emily to say goodbye, but the lead Warrior shook his head 'no'. "You said that they're on foot, walking north? We'll catch up to them shortly and you can say goodbye in person. We have to assume that your cell phone is compromised." He held out his hand and she passed it over to him. In seconds he had completely dismantled it and tossed the pieces out the open window of the truck one at a time as they drove along.

He was right, too, when he said they would catch up to Kimbra and Emily quickly. Tracy pointed them out and the driver pulled up next to them. One of the men let Tracy out the back of the truck and she crutch-walked over to her cousin and her best friend, hugging each of them. "I have to go. I never should have stayed this long. Some day I'll write and explain, but think of this as the Witness Relocation Program. I'll be out of touch a long time. I love you both so much. You and the twins are the lights of my life."

"Trace, what the hell are you going on about?"

"There are two bodies in my unit and two more out back, Em. The police will be all over the place in short order. Don't go back to my place. Em, no worries about your unit—it's safe to go back there, at least for the night. You might want to consider taking your family up to Brisbane for a while, once you've answered all the cops' questions."

"Dead bodies?" What the f...?"

"Kimbra, relax. Where's your laundry?"

"Loaded in my Mini."

"Good. Go straight home after you get Em and the kids safe inside, please. If you can get out before the cops arrive, all the better. Maybe no one has to know you were even here."

The driver rolled down his window. "Gotta go, Miss. Now."

Tracy looked up at him and nodded. Then she hugged the two women again and gave each of the babies a kiss. She was crying when she stood up. "Take care of these two carpet grubs, will ya. Maybe I'll get to see them again some day. I love you both."

"Love you, too, Trace."

"Love you, Cuz. Be safe, wherever the hell you're going."

"No worries. You, too." The Warrior leader helped her into the now-vacant passenger seat and they drove off.

oOo

If Bob had ever had a worse day as a Dark Hunter, he couldn't remember when it was. His body ached and his mind was still a little numb from whatever it was that hit him in the hallway outside the Shield's unit. In one day he'd lost his whole team, killed a civilian, and failed to do anything of note other than get taken alive. His mother was going to kill him, literally.

oOo

Ghazar pulled into the gas station to top up the Harley's tank. If he hadn't stopped at the airport to empty his twisting, upset bowels before buying his ticket, he would have been caught and taken back to DökktEfniTækni to 'answer' for today's mistakes. His nerves were so shot that his stomach churned and bubbled and cranked out acid that ploughed its way through his digestive tract. He'd ducked into the Departures Level handicapped toilet so that he could lock the door and at least have a little privacy.

After he was finished painfully exploding his hastily eaten dinner into the porcelain bowl, he dropped his watch and his Smartphone into the disgusting mess and flushed. The Casio went down and away, but the Smartphone just got caught at the narrow drain and swirled around and around. He didn't care. He just wanted the tracking bug shorted out. He was no idiot. He was quite familiar with the methods DökktEfniTækni used because he was the one who'd been charged with creating the mobile app linking the bugs with the tracker's Smartphone GPS in the first place.

While stopped at a red light on his way to the airport he'd casually reached under the gas tank of the Harley, pried that magnetic tracking bug off and lobbed it into the back of an old Ford half-ton with a box full of propane tanks, so when he stepped out of the toilet, he was 90% sure he was bug-free. Of course today wasn't his day for numbers so he scanned the mezzanine carefully, watching for any kind of seguridad or policía coming for him. He didn't have to look far because there were at least a dozen uniforms coming his way and half that many DökktEfniTækni security suits. He moved back against a wall and walked quickly to the exit stairs.

Once out of sight he raced up one level to the airport's administration level. It was empty at this hour and he sprinted the length of the carpeted corridor and then out through the emergency exit and down those stairs. There was almost no traffic for him to dodge so he walked as quickly and as casually as he could back to the parking structure where he'd left the Harley. He'd never expected to see his two-wheeled baby again, so he was elated that his helmet was still on the handlebar and the key in the ignition. The tank was nearly empty so he planned his new route to go past one of the 24-hour gas stations in the area. The pressure in his belly let up quite a bit when he could see Comodoro Arturo Merino Benitez Airport recede in his rear-view mirror.

He needed to make it to the airport in Mendoza, five hours over the mountains into Argentina, so when he pulled up to the gas pump he wondered if maybe he should buy a jerry can and fill it to make sure he had enough gas. Experience had taught him that as he drove higher and higher into the mountains, the Harley's fuel efficiency would drop drastically as the air thinned out. He turned the engine off, popped the kickstand, flipped up his visor and dismounted. The scuff of a shoe on the pavement behind him caught his ear and he turned, seeing only a muzzle flash.

oOo

Rhianna knew Ghazar well enough to know that he'd avoid capture at the airport and would have to hit the roads. She also knew that he never filled up his motorcycle's tank completely, just dropping in a few pesos-worth of gas when the tank got low. Knowing all of this, she headed to the 24-hour gas bar closest to the airport and parked around back, waiting and watching.

Almost to the minute she predicted he would arrive, Ghazar cruised into the station and pulled up to the row of self-serve pumps. With her hair tucked up under her hat, a loose-fitting jacket covering her few curves, and her little S&W .38 hidden behind her back, Rhianna walked up behind her former supervisor and one-time lover and executed him with a single shot.

She'd hunted with her father plenty while growing up in Minnesota so she knew she had what it took to pull the trigger and take a life, but what she wasn't quite ready for was Ghazar turning at the last second and having to look into his eyes when she pulled the trigger. But pull it she did, and she even kept her wits about her when she turned on her heel and walked away quickly, into the shadows and around to her car.

The newly-installed digital security cameras didn't capture Rhianna's muddied license plate when she drove away simply because the cashier inside was watching Sly Stallone in *Los Mercenarios* on the portable DVD player he'd brought from home and plugged in to where the digital recorder was supposed to be plugged in to. With all of the gunfire in the testosterone- and machismo-filled movie, he didn't even notice the one extra pop that came from out near pump número de cinco; and the murder of the gringo computer geek on the nice Harley went unsolved.

Chapter Nine: The Holy Grail

"This is not a casual game of senet we're involved in. The Balance of All is at stake. There is life and death and sometimes death comes at the hands of the Shields in order to maintain or restore Balance. It is a fact that cannot be argued against or changed."

~Shield Master Wei (180 CE at Hadrian's Wall, watching the Romans retreat.)

oOo

After taking care of the 'Ghazar business', Rhianna drove back to the office, determined to stay up all night if she had to so that she could show Wallace Tabak something solid at first light. As she drove she reviewed in her head the parameters that ShieldBreaker was using now and tried to assess what she could possibly add to the mix to take advantage of DETNADEUX's unsurpassed raw power.

oOo

In his fifty-eight years, Wallace Tabak had experienced his share of muzzle-under-the-chin-and-end-it days, but he'd usually been able to recover semi-gracefully and let time and bourbon dilute the memory of the disaster. But this unmitigated bastard-mess of a day was making him wonder if maybe he should have followed Ghazar ben David out the door. Of course *his* leggy assistant wouldn't catch him off guard at a self-serve before he could enter his own Wallace-Protection Program.

One civilian, five Hunters and the best app programmer money could buy... dead. The app he had been touting to the Board so enthusiastically for the last year was ninety-percent useful which was the same as saying that it was zero-percent useful. If that Sokolowski girl could give him the extra ten-percent as quickly as she settled the ben David problem, he could stay put in Santiago, continuing to enjoy being Wallace Tabak.

Being Wallace Tabak was about as good a life as anyone could sell his soul for. He was a globally respected and feared corporate mover and shaker married to a former Miss Texas, sleeping with the last year's Miss Santiago, and making more damned money than Trump. He had a beautiful daughter, two terrific granddaughters, and a grandson on the way; and when Dark business allowed, he and his wife, Tricia, flew to Curacao to see visit Ashlynn and the girls two or three times a year. Hell, *they* saw their daughter more than she saw her own Dark Hunter husband, Damian, but that was the nature of Damian's job and the benefits outweighed the price in the Tabak family. Of course hostile takeovers at DökktEfniTækni had more than once involved actual gunplay, but one didn't play for the Dark without some serious risks.

It was time to wrap up the day and, since Tricia was in Curacao with Ashlynn prepping for the baby's arrival, he had all night to convince the former Miss Santiago to 'polish his Texas longhorn'. He shut off his laptop computer, disconnected the power supply and the Internet cable then secured it in the fireproof wall safe beside the newly installed HDTV. As soon as he closed and locked the safe, three cameras started recording every movement in the office. Wallace Tabak trusted no one because he knew very well that no one at DökktEfniTækni could be trusted.

oOo

Liam was so exhausted that it took more than a few licks of his face for Phoenix to wake him up. She eventually had to resort to tugging the sleeping bag down away from his face and letting the cutting cold mountain air finish the job.

"Oh! That's so not fair! I was having the best sleep I've had in a month. Just hit your snooze button and give me another ten." He reached for the edge of the sleeping bag to pull it back up but Phoenix backed up with it in her teeth, pulling it out of his reach.

"It's that late, eh?" He looked up at the sky. "It's still dark, P—or have I gone blind in addition to the other crap that I'm dealing with?"

A golden light flashed briefly in Phoenix's eyes, lasting just long enough for Liam to see and know that he wasn't blind.

"Thanks. I guess I could have used the IR goggles to determine the same thing. Tired, lazy and crippled—maybe you'd be safer with Beauty." Phoenix's low negative growl was all Liam needed to hear. "Fine. Then I guess we should get moving."

oOo

By the time *The Pride of Burgundy* reached Calais, Arvinder was long lost Uncle Darshan to the Dhaliwal family and they insisted that he just *had* to join them in Lyons after he was finished with his business in Reims. As a matter of fact they insisted that he keep his taxi fare and ride with them to Reims. If his business was short they could even wait for him and then he could continue on to Lyons with them.

He laughed and thanked them, but his business in Reims could take the rest of the day and possibly the evening as well so although he would accept a ride with them as far as Reims, they might as well continue on from there without him and he would catch up with them

121

in Lyons.

When the Shield disembarked the ferry in Calais with the Dhaliwal family and the Hunter remained on board, leaning back against the rail, not even watching the offloading of passengers, Arvinder felt that he might actually sleep soundly tonight, especially since he would be nowhere near either Reims or Lyons. Visrama and Gaganjot Dhaliwal and their three girls—Kaur, Karuna and Kamalini—were a nice distraction and a perfect short-term cover, but he wasn't about to put them in any further danger than was necessary. As soon as they dropped him off in Reims he would probably be on a train to Paris with Nefertiti's Aten safe and sound.

oOo

Liam noticed the change almost immediately. His left hand had a slightly stronger grip and he felt a bit more stable on his feet. Whatever Beauty had given him seemed to have at least a short-term benefit. Who'd have thought the walking carpet had that kind of know-how?

Thanks in part to Beauty's elixir and much to Phoenix waking him in plenty of time, Liam had everything hauled back up to the car and packed away well before sunrise. His note on the dashboard had a matching one from the Park Warden under the windshield wiper stating that he had until noon to remove his vehicle or it would be towed. If he needed any assistance, he could call the number written on the bottom of the note. It was signed, *A. Bjorn, Warden*.

"We caught a break, P, so let's not push our luck. I say we go vanish in the woods near Lake Louise for a few days. What do you say?"

Phoenix barked softly as Liam struggled to scoop her up and put her on her blanket on the passenger seat.

"I'm glad you agree. So, Deer Lodge or Lake Louise Inn? The Chateau and The Post Hotel are both a little too high-profile for a couple of scruffs like us and I'm pretty sure the Hostel has a no-dogs rule, even if said dog is a famous Pixie Princess travelling incognito to avoid her adoring fans."

The tubby little Yorkie harffed and rolled over on her side, a wide smile on her Ewok-like face.

"A tummy rub? While I try to drive this winding road? No can do, little one, but how about a compromise? Once we get back on the Trans-Canada Highway you can ride on my lap. Deal?"

A soft bark was his answer, as expected. He was pretty sure that Phoenix would gladly spend all day, every day, curled up in his lap if he let her. Of course she might get her wish if it turned out to be MS that was messing him up and it progressed to the point where he needed a wheelchair. Then again, the Dark would probably catch up to them long before then and at that point MS would be the least of his worries.

oOo

Becca decided she couldn't wait for sunrise to get out of Calgary. Her biggest problem was deciding which way to go. After a quick shower she plopped down on the worn couch in the hostel's common area and unfolded her map of Western Canada. She wasn't going too far, too fast on the prairies on her bicycle so she was at the mercy of Greyhound. It wouldn't be her first time running with the Hound and she was pretty damned sure it wouldn't be her last. At least she didn't have to go by wagon train. Once was enough.

She narrowed her choices down to nearby Drumheller and Red Deer; slightly further Medicine Hat to the South, or Edmonton, the provincial capital, to the north. She needed a city big enough to hide in and where she could make some money to buy a car and get clear of Alberta. As much as her heart yearned to hold Skosche again, to love him again, she couldn't risk it—the Dark were flourishing and in her bones she knew that running was her only choice. Her soul mate would have to wait, again.

oOo

Rhianna took a short nap on the couch in the department's lounge then popped open and chugged a can of Red Bull before hitting her workstation.

She'd run the app's parameters through her own superior human processor over and over again and she was sure she was on the right track, the track that Ghazar had shied away from. They'd factored in every aspect of Shield life and history they could, but she realized now that they'd suffered tunnel vision—they'd forgotten that the damned Shields didn't operate in isolation. They were *in* and *of* the real world and it was the real world stats and data that they were missing. Data such as population density and political stability. There was also the simple stuff like the availability of Wi-Fi and the presence of an extensive transit system. The more features she could add that a city boasted of that would make it easier for a holier-than-thou Shield to remain anonymous, to stay beneath the radar, the more likely a Shield could be found there and wiped out.

If she herself were cursed with being a Shield and she had a choice between hiding in a monstropolis like New York City, or a one-horser like Butt-Scratch, Montana, the Big Apple would be choice number one; finding a Shield in an urban jungle of eight million people would be like picking one particular minnow out of a tank of thousands, or one ant out of an entire colony. Hopefully the expanded search-and-analyze parameters she was going to input into DETNADEUX would find all of the ants of Light and crush them so that the strong and deserving could rise to the top and show the bottom of the heap how life was supposed to be lived.

oOo

Downtown Calgary was still wrapped in darkness when Becca pedaled onto the Bow River Pathway heading west from the youth hostel in the East Village across the twenty-three blocks of the city core to the Greyhound station. The lights on the trail were bright enough for her see clearly enough to ride without using the bike's headlight as the asphalt wound between the trees and the river only yards away. Riding with her light off kept her from attracting the attention of the few street denizens who might block her way and swarm her just for her bike and what little cash she might be carrying. In her many lifetimes she'd learned that most of the homeless just wanted to be left alone, but there were always those who would prey on the weak and the available.

She moved fast and silent, past the few early risers before they even knew she was approaching. Curses and shouts of surprise followed her but nothing else. She felt safer riding next to the Bow River than she had in months. The purity of the river wrapped her in a cocoon of security and spiritual warmth. Becca knew it was an illusion, but she felt unstoppable and uncatchable. Like she'd been saying for centuries, the Dark could just kiss her butt.

When she was only a few blocks from where her map said the Bus Depot was, she abandoned the bike in the shadows of Millennium Park Skateboard Park and walked the rest of the way with the panniers slung over her shoulder and the courier tube containing Bunjil's Pipe across her chest.

An hour later she was tucked into the back row of an Edmonton-bound Greyhound coach, glad to feel the road beneath the humming tires leaving Calgary and the Dark Hunters behind. Her last thought before she slipped into a light sleep was to wonder whether or not she would see Skosche again in this lifetime and how she missed him so much that her soul ached.

oOo

Liam knew he shouldn't be driving in the dark, in spite of the supposedly-not-magic elixir Beauty had made for him, but he figured that if he took the slower, less-travelled Bow Valley Parkway from Banff to Lake Louise he'd be fine.

As promised, Phoenix slept on his lap as he cruised along the winding, scenic route that followed the east face of the valley carved by the Bow River long before even *he* was born, the first time. On previous trips he'd spotted deer, elk, moose, bighorn sheep, and even a huge cinnamon-coloured black bear rooting around the undergrowth only a few yards from the road, but the sun was still behind the Sawback Range so it was too dark to see anything that wasn't right on the road or shoulder. He could pass by Beauty herself and if she were fifty feet off the road he'd be as completely oblivious as most of the tourists were. Of course, with his screwed up vision, travelling in the dark was worse than unsafe, it was reckless, but Liam needed to get to the lake, needed to check into a hotel and needed to just unwind for a couple of days. Sit on the shore and breathe in and breathe out. Breathe in, breathe out, and forget about the Dark, the Light, Faerie, Oberon, being sick, or wanting to die once and for all. Twenty centuries of weight on his shoulders would be washed away by the glacial Lake of Little Fishes, or so he hoped. It had worked on previous trips, but on previous trips he hadn't been facing the possibility of life with MS.

He wasn't sure what scared him more, having MS now when Teagan/Phoenix depended on him or the prospect of the MS following him to his next Shield 'assignment' when this one was done. Was it even MS, or was he experiencing a deterioration caused by centuries of being brought back, centuries of living, dying and reincarnation? Could the soul of a Shield be like a strand of DNA and get weaker over time because of replication? All good questions in his mind, but not ones he'd ever see answered if he didn't concentrate on his driving and get to Lake Louise in one piece.

There were no streetlights on the fifty-five-kilometre-long parkway except in the one or two spots where the road split and at the few turnoffs like Johnston Canyon and Castle Junction. There were no Disney World-like floodlights on the mountains towering above him on the east or across on the west flank of the valley as he headed north. The curves had little reflective arrows or chevrons pointing the way and in some cases of extremely sharp turns there were big chevrons, but Liam's not-so-stereo vision was blurry so he slowed, determined not to save either the Dark or Oberon's agents the effort. He drove at least ten k an hour below the limit of sixty and every so often fast headlights in his rear-view simply swerved into the oncoming lane and back again before he had time to react. He squinted into the dark and drove on, envying Phoenix's dog-eyed optimism that it would all be just fine.

oOo

There'd been light drizzle niggling at them for the first eight holes at the Royal Aalborg Golfklub but by the time they were teeing off on nine the clouds above Aalborg, Denmark had actually broken up and the sun was making a valiant effort to burn off the grey. Randolfo didn't care one way or another because he staunchly believed the old maxim that a bad day of golf was better than a good day of work. It hadn't always been the case, but since they'd finally amputated his car-accident-crushed foot and found a prosthetic that didn't chafe like dinner with his stepmother, he'd come back to the game he'd loved since he was a lad.

It definitely didn't hurt that he'd found a true craftsman in the town of Århus—118 kilometres south of Aalborg—who could customize the interior of the false leg so that his Locus fit perfectly and stayed safe. He'd told the Jewish ex-soldier that he wanted the padded insert to be able to hold the small bottle of akvavit he liked to smuggle into football games. The former sergeant smiled knowingly and they had their little conspiracy together. Randolfo wondered what the talented Jew would have said if he'd known that the hollow calf would actually house the long lost, one and true, Holy Grail. Would he even believe him? Probably not.

oOo

When Wallace Tabak called Rhianna Sokolowski up on the carpet as soon as he got into the office in the morning he really hadn't expected to get much more than a few mumbled ideas about what she was maybe thinking of trying at some point. He really didn't expect her to have found four damned Shields of Light.

"Where, and how sure are you?"

He could see she was struggling to keep a satisfied smile off her oddly attractive face. "Saudi Arabia, the U.S. of A., Czech Republic, and Denmark."

Why was getting answers out of some people like pulling bloody teeth? "You'll have to be a lot more specific than that, young lady."

"Of course, sir. They're in Mecca, Manhattan, Prague, and Aalborg. I've given the specific addresses to the Hunters on the ground. I'm just waiting for the confirmations to come in. The Aalborg team is closest. We also have a possible two-Shields Proximity Alert in Calgary, Canada. I've got someone checking on it."

oOo

Kenny had honors so he teed up his ball on Nine and waited a moment for a gust of wind to pass. It was a straight line to the green, five-hundred-and-twenty meters away. Kenny kissed the face of his Big Bertha driver and set his feet. Randolfo laughed.

"You kiss her every time and she still lets you down, Kenny. Maybe if you got some lessons you'd have more success." Standing downwind of his non-smoking chums he took a drag on his cigarette and let the smoke just roll out of his mouth.

Tall, blonde Gamel spoke back over his shoulder on his way to the ball washer. "Are you speaking of his golf game or his love life, Randy?"

Even Kenny laughed at the jibe. Randy blew a smoke ring. "If a lesson will help our forty-year-old virgin in either area, it would be worth the investment. As a matter of fact, Kenny, I know a girl in Rotterdam who will let you chase her around the links all day and then she'll play with your putter all night." He made a circle with his left thumb and first finger then poked the cigarette through it in an all-too-familiar obscene gesture.

Kenny looked up from his stance. "I've met some of your golfing girls, Randy, and I think I'll pass on the offer." He took a practice swing and his friends went silent. He shifted his stance slightly, wiggled the head of the driver, made a slow and steady backswing like he was winding a clock spring and then let the spring unwind. In spite of the ribbing from his three best friends, his shot was low and clean and straight, rolling to a stop a shade over two hundred meters closer to the hole.

"Well done, Kenny."

"Nicely hit, my friend."

"Your best drive of the day. Best drive by *any* of us today."

Morten set up his tee, took a practice swing and hammered off a nice utilitarian drive.

"Good one."

"Solid."

"Playable."

Randy waited for his partner to retrieve his tee and step out of the tee box before stepping up himself, the limp caused by his prosthetic leg a bit more pronounced on the softer turf. "Put it right between the water and the trees, Rand. The way you're playing in the sand today, you'll want to stay away from the bunker on the left."

"Thanks, Gamel. You have a knack for stating the obvious. Just let this old man do his best not to embarrass himself, will you."

"If you hadn't been in and out of the bunkers all the way to here, I wouldn't feel the need to speak the obvious. And you're not an old man until you hit fifty next spring and get the senior's discount at the clubhouse."

"But I'm still the oldest one here."

"And the slowest. Just hit the damned ball."

Randy looked at the green they'd just left and saw the foursome behind them approaching it. Without another word, he teed up, took his two ritual practice swings and gave the drive all he had. The hit was solid and it looked like it might edge past Kenny's, but there was a spin on the ball and it caught the air and pulled hard to the right. There was a loud bang almost like a gunshot when the tree entered the woods.

"Son of a..."

"At least you cleared the sand."

Randy picked up his broken tee and flicked it at Gamel as Gamel stepped into the tee box. "Lick my wedge, Mel."

Two minutes later Randy drove the electric cart over to Morten's ball and dropped his partner off before driving into the woods to search for his wayward Titleist amongst the pines. He parked the cart close to where he thought his ball had landed and climbed out, lighting up the stub of his cigarette that had been tucked behind his ear. He was so sure that he was going to have to chip the ball back out onto the fairway rather than try for the green through the trees that he pulled his nine iron out of his bag and went off hunting.

The grass in the rough was kept reasonably short so he didn't think this would take too long. He heard Morten's club connect with his ball back on the fairway and considered taking the lost ball penalty and just getting on with the game. Then a pair of golfers approached in a cart from the parallel fairway and waved him down. The trees muffled sound so well that if he hadn't seen them they might have driven right up to him unnoticed.

"Did you lose a ball, friend?" The shorter of the two hopped out of the passenger side of the cart and walked over to Randy, holding up a ball.

"You found it over *there*?"

"Just the other side of the trees. You must have had a good ricochet." From three meters away he tossed the ball to Randy in a high, slow arc. Randy reached up and easily snatched it out of the air without even losing the ash on his cigarette. He turned it over in his hand, looking for the *Titleist 1* and his Sharpie marker little green dot that would identify it as his ball. The ball was a Dunlop.

"Sorry, friend, this isn't my ball."

"It's not your *day*, either, Shield." The golfer pointed a silenced pistol at Randy's chest and pulled the trigger three times. Randy was knocked backward. He felt at least one rib break as the thin protective vest under his Nike golf shirt kept the bullets from penetrating. His artificial leg caught on a root and he went over backwards. As he reached for the throwing knife sheathed in the small of his back, he heard the Dark Hunter speak to his partner back in the cart. "Cast the spell and find the damned Locus." Then he shot Randy twice in the head to finish him off.

oOo

Mitchell's tears flowed freely but he wasn't embarrassed one iota. He'd spent seven years studying his ass off, working menial jobs to pay for tuition, and dreaming the huge dream to get here, on the rim of Mount Merapi, the active volcano east of the town of Muntilan in Central Java. He'd always expected to finally be standing here alone, with his camera, but on this, his first trip to Merapi, he led a group of thirty international graduate students in a first-hand examination of the devastation caused by the 2010 eruption that killed more than 350 people. For the next week they would travel every day from Muntilan to Merapi to take air, soil, and ash samples, and update the software on the two seismographs the government had permitted the previous MTU team to put in place two months ago.

They would also take magnetic measurements and tilt measurements, but not today. Today was more spiritual than scientific. Lachandra reached over and took his hand in hers and squeezed. She understood Mitchell's love of volcanoes because she shared his passion completely. They'd met in his graduate *Phreatic and Phreatomagmatic Fragmentation* lecture, fallen in love over chai tea and lava cake, and eventually taken their honeymoon to Pompeii where she finalized her research on ash blankets at Vesuvius for her Master's thesis. It was a marriage made in academia and at least once an hour he had been telling her "I lava you". He was corny and silly and brilliant and she loved him all the more for it.

Three metres away, Italian graduate student Remus closed and locked the sensor's housing and gave Mitch two thumbs up. "Software I have updated and system is reboot while I talk. Should be up-and-jogging in..." he consulted his watch. "Ten...nine...eight...seven...six...".

If a giant had slapped the earth's crust directly under the team's feet, the result would have been no less unexpected or disastrous. The earth buckled and rolled and the rim of Mt. Merapi collapsed in on itself, dragging them all downward. As they tumbled down in free-fall, Mitchell was sure he heard a deep, guttural sigh of relief coming from the lava cap, just before it blew them all to pieces.

oOo

The bus was nearly empty when Becca grabbed her bags from the overhead rack, slung the document tube over her shoulder, crammed her ADIDAS hat down just far enough on her head as to get some shadow on her face without making it look like she was hiding, and disembarked at the Red Deer Bus Terminal. Pulling a pack of smokes out of her hoody's pouch, she drifted out of the station and over to the depot's designated smoking area, which amounted to a tall sand-topped, butt-filled ashtray surrounded by smoker cast-offs and littered junk food wrappers. She wasn't really a smoker, but she'd learned long ago that if you want to stand around and not be seen, then a cigarette in hand chased away suspicion. And *two* smokers chatting in even a thin tobacco cloud were nearly invisible for short periods of time. So Becca had learned to smoke like a pro and always carried a pack of Players Light and a worn Zippo.

Under the overcast sky, alone for a moment, she drew the smoke in, swirled it around in her mouth and blew out a pair of rough smoke rings. Behind her over-sized dollar store sunglasses her eyes were half-closed as if she were savouring the flavour rather than opening her other senses to everything around her. There was only one camera watching the area and it seemed to be crusted over with road dust so it was nearly useless. There had been three cameras inside overlooking the two exits and the ticket counter but they were mounted so high on the walls that her hat needed very little help to keep her from being identifiable just so long as she didn't look up.

Four of the vehicles parked in the angle spots were empty and the fifth held a passenger in the back while a mother helped a daughter load her suitcases into the rusty SUV. The girl appeared to be in her late teens and after her mom slammed the hatch shut the girl jumped into her arms and gave her a big hug, burying her face in her thick sweater like she'd been away far too long. Becca was glad for the dark glasses because it wouldn't do for her to be seen misting up at the sight of a mother-daughter reunion.

She'd been a Shield so long that the faces of her many, many mothers all blurred together, but she always found that no matter how long she'd been Shielding Loci, her current mother always held a special place in her heart. She'd been daughter to one or two useless, abusive couples, but overall she had to admit that her dads and moms had been pretty good people. They'd given her the strength to do what she had to do as a Shield. She did her best to keep in touch with each family as she moved away and found a life that wouldn't get them discovered by the Dark, but good God did she yearn to go home for more than the occasional holiday dinner.

Her father had died of lung cancer last year and although her mother was working hard at being the best nurse on Vancouver Island, she knew Mom hurt deeply. Her brother was a perpetual student and not much for reality beyond campus so it was a blow to Mom when Becca left for the mainland shortly after she turned eighteen. She'd managed to stay anonymous in the Vancouver area for the eight years but it had been exhausting travelling back to the island to help out while Dad went through various life-prolonging-but-not-cancer-killing treatments without creating great, spot-from-space Patterns that would draw the Dark. Every time she stepped foot on the ferry at Tsawwassen and off at Swartz Bay to her waiting mother, she felt eyes on her. She knew what was at stake in the grand scheme of the world at large, but this was Mom and Dad.

She'd lost more than her share of sleep over the dilemma and now, smoking outside the bus depot in Red Deer, Alberta, she cried a few tears for her parents, took a deep breath and went back inside to buy a ticket back south, to Medicine Hat. Somebody on the bus said no one went to Medicine Hat voluntarily, so maybe that was as good a place as any for a girl who'd been first born as Chasina to make for. Besides, it had a cool name and sometimes that was reason enough to go somewhere. Out of reflex she looked up at the big clock on the wall above the ticket counter, and that's when the security camera got a perfectly clear shot of her face.

Chapter Ten: Blood in Mecca

"I feel every death of every Shield as if it were my own. If I could take their pain upon myself to spare each of them the agony, I would, but in each death of each Shield resides their duty and Light and I cannot deny anyone their own Light."

~Shield Master Wei (304 CE, while bowling in a German monastery.)

oOo

The journey to Makkah Al Mukarrameh was a once-in-a-lifetime pilgrimage for every Muslim who was able to do it, yet here Sabir was, making the trip for the second time in ten years. Truth be told, though, since it wasn't Hajj, this Umrah, this lesser pilgrimage, was more to bring his ailing father home to Saudi Arabia for the last time than to make a traditional pilgrimage.

His seventy-two-year-old father, Mohammed—named after the blessed prophet himself—was a simple widower who wanted to sip coffee one final time with his last surviving brother before turning his back on the cancer and surrendering his soul to Allah. Sabir's sisters had offered to make the trip with their father from Cairo and Sabir thanked them from his heart but it was this son's duty, even if he had to take a leave of absence from his corporate law practice in Montreal to do it. What he didn't tell his sisters was that he wouldn't consider himself worthy of the title *Shield of Light* if he ignored the dying wish of the only non-Shield who knew of Sabir's duty to Light.

He'd struggled with the decision of whether or not to tell his father back when he'd been twenty-two and was accepted into McGill University's Law School after completing his degree in Economics at Cairo University, but Dr. Mohammed Kazim had worked hard at his medical clinic his entire life in order to give his three brilliant children the best education they could get. A man who gave you everything deserved the same in return, and so Sabir had told his father exactly who and what he was.

The senior Kazim was a man of science and fact and so Sabir had expected disbelief at the very least; but the man named for the prophet listened silently and seriously to Sabir's tale of his Awakening, and he believed.

oOo

The East Meadow of Central Park was hot in summer, but George always found a nice, shady spot to set up his cribbage board. Unlike the chess players, he kept no routine, followed no schedule. He arrived when he arrived and left when he left. Some weeks he was here every day or so and then he could go a month without dropping by. He also never picked the same shade tree or picnic table for his matches. The only Pattern this Shield consciously allowed himself was making a call to the Rudy Retirement Home On Madison at 102nd to let his father, Bill, know he was on his way. He always called from a different payphone and there was no paper trail to connect him to his dad, but cribbage was their thing and as long as Bill was able, they met and played. In winter they rendezvoused at the Lutheran church instead and played for hours in the parish hall.

Bill's Alzheimer's actually made it easier for George to keep the erratic play schedule because Dad never remembered the last time anyway. This was only the second time in twenty centuries that George had stayed as a Shield in the same area as his family lived. In the Big Apple there was more than enough room for a Shield to slip and slide between the cracks while still living some semblance of a real life. He'd done the same thing in Beijing in the eighteenth century and now that the megatropoli were more common, maybe he could do it more often. Needless to say, a huge factor was always which Locus he was assigned, because the larger the Locus, the less social he could be.

The Sword and the Egg were cumbersome in the extreme but this time around he had Gajaraja's Monkey, the half-inch-tall soapstone carving five-year-old Indonesian Gajaraja had made for his father, Darpaka, to keep him company while he was off fishing. The Monkey was nestled in its velvet wrap in the steel capsule hanging around his neck next to his Emergency beacon and this simplicity allowed him the freedom of the greatest city in the world—at least it was if you believed all the hype from the NYC Tourist Board. He was born in Jersey and loved teasing his Brooklyn and Queens pals about the need to publicize a city the size of New York. It's not like the world didn't know where it was, especially after 9-11. But it was all in good fun because George's buddies teased him right back about the fact that he and Bill lived here in the Empire State, not over in Jersey 'where they belonged'.

It was a busy day in the park so he was forced to set the crib board up on a picnic table a bit too close to a stand of shrubs than he liked. He laid out the two decks of brand-new, sealed Bicycle cards. Dad had been a stickler about new cards ever since he'd started forgetting who George was. He didn't mind playing crib with a stranger but the cards had to be inviolable, virginal, and there had to be two decks so he could choose. Bill liked to have a choice.

He heard a shout of greeting and looked up to see Dad striding down the path with his nurse, Talthea, in tow. Her short legs made it a challenge to keep up with her lanky patient and she railed at him to slow his wrinkly old ass down, but George would have no one else care for Dad. He'd personally selected her from over thirty applicants and made sure she was financially well compensated for all her hard work. Mary, George's mom and Bill's wife, had a care assistant, too, but three strokes had left her vegetative and less in need of a skilled nurse than a nanny. George saw his mother as often as he could but the more restrictive access at her Trinity Home meant that there were better records of his visits, and records meant Patterns.

Bill strode up and stuck his hand out to George. George stood and shook it, returning the strong grip but not battling for supremacy like he had when he was a teen with something to prove. On his eighteenth birthday he'd received his Locus and realized he no longer had anything to prove. Eighteen years later his father still had the steel grip and feel-safe-with-me smile of a former beat cop and George was a Shield who couldn't help but feel the hurt soul-deep when his old man showed no sign of recognizing his only son.

"You must be George. Talthea tells me you wanna to play a little crib with this ol' boy. Well, I gotta tell ya, sonny, I ain't gonna make it easy on ya. Been playin' this here game for more years 'n I can remember. My pop taught me and I taught my boy before he was old enough to count."

"Pleased to meet you, Bill. I'm always up for a good game of crib if you've got the time."

"Got all the time in the world, Georgie. Just so long as you got fresh cards that is. Got a thing about fresh cards, I do."

"Yes sir, so do I."

George was in the middle of losing his second game in a row to his father when a Frisbee disk shot out of nowhere and flew five feet over their heads. The Shield had his hand under his baggy shirt and on the suppressed Glock holstered in the waist of his jeans before the disk landed. A college kid jogged past to retrieve it, tossing out a sincere apology as he went by.

"No worries, kid." George wondered why he was so jumpy. Then he was honest with himself and knew exactly why he was jumpy and asked himself if maybe these seemingly random cribbage games were too risky. Dad might not miss the games if they stopped, but their absence would leave a hole in George's heart he could drive a semi through. His gaze followed the kid and when he bent down to pick up the neon orange disk George saw the gun bulge on the back of the kid's belt. Damn. George jumped up from the picnic table with his Glock so fast that the shot from the shrubs that was meant to take him in the back of the head took him in the middle of the back. His Anti-

Ballistic bulletproof vest took the round and he spun on the shooter, putting two rounds into his centre mass before turning on the kid with the disk.

The kid was obviously no street-recruit, though, because he took cover behind a huge maple, giving George very little target to work with. George glanced over to check on his father and Talthea but Bill had her down on the grass, shielding her with his own body. George had never been prouder of his father than at that moment of unarmed selflessness. "I love you, Dad." Then the Shield ran in the Dark-attack quiet. He sprinted straight at the maple waiting for his target to reappear. Nearly silenced shots tore up the ground to his left as a second sniper tried to track the quickly moving target.

When he reached the tree he realized that the Dark Hunters would naturally all be communicating through headsets so he wasn't surprised to find the kid wasn't thinking of poking his head out. Someone had warned him. In fact, the kid wasn't even behind the tree when he arrived and George had only a blink of time to recognize that the twig snap he heard next came from the branches above him, a split second before the kill shot pulverized the back of his skull.

oOo

Two hours out of Berlin, on their way to Zanzibar Island, the co-pilot of United African Airlines Flight 383 radioed that they were suddenly losing fuel and having electrical problems. That was the last communication from the cockpit, although there were sixteen on-board phone conversations taking place with various parties on the ground when the fireball lit up the sky over the west coast of Greece.

Five-year-old Nomalanga Azikiwe was in the middle of telling her daddy about the beautiful blue-and-yellow-flowered dress she was going to wear to the airport to pick him up later in the day, when the line went dead.

oOo

It started as a hunch, not long after she snapped at Hussein for thinking about his job before the lives of the Shields they served. Coriander knew why she was so sensitive about Shield safety—it was the same reason she excelled at what she did and was the best Spell-Spinner in the complex—her many-greats-grandparents were out there. And when she couldn't shake that thought from her head it coalesced into something more than a tickle, something more than a hunch. An idea.

She could do her job of Shield-tracking because of the links they'd long ago established between Shields and their spell stones, so she had to ask what kind of conduit could she spin if she had a bond stronger than stone-to-Shield. An unbreakable, unique bond. The bond of ancestry. If she shared their bloodline, maybe there was a way for her to establish a link to them. Actually, she was pretty sure that she could do it now that she'd let her brain run around and pick at the problem, but the real question was whether she *should* do it. Whether by making such a connection she might not open the Shields, her greats-grandparents, to detection, tracking and execution by the Dark Hunters.

Could doing what amounted to little more than satisfying her own curiosity end up costing hundreds or even thousands of lives? Yes. Was it worth it? No. Not unless she could find a way to do it safely and come up with a better reason than because she wanted to say 'hi'.

oOo

Sabir freshened his father's and Uncle Jamail's iced tea and sat back with his shisha pipe to watch the rubber match between the two old backgammon rivals. Earlier he'd challenged them both and lost six-straight before retiring to the kitchen to fix them lunch.

Twenty minutes later Jamail doubled, Mohammed accepted, and then stood up. "My old back needs a stretch."

"Your 'old' back, brother, is younger than mine. But maybe you're correct and there are *two* old backs to be stretched, and maybe a bladder or two to be relieved." Both men stepped away from the table and the ivory-inlaid mahogany board. Jamail disappeared into the washroom while Mohammed moved around the room, stretching and twisting his body to get the kinks out of his weary bones.

"How are you feeling, Father?" Sabir put his father's coffee down beside the backgammon board.

"Ha! A loaded question if ever there was one. Now I *know* you are a lawyer! Very well, I'll incriminate myself, just for you. My body is stiff and weary and making obscene noises. My mind is pretty good but has been much better. My soul on the other hand has been blessed by Allah to be in the company of my cherished brother and my honoured son, the Shield of—the *Man* of *Illumination*. If the blessed Father called me now, he would find me at his door wearing a smile and looking for your mother. Now, let's talk about your —"

The rest of what he was saying was lost to Sabir, absorbed by sudden silence engulfing the apartment. He quickly pressed his Shield distress transmitter through his robe—his kandura—then slipped two razor-sharp blades out of sheaths within his voluminous sleeves and motioned his father to get down on the floor.

Over the years, septuagenarian Mohammed Kazim had listened to his son's stories of centuries of life as a Shield and he understood very clearly and quickly what was happening now. He shoved his blessed son back out of the way, grabbed the heavy gammon board off the table and tore open the door, swinging and entreating to Allah for strength in his final battle.

oOo

Being trained, professional killers, the three members of Hunter Team *Kappa Siete Dix* approaching the Shield's lair from the front knew to confirm their target before engaging and to keep civilian casualties to an absolute minimum. But when the crazed old man charged through the doorway and took down their point man with a powerful chop to the throat with some sort of heavy wooden board, all of their calm planning went out the window and six frantic shots rang out from the Hunters disguised as pilgrims.

The board took one shot, one shot missed entirely and the other four caught the old man wearing the white kandura high in the torso, but didn't stop him before he crashed into the second man and knocked him head-long down the wide stone steps. Both men were dead before they stopped rolling—the old man from his gunshot wounds and the Dark Hunter from the blunt-force trauma of having his head bounced off of a dozen steps. The Hunter Team leader dove into the room and came up shooting, catching another old man in the chest as he came out of the toilet, drying his hands. The other half of *Kappa Siete Dix* Team crashed through the back door and two well-placed headshots by the team's armourer stopped the Shield who was rising up from the floor to sink his blades into their Team leader's back.

"Theta, cast the spell, find that Locus and ..." he looked out the door at the bodies of his two men. "The three of us will get our brothers out to the truck. Move, move move! Live feed *off*."

oOo

It was a drier than usual summer and the forest fire risk was high, so there was a ban on campfires throughout the Black Forest region. Freida carefully butted out her hand-rolled cigarette into the tin can she'd carried out from the youth hostel's kitchen, and looked up at the sky. When she'd started her morning food prep shift at Ortenberg Castle Hostel, the sky had been the clear, azure blue she loved in the mountains of southwest Germany; but now, three hours later, the winds were picking up speed fast, it was black as night out, and weird-ass sheets of lightning flashed back and forth from horizon to horizon. It was the strangest thing she'd ever seen.

A sudden gust of wind grabbed the lid of the steel dumpster behind the castle-cum-hostel and slammed it open. Great, she thought, the squirrels and crows will pull out all the garbage and then the coming rain will make a mess in and out of the dumpster. She wouldn't care, except that she was likely to be the one stuck out in the storm cleaning it up, so Freida dropped the can in her apron pocket and charged over to the dumpster to close and latch the lid. The air around her was electrified and she could taste the ozone in the atmosphere as the storm built. She grabbed hold of the heavy lid with both hands and lifted. The wind fought back but she was stronger, and with a loud crash, she got the dumpster closed. She smiled as she slipped the lid's chained bolt through the eye on the container, but the smile went sour when the soft golden hair on her arms and the few strays poking out from under her paper hat all stood straight out. She finished pushing the bolt home and pulled her hands away, but it wasn't enough. Just standing next to the dumpster was enough to make her a conduit for the twin bolts of lightning that smashed down and through her into the ground.

It was as quick and painless a death as anyone could wish for, except that she was only twenty-three. Too young, by far, people would say, but Freida was not the youngest victim of the Black Forest lightning storm today. In the space of time from when Freida butted out her smoke until she locked down the dumpster, there were thirty-two-thousand-eight-hundred-and-twelve lightning strikes in the region. The kindling-dry ancient forest was aflame at all points and the winds picked up power, fanning the fire and herding it over everything in its path, up and down valleys and mountains and straight over top of the three-and-a-half-thousand souls in Ortenberg. As though airborne napalm had hit it, the one-hundred-and-fifty-kilometre-long Black Forest burned to the ground in less than an hour.

oOo

To call the broom-closet an office would be as ridiculous as calling a shoebox a broom-closet, but DW still had a workplace to call his own, even if Master Wei had to stand outside in the hallway in order to confer with him.

"DW, I just got word that their ShieldBreaker went live and within three hours we've lost three Shields and their Loci, not to mention the rising death tolls from the resulting disasters. Tell me what I can do to help you stop this atrocity, my son." He took a sip of his ever-present green tea.

DW spun his chair around to face the Shield Master. "You mean besides getting Maintenance to finish testing the sprinklers so I can get back into my office, sir?"

"I did offer you a space in the Boardroom with Accounts Payable."

"Yes sir, thank you, but I'd rather not have anyone but you looking over my shoulder while I figure this one out. If we have someone inside DökktEfniTækni then it's a safe assumption that they have someone here, or at one of our other facilities."

"Quite true. In the meantime, what do you need?"

"Copies of the algorithms they're using and access to this monster mainframe they've created would be lovely, sir."

"I'll put in a request for you, but in the meantime would it help to actually have one of their Smartphones with ShieldBreaker installed?"

A smile split twenty-eight-year-old programming genius' face. "Oh, I guess it would help a little... or a lot! You've got one, sir?"

"We took it off a Hunter we captured in Tasmania and I'm having it flown in. It should be here by tomorrow morning."

"Cool!"

"I hope so. Now, what do you have in mind to stop it?"

"Well, because it's really all about processing and analysis of data on an obscene scale, we can either attack the data at the source, en route to processing, or after analysis but before the reports are generated and acted upon."

"That's it?"

"Or we could attack the analysis process itself and try to corrupt the interpretation of the data to produce false results."

"Can you guarantee results with any particular approach?"

"The simple answer? No, sir, I can't. The complicated answer is that each approach has both drawbacks and advantages."

"Break it down for me in a report within two hours, please. I wish I could give you more time, my son, but people are dying and if we have to push back to maintain the Balance, then so be it.

"I can have it for you in an hour, Master Wei."

"Then I will see you in an hour." He placed a hand gently on DW's forehead, a blessing.

oOo

"We're talking about an astronomical amount of yen, Tatsu."

"It's not a problem, Jiro."

"You're a professor-in-training or whatever you call it, sharing an apartment with two other post-docs on a university campus and you have more money than Bill Gates?"

"Not yet, but I will by midnight."

"Should I ask how?"

"It doesn't matter. It's all just numbers and numbers are what I do."

"Fair enough, cousin. Should I ask *why*?"

"Honor."

"Honor? Whose?"

139

"Mine. Father's. The family's."

"You would risk prison for *honor*?"

"They killed my father, *your* uncle."

"He died in a train crash, Tatsuaki."

"But they caused the crash."

"It was an accident. A freak electrical problem that caused the switches to malfunction. No one caused it. Who told you this nonsense?"

Tatsuaki didn't answer his cousin immediately.

"Who, Tatsu? Was it Takeko?" Tatsuaki wouldn't look him in the eye. "It *was*, wasn't it?!" He grabbed Tatsuaki by the shoulders and spun him to face him. "Was it your crazy sister? You can't believe the stories she tells you! There's no truth in her words! There never has been. She had crazy dreams as a child and then made up crazier stories since she left for South Africa. I never told you this, but she once told me that her soul was over two thousand years old! You're not risking life in prison or worse because of some lies your delusional sister has fed you."

"It's for honor."

"Then you'll save face and the family honor without me." He took two steps away and turned back, expecting Tatsuaki to once again give in and follow his older cousin's example.

Tatsu stood still as a rock in the sea of commuters. He lifted his chin and finally looked Jiro in the eye. "Loyalty, Devotion and Honor to the Death." The Samurai Bushido Code. The Way of the Warrior. Then he turned and vanished in the crowd, leaving Jiro frustrated and worried. There was a storm coming and he had a hunch there would be no shelter strong enough.

oOo

"What do you mean, 'we have competition', Warrun? We're Dark, they're Light—it's not a competition, it's a *war*." For the third time in five minutes, Mao popped the clip out of his Glock and checked that it was full.

"I mean that I'm sensing someone else in town looking for the damned Shield besides us."

"Are you casting the spell right?" He examined a bullet, looking for non-existent flaws.

"After eight years of tracking this Shield I should bloody well hope so."

"I'm not doubting that you can track a Shield, just that the spell you modified to include the pixie our intel says he has with him will also work on other fairies."

"A pixie isn't a fairy."

140

"Which begs the question again—how do you know the spell works?"

"It's been modified to show me anything with the taint of Faerie on it." He held up the black bone pendant he used for this particular spell. "The strength of the reply tells me how strong the taint is and trust me when I say that there's a pure Faerie 'being' here in Calgary."

"Oberon's people."

"Just one."

"One too many. Can you tell me where?"

"When I cast the spell the first time I alerted the Shield that someone was looking for him. A second cast and he'll know we're close and run, and then we'll be screwed—eight years wasted, not to mention the twenty-four years that Head Office had no idea where to even start looking. I'll cast it if you order me to, but I think it's a bad idea."

"And if this fairy beats us to the pixie?"

Warrun shrugged. "True enough. Catch-22."

"What if we found the fairy and eliminated it before it finds the Shield?"

"Without magic? Not happening."

"Crap! Alright, so what do we know for a fact?"

"Fact? The fairy is somewhere in the downtown core and the Shield is somewhere west of the city."

"So the fairy isn't even close to the Shield?"

"Unless you count the fact that of all the places on the planet they could be, they're both in the Calgary area right here and now."

"Son of a... point made."

"We also know that the Shield is male, over forty and that the pixie must have taken another form, otherwise someone would have spotted her long before now."

Mao's pocket started to vibrate, startling him, and a moment later CCR's 'Bad Moon Rising' started to play. He retrieved his phone and looked at the screen. "A coded text from Regional." He entered his password and pressed his thumb to the sensor, calling the message up. "Up-to-date progress reports needed from all teams. I guess I know what I'm doing for the next hour. Pick up coffee for the team and I'll have them meet you in thirty back at the motel."

"Will do."

"I'll get Dolf to make a few calls and reach out to the street again—the pixie may be disguised but the fairy tracking them might just stand out enough to set off someone's radar."

oOo

Phoenix hopped down to the bottom-most slate step at the shore of

141

Lake Louise. She leaned over and lapped at the frigid glacial water. A D-ring attached her retractable leash to Liam's belt as it extended and retracted while Phoenix moved about on the steps. Park laws required all dogs to be on a leash but the duo had been visiting the mountains for so long that the pixie princess took the harness and leash in stride and was just happy to be out of the city.

Sitting on a higher step, Liam leaned back on the guitar case, his eyes closed and the cane across his lap. The purity of the Light here at the shore was nearly overwhelming. He could imagine what the trapped Chilean miners felt like when they finally came up out of the damp and dark and into the life-giving sunlight after sixty-nine days. It was nearly too much. Without sunglasses and hats they risked blindness and so he felt now, as the untainted lake water burned off his funky mood. He pulled a notebook out of his pocket and started scribbling.

LIAM'S JOURNAL:
I've finally got a few minutes to myself. I don't mean time away from P., but time where I'm not driving or on the move somehow. Just sitting by my favorite lake—5680 feet above sea level, 230 feet deep, fed by six glaciers—a World Heritage Site and as pure a source of Light as this part of the world has. The few pollutants are organic, which can give a drinker 'beaver fever' but only because we no longer possess the enzymes to deal with a few of Mother Nature's bacteria.

Here's a quickie of my favourite place. One little sketch can't hurt.

Good God, that felt incredible! I don't know how to describe the feeling I got making that simple little sketch. It was like the breaking of a fever.

oOo

Liam was in a near-trance state, sitting on the stone steps leading down into Lake Louise when he felt the strange mind reach out and touch his own.

Chapter Eleven: Busted Shield

"A Shield may not know love, for a heart beating with love creates the greatest Pattern of all."
~Shield Master Wei (62 CE while watching a storm gather over Cavalry.)

oOo

The sight of blood—even her own—had never bothered Coriander, so there was no flinching, squealing, or gagging when she pricked her finger and squeezed a droplet onto her singing-bowl's small mallet. Gently and slowly she rubbed her blood over the thickest part of the mallet, the part that she would rub against the outside of the bowl's rim and make it sing. The teak was dense and worn smooth from years of use, but with patience, Coriander worked the blood in and eventually the mallet was ready.

Traditionally, a spell-spinning required both a bowl singer and a spell spinner, because both jobs were really two-handed tasks needing ten-finger dexterity and concentration, but even novices could sing-spin one or two of the simplest spells, such as moving a pencil across a smooth table top. Now, whether it was her dual-Shield heritage or just that she spent more than her share of time practising, Coriander had moved well beyond the pencil-moving spells. She'd worked and worked at it, like a novice juggler alone in the middle of her bedroom, passing, catching and dropping; or the rookie sleight-of-hand artist in front of a mirror palming, sliding, cupping, slipping, until it all came together, all worked smoothly and instinctively.

Crossed-legged on her matt on the floor, Cor placed her three-inch-wide copper bowl on its little, well-stuffed satin cushion to her left. On her right she placed a hammered silver tray the size and depth of a medium pizza tray, but instead of dough, sauce and veggies, this tray held sand from the floor of the spinning cave. It was sand she'd smuggled out in her water bottle more because it was a challenge than because there was any silly rule against it.

With a finger, she drew a simple twice-around-the-tray counter-clockwise spiral, then she leaned over the tray and carefully dropped a bit of spit into the centre of the spiral. The spinning called for water and she figured that water with a little more DNA couldn't hurt her chances of spell success.

Holding the mallet lightly in her left hand she began rubbing it along the outside of the bowl's rim, keeping it upright to maintain a consistent tone. When that tone was full and pure, Cor began a simple vertical-horizontal alternating circular spin with her right hand over the tray of sand and spittle.

The air over the tray grew warm and when she looked closely, she could see power manifesting in the form of faint light rolled up like a ball of luminous yarn. She concentrated on hearing the subtle fluctuations in the tone and willed the spinning energy to strengthen and draw on her blood and the ley lines she sat over. The power grew, expanded, like baking bread—warm and golden brown.

A typically spun spell required a goal, a focus, and actual spoken words for the full manifestation, but Coriander had no name, no location, and no link to call on or follow or speak to, so she simply opened herself up and let her magic flow into and along the ley lines, through the air and into the rocks and sand. Time stopped slowing in the usual way she was accustomed to and instead it seemed to both beat like a heart and move forward and back like the tides. She relaxed and just let it all happen.

And then it *did* happen. It was as if her spell was sniffing for a new scent it was supposed to know when, amongst a world of subtle and not-so-subtle scents, it found it.

"Who?!"

"I am Spell-Spinner, Shield of Light." They didn't speak words so much as trade thoughts.

"How? Who else?"

"Blood song. Just me."

"Blood song?"

"My idea. Blood relation link."

"Blood...? Related?"

"Distant. Descended two Shields, long way back."

"Two... Shields? Me?"

"Must be. Spell work only with blood link."

"Lynette."

"Yes! Skosche, Lynette."

"Me... wow. Hello."

"Hello."

"Where?"

"A base. Details not safe."

"Truth."

"Not Skosche now."

"No. Skosche okay though. You?"

"Cor."

"'Cor'? Nice. What now?"

"Tired. Not easy."

"Go. Sleep. Talk again."

"Okay, *Grandpa*."

"'Grandpa'? Truth."

"Again, soon."

"Soon."

She broke off the exhausting connection, feeling like she was lying on a sun-baked rock, warmed inside and out from above and below. She'd found one of her Shield 'grandparents'. She dragged herself over to her bed and flopped on the covers, wondering where her 'grandmother' was.

oOo

"The parking garage footage is too old. ShieldBreaker has downgraded the success possibility to sixty. She could be anywhere in or around the city. If she found another ride, she..." a chirp from his Smartphone stopped him. He read the message, and then read it a second time, just to make sure he had it right. He wasn't 'leading his team into Tasmania' as they had started calling the mess down in the southern hemisphere.

"Saddle up. She's been spotted in Red Deer boarding a Greyhound for Medicine Hat." Team *Rho Doce Huit* holstered weapons, butted out cigarettes and chugged back the last of coffees, teas, and one unholy mix of whipped asparagus, carrot juice and cod liver oil.

"How the hell did she get up there, just to head back here?"

"Not *here*, Medicine Hat. And we can be pretty sure she'll be tucked in the back of the bus and not leave her seat while the bus passes back through Calgary."

"Which means we'll have to kill everyone on board to get to her."

"Or we somehow get them all off the bus so we can take her outside."

"On the road or at the depot here when they pass through?"

"There's a bottleneck on the route south of Calgary where we can do this fast and easy."

"Follow the bus and make our move on the road?"

"Not quite. We'll go as the electrical crew and get there ahead of them. Ambush. Simple and Solid." He looked at the youngest Hunter. "Jarod, go board the bus here in town and be ready. We'll work out the details en route and text you."

"College kid or hippy traveller dude?"

Mao looked again at the image the alert had forwarded to him. "Judging by the look she's sporting herself, go with the hippy. Let me know as soon as you confirm she's on board and then stay clear of her. Ignore her, even."

Jarod grabbed his kit and started for the door. "Good Hunting."

"Good Hunting."

oOo

146

Becca took the seat right behind the driver where she could not only see clearly out the front windshield, but could also catch glimpses of his mirrors, including the one covering the interior of the bus. She hid under a multi-colored, cyber-goth, dreadlocks wig, her dollar store shades and a baggy two-sizes-too-big army surplus jacket which was more than ample enough to hide the two tanto blades and a silenced Colt holstered under her armpit. Her Kevlar armour was specially designed for flexibility so it didn't bind when she curled up and faked sleep while watching the world in and around the bus from behind the protection of the sunglasses.

The volume of her headphones was low but she nodded her head to create the illusion that she was rocking out, oblivious to the world around her. Her right fist curled around a small punch dagger in the folds of the jacket and she could lash out fast and furious if she needed to. She was heading back toward Skosche and that meant the alarm bells in "Dark Central Hunter Headquarters"—or whatever they called it—would be ringing like crazy and she had to be ready. They couldn't track her by spell without her sensing it, but that didn't mean they couldn't get lucky and be covering the bus depots and airports. She was one Shield against at least one Hunter Team.

The bus driver set up his seat and got out to do one last circle check of the bus exterior before they hit the road. Becca took advantage of his absence to casually check out the controls of the bus. Once she was sure it was one of the models she was familiar with, she leaned back and relaxed. Over the years she'd made a point of knowing how to drive everything from a forklift to an articulated fire truck and everything in between. Knowing that kind of stuff was standard procedure for a Shield. Once upon a time she'd known how to shoe a horse and hitch a team of Clydesdales, which had been a breeze compared to saddling and racing camels across the dunes outside Morocco. Her favourite mode of transport, when time allowed, was elephants. She could spend days riding elephants through jungles and over mountain passes and was as good as any man at controlling the beautiful, gentle beasts. In comparison, a Greyhound bus was simple.

oOo

"*What?!*"

Harff.

"You're bored?" He propped himself up on his good elbow, looked around the room, found the TV remote control on the bedside table and picked it up.

"News, sports, soaps, or cartoons?"

Harff.

"Fine. *You* pick, then." He turned the television on, dropped the remote on the bed beside Phoenix, then rolled over and tumbled back into sleep, this time without dreams of any kind.

Some time later Liam wasn't exactly sure what woke him up from his much-needed slumber, but he rolled over and Phoenix was watching the news as one of Calgary's local anchors summarized a report.

"Did you just wake me up?"

Harff.

"You used magic, didn't you?"

No response.

Crap. He rubbed the sleep away and struggled to a sitting position.

"What's so damned..." A head-and-shoulders shot of a pale, bruised woman popped up above the news anchor's shoulder and Liam's heart stopped. Lynette, now. The anchor went into her summary and Liam leaned forward to both see and hear better.

"R.C.M.P. are asking for assistance in identifying the unconscious victim of the vicious attack near Okotoks. In all there were six deaths and four injuries, including the bus driver who was shot in the leg when he came to the assistance of the young woman. The apparent target of the attack was flown by S.T.A.R.S. air ambulance to Mountain View Hospital in South Calgary where she remains unconscious but stable."

"Damn! Damn! Damn!" Liam scooped up Phoenix and placed her gently on the floor. "So much for relaxing away from the dragon's cave. We gotta go, now. Master Wei is going to rip me a new one, but I'm not leaving her there."

Harff.

"We'll just take the weapons. With luck we can be back here in four or five hours."

Harff.

He shoved his wallet in his pocket, slung his heavy black weapons bag over his back and grabbed his cane from where it leaned against the oak-veneer writing desk.

Harff.

"The what?"

Harff.

"Let's load this up and I'll come back in for the guitar case."

Two hours later Liam pulled into the small pay-as-you-park lot in front of the CareCentre Glenmore Park building in the Mountain View Hospital complex on the bluffs overlooking the Glenmore Reservoir. He backed into a stall, facing the exit, ready to flee.

He reached over and rubbed the top of Phoenix's head on the seat beside him. "We're about to break every rule in the unprinted Shield Handbook, missy. I have to do the impossible and move fast. I'm going to leave you and the sword here, in the car. Stay out of sight and I guess do whatever you have to do to stay safe."

Harff.

"Yes, use magic. It sounds like she's already killed one Hunter Team and we've got at least two more looking for us, so you 'going Pixie' isn't going to do much more than speed up the inevitable. But not until no other options are left."

Harff.

"Thank you." He slipped the Taser out of the leather holster under his left armpit, once again checked that it was fully charged, and put it back out of sight under his jacket.

Harff.

"The .32 is in the holster in the small of my back and the knife is strapped to my right ankle, but I'm in no shape to use it anyway. I'll make do with the Taser and the cane. The gun is my last resort because if I have to use it, I've already lost."

Harff.

Liam reached down inside his collar and withdrew the chain on which his emergency transmitter hung. He slipped it over his head and put it on the seat beside his Locus. "If I'm not back in half-an-hour—or you get attacked—call for help. Hopefully Lynette still has hers if things   go   south   in   there."

Harff.

"Thanks. I need all I can get. Time to go." Beauty's little concoction gave him more control than he'd had when they left Lake Louise, but it was still a bit awkward getting out of the car.

Phoenix stood up on her back legs and leaned on the door, watching her protector hobble off into battle and wishing that there were something more she could do to help.

Liam made his way down the short hill and in through the side entrance of the St. Patricia's Ambulatory Care wing. He squinted at the signs suspended from the ceiling and found the one he wanted—Admissions. No one gave him a second look as he followed the arrow down the hall, past the chapel, and along to the main building which housed the ER, the Gift Shop and most of the labs and staff. When he reached the lobby he took his time to look around, seeing only patients and their family members caught up in their own thoughts and problems. When the Admissions desk came into view so did a hospital security guard. Liam smiled weakly as he approached the tall, elderly guard who had the upright bearing of a former soldier even if he was now close to seventy. The guard smiled back and Liam casually commented on his way past.

"I figured the place would be swarming with police after that silly stuff on the news."

"No sir." Liam stopped to listen and the guard elaborated. "Just the two of them up on 3—a constable and the detective. Pretty quiet and low key right now—just the way I like it."

"The media must be driving you nuts, though, especially the Sun. This is their kind of sensational story."

"Oh, you can bet on that young fella. Got a dozen of 'em corralled down the hall in the Board Room, waiting on the detective and the CPS media lady's press conference."

"So the poor girl still isn't awake?"

"Not that I've heard, but that would be a private patient matter and not for me to need to know. Besides, I just started my shift so I haven't even seen her yet."

"The news makes it sound like she killed four men single-handed and carried the bus driver to safety on her back."

The guard chuckled. "Facts are seldom what you see on the TV, young fella. I haven't seen the news myself but the guard I relieved says the constable told him she took out six, all by herself. That little thing up there is a soldier of some sort, no doubt in my mind."

"Sure sounds like it. Just one constable watching her—I expect they've got her shackled and chained to the wall."

"Most likely, most likely."

Liam looked at his watch and visibly cringed. "Well, I'd best be getting up to my niece's room and see whether they're cutting her loose or I'm dog-sitting for another night. It's been a pleasure, sir."

"That it has, young fella, that it has." His eyes darted down at Liam's cane and curled hand. "You take care of yourself, now, son."

"Thanks. I always do, sir." And with that, Liam made his way over to the gift shop, tweaking his plan as he went, wondering at just how stupid the whole thing was sounding in his head.

Five minutes later he was staring at and memorizing the Fire Route map on the wall outside the bank of elevators. The elevator door slid open and he stepped into the empty box with a stuffed rabbit tucked under his bad arm, a Calgary Flames baseball cap and a copy of People magazine tucked in his back pocket, a disposable lighter in his front pocket, and a pair of ridiculously large I-wanna-be-Paris-Hilton sunglasses in his jacket pocket.

None of the props would be needed if he didn't have one simple thing on his keychain tucked between the car key and the well-worn leather fob—a handcuff key. Since the Spanish Inquisition he'd always carried some kind of skeleton key or innocuous lock-picking tool somewhere on his person. It had taken him three weeks to break out of that prison without a key and he swore he'd never be caught and caged like that again.

Today that simple paranoid foresight might just save his wife's life. Or was she his ex? No, she was probably his widow, since he'd died before her, although it couldn't have been by much because they'd been surrounded by Dark Hunter-led soldiers when the lucky arquebus shot torn open his belly. He'd had just long enough to smile at his one love one last time before he succumbed.

The elevator opened and a bald, black, smiling orderly reached out to hold the door for Liam to exit before backing in with his cart of supplies. Liam muttered thanks and stepped out, into the hallway. He looked left and right, orienting himself, as would any hospital visitor. To his left he saw the cop, chatting with a pretty little Asian doctor. The reception desk was maybe twenty feet to his right but everyone was so caught up in keeping up with their tasks in the understaffed unit that no one noticed the visitor get off the elevator.

Three wheelchairs with attached IV poles sat unattended at the near end of the reception area and right across from the elevator was a pair of his and hers bathrooms. Liam knew he had one chance to get this right. One chance with astronomically stupid odds to make this work. Then adrenalin gave him a boost and he smiled broadly as he retrieved the closest wheelchair. He hadn't aided and abetted an escape in nearly a century but it was all coming back to him now. As he leaned on the chair and limped down the hall with the fluffy bunny in the seat he supposed that technically it was going to be a kidnapping, not an escape, but either way it wasn't his first so he wasn't going to get distracted with worry.

Eyes cast down as if embarrassed at his condition, he limped past the cop. The constable gave him a quick, visual once-over as he approached but obviously deemed that 'the cripple pushing the wheelchair' was no threat, so he went back to hitting on the woman. Liam was grateful that he passed by unaccosted, but was more than a little disappointed that because of his disability—whatever the cause—he'd been dismissed out of hand. If he'd strode up with purpose and full mobility he knew both the cop and the doctor would have taken more notice. He took a deep breath and let his anger flow out and away. He needed all of his energy and focus to be directed at the task at hand.

The end of the corridor came up and he followed it to the left. When he was out of sight he looked and found the fire stairs only a couple yards away. He tucked the chair in beside a cart of fresh linens and entered the staircase. Hopping on his 'good leg', he made his way down one level and out into that hallway, crossing his fingers that this hospital was like most and that the floor plans were repeated up and down the building. Luck was with him and there was actually a small single-person bathroom beside the stairwell. He went in, locked the door behind him and quickly got to work. He dispensed paper hand towels, twisted them into tight sticks, dropping them in the stainless steel sink until he had a small pile of kindling. He sparked the lighter under one corner and as soon as it caught he unlocked the door and stepped back out into the hall. Still no one noticed him. He fled up the stairs as quickly as a man with one wonky leg and a barely cooperative arm could and retrieved the waiting wheelchair. Even the bunny was still sitting, waiting patiently for the next stage of the simple, made-for-television plan.

Liam didn't have long to wait. The soft but clear chime of the fire alarm sounded and the strobe light above the alarm station on the wall began flashing. He counted to twenty and looked around the corner—the cop was now at the unit's main desk. Liam couldn't hear what was being said, but after a moment the officer took off down the stairs closest to the desk. The Shield made his move.

Rolling the chair into the room, Liam closed the door behind him. In the first bed a frail, elderly woman slept, hooked up to oxygen, an IV and an assortment of monitors. In the second bed, by the window, lay the body that housed the soul of the only woman he had and would risk everything for. Once he confirmed that the face matched the one he'd seen from the C-Train only yesterday, he tore open the tiny closet closest to her bed and tossed her clothes onto the foot of the bed. He hung her bike bags and a rigid plastic document tube which he assumed held her Locus, on the back of the wheelchair. Next, he turned his attention to Lynette herself.

Opening the handcuffs barely slowed Liam down but getting Lynette into the chair was where his plan crumbled. His left hand and arm weren't entirely useless, but there was no way he could maintain a strong grip or bear any serious weight. He looked at Lynette, then back at the chair, then back at the bed, and let his mind race through the possibilities. This wasn't impossible, just nearly so. Inspiration struck and he ripped the top blanket and sheet off of the bed and tossed them beside the wheelchair. Then he carefully unhooked her IV bag and placed in on her lap. Grabbing the bottom sheet, he tried to yank its edges out from the between the mattress and the frame but they wouldn't budge. He pulled the corner closest to him and saw the problem.

"Fitted sheets? I'm being beaten by *fitted sheets*?" He reached under the corner and yanked out the elasticized corner then proceeded to hop around the bed and get the other three corners. By the time he got back to the side with the wheelchair and got Lynette bundled up, he was ready to scream. The clock in his head was counting down and he was losing the race. He gathered the four corners in his right fist, twisted his hand around to get a secure hold, then with one back-breaking heave, the Shield one-armed the unconscious patient up and over to the waiting wheelchair. He landed her in the seat with her head up and her feet down, as they should be, but although the landing was soft, it was far from graceful. He didn't have time to make her too comfortable but he did manage to hang her IV bag on the wheelchair's hook, put her bags on her lap, and throw the blanket over the whole lumpy mess.

Ready or not, they had to go. He flipped the brakes off and wheeled the unconscious Shield away from the bed. He pulled the curtain around the bed, hoping that if they needed an extra ten seconds or so, this little deceit might just buy it for them. He scooped her hair up and tucked it under the hat when he stuck it on her head. He steadied his breathing, calmed his racing pulse and wheeled Lynette out into the hallway and away to the left as if they were simply going for a stroll around the corridors of healing.

Chapter Twelve: Demonology 101

"Selection of the Shields of Light is handled in much the same way as my late wives' wardrobes—with neither my assistance nor my consent. I would have it no other way."
~Shield Master Wei (1936 CE to H.G. Wells, over a pint at The King's Head Pub.)

oOo

When it came to thinking and planning on the run, Liam was one of the best, but that didn't mean he enjoyed it. At heart he was a planner. He liked to examine options and angles and ramifications. He liked to be prepared for the worst-case scenario. Crossing his fingers, hoping for the best and diving headfirst into the breach was how Shields got themselves killed. Liam's gut twisted and flopped at the thought that they were now going to have to rely more on luck than on skill in order to get off the floor and across to the other side of the hospital complex.

There were too many variables here, including his own inability to toss Lynette over his shoulder and simply run. Did the freight elevator need a passkey? How far had the cop gone? How soon would the detective be done with his press conference? What if Lynette woke up and called for help? Or worse, what if her injuries were more serious than he thought and she needed medical assistance? With two good hands he was a more-than-adequate field surgeon, but one-handed and on the hobble? There were too many variables, and *he hated variables*.

The bank of freight elevators was well marked and in a quiet part of the unit. Unfortunately it was next to a staff break-room. True to form, though, none of the three heads looked up from their magazines or meals to see who was passing by. They spent their days and nights on their feet and probably didn't get more than a few minutes to eat and relax, so they weren't going to be distracted from their rare moment of peace before they had to jump back into the battle of patient care.

Liam pressed the down button and tucked Lynette and himself into a corner to one side of the doors, as out of sight as he could manage. A chime announced when an elevator arrived and in the silence of the service area Liam was sure it was loud enough to alert the entire hospital that an escape was in progress and where the culprits could be found. The wide steel doors opened and Liam unclenched his jaw only when the compartment turned out to be empty. He pulled Lynette in and let the door close without selecting a floor. He leaned on the chair and took a long, deep breath.

"Cross your fingers my love—that was the easy part." His charge stirred slightly and he smiled. "I'll take that as a good sign." He pushed the lobby button and put his hand on the Taser in the holster. Unfortunately he got little comfort or reassurance from its cold, hard presence.

The trip was both too long and too short. He wanted to get out of there as fast as possible, but he could have used a little more time to relax before stepping out into the heart of the facility. The doors slid open but no one was waiting. The service area was empty. He took a deep breath, twisted his head around in a circle to pop the stress-kink out of his neck, and then pushed Lynette out into the main lobby area. Staying close to the wall he went left, away from the guard who was directing a visitor to the Information Desk a few feet away. Liam leaned hard on the chair, trying to minimize his limp as he turned left at the next corner and started the trip back through the St. Patricia's wing toward the CareCentre building.

It was slow going, but there were no shouts of alarm or shots fired so he began to relax. Then he stumbled over nothing but his own shoe. "Good God I wish it was me being pushed in the chair, just this once."

"Then let's switch places." Lynette looked over her shoulder at him but he didn't stop or even slow down.

"When did you wake up?"

"Fully? Just as you bumped out of the elevator."

"How are you feeling?"

"Good enough. Switch. Now. Quick." He stopped the chair and she flipped the foot pedals out of the way and stood up. She was still a bit shaky but waved off Liam's offer of support, instead handing him the bags she'd had on her lap. She wrapped the blanket around herself while Liam sat on her clothes and flipped the pedals back down. She lifted the IV tube up and over his head so it wouldn't choke him or restrict his movement, then she started pushing the chair. Liam noticed that even at her half-speed shuffle, they were moving at twice the speed as when he had been pushing.

"Where to?"

"St. Patricia's." He pointed at the sign.

"My Locus?"

"Hanging on the left side."

She saw the tube and let out a sigh. "Thank you. Weapons?"

"Taser in a holster under my left arm. Gun in the small of my back. Knife on my right ankle."

"Not great, but not bad." She stumbled, leaning heavily on the wheelchair just as he had shortly before.

"Are you sure about this? I can push."

"I'm good. The shots missed my vest and went through my shoulder. I lost a little blood but the meds I'm shaking off are giving me the most trouble." She stopped suddenly next to a washroom, securing the chair with the brakes and lifting her IV bag off the hook. "Quick! I need my paniers and the clothes you're sitting on."

Without question, Liam handed her the bike bags, stood up so she could grab the clothes and plopped back down while she zipped into the washroom. He waited. A smiling, curvy, little redheaded nurse-practitioner walked past and he returned her smile, resisting the urge to Taser her to keep her from telling anyone she'd seen him. By the time she'd turned the corner and not even glanced back, Lynette exited the washroom, fully dressed. The IV tube came out of her sleeve and into the pack.

"Let's get the hell out of here, Skosche."

"Liam."

"Liam? Nice. I'm Becca now."

"Becca..." He tried it out and it rolled off his tongue easily. It fit her, then and now. He told her as much while she resumed pushing the chair down the corridor.

"Liam's good, too. Solid. Simple. Just like—"

"Don't you dare. He laughed.

"—you."

"Oh, you did! You went for the low laugh." He stuck his left arm out pointing his semi-curled hand at a glass exit door. "Out here, I think."

Becca steered the chair left and Liam swatted the big silver auto-door open button on the wall. They left the cool, filtered, sterilizer-scented Day Medicine unit behind and rolled out into the warm evening summer breeze coming up off the Glenmore Reservoir at the foot of the bluffs. As they cleared the cavity between the two wings of the building and approached the bluff, the asphalt path forked.

"To the right, then right again at the parkade." The first right turn moved them away from a cluster of benches where staff and patients smoked like it was the only thing keeping them alive. Long drags were punctuated by conversations full of laughter and, in some cases, wheezy chuckles. As he was rolled away, Liam's heart went out to them. In his millennia of life he had smoked, drank, and ingested in moderation just about every substance known to man and none of them had come close to giving him the rush he got from opening himself up to nature and filling his senses with the electricity of life.

As if she could read his thoughts, Becca's hand squeezed his shoulder and he reached up and squeezed back. They went on in silence, both tuning their Shield-trained senses to the world around them, listening for the pursuit they knew would come. At the end of the West Parkade Liam pointed again. "Here comes the hard part. Up the hill. We're parked in the upper lot."

"Easy peasey, hon." She rolled him off the pathway and into the roadway, lengthening her stride. She made quick work of the short hill, even though she'd had to snug up against the curb to let a city bus roll past. At the top of the hill she rolled into the small parking lot. "Which one?"

"Second row, silver Corolla. It's guarded, so let me go first. There's no telling what she'll do if she sees you without me."

"She?" Becca rolled Liam through the lot and stopped short when she found the Corolla.

"Just trust me on this. I'll explain on the road." Becca secured the chair and handed Liam his cane. He could still feel the seconds ticking along, slipping away from them. His imagination kept conjuring shouts and running boot steps behind them, spurring them on, but in reality, there were birds and the breeze and the squeaky brakes of a Handi-Bus, but no shouts or boot steps. Yet.

He limped to the car, whistling "If I Only Had a Brain" loudly as he went, his warning to Phoenix that he was approaching. The Yorkie's head popped up in the passenger window and Liam was sure he saw a pixie twinkle in the canine eyes. He clicked the remote on the keychain and the doors unlocked, then he struggled to climb in. Phoenix barked and licked his hand when he tried to stow his cane on the passenger side. Becca chuckled and simply climbed into the back seat, got down on the floor with her belly over the hump in the middle. She pulled Phoenix's blanket down over her, making sure it covered her from top to bottom before she settled in.

"All set back here."

"10-4." Liam pulled out of the parking spot and started down the hill, past the St. Patricia's wing and then past the hospital itself. "This would be a good time to start rubbing your lucky rabbit's foot."

There was a light laugh from under the blanket. "No lucky charm back here. Since I had to cross my fingers, my toes and my legs just to fit back here, that'll have to do."

"It won't be long. Five minutes, ten at the most. I want to be clear of traffic cams before you pop back up."

"No problem, hon. Best to get clear of the city. And we'd better run silent, too. We don't need anyone seeing you talking to yourself, unless you have a Bluetooth headset you can wear."

"Sorry. No cellphone. Low tech all the way."

"Me too."

"Going silent, Sweetheart." The car was only silent for a moment, though, before Liam turned on the radio, with the volume relatively low — loud enough to fill the silence but not enough to block out the world beyond the car. He couldn't see the front entrance of the hilltop hospital from the long exit road so he didn't know if the place was swarming with cops or not, but as he made the right turn onto southbound 14th Street, two cruisers screamed past with their lights and sirens on full get-the-hell-out-of-our-way mode. He risked a glance over his right shoulder just before he merged into traffic and saw that one of the white cruisers had stopped across the road, blocking all traffic from leaving the hospital. The cordon was up, the search was on, and now they had two police forces after them in addition to Dark Hunters and a fairy. Liam suspected that life was going to get very interesting again, and not in a good way.

It actually took fifteen minutes, but Liam eventually got them headed west again, back toward the mountains. After five minutes Becca moved up off the floor and lay on the back seat with the IV bag hooked to the back of Liam's headrest and Phoenix curled up in the curve of her body. Liam could hear the two of them snoring away while he drove into the sunset, concentrating on keeping the little car between the shoulders of the Trans-Canada Highway even though everything was a blur for him.

They got as far as Scott Lake Hill when Liam steered them into the truck pull-off and abruptly parked next to the sign telling everyone that at 1410 metres above sea level, this was the highest point on the 7776-kilometre-long highway that spanned Canada from east to west coasts. Liam didn't give a damn about the elevation or the highway or Scott Lake, which he couldn't even see from the highway at night anyway. He was done. In nearly a hundred lifetimes he'd been to Hell and back. He'd crossed deserts, mountains, seas and jungles. He'd walked, ridden and sailed, but never—*never*—had he been so utterly exhausted, so drained, so tapped dry of every reserve.

He limped over to one of the carved-initials-scarred picnic tables, plunked himself down with his back to the road and wept with his head down on his folded, shaking arms. He could sort of walk, but he sure as Hell couldn't run. He could barely see to drive and knew for damned sure that if he actually had to use a gun the target had better be standing stock-still in bright light no more than ten feet in front of him. As a Shield he was nearly useless. Of course, he'd been worse off before. His second lifetime in Mongolia he'd been born blind and managed to Shield the Wand of Life for twenty-two years before the Dark had found him. In Xaymaca—what is now known as Jamaica— he had developed what he now suspected was emphysema and had never been able to run or swim as far as his brothers, but he had kept safe the small, carved rhinoceros that was the Guardian of Lake Tanganyika. He'd shielded it for seventeen-and-a-half years before his young nephew inadvertently betrayed him to the Dark sailors who came ashore one morning on the heels of a tropical cyclone.

Thinking of the past grief and pain seemed to lessen the present day turmoil and the tears slowed, then stopped. As he wiped the snot and tears with the back of his right hand he felt like he was ten-years-old again and beaten down by the local bully. But none of this should have depressed him like this. None of this should have him broken down and afraid on the side of the road. There was something else eating at him and not knowing what it was, was shredding him up. Something was reaching into his soul and wrapping it up in a gritty, grey blanket of despair. He also knew that he had the answer, had the solution, somewhere in his stretched-beyond-human-comprehension memory. There was something off in his chemistry, he was sure of it. Or it was some spell of despair directed his way by a Dark spell-caster. Or...or...

"We forgot something."

He hadn't heard Lynette get out of the car and approach. No, not Lynette—Becca. She was Becca, now, as he was Liam. He turned and swung his right leg over the bench but her strong, slender hand on his shoulder stopped him from standing up. She sat, straddling the bench, facing him.

"I know we aren't stopped for long, but this will only take a moment and it can't wait another second." Liam felt her warm hands take his own, and in the faint moonlight Becca-who-had-once-been-Lynette leaned in and kissed her one true love for the first time in nearly four hundred years.

All at once, the veil of grey parted and Liam remembered who he was, what he was, and what he had to do. But first, he had to show his twenty-century-old wife how much his soul missed her.

The kiss was everything Liam needed in that very time and space. To use a local prairie analogy, it was a cowboy's first bath after a long, cold, dirty winter on the trail. The power of two Shields in love radiated out from their lips in a slow wave, pushing ahead of it the dust and grit that caked his mind, that weighed down his heart, that was grinding his millennia-old soul down. The wave passed out through his extremities and then, deep down in his chest, the spark of Light he'd nourished and kept alive for so so long flared and grew and spread and burned off the final cobwebs the wave had missed.

Even in her Phoenix form, Teagan's Faerie-born sight could see the warm silvery glow radiating from the Shield and his true love. It was good to see him coming back to life and she smiled; but somewhere a spell was cast and that spell reached out, flayed about, and quickly found her.

Liam's subconscious heard the hoarse barking before his thinking mind knew what it was, but his subconscious was hard-wired to his instincts and reflexes and as much as it hurt him to do so, he broke off the kiss and leaned back to catch his breath.

"Time to run, again, my Love."

"Police?"

"Worse. Two teams of Dark Hunters and a Faerie bounty hunter."

Becca helped him up and handed him his cane. They walked to the car as quickly as Liam could. "But I took out my Hunters. Could their replacements be here already?"

"Make that *three* teams."

"Three? And a bounty hunter from Faerie?"

Liam got in on the passenger side, relieved to have Becca take over the driving. "Okay. Story time. I'll give you the flash-fiction version first, while you drive. Keep going west, into the mountains. Go no more than nine over the limit and at least the law will leave us alone."

"*Should* leave us alone." She adjusted the seat for her shorter legs, snapped on her seatbelt and popped the car into gear. There was a spray of gravel as she left the pull-off and charged back onto the highway.

"First things first," Liam continued. "Becca-who-was-once-Lynette, meet Princess She-Whose-Name-I-Dare-Not-Say, heir to the Pixie Meadows of Compton Down."

Harff.

"An honour, your highness."

"Here in our realm she is just Phoenix."

"Phoenix it is, then."

Phoenix curled up in Liam's lap and drifted back to sleep.

"In a pouch on my belt is Noah's Olive Pit. In the trunk is the Sword. Brother Paul needed a favour and, well, my name came up. I'm guessing that your plastic tube is either the Flute, the Quill, the Pipe, or the Wand."

"The Pipe."

"One of my favourites. Beautiful workmanship."

"Stunning detail."

There was a short silence as Becca concentrated on driving while a big rig roared past them. Once he was gone, Becca spoke.

"How *are* Paul and Ozzy?" I haven't seen them in..." she did some mental calculations but came up blank. "Too long. I saw Brother Abiel in the Maldives just after Lincoln was assassinated over here and I had tea with Master Wei when he visited me on Easter Island around the time Henry VIII was marrying Kathryn Howard, but no Paul and Ozzy for eons."

"They're both good. They look like they haven't aged a day, which I suppose they haven't, really."

"Management gets all the perks."

"If you can call it that. I mean, what would you prefer? To age so slowly it's almost unnoticeable or to be a Shield who lives and dies like the rest of the occupants of this big blue marble in space?"

"Over and over and over again." She sounded weary.

Liam squeezed her hand. "Yah, I know. But think of the things we've seen. To misquote Hamlet, 'There are more things on this heavenly Earth, Horatio, than are dreamt of in your philosophy.'"

"Mmm... so very true. By the way, what's the plan? Where are we going?"

"I didn't think much further than breaking you out and taking you back to Lake Louise with us, but we do need something more than that. I suppose it's time to shatter nearly all of the rules at once and turn and fight. If what we do is all about maintaining Balance, I say maybe just this once we Balance running and hiding with fighting."

Suddenly Liam felt a hot, tingling fire in his left cheek and it quickly spread to his right, then all over his face and head and body and... then it was gone. "They've found us." He looked over at Becca and she simply nodded. "They know we're together," Liam added, unnecessarily.

"How close?"

"The spell was cast from long way off, but it won't take long for them to triangulate with the two of us together."

"Damn."

Becca raised Liam's hand to her lips and kissed his palm. It was her favourite gesture and the fire it stirred in him was as unlike the fire he'd just felt from the spell-cast as could be. He didn't have much strength, but he could hold her hand forever.

o0o

The smell of brimstone filled the air as Juliano lit the braziers and Delecia took a long slow breath to draw it deep into her lungs.

"Mmhmm, hurts so good." She stripped out of her Lemonhead sweats and took her scarlet satin robe off its hook.

Juliano grinned. "It ain't napalm, but it's a great taste to wake up to in the morning."

"Truer words, Jule, truer words." The robe slipped down over her head, the fine satin stimulating the more sensitive parts of her body. Delecia shivered with the exquisiteness of the passing moment. "What have we got?"

Juliano, already in his own robe, which did nothing to hide his swelling excitement, held up his phone. "Text alert. Wellington has picked up two Shields together and they need confirmation, ten minutes ago."

"Nice one! How'd we score that?"

"Norma in Dispatch." The two spell-casters went about setting up their gear as they chatted.

"You're putting it to Sweet Meat Norma Jean? You canine spell-caster you. How serious is it? Piercing? Branding? Suspension?" She laid out the pin board, the flask of corpse ashes and the box of fresh maggots she'd grabbed on her way in to the cell.

"Maybe."

"You've shown her your demon, haven't you?"

"Not yet. Maybe tonight, if we finish here early enough." He retrieved a semi-translucent, eighteen-inch-tall canopic jar from a cubbyhole in the cement wall. In the fluorescent lights it appeared to have an oily bluish-purple surface. Where his hands warmed the jar it changed to a sickly greenish hue. Something moved in the jar, slithering and writhing, slow and deliberate. He placed the jar carefully on the pile of cemetery soil on the tile floor within the six-foot-wide, ivory-inlaid pentagram.

Delecia handed him a canvas bag of black salt as they passed. Their hands touched and their excitement grew. Juliano loosened the drawstring on the bag and began covering the ivory inlay with a solid trail of the dark salt. A single-note doorbell sounded from the ceiling speakers.

"Two minutes, Jule."

"No problem, Del." They both hustled to finish their set-up and be ready in their places in the two minutes. Their bare footsteps slapped on the polished gold-flecked black tile as they hurried. Delecia filled a large bronze bowl with water from the stagnant well in the corner then put it down opposite Juliano's jar. She grabbed a clean obsidian bowl from the stack on the workbench and filled it halfway with naphtha fuel from the tap on the wall. Careful not to spill a drop of the flammable solvent she placed it in the bottom of a two-tiered stand within the pentagram that Juliano was just finishing marking out with the salt. They removed their robes and hung them back on the iron wall hooks.

Long proficient at set-up and 'casting, Juliano and Delecia were both naked and kneeling within the pentagram when the second warning bell sounded. Delecia grinned at Juliano and licked her lips. "Let's get 'er done."

"All the way, girl." With ground-bone-based chalk Juliano drew a second pentagram within the larger one and poured out a small pile of cemetery soil in the centre. He then lifted the jar up and into the newer configuration. Delecia placed the bronze water bowl on the top tier of the stand and lit the naphtha on the bottom tier with a wooden match. She gingerly placed a metal ring lid over the bowl, narrowing the flame to a one-inch hole, slowing the burn. The stagnant, dead water heated quickly.

"Fondue's on," she joked, then opened the flask of corpse dust and ground mandrake and sprinkled it evenly over the surface of the water as bubbles began rising from the bottom of the bowl. Delecia started her incantation softly, under her breath. "Ni koshan orelk madar. Fohr shokan korel ni."

Juliano pressed his palms down on the pin-board, exalting in the moment when the skin stretched tight but was not yet broken. "I love it when you talk Demon to me, Del."

"Fohr shokan korel ni. Ni koshan orelk madar." The water reached the boiling point quickly. Juliano saw this and pushed down with his hands, piercing each palm in thirteen-times-thirteen places. He pushed down hard, fighting the resistance of so many pins in such a small area, feeling the steel points enter his palms and the blood begin to flow.

Delecia watched as sweat beaded on her partner's forehead and his excitement swelled to the breaking point. When she was sure of the moment and could feel the energy building in the cell, she dumped the squirming maggots into the boiling dead water and as they bounced and roiled and cooked, the lid gently lifted off the canopic jar. A dark-scaled, shadowed, humanoid demon poked his little horned head out and spit in the dirt beneath his jar.

"Toh ganensh, Mastra?" Juliano's little subservient demon asked what was his master's will even though it already knew what Master's will was. He was only two months into his thirteen-month term of service but he caught on quickly to the spell-caster's task and what was required from its Hell-spawn powers.

"Viendel loarit divanta." Juliano followed the routine exactly. One did not improvise or cut corners when dealing with demons or one paid a horrific price that death would be a relief from.

"Kwidlack? Divanta?"

"Yes, *two* Shields."

"Da-krem!" There was a moment's hesitation and then the six-limbed creature took the jar's lid gingerly in one taloned hand and placed it upside down on the floor. Now halfway out of the jar, Lectum closed his eyes, tilted his head back and sniffed the air. To him all humans looked the same, but their smell was a different matter altogether. She was here. She would be assisting. He could smell her musk. His tongue flicked out, split in two and sampled the air. Yes, he could taste the rim of her soul—so close, so fresh, and so *corrupted*. When his term was up with Juliano maybe he would ask her to take him on, let him be her demon.

Juliano cleared his throat and drew Lectum's attention back to the task. The demon pivoted his head around as though his neck was on a ball joint and nodded. Delecia ladled out half the contents of the bowl and poured it into the jar's up-ended lid, trying to include as many of the maggots as possible. The demon purred, sniffed the contents of the offering then spat what looked like blood into it. There was a sizzle as the demon sputum reacted to the water, then it began to glow dark red. Juliano's indentured power source held four clawed hands close together over the redness and drew the glow up, into his talons. He nodded again and Juliano quickly lifted his bloody hands off the pin board and slapped his palms together. Blood sprayed and splashed and Lectum purred with unbridled pleasure, then extended his four thin, scaled arms forward, to the edge of the corpse-dust-chalk pentagram restricting him.

Juliano could feel his pulse fast and strong as he bled from the hundreds of pinpricks. Then the power of Lectum slithered through the air across the short gap between them and the spell-caster opened his hands to receive the 'gift' onto his bloody palms. The demon's energy touched the human's life fluid and formed a new force. A globe of crimson power the size of a toddler's head sat on Juliano's palms, growing not in size but in density, drawing blood from the three-hundred-and-thirty-eight tiny open wounds.

Delecia started her incantation but Juliano couldn't hear a single syllable, not only because his blood pounded in his ears but also because he himself had started up with a low guttural hum. Just when he thought his head would explode, there was only the humming and his mind grasped his own sound and rode it down through the floor, through the building's rock foundation, and into the mystical ley line the complex was strategically built over top of. As soon as his mental essence touched the power of the line, he ceased to be Juliano, ceased to be aware of even being alive.

It took two minutes for Delecia to revive Juliano after he'd cast both his spell and his mind outward. Lectum lay curled up beside his jar in the cemetery soil. He was nearly as drained as his master.

"We got it, Jule. There are definitely two Shields together. Let's clean up and get the coordinates to Control so the Hunt can begin."

Juliano nodded and stood, slowly, unsteadily. Lectum reached out hungrily and his master extended his hands into the chalked-out area letting his demon licked off all of the unused blood and healed the wounds of his flesh. The wounds on his soul, though, would probably never heal completely.

oOo

Wallace Tabak blinked twice and took a deep breath to help himself focus. He could feel his blood pressure rising as he stared at the terrified messenger standing in front of him.

"A whole Hunter Team, Miguel? A *girl* eliminated six senior Hunters? Where the Hell did this happen?"

"Canada, sir."

"Canada? Do you think you could possibly get more specific than that? Halifax? Burnaby? Trois Rivieres? *Where did we just lose an entire team of Hunters?!"*

"Calgary, Alberta, sir. More specifically, eight klicks south of Calgary on Highway 2, southbound lanes. They ambushed the Greyhound bus she was on."

"They had her cornered on a *bus* and she *still* did this?"

"They had a man onboard who moved too soon or got spotted before the team was in place and she choked him out with a garrote. She was ready, willing and armed."

"And the remaining five Hunters were *not*?" He pointed at the newly installed flat screen on the wall. "I want a copy of the Live Feed on that screen in two minutes." The young man didn't move from where he was rooted to the Persian rug. Tabak knew there was more. "Tell me, Miguel. Your two minutes are ticking down."

"The team leader was..." He silently cursed his supervisor for being in a meeting when the report came in.

Tabak stood slowly, deliberately, like the predator he was at heart. "Which team was it, boy?"

"*Rho Doce Huit,* sir."

"Damian's team." He dropped back into his chair.

"Yes sir. Your son-in-law's team." Miguel braced himself for the traditional shooting of the messenger, but it didn't come. Instead he watched as Tabak's jaw muscles clenched and his skin flushed. Then the CEO of DET took a long, slow, measured breath. He let it out and took another. Eventually his color faded back to simply tanned and his jaw loosened.

"Miguel, go back to work. Thank you for facing your fear and telling me in person. And when you get home tonight, hug your children. They grow up much too fast."

"Yes sir. Thank you. I will, sir. Can I make a suggestion, sir?"

"If you tell me to see a grief counsellor I'll put a bullet in your head right here and now."

Miguel took his own deep breath before speaking again. "Not at all, sir. There's a team in the air en route from Cape Town with that captured Shield. I suggest redirecting them to Oklahoma City to refuel then on to Calgary to take out this Shield. She was hurt in the attack and is in the hospital."

"Brilliant! Get it done."

"I don't have the authority, sir. Only Hunter Command or higher can give the order."

"I'll take care of it then."

oOo

There had been a layover on some unknown tarmac for a horrendous number of excruciating hours, but they were back in the air again and Takeko felt the jet very obviously bank to the right, the starboard wing dipping a good thirty degrees or more. She slid in the crate but didn't go far before she bumped into what was now the almost downside wall of her pine prison.

"A change of heading? What's happening up there, my velvet-voiced friend?" She tried to sound calm but she didn't like sudden changes that she hadn't initiated herself. Her guard didn't seem to hear her, but rather was listening intently to his headset or earpiece.

"Sí. Sí. Immediatamente! Yo tengo el derecho fundamental arsenal aquí. La cabina del piloto? Sí. En seguida, señor!" Takeko got that he was taking the key for the arsenal up to the cockpit. She heard the scuff of his boots moving away and the jingle of a loaded key ring coming out of his pocket.

"Hello! Mi amigo! Hey! Me tortura mejor con el estómago lleno! ¿Puedo obtener algo de comer ... por favor?" *I torture better on a full stomach. Can I get something to eat... please?* There was no immediate reply. She waited five minutes and still no reply and no return of her keeper. Just when she expected him to return after taking the keys up top, she felt the jet climbing, gaining altitude.

"Now what?" Turbine whine was the only reply she got so she figured that this was as good a time as any to work on getting loose.

oOo

Wallace Tabak made three phone calls before he charged out of his office with his weekender bag in hand. The first was to Hunter Command to redirect the team in-bound from South Africa to Calgary, to take out Damian's killer. The second call was to the DökktEfniTækni hangar to prepare his Gulfstream jet for immediate takeoff. The third and final call was to Tau Drake to explain that he was flying to Curacao to break the news of Damian's death to his Ashlynn and Tricia in person, but he'd be back in Santiago in plenty of time for the Board Meeting.

Drake had growled something about the poor timing of the trip, but Wallace knew his second-in-command understood. The two of them had big plans for Ashlynn and Damian's son in the coming years and for the sake of The Dark, there was no other way for Ashlynn to be told.

oOo

The toilet out back of the petrol station north of Maubranche, France, was small and filthy but the door locked from the inside and that was what Arvinder needed most right now. The layered stains and rancid smells were nothing to a man who had once spent three days in the sewers beneath a Spanish castle in order to elude Dark Hunters and a cuckolded princess who had only just learned the truth about her handsome, baby-faced groom.

He reverently and respectfully unwrapped the sky blue turban from his head then wound it around his waist and pulled his sweater down over top. Gently, he pulled off the fake beard and dropped it in the cracked, ancient toilet. With a pair of barber's scissors, Arvinder's skilled hands swiftly cut his thick, black hair off, dropping the cuttings on top of the now soggy false whiskers.

When he had his hair as short as he could possibly get it with the scissors he slipped the tool into his back pocket and retrieved a cordless trimmer from his bag. Going by touch, he shaved the remaining choppy stubble down even further and when he was done he flushed the toilet for what was probably the first time in days or weeks. He watched the evidence of his old self go down the drain, and then he walked out into the sunlight, the transformation complete.

The Shield who had recently been Arvinder was gone and in his place was Hassan from Morocco. Within the hour he managed to hitch a ride in a Geneva-bound lorry and once again a Shield and his Locus had broken Pattern, eluded the Dark, and vanished into the wide, wide world.

oOo

Tracy had the rescue team's driver drop her off at the Devonport Airport where she waited until they'd driven off and then immediately made her way by two taxis to a rented garage where she kept her back-up vehicle—a dirty, dinged-up '05 Ford Territory SUV—and a load of supplies. From clothes to new identification, cash, weapons, hair color and a few more odds and ends, she had everything she needed to change her identity and disappear. She even had a crate of non-perishable food should she have to take to the outback for a while. Her only concern was that the brace on her leg would make her easily identifiable until she was able to walk without it. She'd have to do her best to stay in the car as much as possible until her bloody leg was stronger.

She looked up and down the laneway, taking in every detail, seeing the rusting, discarded stove, the five worn tires of various sizes and the aluminum shed with the padlocked door. Only when she was sure no one watched did she stump inside, turn on the bare bulb, grab hold of the rope over her head and pull the garage door back down. She locked the door, set the aftermarket alarm, and stashed the Egg on the floor in the front passenger seat of the Territory before doing a walk-around of the vehicle. She checked the tire pressure, the Best Before sticker on the license plate and then popped the hood and checked the various fluids. It had only been six months since she'd last checked everything so all was good and ready for the road.

It was the thought of the exhausting road ahead—and the sea trip to the mainland—that made up her mind that she needed a nap. She folded down the back seat, climbed in a bit awkwardly because of the brace, and then locked the doors. There wasn't much space, but when she shoved everything to one side there was enough to stretch out with the blanket and old foam pillow. She applied a precise amount of pressure to the largest crease on the inside of her left wrist, circling her thumb around, massaging the point, willing herself to relax. It worked, and she shoved back the adrenalin and fell down into sleep with two guns and a sword within easy reach.

Chapter Thirteen: Bob

*"I, too, have read the Venerable Sun Tzu's **Art of War**, but I have found over the centuries that few people who spout the words live the life."*

~Shield Master Wei (1471 CE while playing dice with Tower of London guards.)

oOo

The offer they put on the table made Bob's eyebrows edge up. He had jumped from a tedious, dead-end life in police work for the league of Dark Hunters because they'd simply offered him too much money to ignore, but on the piece of paper this Brother Abiel had just put on the table in front of him was an amount that wouldn't even cover a year's worth of payments on Bob's Range Rover. Then the good Brother of Light put three 4x6 photos on top of the salary offer and Bob's attention was fully his.

"You're threatening my niece and nephews?"

Abiel laughed but Bob heard no cruelty in the mirth. "My friend, you have been playing for the wrong team for far too long. I'm showing you these smiling, mischievous faces because I want you to ask yourself what kind of world you want them to grow up in."

"Why should I care?"

"You *do* care, because their cousin, your late son, would have been fourteen last month and when that drunk driver killed him eleven years ago it was a dark act in a dark moment that took away the boy who was your Light. We can't bring John back, but we can and will fight to keep this world bright."

Bob was silent. There was nothing he could say past the lump in his throat that wouldn't be a lie right now, no denial he could make. He knew his loyalty had a price because eleven years ago the recruiters at DökktEfniTækni had written the check and he'd cashed it.

"Tell me about this app, Bob."

And he did.

oOo

"So you've got a room in Lake Louise. Is it a good place to hide out for awhile?" Becca drove the Corolla through the Bow Valley, past the lights of Canmore.

"It would have been, but we've got to be drawing Dark attention like bad meat draws flies."

"Nice. Can we be honey attracting bears, instead?"

"You can be anything you want... Honey."

"Thanks, Sugar Lips. How's the Lake for an ambush?"

"Or a Last Stand?"

She glanced over at him. "When did you go over to the glass-is-half-empty side of the party? You used to laugh in the face of the Dark before slicing them open and running off into the shadows with both your hide and your Locus safe and secure."

"I don't run anywhere any more."

"I noticed that. What's up? A stroke?"

"My neighbor, Norinne, made a pretty good case for MS. The usual signs of a stroke aren't there."

"How long?"

"Two weeks-ish." Maybe longer, for minor symptoms I didn't notice or more likely ignored."

Becca reached over and caringly rubbed Phoenix's silk-soft head. "How long have you two been together?"

"Thirty-two years yesterday. Time moves a lot slower in Faerie." He put his hand on hers and she spread her fingers for his. Their fingers interlaced and their love pulsed to their heartbeats.

"Yesterday was your fiftieth?"

"Yup."

"Wow. Happy belated birthday. Here's to the next fifty."

"The *next* fifty? Do you think we'll even make it to tomorrow?"

"Well, Shield of Sunshine and Optimism, that depends on whether or not we can defend this place in Lake Louise."

"We can't. It's a hotel."

Harff.

"Oh, you're awake now."

Harff.

"Run? Sure we could. But once their spells pinpoint our locations they can track us like bloodhounds until they catch up to us. With three Loci and two Shields together, we're a Dark magnet. Throw in Oberon's pet hunter and we run out of options fast."

Harff.

"True enough. If we fight and lose, the resultant disasters could kill hundreds of thousands. If we run, they'll eventually catch us anyway and the result will be the same."

"Or we could fight and win. Or run and evade."

"Not together. We did it once, but that was a long time before technology made both communication and travel faster. They're probably plugged into most of the world's security systems at one level or another. I've been off-grid for a long time. I have no identity on the Internet, but with the two of us together, their spell casters have got to be feeling like they won the jackpot. They'd hardly need Facebook to find us."

Harff.

"Teleport?"

Harff.

"It wouldn't..."

"Wouldn't what?"

"Work. But it *might*. Like crossing a creek to break the scent trail when the hounds are following."

"I've done *that* once or twice over the centuries."

"We did it together, right after Constance was born."

"Would teleporting work?"

"Yes... no."

"Maybe so?"

"Again, the two-Shields thing. If we called for back-up and they did teleport us back with them, we'd draw the Dark right along with us. I don't know all that they're capable of in terms of tracking us with magic or tech, but I won't risk leading them to a spell-spinning Warrior Base."

"If we separated?"

"We'd have to be picked up by separate teams and go to separate bases. Master Wei is right and has always been right. Two Shields can't be together."

"I just found you. I'm not losing you already." She squeezed his hand and he squeezed back.

"We're Shields, Becca. We're not like everyone else. We have a responsibility, we made a commitment." He raised her hand to his lips and kissed it. "I can't believe I'm saying this, but we have rules for a reason. We can't just toss them away because they don't suit our needs of the moment."

"You're the only man I've ever truly loved with everything I've got. We had children..."

"You've never had other children?"

"Yes, of course I have. Ten in total. But only three of them were with you. Only three of them were born to me as a Shield who knew I was a Shield, knew what it was to be a Shield. Didn't you father any children other than Constance, Eric and Samuel?"

"Just our three."

"Really?"

"I always became a Shield before I could get 'busy'. There were a few close calls, but Constance, Eric and Samuel are the sum total of my progeny."

Becca drove on in silence for minute before Liam realized that she was crying. He kissed her hand again, and then held it to his heart. "Three with you was all I needed, my Love. They were beautiful and brilliant and gifted children. But knowing that they weren't Shields and that when they died, they died, they didn't get 'recycled' like us...

I couldn't go through that again. I have been in love at least once in nearly every life I've lived, but there was only one you. Only one Shield who was also the Locus of my soul's Light."

"Oh Skosche... Liam... I'm so sorry."

Liam suddenly remembered a certain young spell-spinner in the here-and-now. "Don't be. In all the rush to save my damsel, I completely forgot to tell you about our granddaughter."

"Granddaughter?"

"Actually, our too-many-greats-to-count-granddaughter. Cor. She's a spell-spinner on our side."

"How on earth did you find her?"

"I didn't. She found me. She used our blood bond to spin some kind of spell and reach out to touch my mind. We chatted, but only briefly. I guess this spell was her own little creation and it tuckered her out to use it. We were also a bit worried about it being traced."

"How do you know it isn't a trap? That they haven't found a way to reach out to us and they started with you?"

"She knew both of our names."

"That would do it. I suppose the other side could have that information in their archives, but how would they know to reach you, of all the Shields out there."

"Exactly. I trust her. There was more than words in the conversation. Of course, if it is a trap, it won't be the first one they've laid for me and it won't be the last. While *we* fanatically avoid patterns, *they* seem to rely pretty heavily on repeating what went before and fine-tuning it."

"Speaking of which, is this the same route you always take to the Lake? Shouldn't we be changing it up?"

"There aren't a lot of choices without adding hours to the trip. Millions of people travel this road every year, so the ones who don't are more likely to stand out."

"So, what are our options when we get there?"

"God, I really don't know. Only separate teleporting makes any sense at all. Everything else results in too much death. Death is a part of life but every time I Awaken as a Shield my heart cracks just a little bit for everyone who died because I failed, eighteen years before."

"Me, too."

oOo

With a baseball cap and his sweatshirt hood covering his head and shading his face, Dax was able to move around Calgary within the layer of human civilization known in Faerie as The Invisibles, the ones no one sees. It wasn't the first time he'd ventured out of Faerie into the human world, but it was most definitely the first time he'd done so at the behest of his father, the all-powerful, throne-warming King of the Fairies himself, Oberon.

Dax loved this rough, dirty, violent world of the short-lifers, but the stench was almost enough to send him fleeing back home. Even a fortnight tracking a pair of rank, half-dead, diseased ogres was better than the reek of exhaust fumes, grease-soaked substances they mistook for food, and the burning-chemical-and-beast-urine concoctions they dared call perfume. Nineteenth century London was atrocious as they industrialized their world, but at least a short ride out into the countryside could clear the senses. In this new century of theirs the humans were killing their world and Dax just wanted to be quit of it.

This Princess of the Pixies he was tracking had changed her form and thereby cloaked her magical nature, but to an elf with his skills and experience, she couldn't hide completely. Her scent was cooling, here in this deadly, iron-filled city, but there was still a trace of Faerie he could reel in and follow. Not even the stench of diesel and deep fryers could hide her essence from him. He'd lost the trail down by the river that bisected the metropolis, but with a few notes from his flute he found a thin thread upstream where she and her human protector had left the pathway and moved away from the protection of the river.

Earlier on in the day, or was it the day before? His sense of time was all askew in this world. *Whenever* it was, he'd felt the slap of a clumsy spell as it identified him and then passed him by, but there had been nothing since. Someone else was tracking the pixie, but he'd been warned about the possibility and his blades were ready.

oOo

"I'm of no use as a Shield. I'm broken." Liam wanted to scream his frustration but instead spoke softly, barely above the radio.

"Of course you're broken—you're human. It's not being broken that matters, it's what you do in spite of the condition, which, by the way, is the human condition. 'Perfect' is an illusion."

"I know. It's an illusion perpetuated by the spiritual leaders and now by marketing wizards."

"Exactly. If God can work with imperfect tools—us—then it behoves us to do the same."

"*God.* You know, considering what we do and why, you'll probably find it odd that I don't really pray. I'll say a blessing once in a while but I don't pray in the traditional sense."

"Neither do I. I haven't prayed since you died in my arms, with an arquebus shot in your belly. I *talk* to God all the time, but I don't ask for anything other than advice because he's already given me all the tools I need to achieve everything I want to."

"That's easy to say—we're Shields."

"Is it? Really? We live life after life, every time with the same task and every time with a guarantee of failure. *We* are the ones who truly, simply, just live our lives the best we can and that best is to soldier on. To run, hide, and outwit an enemy who will not relent, not surrender, not give up nor give quarter. Their army is endless and we are, each of us, together, alone."

"Then why do we do it, Becca?"

"Because we're servants of Light, not slaves of Dark. We're Shields of Hope, not Spears of Despair."

"Well put."

"A long time ago I was outside a temple in Jerusalem that the faithless had turned into a marketplace and a madman burst in and tore the place up, driving out the animals and overturning the tables, shouting about 'his Father's house'. He wasn't worried about making enemies because he had a responsibility to his beliefs."

"I know. I followed him into the temple and nearly got trampled by the little stampede he caused."

"You were there, too? We were that close?"

"We were *all* watching him, expecting great things from such a charismatic prophet. We knew he was going to inspire, but I'll be honest when I tell you that we had no idea how big it would get."

"He was something else, wasn't he?"

"Did I ever tell you that I was the one who collected the Grail?"

"You? *Really?*"

"Like I said, Master Wei had a couple of us watching him, following him. He was making a lot of noise and garnering a lot of attention, so we stayed close. I was a server at the home in Bethany where he held that final supper in the upper room. When he spoke that evening, the air was electric. I could see his aura as clearly as I could see my own hand in front of me."

"I heard his sermon on the mount and would have followed him anywhere."

"Me, too." Liam took a slow breath, smiling, remembering. "You know, the same has been said about Hitler, that when he spoke few could resist his words."

"Please tell me that you didn't just compare Jesus Christ to Adolf Hitler. They're... is there something more than polar opposites?"

"Not that I can think of."

"Christ and *Hitler?*"

"Of course they're opposites, but deep at the root of both of them, at the root of all of us, is life energy and choices. The Hitlers, Amins and Dahmers chose Dark, and it's our task to support those great souls who choose Light and maintain the Balance."

"So true, Love. I've Shielded the Grail three times and there's something special about it."

174

"There's something special about all of the Loci, which I suppose is what's at the heart of why they're Loci, why their mere existence inspires Light in the worlds."

"But I've always had a special spot in my heart for the Grail, even before the movie."

"Indiana Jones or Monty Python?"

"Python."

"Good choice. By the by, you should have felt the cup when it was still warm from his touch."

"Really?"

"I was its first Shield. We had no idea how the next few days were going to go but we knew that his new covenant was going to change things. The Light was strong that night."

"The Force was strong in him?"

"Oh, you didn't just say..."

"Yah. Sorry. You can spank me later."

"Promise?"

"I'll be devastated if you *don't*."

"Me, too."

The music from the radio filled the silence as Liam raised Becca's hand to his lips and kissed it.

She purred with joy. "Mmmm..."

He placed her hand back on the steering wheel. "Better let you drive."

"Fine. Spoil sport."

Liam chuckled darkly. "Headline news: Two Shields of Light died tonight when the car they were in left the Trans-Canada Highway and slammed into Lac des Arcs in the Rocky Mountains. They died instantly but both wore inexplicably large grins."

Becca slapped his leg gently. "Phoenix, is he always this much fun?"

Harff.

"I thought so."

"I'm being ganged up on."

"Give it up, mister. You're outnumbered."

"I surrender. Unconditionally."

"Good. Now, I want to go back to what we were talking about. I realize that we've all seen and done things that only other Shields can appreciate the magnitude of, but... *you were at the Last Supper*. That's huge! How close was the description in Paul's letter to the Corinthians? Does the Bible have it right?"

"Don't get me going on the Bible, woman."

"Why?" She smiled, goading him on.

"I believe that the Bible, like the history books, is subject to intentional revision and unintentional mistranslation."

"How so?"

"Let's just say that there are statements attributed to him that he never said and things he preached that no one recorded. We remember of history what we want to, like the Irish clinging to the belief that their Blessed Saint Patrick was Irish, or, more recently, the U.S. Navy remembering that Captain James Lawrence's last words on the deck of the Chesapeake were 'Don't give up the ship!' and made them a battle cry still used today."

"Those weren't his last words?"

"Sort of. His last words were actually 'Don't give up the ship! Burn her!'"

"And you think they were wrong to forget the part about burning the ship?"

"Not at all. He was my uncle and a good man and I'm proud his death has brought inspiration, but my point is, they took what they could use and left the rest out."

"Like the Bible?"

"Like some of the translations floating around, yes."

"Wow. You sure know how to heat up a conversation."

"This is the only the second time I've ever spoken the words out loud."

"What happened the first time? Did you shut the party down with your controversial cocktail conversation?"

"I got burned at the stake. My Locus, the Bowl, burned with me."

"Oh my... I'm sorry, Love. I didn't realize."

"It was a death, like all of the others. You once took three long, hellish months to die of the plague. Give me a fast fire any day over that."

"I guess. But the *pain*..."

"...was unbelievable, true."

"Ours is not to question why, but to be a Shield until we die... and die and die and die."

"It's not like we haven't done our share of killing, Love. I've killed four-hundred-and-six men, twenty-one women and one child. I don't like it, I'm not proud of it, but it *is* what's required of me."

"My numbers aren't much different, except I've never had to kill a child."

"It was an accident, but the sword was in my hand so I was responsible, and when the time comes, that soul and all the others will be counted against me and the debt will have to be paid."

"To whom?"

"It doesn't matter."

"What do you mean, it doesn't matter?"

"I don't need to know the name of a bank's CEO in order to know where I keep my money; likewise with my Faith—the name isn't as important as the investment I've made with my soul."

"So 'Jesus', 'God', 'Gaia', 'Satan'...?"

"None of the names matter, only that you've invested and can live with your decision for whatever kind of eternity you believe in."

"No wonder they burned you at the stake. There are plenty of people even now who would throw the Liam on the barbeque if they heard you."

"We—you and I and all the other Shields—have been raised in pretty much every religion known to man and a few that have been forgotten. They're *all* right. And they're all *wrong*. In twenty-some centuries of life all I really know for certain is that it's what's at the heart of the beliefs, not the ceremonies and rules the leaders dictate and impose in order to maintain *their* hold, *their* control, *their* power."

"Wow."

"The best church I ever attended was run by a priest who, when asked how to perform a certain rite, said 'I don't know, and I don't care.' He went on to tell the congregation that it didn't matter if you used your left hand or your right, if you're a man or a woman, if you use gold or tin or wood. What mattered was—*is*—your intent. What do you want to achieve with the rite, the ritual, and is your heart in it?"

"Wow. You've put a lot of thought into this."

"And you haven't?"

"Of course I have. It's just that as a woman my rights and exposure to all of the doctrines has been so different from yours. Don't forget that relative to my whole life, I've only just been allowed to vote. I still can't step foot into some of the temples, simply because of my gender."

"I guess if anyone ever writes about the life of a Shield it'll make a few waves."

"Probably not."

"No?"

"No. Who'd believe it?" She smiled.

oOo

Tao Drake sat with his back to the smoked-glass window overlooking the mountains outside his office at DET. As Wallace Tabak's second-in-command, he was responsible for putting together the upcoming Board Meeting. He could easily have delegated the task as he did so many others, but trusting the Board Meeting to anyone else was just too great a risk in these turbulent times. He needed control.

The Smartphone on his massive carved basalt desk buzzed with an incoming message. He picked it up and read the text, then without a word he dialled the number in the message.

"I don't remember giving this number to you, Nickols."

"You didn't, Drake. Tabak is in mid take-off and can't be reached for another twenty minutes."

"Twenty minutes? What in the Hell couldn't wait twenty minutes?"

"Our stock is going through the roof. There's something up."

"Who's buying it? What's his name?"

"That's just the thing, it's not any one buyer. The only reason the sales got flagged is that they all happened within a five-minute window of time."

"Shell companies. A creeping tender offer? Of DET? We do the taking over, we do not *get* taken over. Can Tabak's techs track the transactions?"

"Most likely, but with him off-site, the chain of command goes to you and so I need you to give the order. Put me in charge, but the initial order has to come from you."

"Who do I call to get this fixed now?"

"Her number is at the bottom of the message. I'm on my way over there now so I need them ready to roll when I arrive."

"Nickols, are you giving me orders?" His voice got low but didn't falter in clarity or menace.

"We're about to lose *everything* so I'm not wasting time with hand-holding. This is what you pay me to do so let me do it. As soon as I've got hard data I'll pull every available spell-caster with a pet demon on it and find these sons-of-bitches. After we do, and after we stop the bleeding in the markets, you can kick my ass then. In the meantime, I'm two minutes away from Tabak's tech-freaks so get off the phone and make the call... please, *sir*."

Drake hung up. He knew Nickols was right and they needed this done now, not in twenty minutes while they try to reach Tabak. Where the Hell was Tabak going, anyway? He'd have to solve that mystery after he set the dogs loose on the takeover. He pulled up the text message again and called the number at the bottom.

"Rhianna? This is Tau Drake and this is a priority command. Confirm my ident with VoiceSekure." He waited while she did exactly what he said. "Got it? Good. In about thirty seconds Rance Nickols is going to be standing at your desk. He needs all the resources you have available and you're to give him your full cooperation. There's no time to consult with Wallace Tabak. This is now your one and only priority. Do you have any questions, young lady?"

She had only one and she asked it.

"Put ShieldBreaker on auto-pilot or whatever the Hell you do and concentrate all of our electronic resources on the problem Nickols is about to drop in your lap. If you can't solve this problem in the next fifteen minutes, then there won't be anyone left at DET to care about the goddamned app. Any more questions? Good. Get this done." He disconnected the call and resisted the urge to crush the phone in his hand.

oOo

Even in Faerie Dax was considered handsome by many, beautiful by some, and even downright delicious by a few. He had the exotic looks one would expect of mixed-race royalty. His father, Oberon, was pure elf and his mother was a pixie. At six feet in height he was tall for an elf, a giant for a pixie, and barely above average amongst the humans he now mingled with, but his twinkling gold-flecked, emerald-green eyes were spellbinding, and his thick, short, blue-black hair just begged to be ruffled. He was so slender as to appear skinny but he was faster and stronger than any pure human and had the reflexes of a dragonfly.

All of these physical attributes and gifts made Dax the centre point of any hall he entered, unless he wanted to remain unseen. The one gift that he treasured most from his mother's side of the family was his ability to pass completely unnoticed through a crowd. Many an hour he had spent in his father's lush garden simply reading and sketching while servants, siblings, and even party guests strolled within reach of his long arms without knowing he was present.

It was this little talent of his that enabled him to follow the frumpy human man into the Shield's residence without his so much as blinking in his direction. As the inner door swung closed he slipped a green oak leaf into the latch and the lock was prevented from catching. He quickly slipped out his flute, faced the enormous list of what he assumed were building residents and played two phrases of his hunting tune.

The pure faerie notes filled the vestibule, echoing joyously back and forth between the glass and stone. Into that echo he played one single note, and willed it to the resident board. A soft green pinpoint of brightness flicked across the names and around the buttons, seeming to follow a scent search for a snicket of like, a dollop of faerie. There were well over a hundred names on the board but the music still echoed in the small space as the green brightness considered each one, back and forth, seemingly at random. And then it picked one, circled it and bounced up and down on it to signal Dax it had done its job. The nameplate said 'Smith, B A'.

Dax reached out with his silver flute and the green brightness returned to its source, its home. "Well met, little one. We enter now the lair of the Shield. I would suppose these white circles are for summoning the tower occupants from their quarters. Could it be that easy? Wouldst he come if we summoned?" He pushed the button next to 'Smith, B. A.' with the flute and waited. And waited. He pressed it again and this time his elven hearing detected a faint, raucous buzzing sound somewhere in the tower above him. He lifted the flute and the buzzing stopped, pressed it down again and the buzz returned.

"Primitive, yet effective." He removed a tiny leaf from his cuff, pressed the flute down once more and slipped the leaf into the thin gap between the button and the board. He lifted the flute and the leaf held—the buzzer continued to sound above. Dax slipped on his thin gargoyle-leather gloves to protect his hands from the iron of the door handle then gripped it and swung the inner door open, deftly catching the oak leaf as it fluttered away from the mechanism. Once he was in the large, unoccupied lobby the buzzing sounded much clearer. Dax quickly found the stairs but a wave of nearly debilitating nausea struck him as he reached for the door. He leaned toward it and confirmed that it wasn't just metal; it was cursed iron—iron by its aura and smell. Iron... his bane, the one thing in this world that was sure to kill him.

In the last Faerie-Human war it was the iron blades and armour that turned the tide in favour of the short-lifers and forced the Faerie folk back into the Shadows. Dax had been told that his pixie blood was the only reason he could even breathe the iron-dust-filled air of this world, but he wasn't immune to the ferrous poison, just a bit more resistant.

His gloves kept his skin from burning but couldn't protect his Faerie essence from the overwhelming abundance of iron in the stairwell. As he forced himself to mount the steps, following the buzz, he theorized that the humans used steel to make up for their inherent lack of natural magic. He had visited elven cities with towers twice as tall as this clumsy block but they were constructed entirely of living wood, bound by earth magic.

Somewhere after the fifth floor Dax lost count of how many levels he had climbed but when the buzzing began to fade he knew he'd gone too far. He backtracked clumsily and exited the Stairwell of Death out into an uninteresting corridor lined with more iron doors. Exhausted, he took a moment to get his bearings then went left. As he followed the buzz he looked at his flute, his gloves and the doors and knew that the protection of the leather was more important here than calling up his magic through his music. He tucked the flute in an inside pocket and loosened the silver dagger in his sleeve. He was without magic for the moment but he wasn't completely defenceless.

He padded down the corridor and felt some of his strength returning. The further he walked from the iron staircase, the less oppressive the edifice felt. By the time he reached the door numbered '806', from behind which the buzzer sounded, he could walk without wincing and breathe without pain in his chest.

This was where the Shield's trail had brought him and in spite of the suppression of his senses by the iron around him, he knew without a doubt that this was where Princess Teagan Wayfellow made her home with a Shield of Light. Dax looked at the lock and realized that if he knocked politely he would announce his presence and defences would be set. This was too important to lose his advantage. He removed the grey gloves, tucked them in his pocket and pulled out his flute. He thought he heard the muffled scuff of cloth on cloth nearby but a quick look left and right confirmed that he was still alone. He played a perfect C to clear the air and when the echo died, he leaned close to the two locks and played a light, delicate tune with a Celtic bounce to it.

As his magic reached out he could feel the tumblers within the locks shift and move ever so slightly, but they stayed locked. He tried a different tune, slower in tempo and deeper in tone, concentrating so hard at making his magic work its way with the iron locks that he didn't hear the woman approach from behind. He nearly dropped his flute when she spoke.

"He's not home. I have a key. Want to try it?"

Chapter Fourteen: Oberon's Bastard

"It takes great skill to be both seen and unseen, both heard and not heard. The most difficult skill to master and yet the one a Shield cannot survive without, is attaining Balance."

~Shield Master Wei (circa 200 BCE while proofreading the Rosetta stone.)

oOo

Dax spun around and looked down at the woman. She was another beige, non-descript human exuding sadness and melancholy from every pore. She held out an aluminum key. He looked her in the eyes and smiled, knowing full well that this was magic he didn't need the flute for. She smiled back and pulled the key back a bit, coy in her own way. Dax stepped to her and took the aluminum key gently from her fingers. She was reluctant to let it go but couldn't resist his will. He held it up to the light, as if he could discern the secrets of the human world from its grooves and notches.

"Thank you Lady..."

"Norinne. My name is Norinne." She leaned in, as if expecting a kiss or a caress.

Dax obliged her and ran the back of his left hand gently along her jaw line, strengthening the spell. "Feicim spéir i do shúil, mo ghrá." *I see Heaven in your eyes, my love.*

Norinne smiled again and pressed her head against his lingering fingers. "Ach tá sé Ifreann a bheidh tú ag féachaint go luath, a ghrá." Dax's eyes went wide and with snake-like speed, Norinne stabbed him in the arm with a small, steel, throwing knife. "Yes, Son of Oberon, it is *Hell* you will be seeing soon, my love."

Dax collapsed to the floor and Norinne quickly dragged him back into her apartment. Once his feet were clear of the door she closed and locked it. The hunter from Faerie looked up at her from the carpeted entryway, in shock.

Norinne could see the darkness of the poisonous iron spreading out from his wound, snaking slowly along the veins under his pale, nearly translucent skin. "It's only a flesh wound, but the blade is iron so you'll not heal easily. As a matter of fact, if you don't get help soon, you'll die, and that's not what I have in mind for you." She nodded toward the interior of her apartment. "Follow me."

Lacking the strength to lift himself up, Dax stayed where he was. Norinne kicked the sole of his boot, though not too hard.

"Get up, elf. You may be fey, but you're no weakling. Like I said, it's just a flesh wound. Walk it off, or crawl it off. I don't care which, but bring yourself into the living room where we can chat." She left him where he was and walked through the galley kitchen and into the sitting area. Dax couldn't move. He tried, but the iron piercing his arm in conjunction with the iron surrounding him in the building was too much. When he didn't follow her, Norinne returned to his side.

"Really? Oberon's bastard half-pixie son can't handle a little iron? Well, that makes this all the easier." Norinne reached down and before Dax could react she plucked the silver dagger from his sleeve then snapped a pair of steel cuffs around his left wrist. He screamed when the iron touched his skin and Norinne pulled his sleeves back down and under the cuffs so that they formed a thin layer of protection for his skin. "You're dying, and that's not what I want. If you won't get up and walk, then we'll chat right here."

"The wound is great." His voice was weak and held no magic.

"The wound is minor, but I realize now that there's more iron at play than what I just stuck into you and locked onto you. The whole city must be making you sick." Dax nodded. "Then I'll be quick. My desire is not for you to suffer long, nor to die. I need you to carry a message back to Faerie, to your father. Will you do that willingly? Will you give your word or do I stick the iron in your heart and save myself the trouble of having to hunt you down?"

"I promise."

"You promise to risk your father's wrath in order to keep your word?"

"It would not be the first time."

"No, I suppose not." She helped him to sit up and leaned him against the wall. "This message is directly from Shield Master Wei himself. The Shield is not for you. Neither is the Princess. The debt owed by her father will be negotiated but not at the cost of lives here or in Faerie. Your father may have an almighty high opinion of himself but he will find the Warriors of Light inside his keep, armed with enough iron to end Faerie itself if he doesn't parlay and find a way past this perceived insult. We fight Dark because we *have* to. We have no desire to fight Faerie but if we do, it will be because we *want* to. We agreed to protect the Wayfellow Princess because it was the right thing to do. Your father has shown moments of inspired compromise and negotiation over the centuries, let this compromise be remembered for the compassion he will show in this matter."

"He will not be happy when I return with this message."

"Then this son of his will die, because I will follow you into Faerie myself and sheath my iron in your beautiful heart."

Dax's eyes went wide. "You would...?"

"We would do what we have to. No more, no less. There will be Balance even in this."

"And if my father simply kills me and sends another for the

Princess?"

"We have allies deep within Faerie. It's how we came to be protecting the Princess in the first place."

oOo

DW's desk was tiny but the computing power he could access from it belied the miniscule dimensions of his workspace. In his efforts to find a way to break the ShieldBreaker app that was getting their Shields slaughtered, he had decided to go with a worm that watched for one single source picking up massive amounts of surveillance data and then foul up the data on its way in.

His worm would twist and jab at and render every piece of digital data point-two degrees off of accurate. Facial recognition algorithms would miscalculate, GPS data would shift slightly, and chains of commonality would be severed and reconnected where they shouldn't be.

One at a time it wasn't much, but since the worm would do its work worldwide and then release the data back into the collection stream where it would be added to a whole and worked on from there by whatever massive cruncher the Dark had, the resulting mess would look close enough to the expected truth that they would go along with the findings until there was someone on the ground to actually contradict the data, to witness the errors first hand. By then it would be too late to backtrack and since he was using a randomly-generated sixteen-character alphanumeric signature key for each twist, even if they had all of his work, they'd never know which data to trust and which to toss out. It was simple, elegant and just might work. All he needed now was the go ahead to launch, and he wanted to see Master Wei's smile when the Shield Master gave it.

oOo

"We move, now!"

The members of Team *Zeta Cero Onze* were already fully suited up and armed so their response to Mao's command was immediate.

"Portman's in the can."

"Then kick the door down and drag him out. And while you're hauling his ass out to the truck, tell him no more double-bean burrito breakfasts—not while he's on my team."

"10-4."

The team scrambled to grab the gear they didn't already have strapped on and Warrun, the second-in-command, zipped up his web vest and followed Mao out. "What have we got?"

"*Rho Doce Huit* got themselves dusted by their target not thirty miles south of here. *Our* Shield just broke her out of Mountain View Hospital and they're travelling together, setting off alarm bells with every spell-caster in both hemispheres."

"Perfect! Where are they?"

"Major Spells says they're heading west but I just got an update on that ShieldBreaker thing that we're looking at a one-hundred-percent that our Shield is in a silver or grey Toyota Corolla."

"How the Hell did they narrow it down so fast?"

"He prairie-dogged when he sprung her, and based on the security video from the hospital and the traffic cam footage, we've got him. Last seen westbound on Highway 1 an hour ago."

"An hour? That's a big bloody lead. I thought this app was the latest and greatest. What took so long?"

"Apparently there are two-hundred-and-nine silver '94 Corollas in this town and since this damned province doesn't issue front license plates, analysis was bogged down. I guess they had to cross-reference with spells to give us this one-hundred." They tossed their gear into the back of the leased Ford Expedition.

"An hour? Hell, my grandmother could do better with stale black salt and a borrowed cauldron. Dammit. An *hour*. This thing has how many petaflops of power and the best they could give us is an hour old. I'm glad it wasn't *my* money they invested."

The rest of the team arrived carrying their gear, with Portman the sniper skilfully buckling his belt with one hand and carrying his rifle case with the other. "What's an hour?"

Warrun grumbled. "The lead he's got on us."

"Ouch."

o0o

"You've done well, DW. How soon can you put this in place, my son, and how long will it take to start getting results?" A wisp of smoke rose from the incense stick as Master Wei walked it over to the jade dragon holder on the shelf next to his elegant, white ceramic Buddha.

The young programmer grinned. "It's ready to go now, sir. I can give the command from my iPhone. As for the results..." He shifted where he stood, back and forth from foot to foot, knowing that this was the answer that mattered most. "It's an accumulative thing, sir. It'll multiply geometrically so it will move fast, but the results will be subtle. I'm monitoring a half-dozen controlled feeds from source to destination so I'll be alerted to even the slightest change."

"It sounds 'insidious', almost like something the other side would appreciate. Once again, my son, I am very glad you are on our team. Somehow please relay to your friend that I—*we*—are eternally grateful for her assistance and we most definitely do not underestimate the risk she has taken."

"Thank you, sir, I will."

"You trust her implicitly?"

"I do, sir."

"Then release your worm." DW took out his phone and sent the command. "Knowing you as well as I do, my son, I'm sure you've given it a cool name."

"Trickle."

"Trickle? An interesting choice. Enlighten me, please."

"Well, a trickle of water can adapt to any terrain and given time will wear down even the largest mountain."

"That, my son, is perfect. Sublime yet succinct. Of course I do hope that our Trickle doesn't take an eon to wear down this ShieldBreaker."

"If my calculations are even close, ShieldBreaker could be in serious trouble within forty-eight hours."

"Ah, so you do have a number."

"There are so many variables, sir, that I can't make any promises. If they're prepared for this eventuality they could have countermeasures in place."

"And they will *kill* this 'Trickle'?"

"No, but they could reduce its effectiveness and speed enough to get a bit more mileage out of ShieldBreaker before it grinds to a halt."

"I have faith in both your own abilities and in Trickle's potential. Be proud of what you've done."

"Thank you, sir."

"Now, I believe you have just enough time to get to Brother Paul's service for the victims of the three 'events'."

DW checked his watch. "Thank you, sir. I'll let you know as soon as Trickle shows any results."

"I appreciate that. Now go. I'll be along shortly."

DW left and the Shield Master picked up the wooden mallet beside his contemplation mat and hit the brass gong with a short, sharp strike. The deep tone filled the sanctuary and he let it vibrate through his system feeling it deep in his millennia-old soul. These were off-Balance times, but he managed a small smile as the tone faded away, leaving him alone with the tinkling fountain in the corner while his own 'trickle' eroded the sense of Dark that couldn't help but creep into his sphere.

oOo

Brother Paul watched the nearly one hundred Campus Lux staff file out of the massive, glass-roofed, sod-floored Peace Lounge, their conversations as upbeat as could be expected. It had been the darkest day any of them could remember but he'd tried to make it a celebration of Life and Light, not a bitch session about the shift of Balance with a plane crash, a volcano, and the stunning fire that had wiped the ancient Black Forest off the map.

He himself was still struggling with the power of the lightning storm that had manifested in Southern Germany. When Brother Abiel interrupted the service with the breaking news that they'd recovered the Bracers of Atlantis in a shock-troop raid on the ground in China, the spirits of those in attendance rose up and Paul was able to send them away with hope. He kept mum on the fact that they were still missing the Holy Grail and Gajaraja's Monkey.

Ozzy lay with his head on his paws in the grass next to the forty-foot-wide circular sand garden as his master walked the rake back and forth across it, erasing all signs of staff interaction, including his own footprints. Barefoot, Paul moved slowly and deliberately, feeling the fine coral pink sand caress the bamboo rake, his eyes half-closed as he let the task draw away the darkness while the sunlight slanting through the glass above warmed his robes and the body within. So closely bonded were dog and master that as Paul's breathing slowed and his chi evened out and leveled off, so did Ozzy's.

By the time Brother Paul was satisfied that the sand garden was in order and his soul was settled, he placed the rake in its stand and nodded to Master Wei who relaxed in the shadows.

"That was a beautiful service, Paul—and much needed."

"Thank you, Brother. As always I'm honored to be able to acknowledge the sacrifices and losses, but it is a task I wish never had to be performed again."

"The Dark is as necessary for Balance as Light is, but I do understand what you're saying. I, too, wish there were a better way. I would step up and into the blade of Dark myself, if it would end the massive losses of innocent lives and achieve perpetual Balance."

"As would I." Ozzy nuzzled Paul's leg with his large head and Paul smiled. "We both would."

"There is some good news, though, Paul—a card I've been holding close to my chest in order to keep the curious ears from grasping it and the wayward tongues from forwarding it beyond our walls. It's time I brought you up to date." He motioned to the freshly raked sand and made a circle motion with his hands. Paul understood and nodded.

The two men closed their eyes, took two deep breaths to focus their chi and stepped from the grass onto the sand, except that this time Paul's feet made no impressions. Likewise, Master Wei moved to the center and sat, all without the sand showing any sign of his passage.

As soon as Paul left his side, Ozzy stepped onto the narrow stone border between the grass and the sand and paced the circumference of the meditation area. With every step he left behind a glowing paw print, and when he finished the first circuit the glows floated above the stone, spread and joined together to form a ring of pale yellow light. On his second circuit, Paul's faithful companion moved faster and more sure-footed and the glow deepened. He nearly sprinted the third trip around and when it was done he sat on the stone and barked once. The result was immediate and within the circle Paul felt rather than saw the ring spring up and become a golden dome of power over their heads, nearly touching the skylights of the Peace Lounge. As long as Ozzy remained in place, on guard, the two men were completely isolated from the outside world in both time and place.

Master Wei looked down and confirmed that the glow passed beneath them, making the seal complete. "Very simply put, DW has developed—at my behest—a countermeasure to this ShieldBreaker app of theirs. He has applied his usual brilliance to the problem and we should be seeing the results very soon."

Looking around him at the security measures they had just enacted, Paul raised one eyebrow in question. "You couldn't have told me this in your secure office?"

"Yes, of course I could have, but the Dome of Silence is more fun, don't you think?"

Paul smiled. "Yes, it is."

"It's also very cleansing."

"Mmm, yes." He could feel the gold light touching his soul and pushing out the grayness that gathered there over time.

"My office *is* secure, but only this is one-hundred percent. We are here and not here and anyone not here with us, can neither see nor hear us in the here and now. You know?"

Paul roared with laughter. "You've been saving that one, haven't you? Working it over and over in your head to get it just right so you could spring it the next time we came in here, haven't you?"

"Not quite, but close." His smile widened in a momentary admission of guilt and then slipped away. "To be truthful, we are here about Brother Eleazar—Liam. I read your report about your recent visit with him and I'm concerned that we've put too great a burden on him. Between this illness of his, the fact that he has both Dark and Faerie pursuing him, and then we burden him with another Locus, one which is nearly impossible to conceal and almost as awkward as the Egg, we are asking one man to do so much."

"There is no one I trust more to carry this burden than Brother Eleazar. Even in his limited capacity he is the one Shield capable of staying below all radar. He has been with us since the beginning and has reservoirs of strength and wisdom we have yet to see the bottom of."

"And yet he has just broken Sister Chasina out of police custody in a hospital and they are traveling together."

"He did *what?!*"

Master Wei smiled kindly. "You were busy dealing with the disasters, so I kept the report to myself. But now that we are moving to stop this ShieldBreaker evil, we can look to our own house."

"He's with Chasina again?"

"We knew it would happen eventually. They are true soul mates and the more time that passed, the more likely it was that they would stumble upon each other once again. Of course, it certainly did not help that in surviving the most recent attack and killing all six of her Hunters in front of witnesses, she made the news at least locally. Thank goodness there was no video or it would have gone viral by now and we'd never see the end of it."

"What do you propose?"

"I was hoping you might have a suggestion. I would love to send in three or four heavily-armed retrieval teams to back them up, but until we know for a fact that ShieldBreaker is no longer in play, we can't risk having teams away from their bases trying to keep up with two Shields on the run."

"So we keep their own teams on stand-by and wait until they call for help?"

"We do. Which makes me wonder why Chasina did not call for assistance when she was under attack."

"The system is still new, relatively speaking, and it's possible that she just forgot."

"Or was out of range. Please have someone in Systems Diagnostics look into it, just to make sure that DET hasn't devised a way to block our signals. I don't understand all of the technical details, but I was sure we had designed the Emergency Transmitter System to be self-testing and capable of avoiding any tracking not keyed to our codes."

"That's my understanding as well, but I'll have them investigate immediately." He took a long breath and focused his thoughts. "Are we coming up on a Great Shift? Is the Balance about to be lost?"

"My heart tells me 'no', but the tingling in my spine tells me it's time to go to DEFCON 1, as our American friends say."

"Then I'll do as you've asked, immediately, and I'll personally oversee what's happening with Liam-who-was-born-Eleazar. Would that we could bring them here and protect them within this dome."

"A good thought, but we could never protect them en route and they would be tracked to our door. We might be able to hide them once they arrived, but there would be an army on our threshold ready to burn the place down around our ears. No, they have to stay in play, stand their ground."

"You don't think they'll split up and go underground, back into hiding?"

"Their love is too strong and his need is too deep, Paul. She won't leave him to face his two teams of Hunters alone, especially since he's guarding the Princess. I know they will stand and fight, whether or not they know it yet themselves."

Ozzy barked his warning that the dome was about to fail and the two men stood, signally him to end it. The dog nodded once and the golden dome dissolved and floated off in all directions, back into the rarified mountain air. Wei and Paul stood and walked back to the grass, this time leaving their marks in the sand. Paul looked back at the footprints and shook his head.

"I just finished raking."

"Leave it. Break your Pattern. Someone will come along and take their own pleasure in the raking. We cannot do everything ourselves, only that which we are uniquely qualified for."

"Amen, Master."

Time was running out for the Forces of Light to prepare for the battles ahead so the two men split up and sprinted off to their tasks, Ozzy racing alongside his master.

oOo

Tatsuaki picked up his skim milk latte from the counter and worked his way through the forever-crowded coffee shop to the street counter seat Jiro was saving for him. Tatsu watched the lunch-hour sidewalk crowd flow past, a river of humanity oblivious to the genius sitting an arm's-length away, getting his caffeine fix.

"You're late, cousin."

"Encryption problems." It was a statement of fact, not an apology.

"You really went ahead and did it?"

"Yes. Here, I'll show you." He pulled out his tablet and with a few deft strokes pulled up the live feed of his stock transactions.

Jiro flinched when he saw the numbers flashing past showing Tatsu's redirected funds make sashimi of some corporation with the strange name of DökktEfniTækni. "Am I an accessory now because I've seen this?"

"I don't see why you would be. You know nothing about the company or exactly what I'm doing. What would you do? Tell the police that your crazy cousin showed you some flashing numbers on his computer and it might mean something big to some corporate Godzilla?"

"I suppose not..."

"Even the Securities Exchange would shake your hand, say 'Thank you for your concern' and walk you back down to Kasumigaseki Street. Cousin, you worry too much. This will all be over by the end of the day."

"What about the profits?"

"There won't be any. It will all collapse in a heap when it's over."

Jiro lowered his voice. "They will hunt you down like a dog, Tatsu, and so will the people you are stealing the money from."

"What money? It's all just numbers. Besides, I hacked their own bank accounts to finance the whole thing."

"Their own accounts?!" His voice raised but he caught himself before he was shouting. "You... you... that's... *brilliant.*"

"Yes, thank you."

"But what if you're caught. You'll spend the rest of your life in prison."

A woman's voice interrupted them. "Oh, Tatsu is too smart for that. There will be no prison for Tatsuaki."

The cousins turned on their stools to face the young Japanese woman looking up at them from the sidewalk through the open window. She held a student's book bag and looked like a sad, half-smiling university student. "Tatsu, I'm so sorry to hear about your sister."

Tatsu stood up so fast he knocked over his stool. "What about Takeko? What's happened?! Who *are* you?"

"I'm just a friend of a friend."

"But what about my sister?"

"Oh yes. So sad, her losing both her brother and her cousin on the same day. Quite tragic."

"But I'm her brother and this is her cousin."

"Yes, of course you are." She then pulled her left hand out of her bag and before either of the young men recognized the silenced gun for what it was she shot them both twice in the chest and once in the head.

The two girls at the next table interrupted their texting only when the corpses of the two men slumped to the floor but they didn't start screaming until they saw the blood spreading out on the polished white tiles. In all the confusion and commotion no one saw a young woman take a step back from the coffee shop window and get swept away with the river of pedestrians.

o0o

"Don't even open your mouth if the news isn't good, perfect even." Tau Drake glowered at Rance Nickols who stood on the other side of Drake's desk with his hands in his pockets.

"He was brilliant, but our people were better, especially that Sokolowski girl. We've stopped the hemorrhaging and are well on the way to reversing it."

"*He*? One son of a bitch did this? Does he have a death wish?"

"If he did, it's been granted. He no longer poses a risk."

"Perfect. Now kill everyone in his family. I want his gene puddle dried up and wiped off the planet."

"Gladly. Except for his sister."

"I don't care if she's Jennifer-Connelly-gorgeous, kill her. Spare no one—not Grandma, not baby Huey. Kill them all." His tone left no room for argument.

"His sister is the Shield we just captured in Cape Town."

"A Shield?!"

"She's chained up in one of our corporate jets right now."

"Double the guard on her. I want her alive and healthy when she arrives. Not a break, a cut, or even a bruised hymen. No one touches her. No one is to get more pleasure from her torture than I will."

"I'll set it up myself."

"Of course you will."

oOo

The blood made her bindings slippery so Takeko twisted, ignoring the pain rampaging through her muscles, especially her shoulders and thighs that took the brunt of the abuse. On her side in the crate she arched her back to get as much slack as she could into the cord hog-tying her hands to her feet behind her back. She knew that if she could get her right sandal off there was a small razor-sharp ceramic blade in the sole, beneath the heel pad.

She took a deep breath, let it out slowly and arched, then she arched her back a bit more and, certain she was close, squeezed the last vestige of air from her lungs and arched beyond the pain. The fingers of her right hand reached out and at last found the heel strap of the sandal. She concentrated on what her numbing fingers were telling her and pulled the strap down and off. The sandal slipped off her foot and dropped the two inches to the bottom of the crate.

She relaxed her back and let her wrists and ankles take back the pressure of the cord. The fresh pain made her cry out but she bit her lip to contain it, to keep her captors from wondering what she was on about. Takeko wept in silence. She had never known such agony and if she had, somewhere in her centuries as a Shield, she couldn't remember it right now, in the ass-end of the beast thirty thousand feet up. Ignoring the tears, she felt around behind her and found the cast-off sandal. Her fingers getting more numb, she fumbled with the heel pad on the sole. Once it was free she went after the blade. She nicked her thumb on the blade as she pried it loose but she managed to hold on to it.

She cut the cord connecting her wrists to her ankles and the release was almost as excruciating to her joints as being tied had been. She cut herself twice more trying to get the blade onto the cord binding her wrists but once she did it went through effortlessly and the cord snapped like a guitar string breaking.

Even with her hands free, the strain on her shoulders had been so bad that it took a minute of gentle twisting and turning before Takeko could get her right arm forward. She rolled over on her back, her knees tight to her chest within the claustrophobic crate and once her weight was off it, she brought her left arm forward. The relief brought more tears but they didn't keep her from cutting her ankles free. As the blood flowed back into her extremities she wanted to scream out, to rage against the shafts of red-hot agony spiking in her hands and feet but instead she rejoiced in silence.

o0o

"Lost three, in hours." Coriander had found Liam again through the blood spell and Liam got Becca to pull over in the dark parking lot at Castle Junction.

"Three?" Liam didn't doubt what Coriander was telling him, he was just simply astounded at the sudden loss of Shields. If not for her own vigilance, Becca would have been number four. "Traitor?" he asked.

"No traitor. Smartphone app and supercomputer."

"Inevitable, I guess. Resulting disasters?"

"Mediterranean plane crash, Javanese volcano, Black Forest lightning storm."

"Just a storm? Not bad."

"Forest burned. All gone."

"Black Forest *gone?*"

"Truth."

"Damn."

"Double damn."

Becca put her hand on Liam's arm to remind him that she was there. As soon as her skin touched his she felt Coriander as a presence in the car with them.

"Grandma here, too. Want to try and talk?"

Silence echoed from Coriander's end of the blood link and Liam thought they'd lost the connection. "Cor?"

Her 'voice' was shaky when she spoke again. "There? Lynette *there*? Oh, no. Not good. Dark tracking…"

"Becca. I'm Becca now. Short talk. You're right. Not good, but maybe our only chance."

"Oh-kay. Short. Must be."

o0o

It had been raining for three straight weeks in Prague and Anton was ready to stand on the roof and scream at the clouds, but he resisted the urge, knowing full well it was the kind of attention a Shield had to avoid. The rain was making him crazy, though, and he had to do something. He wasn't due down at the docks for another three hours so maybe the roof wasn't such a bad idea, provided he resisted the urge to scream his frustration out across the Old Town Square. The lights of European cities stirred his blood, making him rejoice in his soul's antiquity, and none did it more so than the capital of the Czech Republic.

From the rooftop he would see the whole city laid out before him. He looked out the window, his Shield's caution making him stand to one side. It rained still, but it wasn't coming down nearly as heavily as it had been a few hours ago. He scratched his moustache, looked at the old grandfather clock staring impassively back at him, and made up his mind. If he couldn't redirect the rain to Germany's Black Forest to extinguish that disastrous inferno filling the news broadcasts, then the least he could do was wander up the stairs and let his soul be scrubbed clean along with this magnificent city in the hours before dawn. The news footage of the ravaging of the Black Forest was a blot in his heart.

Anton checked his Locus—the last vial of the Lemurian Pollen— in the pouch on his belt, clipped his always-loaded Colt next to the pouch, tossed on his dark wind-breaker, grabbed his umbrella, hung his Nikon around his neck, and locked the flat behind him. He moved silently toward the narrow stairs leading up to the tiny rooftop garden he'd built last summer. The building was its usual waiting-quiet at three-o'clock in the morning, though there seemed to be a faint light and a bit of movement within the flat of his new tennants. He slipped the Colt around to the front of his belt and unzipped his jacket a few inches up from the bottom. They were a nice couple whose young baby never seemed to fuss much during the night, but he was a Shield, always and forever, and that meant caution when others usually trusted.

The humidity made the door to the roof stick so Anton leaned the umbrella against the yellowed plaster wall, got a better grip on the door and pushed. A powerfully built stevedore, he didn't have to push too hard, but the door shrieked insanely as it swung open. He stopped it mid-scream, hoping no one had heard. It was a solid building but that was one helluva banshee's wail. Tomorrow he would oil the hinges, but in the meantime he propped the door open with an old brick so he would only have to squeak it once more, when he came back in. Opening the umbrella, he stepped out into the hot, damp summer air.

The clouds seemed to recognize him and the rain petered off to stop completely by the time he reached the low wall overlooking the street a hundred feet below. Prague sparkled, washed clean, with the Žižkov TV Tower dominating the skyline off in the distance. He looked up at the clouds one more time as if he could confirm they weren't going to dump a deluge on him, then he put the umbrella aside so he could raise the Nikon to his eye. He checked the meter and knew that it was too dark out to shoot hand-held but his tripod was back downstairs. Compromise was his watchword so he leaned against the building's west chimney, let out his breath, held it, and took the photo. When it popped up on the three-inch screen on the back of the digital SLR he saw that at least at that size it was a crisp, clean image. A soft voice behind him gave him a start.

"Such a beautiful, peaceful time of the morning." The somewhat chunky but still quite pretty young neighbor stood silhouetted in the doorway, rocking her blanket-wrapped baby gently in her arms. The old incandescent bulb in the stairwell shone through her nightgown and Anton found it difficult to look up at her face rather than stare at her legs, naked beneath the thin cotton. He felt his face flush when he couldn't keep his thoughts as pristine as a Shield's should be when in the company of another man's wife.

"May I join you?" She waited for an invitation, understanding that he was having a contemplative moment in the night.

"Of course. Please. It's too beautiful up here to keep it to myself."

"Thank you." She moved forward, her bare beet padding gently on the damp stepping stones of the garden. "I'm Kuba." Her smile was a little crooked, her teeth needed a bit of straightening, but her eyes sparkled like the city lights and Anton had another most inappropriate thought. Then Kuba tripped and fell forward, the swaddled infant leaving her arms as the young mother flung her hands forward for balance.

Anton let go of the Nikon and grabbed for the baby now in mid-air, but it was too late. At the same split second that he remembered that Kuba had used the singular when she asked 'May *I* join you?' he realized that the 'baby' was just a bundle of unoccupied pink blanket. His Shield instinct told him to grab for the Colt but his primitive protector's mind made him grab the blanket, just in case he was wrong, and there was indeed an infant in danger.

He caught it and the blanket truly was empty. Part of Anton was relieved, but it wasn't the part that saw the three muzzle flashes nor the parts that felt the bullets tear through and send the Shield's soul spinning to its next life. It was simply the part of the Shield that was grateful that no matter what happened, no child would be harmed here on his Prague rooftop.

Chapter Fifteen: Chocolate & Apologies

"If a Shield sees a tree fall in the forest and tells no one, did it still fall?"

~Shield Master Wei (942 CE while teaching a novice how to milk a yak.)

oOo

Liam and Becca both felt Coriander's mental scream and for the first time in over twenty centuries, the two Shields knew what the collective soul felt when a Shield died. The warp and weft of the tapestry of Life unraveled in one tiny little corner and they could suddenly see it in their minds. There was a flare of Light and then a little darkness in that spot before a tiny flare lit up far away in a distant corner of the tapestry. They all spoke at once, overlapping in the blood song.

"What in God's name...?"

"Was a *Shield*?"

"Think so."

"Means there's ..." Becca was ahead of the other two but Liam was close behind.

"...disaster coming." He finished her thought.

Coriander was stunned, but was still alert enough to maintain the link and to see what the other two couldn't. "Tornado!"

"Where?!"

"Manifesting..." She concentrated hard. This was what she did for a living and so it should be easy for her. There it was, a twisting of the pattern in the weave. "...manifesting... outside Houston, Texas. Oh God! It's F-5! Will kill thousands!"

Liam couldn't focus, couldn't see what she did. "Where? I'm not..."

"I see it!" Becca seemed to be more in tune with Coriander. "Huge! There'll be nothing left! Can we warn?!"

"How?" Liam could feel Becca's grip tightening on his arm, and then he felt something else—something small and hairy, with claws. "Phoenix? What are you doing?" Somewhere in his mind Liam heard an answering whistle but then Becca cut it off.

"Yes! That's it! Push it! Will away from city. Come on, think shifting in weave, ripple of 'away' and push up. Push out into Gulf! Keep from touching down!"

"How?" Cor sounded like panic was going to derail her at any moment. "*Can't!* Can't! I... too... it's... *working*! It can't touch down!"

"Push!" Becca directed the other two. "Will away! Redirect! Refuse let it down, make go to Gulf! Force it! *Let know who in charge!*"

"Can't see damned thing?! Can't help!"

"Liam! Picture Gulf of Mexico in mind. Picture ocean! Imagine power to shift wind and control it! Be Zeus and force will on it!" Pixie whistles and human grunts of strain were all Liam could get from the three women, but he did as he was told. He imagined the Gulf of Mexico and the salt of the sea spray. He pictured the white beaches and the blue-green waves and the deep, deep water. He tried to wrap his mind around the idea that he had a colossus' hands and could mold wind like clay and bend it to his will. He couldn't see what they saw but he could lend them whatever power he had here, in this place between realities.

Whatever it was he was calling upon, whatever it was they were trying to do, it was over as quickly as it began and the link snapped. They lost the connection to Coriander and found themselves exhausted, flaked out in the Corolla. Becca's fingers were still dug deep into Liam's arm and poor Teagan was collapsed across his chest. Liam was so drained that he could feel a deep sleep calling him down, but something in the situation gripped him harder than Becca's hand. He opened his eyes completely and looked around inside the car, looked outside the car at the world around them. Then he saw it.

"Phoenix! *Teagan!*" The pixie princess was in her own form, her spell having failed. "Becca! Wake up! Drive! Now!"

"What?"

"Her spell has failed. They're going to know where she..."

Teagan arched her back and woke up with an ear-piercing whistle. She shook her head to clear it, then looked at her hands. Seeing hands instead of paws she whistled again and a moment later was once again a Yorkshire terrier in Liam's lap.

Becca was sluggish, slow to react, but she was trying to focus, to see the situation. "She's back. She's a dog again."

"But she was full pixie long enough for Oberon's hunters and anyone else to zero in on her. We have to move and move now."

"Where to?"

"Back to Bankhead."

Harff.

"What do you mean, not yet?"

Harff, harff.

"Good thinking. Okay, get driving, take a right out of the parking lot and follow 93 South. We'll get up and over the pass toward Radium where she can 'go Pixie' again. They'll zero in on that and plot a likely intercept based on the two points and the time frames."

"We want them to follow us?"

"No, we want them to waste time trying to head us off, setting up an ambush in the wrong direction, while we go elsewhere."

"And you think they're stupid enough to fall for it?"

"It'll take us twenty minutes, tops, and if it doesn't work we won't be that far from Bankhead anyway."

Becca got back on the road and followed Liam's directions. Soon they were driving past Storm Mountain and west into British Columbia. After five minutes of driving on the dark highway, Liam covered her in a blanket and had Teagan revert to her pixie form for one minute, just to make sure the spell-casters and whoever else found her. She took a moment to give Becca and Liam both big hugs and then she became Phoenix once again. Becca took that as her cue and turned the car around.

"Back where we came from?"

"Back to the Trans-Canada then up to Lake Louise. We'll get our crap from the inn and then double back to Bankhead. It's the only place they can't sense her, no matter what form she's in."

"Really? Why?"

"The coal. Bankhead is an old coal mining town and the coal is everywhere on the ground."

"Dark Hunters can't find her in a coal town?"

"No, *fairies* can't find her. I'm pretty sure the coal doesn't affect the blood-casters doing the magic for the Dark. We'll still have to deal with them when the time comes."

"So it won't affect our Warriors when we call them?"

"I have no idea. It's not like we've had a chance to try this before. Just like always, we're flying by the seat of our pants."

"And such a cute seat you have, too." "I'm old enough to be your father, young lady!"

"Only this time around, old man." She smiled quickly at him, keeping her eyes mostly focussed in the dark road.

"Let's just concentrate on staying alive and worry about the flirting later."

Becca was quiet for a moment. "You really are scared, aren't you?"

"Terrified. Death I can deal with. Torture, pain, all of it is what we've faced over and over." He stroked Phoenix's head with his good hand. "But this isn't Buddha's Pebble or Ilo's Soapstone Ostriches. If they catch us, they'll kill her, or they'll trade her to Oberon and *he'll* kill her, or imprison her or whatever he feels will pay the debt owed by her father. I've been her protector for thirty-two years and I'm about to let her down in a way I'll never be able to make up for." Phoenix licked his hand. "I know you won't blame me, kiddo, but that won't make it any easier."

"So, you're saying we have no plan. Again."

"Pretty much, yah."

"Then this is the perfect time to talk about what the hell we just did with that tornado."

Liam chuckled. "As good a time as any."

"It looks like we affected it. Like we took control and redirected a post-Shield-death disaster. That's huge."

"Almost as huge as having the Dark surrender."

"Let's not get carried away. As long as there's Light, there'll be Dark. When you shine a Light on something it always casts a shadow, and within the shadow is Darkness. I'm just thinking that if we can redirect the inevitable disasters, then we can seriously shift the Balance our way for the first time in a long time."

"Sure, maybe. But look at the conditions we just created in order to do it. We had to have two Shields and their Spell-Singing descendant linked up in a blood-song with a pixie. How long do you think it'll take the Darknuts from zeroing in and just dropping a nuke on us."

"So you're saying it's not likely going to be a regular occurrence, this redirecting of disasters?"

"Not even close. Once more, maybe. We really haven't made any big long-term change."

"Damn."

"Definitely damn. Unless..." he let the statement drift off as he thought through the idea he was percolating.

"Unless *what*?"

"Unless we only do it once more, but use it to seriously shift the Balance."

"How? What's one disaster in the big scheme of things?"

"That depends on where it hits. They have to have a headquarters somewhere."

"A *headquarters*? They're not movie villains, Liam."

"No, they're the bad of the bad, the Dark that goes bump in humanity's life. They're ego personified and power most corrupt. They're tracking Shields with a supercomputer which means that they've truly embraced the Darkness in mankind."

"You mean they've become a corporation?"

"Exactly. That's always been the primary difference between Dark and Light. The individuals of Dark never have the same power and influence as the individuals of Light. A Locus is taken into hiding for a lifetime and it takes a team of Hunters to track and kill the Shield guarding it. A *team* against one. They've always been a numbers-based operation. There are one-hundred-and-forty-four Loci. No more, no less. There are thousands or tens of thousands of them. If we can hurt their numbers *or their leadership*, they could falter and there could be a shift in Balance that just might give us a chance to catch our breath."

"You really believe that, after more than two thousand years as a Shield?"

Liam shook his head, sadly. "Not really. But after two thousand years I feel like I need to do *something* to fight back. People die to protect us every day and I'm bloody tired of being one who gets to come back while others don't. I want to reach out my hand and crush the Dark into submission for a century or two."

"Now you sound like them."

"Of course I do. We are them and they are us. Maintaining a world with a Balance of Light and Dark is useless if we don't acknowledge our own internal Light and Dark sides. Ignoring our own Darkness is as useful as ignoring the world's Darkness. It won't go away. It'll fester and infect and grow."

"So we'd all be better off if we embraced our personal Darkness and let it free?"

"Don't twist my words, missy. We each need to look our Darkness in the eye, see it for what it is, and take away its power over us by not letting it run things. Can we use what we did tonight to take away their power, at least temporarily?"

Becca lifted his hand to her lips and kissed his palm. "That's what I've always loved about you—your ability to see things from a different angle than the rest of us and your desire to go left when the world is marching right." She took a deep breath. "Yes, I think we can do something, and yes, I think it'll be a one-shot opportunity. Don't ever tell Master Wei or Brother Paul this, but there are days when I want to kick the Dark in the nads over and over again."

"Ouch."

"And it would feel *so* good."

"Yes, it would. You do realize that whatever we do to them, no matter how hard and fast and deadly we hit them, there will be more to fill the void they leave?"

"Like you said, Dark is in our nature."

"But this once, let's at least give them one big boot in the 'sensitives' before they take us down."

"Count me in." She saw the lighted white-on-green sign indicating the exit to Lake Louise, signalled and followed the ramp off the highway. "But let's at least try and come up with a plan that will let us live long enough to get that kick. Do we have any allies at all we can count on out here or is it pretty much a matter of letting the Hunters surround us and then press our little beacons?"

"Well, we have a Sasquatch on our side, and that counts for something." He pointed to her left. "Left here then across the bridge and right at the next stop sign."

"A Sasquatch?"

"Beauty. She's a big sweetie."

"*Bigfoot?*"

Liam laughed full and strong. "Yes ma'am, though I wouldn't call her that to her face if I were you."

oOo

Liam gave Becca the key card and guarded the car with Phoenix while the Shield of his heart grabbed the few things they'd had to leave behind in their rush to rescue her in Calgary. Becca was quick, efficient and quiet, and they were on the road again in ten minutes.

"Back the way we came?"

"I'm torn about that. There're two roads from here to Banff. There's the Bow Valley Parkway which is a slower speed, two-lane back road, and there's the massive, twinned Trans-Canada Highway."

"Why are you torn? It's a no-brainer. First off, we need speed. Secondly, we have a lot more room to maneuver on a big, multi-lane highway. I'm sure the back road is pleasant and scenic, but it also sounds too easy to set up an ambush on."

"Then take this exit and get us back on the Trans-Canada."

"So, back the way we came, then?" She followed his directions and sped down the on-ramp from Lake Louise Drive.

"Yes, smart ass, back the way we came."

"Good idea. I'm glad you thought of it."

"Just shut up and drive, Lover. Gloating is such an ugly habit."

"Yes sir." She laughed and Liam wanted to kiss her but also didn't want to distract her at highway speed. Instead he reached over and squeezed her hand on the steering wheel then lifted Phoenix up and between the seats and gently placed her on the back seat on her blanket. He tried to reach his nylon weapons bag but his body betrayed him again and he had to both unfasten the seat belt and recline his seat in order to make the grab. He hauled everything up front and when he got the seat back upright and his seatbelt back on he started in on the weapons. One-and-a-half-handed, he checked every clip, tested every firing mechanism and when he was done, he moved onto the blades. He checked each scabbard snap, each closure, making certain they were going to open when they needed them to.

They pulled over just south of the halfway point at Castle Junction so Becca could retrieve the weapons in the trunk and after she'd strapped on one of Liam's holstered side-arms and the brace of throwing knives he kept hidden with the spare tire, she felt less naked and nearly ready for battle. Liam continued the prep of their back-up weapons.

Becca chuckled softly. "It's a good thing we're at war, Sweetheart, or I would be concerned about your predilection for toys that shoot, stab, and slice."

"I just wish I had a couple grenades, but shrapnel doesn't care who it takes out and I'm not the only one who has to stay alive here."

"You're so considerate, Li. Have I told you lately?"

"Every time you look at me."

"Well, sometimes the words need to be said out loud. I love you, Eleazar. I've missed you."

"Right back at you, Chasina. You're my soul and always have been."

"Good, because I could really use a cheeseburger right now and I think the police took my cash along with my weapons."

"I have cash."

"I love you," she answered in a mock little girl's voice.

"Yah, at least until I fill your belly with food and then you'll drop my crippled ass by the roadside and drive off with my dog."

Becca slapped his chest hard with the back of her right hand. "Don't you *ever* say that again!" The fun note in her voice was gone.

"Ouch. Say what?"

"That you're a cripple."

"But I am."

"No, you're not a cripple. You move slower and more awkwardly than you used to but you are not a cripple. I hate that word."

"I'm sorry."

"It's such a negative word. We of all people know that no one in this world has ever been perfect. We all have strengths and weaknesses and things we do well and things we do badly and things we can't do at all. Calling yourself a cripple is a cop-out, an excuse for not trying. Calling someone else a cripple is an insult and a devaluing of their humanity."

"Becca, I'm truly sorry."

"I know you're frustrated, Liam. I know you feel that you're useless as a Shield if you're not able-bodied. But you have your mind. You are the most brilliant tactician and most efficient warrior I've ever met, and you *know* I've met a few."

"I promise I won't ever use the word in that context again."

"Good. The most beautiful souls can reside in the most shattered shells. You're only a Broken Shield when you give up and stop fighting."

Liam caught the subtext in Becca's rant and finally understood. "How bad was it?"

She took a breath. "It was polio."

"Son or daughter?"

"My son, Mtima."

"I'm sorry. Polio can be rough."

"Not as rough as the teasing and taunting and beatings he got from the boys and men in the village."

"His father?"

"Mudada was a good man, but he was taken by the slave traders and we never saw him again. The following year I became a Shield and having the responsibility of both a son and Mingmei's glass dragon kept me busy enough. I refused to take another husband, and so Mtima and I were ostracized and forced to live outside the village proper. Even our family turned their backs." She cried.

Liam pulled a handful of napkins out of the glove compartment and handed them to her. "Cruelty is unforgivable."

"Mtima was nearly ten when the shaman—*his own grandfather*—blamed my son's withered leg for the curse that the elders claimed was killing our livestock and withering our crops. The people shamed him, and when he fled back into our hut they threw stones at our home and shouted curses well into the night."

She drove on in silence, splitting her attention between driving and swiping at her tears and runny nose. Liam let her have the silence. Eventually she finished the story. "When the sun rose the next morning there was an unnatural silence in the hut. I'd been half afraid that they would burn us alive in our home but when we didn't fight back they all returned to their own homes. Even the jungle seemed to be quieter than usual and I soon discovered why. Sometime in the night, after I'd drifted off from sheer exhaustion, my baby boy had hung himself from a roof beam." She swerved the car over to the shoulder, slammed it into park and punched on the flashing hazard lights.

Liam released his seatbelt and pulled her into his arms as best as he could in the small car. Becca wept and he let her. He had absolutely no words that could possibly comfort a mother mourning her child so he didn't even try. He just held her tight and lent her whatever strength she needed.

oOo

The London office of DökktEfniTækni was much livelier with Mick away. The element of fear that ran through the cubicles and hallways was never completely gone but the pervasive dark mood lifted a little when Mick headed off to Santiago. There were conversations and laughter and even the occasional joke shared at or near the water cooler. For Simon, the best part of coming in to work while Mick was flitting about with the other pinstripes in South America was the amount of time he could spend naked with Marguerite, Mick's assistant.

Mick had left him with the warning that if he didn't find the Shield then he'd feel the wrath of Head Office, but Simon had people watching the airports, bus and rail terminals and even the ferry docks, so he wasn't worried. He even had some little wanker geek in Systems watching the video feed from London's two-hundred-and-seventy Underground stations. The bloody poof Shield would be found again now that they knew exactly what he looked like. The two spell-casters in the basement took turns reaching out along the ley lines and through the ether but the scent they'd originally caught that led them to this Shield in the first place was gone. He suspected that their problem was more with getting their little demon to cooperate than with any countermeasures taken by the Shield.

He opened the banking app on his phone, punched in his passcode and checked his balance. He'd been down to four quid when he'd finally passed out beside Marguerite last night so seeing his account flush and full meant that payday had rolled in again and he was ready for more fun. Marguerite's flat was fine for an occasional frolic and bounce but he thought maybe the two of them needed a night at the Savoy with room service and uncounted hours of playtime with all the 'toys of joy' Marguerite kept in her weekend bag.

Knocking back the last of the Bushmill's whiskey coloring the bottom of his tea cup, Simon left the fine china on his dishevelled desk and wandered down the hall to Mick's office where Marguerite was sure to be plugging away on her computer making his cousin look good with Head Office.

"Hey luv, anything interesting in the DET world?"

When Marguerite looked up from her desk she almost looked pissed that he had the nerve to interrupt her at her menial secretarial shite, but the smile she flashed changed his first impression and also changed direction of his blood flow to down below his belt.

"Just taking care of a few little things for Corporate, hon."

"Anything earth-shattering I should know about?"

"No, just some silly stock market alert, and a request to clean up a clerical error that's been on the books for too long."

"Finish that shite up and come into Mick's office—I need you to take some 'dictation'."

Marguerite giggled. "Ooh, Sy, I love it when you 'give me dictation'."

Loosening his tie while he strolled into Mick's empty office, he called over his shoulder. "How about the Savoy tonight? We could 'dictate' all night long in the lap of luxury."

"You're a naughty boy, Sy. Just let me send a confirmation to Corporate and I'll be right in."

Simon had his pants around his ankles and was making room on Mick's desk for Marguerite when she closed the door and came up behind him, encircling him with her arms. She hugged him tight and pressed her naked breasts against his back. When she wiggled he reached behind her to grab her backside and pull her closer, grinding back. Her left hand went to the waistband of his boxers and his moan filled her ears. He closed his eyes and tilted his head back and that's when Marguerite cut his throat and cleared up the 'clerical error' that Tau Drake emailed her about from Santiago.

It took a few more strong cuts but the former Dark Hunter quickly removed Simon's head and placed it on the desk for his cousin to find upon his return. Of course Mick's return depended entirely on whether or not Drake deemed him to be another clerical error to be cleaned up.

With no one to interrupt her, she had plenty of time to use Mick's private shower to scrub off the blood, get dressed, and get back to coordinating the fresh Hunter team trying to find the scent of the Shield DET had tracked as Arvinder.

oOo

Hussein put the box of Godiva chocolates outside Coriander's door then ducked back into his own room across the hall. He left his door ajar just enough that he would hear when she left for work. Cor's shift started in fifteen minutes so she'd be leaving for the caves any second now, he hoped.

A minute ticked by. He thought he heard her moving around in her unit but still no exit. He prayed that she didn't leave it too long or she'd be in too much of a rush to hear his apology. Just as he finished the thought, though, he heard the 'thunk' of her deadbolt sliding open, followed by the door. He waited behind his own door.

"What the...? Godiva's? Raspberry Dark? Who on earth?"

Hussein stepped out into the hall, nervous but trying to smile. "Me. An apology. A peace offering."

"You didn't have to, H. I'm sorry I snapped at you. I know you're not Dark." She opened the chocolates and offered him one, which he gratefully accepted—spell spinners and bowl singers were notorious for their sugar cravings.

"I *was* out of line, Cor. Some days I have to think this is just a regular job with regular hours and regular pay or I can't handle the idea that we're partly responsible for maintaining Balance."

She closed her door, locked it and started off toward the caves and work. Hussein fell into step beside her. She offered another chocolate but he declined this one, having eaten half a box of his own while he waited for her. Instead he dropped a bomb. "We know where they are."

Coriander nearly tripped on her own feet. Of course they knew two Shields were together but how would they know they were *her* two Shields?

"Um, who?"

"The Dark. This new tech of theirs gave them away. One of our guys followed data stream after data stream until it led to a complex on the outskirts of Santiago, Chile."

"Chile?"

"Yah, some major corp called DET—DökktEfniTækni. I guess Master Wei has suspected DET for awhile but that Hunter we caught gave them up."

"A crisis of conscience?"

"It sure wasn't for the money."

They left the carpeted hall of the staff residence and walked onto the polished floor of the outer caves. "How do you *know* all this stuff, Hass?"

"I keep my ear to the ground."

Coriander stopped in her tracks in the middle of the short corridor before they went through the security checkpoint and into the restricted work area. A 'eureka' moment struck her right between the eyes. She turned to her teammate and lowered her voice. "H... could you get me the *exact* coordinates of this DET place? I mean right down to the second, but without anyone asking why?"

"Why?"

"I have an idea, but if it doesn't work I don't want to look stupid."

"Will it put anyone here at risk?"

"Not at all. No. Probably not."

"Can I help?"

"Get me those coordinates and you could make all the difference in the world. Literally."

"You got 'em. Do you have to do whatever you're planning to do here, on site?"

"I guess not. Why?"

"What if you took my truck and drove out into the desert for an hour? Would that work?"

"I guess, but, again, *why*?"

"Because I think you're going to try something dumb and although I love 'dumb', I know it can turn around and bite you in the ass. If you do something and the other team tracks you and calls in an airstrike..."

"An *airstrike*? Are you serious?"

"Dead serious. Who do you think finances most of the military regimes in the world? Who do you think is the major military contractor supplying half the weapons to the troops in the west?"

"This DET?"

"Exactamundo, Cor. *The Dark*." He pulled a small ring of keys from his pocket and slid one off the split ring. "Here's the spare to my truck. I'll text you the coordinates by the end of your shift if you promise to tell me if you need help. I'll go fill it with gas now so you can use it any time."

"Deal."

"Cool. Go to work, show them why you're our number one spinner and, again, I'm sorry about my crack earlier."

Coriander leaned in and kissed him on the cheek. "It's cool, dude. We're all family." She stepped up to the retinal scan, spoke her name to the microphone and when the door swung open she jogged off to the caves.

oOo

"Are you ready? How far away is your access portal back home?"

"Not... far." Dax was having trouble focusing on the world around him.

"You'll have to do better than that, Dax. I can't get you there if you don't tell me where we're going."

He knew the place was dark and steeped in iron. He'd almost died there. "A tunnel."

"That's a start, but only half-a-step above useless."

Iron everywhere. He'd be forever indebted to anyone who could aid him in being quit of this poisonous middle realm. "It was abandoned. A Tube station."

"Tube? Oh, a *subway* station. That narrows it down a lot. The only one in town is the old City Hall station." She lifted the loose dressing on his arm and examined the blackening wound. "That doesn't look good at all. Stay put." She went to the kitchen and returned with a brown glass bottle, opened it and withdrew an eyedropper. "This is going to hurt like hell for a second or two but that'll pass quickly." She squeezed two drops into the wound but Dax didn't scream as she'd expected — he fainted. Passed out cold.

"Hmm, I didn't see that coming." Norinne replaced the dropper cap on the bottle and slipped it into her pocket. The wound smoked a little where the colloidal silver solution met with the iron and dissolved it but there was still enough of the toxin in the wound to keep the half-elf pliable and reliant upon her.

oOo

Rhianna glanced down at the beeping Smartphone on her desk and hit the 'Acknowledge' icon that popped up with the ShieldBreaker Administrator Alert. She barely glanced at Nickols sitting next to her. "This will only take a second. Two Shield locations confirmed one-hundred-percent in Seville, Spain, and Alexandroupolis, Greece. For the time being we have a human being..."

"You've got ten seconds."

She nodded and tapped the new icon for "Take Action". A message was forwarded to the Hunters in Seville and Alexandroupolis and the take-downs commenced.

Chapter Sixteen: The Indra Jatra Bells

"There will come a time when Dark will find Light faster than Light can run, and I weep now for then."
~Shield Master Wei (2006 CE at a cocktail party overlooking Park Avenue.)

oOo

It was a hot August afternoon in Sevilla, Spain, but the weather man on Canal Sur had called for cold and rain tomorrow so Lucia decided that a quick ten kilometre run would get her blood pumping before she sat down on her little balcony and settled in for an evening of editing her latest book of poetry. Dinner with Antonio was to be a late one so it was run now or run in the rain tomorrow. The decision was her favourite kind—a simple one.

She removed the synthetic bladder from her Platypus hydration pack and slipped her Locus into the bottom, before replacing the bladder. The oil-skin-wrapped case containing the Indra Jatra Bells fit snugly and with the tiny pillow of sky blue silk gently but tightly tucked between the two ornate brass disks, her Locus would be safe and silent while she ran. The Marathon de San Sebastian was only three months away and her time was still too slow. She was running a three-hour race and wanted to bring that down under two-forty-five before Spain's biggest marathon.

Her palm pressed against the sensor pad on the wall inside the flat's door and a soft beep told her it was armed and she had twenty seconds to get out and close the door. She was quite proud of the security system she'd designed to protect her Locus—bullet-resistant glass, steel-reinforced doors, Kevlar-mesh-backed walls, floor and ceiling, and a thorough complement of motion-detectors, cameras and a short-term, stand-alone, back-up power supply to keep it all running when the crap came down. The Dark would never breach her defences again. She was even considering contacting Master Wei to offer the designs to other Shields, all with Pattern-breaking variations, of course—it wouldn't do to create security systems for Shields that could be used to track the very men and women and Loci they were designed to protect.

A quick touch to confirm that her distress transmitter hung under her shirt, next to her crucifix, and then Lucia was down the stairs and out onto Calle de Colombia for her morning run through Sevilla. She felt alive and energized and ready to take on the Dark single-handedly. It was her last thought as Lucia.

The sniper was so far away when he sighted on the slender, athletic Shield and squeezed the trigger that Lucia only had time to subconsciously register the sudden silence of the street traffic around her before she was dead.

A little Fiat van pulled up next to the downed runner, two coverall-clad men jumped out, threw a plastic bag over her gun-shot-ruined head, tossed the body into the van and drove away, turning south toward the roads that would lead them to Gibraltar.

oOo

The afternoon traffic on the Egnatia Odos highway connecting Kipoi in northeast Greece to Igoumenitsa in the northwest was slowing. As the Greek portion of the E90, it traversed mountains, zipped through tunnels and roared over bridges, and Riccardo loved every one of its nearly one hundred kilometres. It was the perfect way for the thirty-seven-year-old Shield to get out on his BMW R 1200RT and get the dust out of his sinuses from working all week in the archives of the Ethnological Museum of Alexandroupolis.

He tried to pick less congested times to go but he had to be in Kerkyra on the island of Corfu for the evening meal at the monastery so it was now or not at all. His bed roll, a clean robe, sandals, his workout clothes and his lecture notes for tomorrow's workshop on Thracian Folk Culture were all packed on the bike, and his Locus—a fragment of Frejya's Midsummer Spar—in the wolf-fur-lined heavy leather pouch on his belt. Flexible steel blades were within easy reach in the thigh pads of his Kevlar riding pants. It was too hot for his jacket at this hour so he was stripped down to just his leather-faced Kevlar armour vest on top of his t-shirt. Wrapped up in his robe but easily accessible in the unlocked hard case behind his right hip was an Uzi with a long clip. It was noisy and messy but sometimes there was no other choice.

As he approached the Komotinis-Xanthis exit, traffic dropped to a crawl and Riccardo could see the flashing lights of the emergency vehicles ahead. Sweat trickled from under his helmet and down his back, under the vest. He was broiling in the afternoon sun but a chill followed the sweat down and he pulled over to the shoulder of the highway, trying to get a better look at what lay ahead. It didn't look great. The westbound lanes were a car park for almost a kilometre but he thought he could see it clear up before the off-ramp from the southbound Komvos Xanthis Anatolikos, which meant that he could avoid the whole mess if he just got off the E90 here and went north to the southbound-westbound ramp. Quick and easy. The traffic ahead bottlenecked past the accident just past the overpass and his Shield instincts were humming with warning. A narrow bottleneck would a perfect place for an ambush, especially if the Hunters were doubling as national Hellenic Police.

Riccardo climbed back on his bike and drove slowly down the shoulder of the highway, passed the stopped vehicles until he got to the northbound off-ramp. He kicked his speed up and cruised along north. He checked over his shoulder and no one was following him so he suspected that if there really was an ambush, it was within the accident scene and he'd just evaded it. He grinned and mentally patted himself on the back as he continued on. Traffic north to Komotinis-Xanthis was sparse so he got to the southbound-westbound exit quickly. An ambulance sped south toward him with the lights and claxons on full-tilt so Riccardo waited until the emergency vehicle turned onto southbound Highway 2 then followed it.

When Riccardo was past the farm buildings on his left he strained to see how serious the accident was on the E90, which is probably why he didn't notice when the ambulance slowed a trifle and the rear doors swung open. The first two rifle shots took out his headlamp and windscreen before the shooter got the range and hit the Shield in the chest before Riccardo could recognize and evade the assault.

He was punched clear off the back of the bike, which continued on without him for a short distance before slowing and tipping over into the gravel. As he got to his feet he heard brakes squeal to a halt behind him and reached for his blades, but he knew it was too late. To no one in particular he whispered "I'm sorry" just before automatic fire took his legs out from under him. His bike and the gun were too far away so, ignoring the pain, he simply rolled over to face his Hunters. A shotgun blast ended his agony.

oOo

The wind was crazy as it swept in over Aruba, but the cruise ship's crew had all seen wild weather before so the Platinum Sea Queen continued out of harbour to open water to wait out the storm in the lee of the Caribbean island. The weather warning alerted the bridge crew that the Szilagyi Waterspout Index was +9 out of a possible +10 but the Platinum Sea Queen was over a thousand feet long and had laughed at all previous storms. Besides, dinner was being served and it was the liner's famous once-a-voyage Seafood Spectacular.

The first dinner seating was just reaching dessert when the storm winds whipped into a funnel-shaped vortex, swept around southern tip of the island and tore the ship apart in a tornadic frenzy. Two-thousand-nine-hundred-and-eighty-three passengers and crew perished that night, including three-hundred-and-four children. Of the sixty-one survivors, forty-nine said the vortex looked like the hand of God reaching down out of the roiling black clouds to grind the ship to pieces. The remaining twelve said they were standing in line for the second seating for the Seafood Spectacular and saw nothing until the ship hit the fan, so to speak.

oOo

Estadio de Fútbol Maya was packed to the brim. Wikipedia had listed the brand-new stadium's capacity at 100,000 but Maria was sure they were pushing it to at least 110 or 120 k. She'd done a little research online before driving down from Corpus Christi to Mexico City to see her nephew's first professional match. Football was the beloved pastime of every man in her family but Carlos was the first to make it out of the barrio and into the big time. At seventeen he'd been at the University of Arizona on a sports scholarship but when the Mexican Football Federation knocked on his dorm room door and invited him to 'kick it around a little' at a few practices with the national team, Carlos was on the next plane south with a leave of absence, a pat on the back, and a 'go get em' from his U of A coach.

That was three months ago and now he was playing on the second line at the massive Mayan Football Stadium. Sure it was only an exhibition game to raise money for rebuilding schools after last year's devastating earthquake, but *her nephew was playing professional football!* She wasn't due in court back home in Texas for four days so she had plenty of time for a 'little' family reunion on her brother's farm. But first, the game.

The entire section she was sitting in had erupted out of their seats when Carlos ran out on the field with the rest of the second line and Maria's ears were still buzzing. She realized how much she was missing her family, especially after spending the last ten years busting her butt to make partner at the little criminal law firm her former UT Austin law professor had started up. There was passion and excitement here, south of the border and she missed that. Right now, at this game, there were no suits, no dockets, no continuances... just an unbridled love of life and the smell of natural gas. Gas? Why would she smell gas here? Food, sweat, beer, perfume, yes, but *gas*? She turned to her sister-in-law next to her. The crowd was still on its feet cheering the teams as they lined up for the playing of the anthem.

"Consuela, tell me I'm crazy. Do you smell gas?"

"What?!"

"DO YOU SMELL GAS?!" She had to shout to be heard.

"Did Papa fart?! He's always doing that! With him it's a good sign!

"No, not *farts*! Gas! Like for cooking!"

"No I..."

The gas leak was officially blamed on the minor ground-shaking they'd had earlier in the week, but the filed paperwork all said that the post-quake safety inspection of the stadium had been thorough and it had passed with the usual flying colors. Unfortunately no one could question any of the ten inspectors because they were all sitting in the stands behind the national team bench when the series of forty-two explosions ripped through the massive stadium and brought it crumbling down into the dust.

The pillar of black smoke could be seen as far away as Veracruz on the Gulf of Mexico and the fire would go on to burn for twelve hours before they could cut all gas supply lines to the stadium and fire crews could get the blaze under control. The screams of the trapped and dying spectators would forever live on in the nightmares of everyone present.

The next day a small law firm in Corpus Christi, Texas closed for a memorial service, and a teary office manager quietly composed an ad announcing an opening for a bilingual criminal lawyer with a shining smile and a huge heart of gold.

o0o

Master Wei found DW in the Peace Lounge, walking a circle around and around the sand garden, dragging the rake and weeping. The young man was so exhausted that he could no longer even lift his feet as he walked. The Shield Master stopped him with a gently placed hand on his chest and DW didn't resist when the rake was taken out of his hand and placed to one side. Nor did he complain when he was led by the elbow to the middle of the disk of sand and made to sit. Strong, wiry arms encircled him and he leaned on the shoulder of the man who had been everywhere and seen everything.

"Release the pain my son. First you must purge the poison up and out. Your thoughts are mistaken but they are still your thoughts and have weight. Pull them up, push them out, expel them into this place of peace and led the world carry them for you."

DW sobbed.

"Scream, my son, my brother. From the root of your agony, scream." DW kept sobbing so Master Wei took a deep breath, tilted his head back and punched out a scream from as deep a place in his history as he could reach. It was piercing, and startled the doves and pigeons roosting in the eaves of the building. Then he took another breath and screamed louder and longer. When he was finished, he panted to catch his breath.

"Again, please." DW looked up with a teary half-smile.

They screamed together and screamed together and screamed together. As the news spread around the campus of the two most recently lost Shields and the incredible disasters that followed, others joined in the ritual purging. Ten minutes later the campus was silent and the Dark had been banished once again from their thoughts. Exhausted souls fell into sleep quickly and quietly. Master Wei lay DW out on the warm sand and sat beside him.

"It is not your fault. You did not kill these or any other Shields."

"But I can stop the deaths."

"No, you are one man with a brilliant idea. You will not stop the deaths, although you may slow them and help maintain Balance."

"Trickle has failed."

"We don't know that for a fact. You yourself said it would take time. And how do we know that these two are not just two of the ten, which might have happened regardless? Maybe instead of losing two we saved eight."

"But that cruise ship and that stadium..." He sat up, slowly, exhausted.

"Yes, evil does seem to be winning, but we must look at the large picture, DW. After the Indian Ocean tsunami in 2004, then Hurricane Katrina in 2005 we thought Balance was lost. Then the Haiti earthquake in 2010 tore our hearts out and made us question our chances. But in the historical perspective, these are neither the biggest nor the worst losses we ever have faced."

"But..."

"But *any* loss of life is a disaster. The loss of any soul in this battle is a tragedy. In 1839, a cyclone in India claimed nearly 300,000. In 1887 the Yellow River in China flooded and claimed over a million. Less than a century ago, the Central China Floods of 1931 took between one-point-three million and four-million people."

"*Million?*"

"Million. My point is that we didn't lose hope then and we are not going to lose hope now. I have faith in your Trickle and you must, too. You are part of this team and you serve an integral role, as do we all. No one of us is more important than another, even amongst the Shields." He stood up and sand tumbled off his robe. "Take whatever time you need, DW, but do not waste it feeling sorry for yourself or taking the blame for the actions of others. *You* killed no one."

o0o

The Gulfstream GV was on final approach when Tabak's Smartphone buzzed with an incoming text message. He took a lazy sip of bourbon before picking up his phone to see who couldn't live without his business acumen for one single day. The caller ID simply said "L" but that single letter was sufficient to make Tabak sit up straight, rub his eyes alert and forget the bourbon. A tap on the screen brought up the brief text.

"ShieldBreaker is dead. Transfer to London Office effective immediately. Continue to current destination. Give your family my condolences. L."

Tabak read the message a second time, looking for any subtext, any reason not to take the message at face value. Nothing. It seemed fine. The third time through, though, he saw it. Nowhere did it mention Damian's name. This wasn't about Damian's murder at the hands of that damned Shield, it was about *him*. It was his termination notice. He took a deep breath. His heart pounded, so he knocked back the rest of the whiskey. Another deep breath and he pressed the intercom button connecting to the cockpit.

"Yes sir, Mr. Tabak. This is Captain Petch. How can I help you?"

"Reroute us to Dallas, Captain."

"But we've been cleared..."

His order was being challenged? "*Un*clear us, Captain. We land in Dallas."

"Yes sir. Dallas."

Tabak decided right there and then that Captain Attitude would be the first of the three-person crew he would kill once they'd landed. He replied to the text with a quick 'Acknowledged', and then sent a nearly-as-brief one to his wife. "Plan B." He didn't need to say another word. They'd long ago discussed the possibility that playing for the Dark would be a fatal decision so they'd set up a contingency escape plan and a coded message to implement it. With that single message his wife, Beth, would vanish, but not before forwarding the message to their daughter. They would meet up down the road, at a pre-arranged location, after a specific amount of time had passed. The Tabak family had just ceased to be. Miss Santiago was on her own.

The former executive sitting alone in the passenger cabin of the DökktEfniTækni Gulfstream jet opened his attaché case and under cover of the lid he screwed the suppressor onto the little Remington he carried, then he slipped in a full clip of subsonic rounds. The pilot *deserved* early retirement, but the stewardess gave great in-flight so he might even have a moment's regret after he pulled the trigger.

The jet banked hard to port and gained altitude, clearing Austin airspace quickly.

oOo

The return message came back as simply "Acknowledged."

"He's running." The Lucifer put the phone back down on the desk and leaned back in his chair.

"What did you expect?" Millicent used a tone with her father that no one had ever dared and lived. "Want me to intercept him? Pick up his family?"

"No. Let him run. We know where he's going and I'm not sure I want to lose his brilliance quite yet. Let's give him a year or so on his own to reconsider his decision and then we'll approach him from a stronger negotiating position."

"And Santiago?"

"They have at least one leak. Tell Drake the show is now his and he's to plug the leak if he has to call everyone back to take a lie detector... or he can follow Tabak into the wilderness."

"Done."

"Of course. Now, any progress on the Facebook deal?"

"There *is* no deal. We've got nothing he wants."

"Nothing? That company is a data mine and I want it."

"You're just jealous you didn't think of it first."

"Of course I am. Is there nothing we can offer this weisenheimer?"

"He already has everything. His net worth rivals yours."

"I hardly doubt that, but I get your point. I'd prefer full financial control but I want the data so have Tech get us in through a back door and we'll pilfer what we can while we wait for the cracks to appear in his armour."

"Yes sir."

Chapter Seventeen: Light Offensive

"It is because we are unnoticed by the scholars and forgotten by the history books that the Shields can do what we need to do, for the sake of Light everywhere."
~Shield Master Wei (1921 CE in the gallery of the U.S. Open.)

oOo

By the time Norinne and Dax got into City Hall by picking the lock on an Emergency Exit and then down to the locked steel door leading into the never-finished subway beneath, Dax was looking like he might not actually make it back to Faerie alive. At the bottom of the fire stairs he had led Norinne to an unmarked door beneath the suspended steps.

"There's a lot of iron down here, Dax, I'm impressed that you got past it all. How are you doing? I can take the cuffs off if you give me your word that you consider this matter settled, that you're going directly back to your father with the message that this will be negotiated."

Dax nodded and Norinne saw that the elf was weakening. She quickly unlocked the handcuffs and freed his wrists. Once she slipped the steel cuffs into her back pocket, she massaged his wrists to get the blood flowing again. Eventually his color improved so she sat him down on the stairs and went to work on the lock, listening for the sound of any security guards doing their rounds.

"Are you sure you can make it from here? Is it far?"

Dax took a deep breath and answered. His voice was soft and a bit raspy, but at least he had the strength to speak. "All will be fine, m'lady. Beyond this door sleeps a dark elf—a dwarf you would call him—who will guide me back. The natural tunnels start nearby so the journey will be quick. You have my word that I will settle this with my father."

"That's good, because I'm not really a killer but I will if I have to, I suppose. Besides, the Princess and Liam have enough trouble with the Dark Hunters after them, so not having to worry about an attack from Faerie will take some of the pressure off."

"They are hunted by others?"

"You didn't know? When Master Wei accepted the responsibility for her safety on behalf of all of the Shields, the Dark took notice of her. They've been tracking Liam—and Phoenix—for thirty-two years of our time."

"What will these Dark Hunters do with the Princess when they catch the Shield?"

"Kill her or take her God-knows-where. They want his Locus

most, but may see value in her as a bargaining chip of some sort."

"Then consider Faerie no longer a threat."

"You can speak for your father?"

"Let us say only that I am my father's son and not without my own resources in our realm. He will listen because I will make it in his best interests to listen." He glanced at the still closed but unlocked door leading into the abandoned subway. "It would be best if you leave. My tunnel-dwelling friend is of strong heart and stronger arm but not the sharpest pebble in the pond. If Halvor sees you, he may think I need protecting and there will be little I can do to stop him in the condition I'm in. I give you my word again, m'lady, and also that I will lock this door when I am through." Standing slowly but much steadier than before, Dax took Norinne's hand and kissed it. She blushed.

"Be well, Dax. You know where I am if you want to spend some time away from lithe, delicate, beautiful fairies."

"That is a most tempting offer, m'lady. Now, please, go. I may not be as strong as I'm letting on and will be needing the healing of Faerie very soon."

"I am sorry about that."

"It was your duty. I am sorely wounded but not yet mortally so."

Norinne kissed him on his pale cheek and trotted up the stairs and out into the warm evening air of downtown Calgary. It wasn't until he heard the latch of the door closing up at street level that Dax pulled his shirt sleeve down over his hand and opened the door into the dark tunnel. As soon as he saw Halvor, his short, broad, long-bearded guide, Dax stepped out of the harsh artificial light of the stairwell and into the tunnel, pulling the door closed behind him. He managed enough strength to throw the latches and relock the poisonous door before he collapsed. His last thought was that he couldn't die until he had entreated his father on behalf of the Pixie Princess and the humans who risked their lives for one who was not even of their world.

oOo

Warrun wiped the mustard off his moustache and glared at Mao. Their team leader had insisted on driving ever since the team left Banff. "Was the sudden stop absolutely necessary? It's a damned good thing I wasn't drinking a McDonald's coffee."

"It wouldn't have been necessary if we had accurate intel or a spell-caster who knew which end of his wand is up." Somewhere in the darkness, the Rocky Mountains stood huge and implacable around them. Hunter Team *Zeta Cero Onze* had passed into British Columbia from Alberta when they drove up and through the pass where all of the alerts had pinpointed the two Shields and the pixie to be but there was no sign, no clue as to where the Shields had gone.

"So they pop up on the radar here and then they vanish?" Mao was ready to put a bullet through something, preferably something fleshy.

Dolf, the team armourer, unlocked the rear door and climbed out of the SUV, stretching his back and arms when he was free of the cramped space. The rest of the team followed him out into the parking lot. They were close to their prey after a long hunt and they were getting worn out. Everyone just wanted to put this Shield down, recover the Locus, get the stupid pixie-thing back to Chile, and take a much-deserved vacation.

"What does ShieldBreaker say? Hit 'Refresh'." Portman scratched himself, pulled his underwear out of his crack and lit up a cigarette, making sure to step downwind and away from Mao.

"I just did. There's no reception up here in the pass. We have to relocate."

"No problemo." Juarez was the most relaxed of the team, but he was also the shortest at five-foot-ten and so his legs weren't quite as cramped as those of his teammates. "Let's drive a couple miles down the road and try again."

Mao took a swig from his water bottle, swirled the cool liquid around in his mouth and spit it out. "That's the damned problem." He pointed at the map Warrun had just pulled out. "We have four choices: north, south, east, and west. That may sound simplistic but it's the truth. Unless they're on foot, those are their choices, too. Highway 1 toward Lake Louise, back south toward Banff, 93 here west to the interior of British Columbia or, beyond Lake Louise, north to Jasper. There are also a couple minor choices. It's not like we can get parallel to them and then cut across and ambush them. We could travel ten or twenty miles before there's a road that crosses over."

"What do your instincts say?"

"My instincts say we're in the wrong province. She just came from here, or so says the last report her Team filed before she butchered them all. They know we were on to them in Calgary so I think this is a panic run. But they're not stupid, so they won't run blindly. I say we go back across the pass into Alberta and then I'll try for another update. We'll see what happens from there. We've got their goddamned photos and vehicle description so unless they've stolen something else, a camera somewhere has got to pick them up. It's just a matter of time. If we have to, we'll rent one of those cabins back at the junction and see what the morning brings. More damage will be done if we head off in the wrong direction in the dark."

"Works for me."

"Load it up."

o0o

Bob looked at the document in front of him. It was a mission statement and although he'd read it twice, the only words that stuck in his mind were 'Honesty', 'Integrity' and 'Trust'; but those three words were more than enough. He signed on the line to acknowledge that he'd read and understood it and in that single act he turned a corner and once again felt worthy of his son's memory.

oOo

Coriander tried not to think about the part of the equation they had avoided talking about, the part that made them all seem no better than the Dark. With the coordinates of the Dark complex in hand and two Shields and a spell-spinner prepared to direct a disaster to those coordinates, they hadn't discussed how they would control the timing. In order for the whole thing to work, a Shield had to die. It's not like they could just sit on hold and wait for the Dark Hunters to catch up to a Shield and execute them. She didn't have that kind of power and they couldn't maintain a link for that length of time. They needed complete control and that included the death.

She knew what Liam was going to suggest and the idea broke her heart. Her grandparents had only just found each other again. It wasn't like they could stay together, but that wasn't the point. They could keep in touch through Facebook or Twitter or just by old-fashioned email. It shouldn't have to end.

oOo

When they reached Banff Liam had Becca take the turnoff to Lake Minnewanka, but instead of pulling into the parking lot overlooking the ruins of Bankhead, he directed her a few dozen yards further down the road and up the fire road to the north. They bounced along the dirt track only until Liam was sure headlights from the main road wouldn't reflect off of the hidden car and give it away. He struggled with his seatbelt for only a moment before he released it. Becca was out and reaching for Phoenix in the back when Liam found his footing on the dirt and pine needles. They each took deep breaths and straightened the road-kinks out of their backs. Becca had had a bit of a break when she rushed in to McDonald's to grab them some sustenance, but he knew her pain-killing meds had worn off hours ago and her body kept reminding her that she'd been hurt.

The air was crisp and clear and fragrant with pine and spruce and clean soil. "This is amazing, Li. I could live in a place like this forever."

"I think we did." He rolled his neck to get the kinks out then addressed Phoenix. "Your Highness, I think it's time for you to go find

Beauty. We'll go down into the town and dig in. Will you be okay?"

In answer to his question she stood up on her back legs so he could pick her up. He tried but couldn't keep his balance so Becca stepped in and lifted the little Yorkie into his arms. She licked his face and nuzzled him closely. She knew she had to go and she knew this all had to be done, but after thirty-two years of being inseparable, this was the first time she'd be more than a few yards away from the person who had given up this lifetime to keep her safe.

"I love you, too, Missy." He handed her back to Becca who gently placed her on the ground while Liam brushed away tears with the back of his hand.

In a moment the air around the dog began to glow as she began her transformation. Liam sat back down in the passenger seat with his legs dangling out of the car then he tossed the pixie's t-shirt and tights next to the glowing maelstrom. Becca simply sat down on the road, unwilling to miss a moment of the magic. They both wept with joy as the lights and sparkles and magic spun and danced and cavorted before them. In spite of the Darkness they would soon face, the two Shields felt hope and love and Light there next to the ghost town in Banff National Park.

Eventually the tiny sparkling arm came out of the light and grabbed the t-shirt and tights and yanked them back inside. Not long after, the sparkles stopped spinning, the pixie lights faded and Princess Teagan—Heir to the Royal Pixie Meadows at Compton Down—jumped straight up into the air, did a double back-flip and landed her full two-foot-nine height in front of Becca. She hugged her and kissed her and giggled like the world was her playground. Leaping through the night air she landed gently on Liam's lap, grabbed his face with both of her tiny hands, and leaned in and kissed his forehead. Sparkling imprints of her little lips hung there, a blessing and a wish. She whistled once and was gone, off into the woods to find their giant friend. As she flitted through the trees, pixie lights appeared and disappeared along behind her.

Becca looked over at Liam and his tears mirrored her own. "That was... in over two thousand years, that has got to be... I'm absolutely..."

"I know. Me, too. Every time." He levered himself up out of the car and held his hand out to her. "It's a marvellous night for a moon dance..."

Becca stood, brushed off her jeans and took her husband's hand. "It most certainly is, Shield of my Heart." Then they danced and hummed and tried to remember as many of the words to Van Morrison's hit as they could. They swayed and stepped and leaned and shifted back and forth like they'd never been apart, never lived and died without each other there to protect and hold them.

At some point under the stars and sliver of a moon above, they made love. There was both the tenderness of centuries of heartache and the urgency of the reality approaching much too fast, all wrapped up in the moments they could steal, there on the forest floor on the pine boughs and the blanket from the back seat of the car. Becca lowered Liam onto his back and took control, allowing him to relax and concentrate at the same time. They got swept away in the long pent-up passion and when they were done and sated and exhausted, they held each other, breath-to-breath, heartbeat-to-heartbeat.

It was Becca who finally pried herself away from the melding, reaching for the dregs of the reserves of strength she had nearly tapped dry. "We have a battle to fight, my Love."

"Naw. Let's just lie here and let the world figure it all out without us." Liam smiled up at her as she dressed.

"Okay. Sure. But after that universe-tilting we just did do you think either side is going to ignore the fact that there are two Shields together in one place, doing the Hokey Pokey? If the Dark doesn't show up to kick our asses, then Master Wei should be along shortly to give us the lecture of a hundred lifetimes."

"Fine. Be right. Again." He sat up and pulled down the sweatshirt that had gathered up under his chin during their little romp. He had difficulty with it and stopped. Reality crashed down on Liam's head but Becca saw his frustration and knelt down beside him.

"Please. Let me." And she dressed him, with kisses between buttons and zippers and laces. Liam didn't forget the situation but he did let go of much of the funk and soon was being helped to his feet.

"What do we need, Li?"

Liam laughed softly. "Just all of the guns, ammo, armour, the Night Owl goggles, the guitar case, your tube, all of the blades—both throwing and slashing—and the blanket."

"Not a problem. My natural night vision is pretty good so you get the goggles. If you can walk, I'll hang stuff off of you until you say when, then I'll grab everything else and we'll get going."

"From lover to pack mule in three minutes—life is looking up." He quipped as she slipped the strap of her Loci's tube over his head to hang on his good shoulder, and she kissed him quickly.

"But such a sexy pack mule you are. I'd ride you down into the Valley of Paradise any time."

"I'll bet you say that to *all* the jackasses you go into battle with."

"Yup. Pretty much." She gently slipped the night goggles on his head then let him adjust them while she pulled his shoulder rig into place and added his two side arms and the three spare clips. He fixed a twisted buckle then Becca added the canvas knife bag with a long strap over his head and that was his limit. "When."

"You're sure?"

"Yah. Any more and I'll tumble down the steps and skewer myself on a tanto."

"Then that's your limit. Give me a second to load up and we'll get out of here." She picked up the heaviest bag, the one with the sound-suppressed rifles and their boxes of ammunition. "Will Phoenix know where to find us?"

"Not a problem. Both she and Beauty can see quite well in the dark."

Becca struggled to get the forty-pound bag's strap over her shoulder when she felt the weight lifted up from behind her. She swung around with a flash of speed, unsheathing her throwing knives in a blur. Then she dropped the blades and leaned hard against the car. "Holy sh—!" Behind her, Liam chuckled.

"Becca, meet Beauty. Beauty, as I'm sure Phoenix told you, this is Becca." The seven-foot-tall Sasquatch reached ever so gently out and brushed a strand of stray hair from Becca's face. Becca took Beauty's massive fingers in both her hands and held them to her face.

"You *are* beautiful!" She released the hairy, leathery hand and stepped into Beauty's embrace. They hugged like old friends. When the moment was done Becca stepped back and smiled. "I almost met your Chinese cousin a few centuries back. I don't know who was tracking whom, but we kept crossing paths in the high Himalayas for about a fortnight."

Beauty grunted and flashed her version of a smile, and then she held out her hands and motioned Becca to load her up. The weight the humans struggled under was nothing to the Sasquatch so Becca even took the blade bag off of Liam and hung it on Beauty instead.

"Where's our little friend, Beauty? She was supposed to stay close to you. I don't want her getting blindsided by a wolf or a Great Horned Owl out here. Beauty grunted and Liam gasped. "She went *where*? And you helped her?!"

There was a series of grunts and a snort this time and Liam relaxed a little. "I'll take your word for it, but only because you're as protective of her as I am; but I wished you'd stayed with her."

Grunt.

"Well, since she told you to come back and help us, you're forgiven. Neither one of us has ever been able to say no to her when she's being an imperious Pixie." He looked in the car and at the loaded females in front of him. "I think that's it. We gotta move, folks. Those spells-casters will have us cornered too damned soon.

o0o

"That son of a —!" Mao slammed his fist into the SUV's dashboard, denting the integrated plate covering the airbag.

"Who?" Portman was driving now and he voiced the question the whole team wanted to ask but didn't dare. In a car-full of weapons a furious Hunter Team leader was best handled with kid gloves.

"The Shield. He's double-backed to Banff. He just got spotted in... Vera Cruz? What the hell? This stupid ShieldBreaker thing is..." His anger subsided a bit. "... compromised. Total shut down. Effect immediately. Pull over, now. Before we drive another yard I want Warrun to cast and find this Shield." His phone beeped with a waiting message and he touched the screen to open it. Portman pulled the SUV over onto the paved shoulder of the highway, and then Warrun hopped out and quickly moved off into the ditch to cast his modified spell.

"It just hit the fan, lads. There are three teams in Banff waiting to rendezvous with us and share intel. There are two Shields together with three Loci and we are *not* to lose them. Hunter Command isn't taking   any   chances."

"We don't need help. We can *do* this." Dolf puffed proudly in the back seat.

Mao turned around to face him. "Really? This little girl just took out an entire team of Hunters. *Our* Shield has eluded detection for over thirty years. He's one of the originals and he's probably the best. Do you want to die as part of a team of six or live as part of a larger force? I've got a thing for living so you can probably guess which way my vote is being cast."

"Yah, I suppose."

"You suppose? There's no room for ego here, Adolf. During the Hunt it's one thing but this is Kill Time. We work together with however few or many we get and we make the takedown. If you don't like this then step outside because every one of the Hunter Team leaders on the planet has a standing order to immediately execute any team member not willing to play ball. I need to know now and so does everyone else that you're going to follow orders without question." His voice dropped to a rumble and Dolf's teammates shifted away from him. "Decide now, Dolf. Decide whether I arrive in Banff with five men behind me or just four. Decide for me whether I tell your parents that you're a man I'm proud to have watching my six or whether I get to tell them their little boy died in the dirt in a Canadian ditch with *my* bullet in the back of his head. Decide now and never make me ask you again."

"Yes sir," Dolf squeaked. There was no gun drawn, no weapon facing him, but he knew Death when it looked him in the eye. "I'm one-hundred percent yours, sir. I was just... I'm proud to be on this team. *Zeta Cero Onze* can handle what is thrown our way. But if orders are to be part of a larger force, then I'll do it and make you proud."

Mao tossed him the Smartphone. "Then reply to the message that we're twenty minutes out and will meet them behind the Whyte Museum, next to the Bow River. That's Whyte with a Y. It's a name, not a description."

Dolf started thumb-typing and a moment later Warrun got back into the Navigator. "Bingo. Looks like they're camping just northeast of the town, on the Lake Minnewanka Road. And no sign anywhere of the hunter from Faerie. I think they left him back in Calgary."

Dolf leaned forward in his seat and handed the phone back. "Message sent. Chief, are we good?"

Mao smiled. "We must be because you're alive to ask that question." Portman got the vehicle back on the highway and heading toward the rendezvous. "Now, everyone, it's game time. This will *not* be Tasmania. We will be *victorious*. The only prisoners to be taken will be the ones *we* take, which, by the way is the girl only. Our Shield is to die as planned but orders from Hunter Command have us bringing the girl back."

oOo

Beauty had insisted on staying at Princess Teagan's side but the pixie princess had whistled her friend away. Once they'd found the mine entrance and Beauty had made short work of the boulders blocking it, Teagan felt it was safest if she did what she had to do alone. She would never forgive herself if Beauty got hurt, and she couldn't predict exactly who was going to answer her call.

Once she was sure the air was good, Teagan climbed through the narrow gap into the old coal mine and sent a pixie light down into the darkness. Down and down it went and when it didn't return, she knew this was the right place. She started whistling a simple lullaby, urging the notes down into the blackness after the pixie light. The notes echoed off the dark, moist rock walls and strolled languorously down into the depths.

She looked at the parallel rails spiked to the rock under her feet and wondered if the iron would be much of a problem. It was too late to worry about them now, though. She picked up the tempo of the tune a bit and whistled a waltz away into the heart of Cascade Mountain. The waltz became a jig and the jig became a reel until her notes overlapped, layered the darkness and banished the melancholia of the capped mine shafts. Pixie lights sprang up around her spontaneously and she danced with them, whistled with them and called each by name. It had been but a moment in Faerie that she'd been gone, but a lifetime of hiding for her here with Liam in the upper realm.

She whistled and hummed and tapped out rhythms and songs both old and new. She made it up as she went along and then tapped into her memories for the old and faithful. She threw everything she had

225

into the calling, because everything she had was at stake. Her father's debt was nothing. The price on her head from Oberon the Overbearing was nothing. The life of the Shield and his true love were everything, and they were at stake. This beautiful, smelly, nearly magic-free world of iron and plastic and reality-trash television was all at stake, and she was a Princess of the Realm with the right to call armies forth, dammit, and that's what she whistled into the echoing hollowness of the Pacific Coal Company mines.

And then the mines weren't so hollow, nor so empty. The echoes seemed to get flatter and flatter until there was only the echo of a duck's quack, which was no echo at all.

"Is é sin an t-amhrán álainn, do Mhórgachta. Nó is féidir liom a ghlaonn tú Teagan, ó mé ar ríoga mac?" *That is a beautiful song, your Highness. Or may I call you Teagan, since I am a royal's son?*

Teagan stopped whistling and the mine was nearly silent. The bastard son of Oberon stood stock still, his sword sheathed, his hands away from his body in supplication and surrender, waiting for her reply; but there was a shuffling sound coming from behind him, from deeper within the earth. She saw a glow, a light, too, but it was no pixie light of hers.

Whistle.

"Níl mé ag iarraidh ort teacht liom. Tá mé ag iarraidh dul in éineacht leat. d'iarr tú agus mé ag teacht." *I am not asking you to come with me. I am asking to accompany you. You called and I have come.*

Whistle.

"Ah. Tá an scéal fada agus is é an ama gearr. Tá d'athair fiach atá faoi chaibidil go réasúnach agus tá mé a bheith saor ó rianú tú ionas gur féidir liom a sholáthar ar bith agat agus gach cúnamh. Is é Dorchadas an namhaid go léir." *The story is long and the time is short. Your father's debt is being negotiated reasonably and I have been freed from tracking you so that I may render you any and all assistance. Darkness is the enemy of all.*

Whistle.

"Táimid ag do sheirbhís. Is é an t-arm mianach ach tá mé leatsa a ordú. Ach is féidir linn le do thoil fháil amach as na ráillí iarainn... sruthán siad cuid againn níos measa ná daoine eile." *We are at your service. The 'army' is mine but I am yours to command. But may we please get away from these iron rails... they burn some of us worse than others.*

There was a loud shuffling from behind Dax and a troll stepped gingerly into sight, trying to avoid the rails. It wasn't so much that her excellent dark vision allowed her to see the great creature, but that he was surrounded by glowing pixie lights. Out from behind his hairy, muscled mass there came a giggle and a face peeked around his wide butt.

Whistle! *Cousin!*

Whistle! *Cousin yourself, Nóinín!*

Dax cleared his throat. "An féidir linn an deis seo le do thoil le chéile taobh amuigh? Gheall mé an troll mbeadh roinnt daoine olc a ithe." *Can we please take this reunion outside? I promised the troll there would be some evil humans to eat.*

Teagan pointed at the rocks blocking the mine opening and whistled. Dax pointed at the blockage and nodded to the troll. With what may or may not have been a smile of pleasure, the creature slumped up to the rock and very gently pushed it all outward, with very little effort. Teagan was immediately glad she sent Beauty back to the Shields. Next to the muscle from Faerie, the gentle Sasquatch would be but a scrawny weakling of the upper realm. With that thought in mind she turned to Dax.

Whistle.

"An féidir é seo a rialú? Abair liom a is féidir leis a itheann agus a bhfuil nó cad nach féidir leis agus beidh mé ag ceangal air sin. Sé le bheith lenár teaghlaigh ar feadh na mblianta Beidh déanamh amhlaidh dom ar an litir." *Can he be controlled? Tell me whom he can eat and whom or what he cannot and I will bind him to that. He's been with our family for years so will obey me to the letter.*

Whistle?

"Then let us go to battle, your Highness. You can explain to me what we are up against as we walk." They followed the waiting troll out into the Rocky Mountain air and were followed by a dozen pixies, twenty elves, and thirty dark elves that hated being called dwarves by anyone other than their mothers. Teagan whistled a command to the pixies and the lights were doused. There would be plenty of time for play when the battle began.

oOo

By the time they reached the parking lot above the ghost town known as Lower Bankhead, Mao had twenty-three Hunters under his command and enough experience and materiel to wipe out a small island nation. Against two Shields and a pixie, it would be quick and painless, even if they called in some Warriors of Light. He assigned half of the Hunters to switch to non-lethal means only and it was their task to bring down the woman. The male Shield was fair game and in the darkness of the mountain night they looked like a huge, shadowy Ninja force moving in on a helpless camp. Overkill was never a problem with him if it kept his team alive.

oOo

Liam and Becca holed up in the ruins of the Power House while Beauty hid herself up the coal scrap path and out of direct line of the Shield's weapons. Liam wanted her to stay safe behind them but Beauty insisted on being forward to watch for Teagan. Becca found the compromise position for the Sasquatch and they all settled in and waited.

Liam heard the approach of vehicles up on the road above at about the same time he saw what looked like dancing lights up the mountain face a ways. The lights were quickly doused and Liam just hoped it was in time. Beauty had explained that Teagan was calling for help through the mines and the Shield just hoped to God that whoever showed up would be friendly to their cause. It would suck to have armed Hunters in their face and elves on dragons coming at them from above.

"It's time." Becca took out her emergency beacon and darted through the trees to the shelter of the Briquette Building where Bankhead's brittle coal was once combined with Pennsylvania pitch to make usable briquettes. When she was sheltered, she pressed her beacon and waited. Back between the giant floor slabs of what had been the Power House, Liam was doing the same. He thought it best to have the two teams of Light Warriors teleport into different locations so as not to have them start shooting at each other. Besides, three Warriors were easier to hide than six.

oOo

The troll, Rinceoir, was hungry and as soon as the pixie princess explained whom he could and could not eat, he trudged off to find some supper. Man flesh was usually too fatty, but she promised it would be strong, muscled warrior meat tonight so he was happy. She did warn him to be quick and silent and not be seen because they would shoot arrows of fire that would pierce his hide and kill him fast, but he'd always been quick and silent so he wasn't worried. These silly pixies never thought trolls were smart.

Rinceoir had two flesh-stripped Hunter corpses in front of him and was sucking the meat from the leg of a third one when Teagan and company came upon him in the roofless ruins of the Lamp House a short time later. Trying not to be ill in front of the troops, she quickly rifled through the battered and bloody pile of gear Rinceoir had peeled off the Hunters and found what she was looking for. She handed the headset to Dax and pointed to his ear. He inserted the rubber earpiece into place and smiled widely when he heard a deep human voice directing what seemed like a small platoon of Hunters. He turned to the captains of the Faerie force and spoke quickly and softly. He pointed to the pile of gear and the captains quickly relayed the orders. Within moments every one of the Faerie force had rushed forward, taken a good strong sniff of the Hunter gear and clothes to get the scents in their noses and then gone off in groups of five, each one with at least one pixie ready to distract and confuse the enemy with pixie lights and giggles of mock innocence.

The troll burped softly and stood back up, stretching to his full height of close to twelve feet. Teagan smiled at this massive innocent creature willing to come along and fight by their side simply for the price of a good meal. She kissed her former bounty hunter on the cheek as thanks and then led her own little force of Dax and captains down the trail to the ruins below. Her cousin, Nóinín, tagged along beside her, obviously smitten with the tall elf captain who walked in silence behind Dax. Nóinín kept looking back and giggling. The captain smiled once and regretted it immediately because half-his-height Nóinín fell into step beside him and insisted on mimicking his every move as they slipped through the dark woods.

Dax heard something on the Hunter headset and motioned for them to halt. He listened closely and then explained quickly to the two captains. The elf captain lifted an elk horn from his belt and gave two blasts. Even to a human born and raised in the area where elk herds were common and the beasts grazed on lawns and wandered the streets, the bugles would simply be night soundings by a bull. To the elves, they were the command they awaited.

The dark elf captain took his hammer and struck a short pattern on a boulder next to the trail. The dwarven hammer code went deep into the rock and his troops got their orders. Dax quickly hustled the little group over to a stand of trees overlooking the plain of Lower Bankhead.

oOo

There was a lot of open ground in Lower Bankhead so Mao had the troops move out and stay in the trees around the edges of the manufacturing part of the early twentieth century town. His night goggles picked up movement on the far side of the meadow so he switched to his rifle and the telescopic night scope mounted on it. He watched and when he saw the elk bull lift its massive head and move off into the trees he lowered his rifle.

"There are elk out here and probably coyote as well," he said into his microphone. "Let's not get spooked and start popping off at the wildlife. Two Shields, one pixie. The male Shield dies, the female Shield *and* the pixie, live. Reports say that the pixie may be in the form of a small dog so don't let any puppies get away."

"Did you say 'pixie'?" The voice over the headset wasn't one of his own team.

"I did. The pixie is not a Locus but is as important to Corporate as if she were. There's also a sword, an olive pit, and a wooden pipe. We need all four intact."

"A pixie? We flew in from Montana for a pixie? Next it'll be a dragon or an ogre."

Mao was ready to slit the throat of the idiot arguing with him. "Would the Alpha who owns the moron please shut him up before I do."

"Nobody *owns* me, buddy, especially y—". There was a choked cry and a gurgle and then radio silence.

"Thank you." Mao would have liked to do it himself but one of the others had saved him the pleasure. He didn't care, just so long as the idiot was stopped from jeopardizing the mission.

oOo

The elf warrior wiped his blade on the Hunter's own jacket and placed the severed head down onto the coal-covered ground—this was no time for taking trophies.

Chapter Eighteen: Pixie Lights & Death

"The weight of responsibility borne by each Shield is incalculable. Self-termination of an assignment is uncommon, but not unheard of over the centuries and no one judges the Shield harshly. We can only bear what we can bear."
~Shield Master Wei (1528 CE, while peeling potatoes with Martin Luther.)

oOo

Becca's three Warriors materialized in the middle of the Briquette building and she welcomed them with her arms above her head and her weapons holstered. "Shield of Light here," she whispered. "Thanks for coming to the party. Get down, stay quiet, I'll fill you in."

The Warrior lead nodded and the three of them joined Becca with their backs to the walls.

oOo

The gap between the concrete slabs of the Power House was wide and the spell used to transport Warriors of Light kept them from materializing inside solid objects, but the three of them appeared in a semi-crouched position and their heads were exposed above the slabs.

"Get down!" Liam whispered as loud as he dared. Two of the Warriors responded immediately but the third one was a bit disoriented, having been told they were going to a national park in the Rockies. One of his teammates tackled him and then there was silence.

Liam raised his head to near level with the top of the slabs but could hear nothing unusual above the breeze. He knelt back down.

"Sit Rep. Two Shields, three Loci. Unknown number of Hunters. Assume six per Shield or six per Locus. Minimum twelve. Also present, one pixie, one very large hairy creature that looks like Bigfoot."

All three Warriors lifted their night goggles to stare at Liam. "Okay, she *is* a Bigfoot, but she's on our side. Also, we're facing possible friendlies from Faerie. We have no idea whose side they're on, yet. Just aim for Hunters and don't attack anything non-human unless it's to save your own life."

"Have you got any *good* news, Shield, sir?"

"Would another team of Warriors help?"

The Team Leader grinned. "Just a little, sir." He made an adjustment to his headset and spoke into the mic. "Light Leader respond." What he heard satisfied him. "Roger." He turned back Liam.

"The other team is here and briefed. Whereabouts is the other Shield, sir?"

Liam pointed with the cane. "That way. Thirty yards. Enemy starting point is two hundred yards that way." He pointed toward the parking lot at the top of the steps built into the hillside. "Faerie friendlies starting out above and slightly east of enemy. Been blind here since taking cover minus ten."

"Roger that, sir." He looked at the cane and Liam's curled left hand. "Are you injured, sir?"

"No, sick. But I'm armed to the teeth so go do what you do best and I'll cover your retreat if needed. Unless you've got orders to the contrary, we're full lethal on all non-friendlies."

"Copy that, sir. Lethal. No orders to contradict. It's nice to be called in before it's too late." The leader then used hand signs to instruct his men and all three dropped their goggles into place and slipped out into the night. Liam watched them go and whispered a prayer for their safety. A moment later Becca scrambled back into the weed-choked ruins beside him.

"All set, Lover. Shall we move into position?"

"Roger that, Gorgeous."

They each clicked the safeties off of their rifles and wiggled to opposite ends of the gap, Liam with the night goggles and Becca with a night scope. Then they waited.

oOo

Mao saw a burst of suppressed muzzle flash from across the meadow, but then nothing. There was no radio confirmation, no answering fire. "Delta One, did you copy that flash?"

Warrun was quick to answer. "10-4. Investigating."

"Copy that." At least he could rely on his own team to do the job professionally.

"Alpha One to Alpha Two... report."

"Lost contact with Gamma Two."

"Copy that. Alpha Three?" Silence answered him. "Alpha Three, do you copy?" There was no reply, and that's when Mao realized that this wasn't going to be quite as simple as he'd expected. "Alpha Four, I need you to —" A distant male scream interrupted him. It was to the west and it sounded too much like Dolf for his liking so he took off at a run, trying to stay as low as possible within the trees. Muzzle flashes appeared from the same direction but aimed at him and he hit the dirt. Slugs took chunks out of the pine tree to his right.

"Dammit Portman, it's me!" More muzzle flash and the soft thup-thupping of the suppressor not quite silencing the shots. It wasn't Portman. He raised himself up and fired a triple burst into the trees where he'd seen the flashes. No scream followed but neither was there any further fire. He moved forward in a zigzag pattern, doing his best to keep bigger trees between him and the target.

"Alpha One here. Has anyone sighted a bloody Shield yet or are we shooting at each other?"

"Negative. No Shield in Quadrant Two."

"Negative Quadrant Three. We had movement but I'm pretty sure it was a bear, though it was on two legs and moving damned fast."

"Quadrant Four... anyone home?"

"Negative in Quadrant Four. Wait... I see lights. I've got them! Moving north toward that coal pile we passed on the way in. Looks like the idiots are using headlamps. I'm in pursuit."

"Quadrant Four, you *must* confirm target is Shield before engaging. This is a tourist area and we are *not* to take civilian lives. Repeat: no civilian casualties. If in doubt, go non-lethal."

"Copy that." His voice was barely a whisper. "I'm gaining ground. Can't see targets beneath the lights, but man are they beautiful. Just like—" The was a short gasp and a sigh, like air being let out of a bag.

"Quadrant Four? Quadrant Four respond. Dammit. Does anyone have eyes on whoever that was in Four or the lights he saw?"

"Negative on Four, but I think I see the lights. Pursuing with extreme caution."

"I've got the lights crossing into Two."

"No, they're in Three, clear as day."

"Confirming Three. Hey! I've got some over in Two as well. Hey Alpha One, check your six. It looks like you've got three behind you and up about eight feet in a tree."

"What the hell?" Mao started to turn around but the bugling elk started up again. There was something odd about this one, though because to Mao it sounded more like a battle cry. If he didn't know better, he could have sworn it was a signal of some sort, but—".

Mao's thought went unfinished. The elven arrow pierced his throat and dropped him. Arrows and hammers and daggers and claws flew and smashed and slashed all across the ghost town of Lower Bankhead, illuminated only by the stars and a few pixie lights. The remaining Hunters died almost as one, with the exception of Portman.

The last remaining Hunter stood face to face with what he swore was Bigfoot, and he truly knew fear for the first time in his life. He carefully placed both weapons down on the ground. Then he unbuckled his ammo belt and dropped it. With two fingers he bent over and slipped his boot-sheathed knives out and tossed them away, out of reach. He removed his body armour and dropped it as well, showing that he was giving up his protection. He removed his night-vision goggles and turned slowly to show the beast that he was no longer a threat.

A twig snapped behind him and a deep, low, beastly growl released the muscles controlling his bladder. By the time he turned around to face the Bigfoot again, his pants were soaked with his own urine, but there was nothing and no one to see his humiliation. It was gone, as were his weapons and gear. Without the goggles he could barely see his hand in front of his face so the lightly accented voice that came from the trees to his left nearly stopped his heart.

"Run, Human Hunter. You have been spared. Return to your own as a coward who survived when others did not, or run and make a new life. You will be remembered in two realms so change your ways and you'll live to see more sunrises. You have five heartbeats to make the roadway and ten more to get far enough down it that we don't change our minds. Remember that you have seen *nothing* here tonight."

Portman ran. In his combat boots, piss-soaked pants and sweat-soaked black t-shirt, he ran. He ran like Lucifer himself was on his heels, which is exactly what would happen if anyone from DET ever found out that he had survived this night. He stumbled as he ran, seeing only the most rudimentary pathway.

As Portman passed the Lamp House the troll caught his scent and considered giving chase but Rinceoir's belly was full and the smell of the fleeing human wasn't particularly pleasant. That meat had soured.

Portman reached the top of the steps and considered taking the SUV but the keys were on his belt back with the monster. He ran on. He ran right past Nóinín who stayed hidden behind the tree until he was past and then shot him with a sliver-thin dart. In his haste to quit the death zone he felt nothing of the pinprick, and he definitely felt nothing when it was absorbed into his skin and marked him for all Faerie creatures to know. Beauty and Dax may have let the human live but that didn't mean they couldn't keep an eye on this enemy and finish the job if ever the need arose.

Nóinín covered her nose at his unnatural, animal-strong, human stench, and wandered back down to join the party. A hint of sun was starting to light the sky when she found her elf captain and hopped into his lap.

oOo

After wishing Liam and Becca well but reminding them in no uncertain words that two Shields together was expressly forbidden for a reason, the Warriors of Light broke their vials and returned to their bases without having fired a single shot.

Liam wanted to leave the Hunter corpses in their vehicles so they would be found and send a message to the forces of Dark, but after a brief, heated discussion they decided to allow Dax and his elves to drop them into a dead-end branch of the mine and block it with rocks. The masters of the dead Hunters would never know for sure where all of the men disappeared to and that would send a much stronger message than a pile of bodies in a parking lot. There was nothing they could do with the rental vans and trucks so they left them untouched, a problem for the Park Wardens and RCMP to puzzle over.

Sunrise was close when the last of the Hunter corpses were tended to. Liam said a blessing over the mass grave, sad at the waste of life and wondering if this was the right decision, not letting the Hunters' families have closure, but he'd been outvoted. At least he knew where the men and women were so that an anonymous tip someday down the road might set things right.

The dark elves led the sated troll back into the mine, followed by the elves and the pixies. Even though Dax assured her that it was safe for her to return to Faerie, Teagan opted to stay with Liam until Master Wei could confirm with Oberon himself that her time in the upper realm was at an end. She hugged Nóinín quickly, then kissed Dax on the cheek and walked back over to Liam's side. She could see that the Shield was mentally and physically exhausted and leaning heavily on Becca. Dax and Liam shook hands as silent allies who know that the war against the Dark was never over, and then the Fay folk from Faerie slipped back into the mine to make their way home.

Beauty rebuilt the wall as quickly as she could and walked her friends back to the Toyota. She hugged them all and kissed Liam on the top of his balding head. Then she put one huge hand over her heart and the other over Liam's. She grunted, then very clearly said in English in a gravelly voice, "Be well, Shield of Light. Love you."

Liam had said far too many goodbyes in two thousand years to break down and weep at Beauty's feet, but that didn't mean he didn't want to. A kinder soul he had never met. Tonight she could have killed and had good reason to, but she'd spared a man's life after joining a battle that had nothing to do with her other than her friends had asked for her help. Liam stood as tall as he could and covered Beauty's hand with his both his own. "You be well, Beauty. I love you, too. We will meet again."

A car drove by on the road below and Liam snapped out of his reverie. "Time to go, everyone. If we get caught here it will have been a complete waste." Becca hugged Beauty and then Teagan jumped up on the Sasquatch's shoulders and smothered her head with silly kisses before hopping down and spinning back into her dog form. Beauty ever so gently picked up the little Yorkie and kissed her on the nose before handing her to Becca.

Liam lowered himself backwards into the passenger seat and swung his legs up and in. Becca put Phoenix on his lap then buckled his seat belt around him before climbing in the driver's side and starting the car. Beauty turned and loped up the path away from the mine, up toward the valley where she made her home. As they drove away, three sets of eyes cried, as is proper at good-byes.

"Where to now, Loverboy?"

"Back to Cowtown. I have a little place where we can change vehicles and hole up until Coriander gets in touch and we can take this battle back to the next level."

oOo

Baldur, Eilif and Ansfrid materialized quickly and cleanly on their polished agate pads. Liv stood up from her cross-legged lotus position in the centre of the spell-spinning formation and aimed a raised eyebrow at Baldur whose knees and elbows still had sap and pine needles stuck to them.

Baldur smiled. "There and back again. You four are the best."

"Thank you, but you three look more like you were hiking through the woods than battling a small army of Hunters."

"We didn't fire a single shot. The Shields are fine."

"'Shields'? As in plural, more than one in the same location?" She walked across the stone framework separating the sand and the water and met him at the bottom of the steps. "That's why my far-sight was confused."

"Two Shields."

"How many Hunters were there? I counted at least two teams before we sent you."

"Try *four* teams. We weren't there for the final body count but best estimates put it over twenty. It was hard to tell because the troll kept pulling them apart, sucking the meat off them and tossing them in a pile."

"Trolls?"

Ansfrid and Eilif were hanging up their gear and locking their weapons in the safe. Eilif looked back over his shoulder at the little gathering around Baldur. "Just one. But there were elves and dwarves, too, so one troll was plenty."

Ansfrid pulled his Kevlar vest off and hung it on the hook under his nameplate. "Don't forget the pixies. The lights were beautiful. Almost followed one myself."

Jorunn sat down on the steps and sighed. "You guys get all the fun. Trolls, elves, dwarves, pixies and *two* Shields."

"I'm calling 'bollocks' on the whole story." Peder crossed his arms and dared Baldur to keep lying. "It was a false alarm and you three are just having us on."

Baldur looked straight at Liv when he answered Peder's accusation. "There was a Sasquatch, too. Ask your brother—his team was covering the second Shield."

"You saw *Lothar*?"

"Briefly. He looked good. Married life is treating him well. He says 'hallo'. Call him and he'll back us up. In the meantime, I have a report to file. There are some things Brother Paul needs to hear."

"Elves and dwarves and pixies…"

"Oh my."

"I still call 'bollocks'."

oOo

Liam had Becca take the long way around to the storage garage he owned on the east side of Calgary. His corporation owned the rented-out duplex that the huge storage barn backed on to but he'd always kept the barn for himself. The building looked scruffy from the outside with cracked windows and plywood curtains but inside it was fireproof, alarmed and immaculate. It was where Liam kept all of his family's memorabilia as well as two spare vehicles, which, like the storage barn, were better maintained than they appeared from the outside.

The silver 2000 Chevy Cavalier had a couple rust spots but the engine was a turbocharged 350 out of a Camaro and tuned up once a year. With gas from the sealed, hand-pumped reservoir in the corner it would be ready to roll quickly. It was a manual transmission and would be perfect for Becca. Liam's days of driving a shift were done and gone, so the dented-up, packed-with options 2005 Grand Caravan was going to be his new ride.

Phoenix wandered around the building, sniffing out the corners, looking for anything new since they were last here. Becca unloaded their gear from the Corolla on to the cement floor, and Liam leaned against the workbench, watching the two of them and rethinking his decision. He hadn't said it out loud to either of them, but this little assault of theirs on the Dark Complex was going to need a Shield death to make it work and between the two of them he was really the only logical choice. He was fifty years old and struggling to dress himself in the morning, so if his controlled death could strike a deep, bloody blow to the forces of Dark and shift the Balance in favour of the good guys for a while, then this was his time. Which meant that he wasn't going to need the Grand Caravan so Becca might as well take her pick.

He saw no point in bringing that up now, though, because she could take care of it all after he was gone. What he did need to take care of here and now was a little paperwork. He slowly lowered himself down onto his knees on the cement floor and opened the cupboard door, revealing a small fireproof safe. He spun the dial left and right and back left and popped it open.

"Can I help?"

"Please. We'll need that manila envelope." He pulled himself up and Becca took what he needed out of the safe and put it on the workbench. When she turned to face him he looked her straight in the eyes and took her hand in his. "The following is not open for discussion. It's what needs to be done. I know I can count on you. As a matter of fact, you're the only one I know who *will* understand why everything has to be done as I say."

"You're getting bossy in your old age, mister."

"Yes, I am. So here it is. We both know where this is going. It's not our first choice, it's our *only* choice."

"Li—"

"You know I'm right. We're Shields and we do what has to be done. It's never easy but it's what's required of us." He handed her a thick manila envelope. "Call the lawyer on the card inside—he'll know what to do. Please take out the top sheet for me to sign and then it's all yours. He knows to expect a call some day. Half of my revenue stream will pass to you while the other half will be invested until my Awakening. He's my cousin and will do exactly what I've asked, legal or not."

Becca placed the paper in front on Liam and passed him a ballpoint from the pen-and-pencil-filled coffee cup on the bench. He tested the ink on an old newspaper then signed and dated the form.

"Don't you need a Notary to witness it?"

"My cousin will take care of it."

"Li—"

"I also need you to fill in the recovery team when they arrive. They'll take the sword and the Olive Pit off your hands, and get a message to Master Wei about the Faerie situation. Do you mind watching Phoenix until Wei and Oberon reach an agreement?"

"Of course not!"

"It could be awhile. Two days of negotiation in Faerie could be twenty years here."

"I wouldn't have it any other way." She picked up Phoenix and placed her on the bench next to the envelope. "You're welcome to hang out with me as long as you want, just so long..." a tear rolled down her cheek. "Just so long as you don't mind a life beneath the radar."

Phoenix looked at Becca, confused.

Harff.

Liam rubbed her head and his voice cracked. "We're coming to the end, my dear friend."

Phoenix barked sharply and snapped at Liam's hand. She missed, but intentionally.

"Yes. We knew this day would come. Frankly, it's taken longer than I expected and I'm thankful for every extra minute we've had together. I'm also grateful that we actually have time to say good-bye and that you're going to be safe. The expectation for the last thirty years was that I would keep you safe as long as I could and then either Oberon or the Dark would put me down and take you."

Harff. Harff.

"Becca would you please find her Highness' clothes. She wants me to say this to her real face."

"Of course." She went in search of the t-shirt and tights she was pretty sure Beauty had tossed in the back seat. Liam turned back to Phoenix.

"Miss P, my biggest fear for the last three decades has been that I would fail and you would die."

Harff.

"We always knew we couldn't run forever. This isn't a battle, it's a war."

Harff.

Becca found the clothes and put them on the front passenger seat then lifted Phoenix up and into the car. She and Liam turned their backs and the lights swirled and flashed behind them, as Phoenix became Teagan once again.

Whistle.

The two Shields turned in time to see the pixie leap from the car to the workbench where she grabbed Liam by the end of his nose and squeezed hard.

"Hey! Ouch!"

Whistle, whistle, whistle!

"Am I wrong? Does this have to be done?"

Whistle.

"None of us like it, but without sacrifice there is no honour. I have to die sometime and if this one act could save thousands or even millions of lives and shift the Balance our way for a few decades or even just years, then I don't see how there's much of a choice."

Whistle?

"Of course I love you. You're my family." He did a quick mental calculation. "You've been with me longer than anyone, including Becca, who was Lynette at the time."

Whistle?

"Yes, really. If I could have you with me forever like Paul has had Ozzy by his side, I would. But Paul is more than just a Shield and Ozzy is a dog. He's a very special dog, but he's still a dog. You're a beautiful, brilliant Pixie Princess who has a life to go live. You have love to find—"

Whistle!

"When? Oh, no, not the elf?!"

Whistle.

"Well, there you go, proving my point. Go, have your life. Get married and have pixelf babies. Or would they be elfixies?"

Whistle!

"I am *not* being a smart ass. It's an honest question."

Whistle.

"My point is, I have to do this and we all know there's no choice."

Teagan threw her arms around him and Becca stepped in and hugged them both. The three of them stayed like that for a while before Liam tapped out.

"We don't know when she'll 'call' so we'd better get some sleep. We'll fold the seats down in the Caravan. The building is alarmed and reinforced and we're armed. Besides, I don't think there are too many Hunters in the vicinity to take up the chase right now. We have some time."

The three of them curled up together and slept as a family, their first and last time.

oOo

Coriander pulled Hussein's truck off into the scrub and shut it off. She was a long way from civilization but Hussein was right when he suggested that it would be safer for everyone if she were away from everyone when she did what she was planning. She took the blanket she'd brought and placed it on the ground, then thought twice and laid it out in the bed of the truck. She wasn't particularly squeamish but tarantulas and scorpions were more than mere bugs.

She got set up as quickly as she could but when she reached for the mallet and bowl she hesitated. She took a deep breath and looked up at the stunningly star-lit night sky. This far from the lights of town the Milky Way was easy to see as she gazed at their galaxy edge-wise. It took that breath away and the next few, too. They lived in a magnificent world and if there was something they could do to help save it, then Honour, Trust, and Integrity demanded that they put aside personal agendas and do what they could. She smiled and found another breath, then pricked her finger and drew blood.

oOo

The jet was beginning its descent when Takeko finally got free of the crate. Getting out wasn't the hard part; it was doing it without alerting the Hunters seated a few metres away that was the challenge. She lowered the lid back in place and re-latched the lock, just in case she needed to buy herself some time. The tiny door leading into the cabin proper was closed but she knew that would change, sooner or later. She looked around for a place to hide but other than her crate, there was nowhere even her slender Japanese frame might squeeze into. She rubbed her wrists to get the circulation back in her hands and rotated her shoulders slowly. They hadn't actually been dislocated, they just felt that way. Her nerves screamed at her to stop the rotation but she knew there was no choice. She no longer had the luxury of time. She had to be ready to move when the opportunity presented it—

The door opened and a Hunter stepped into view. Without finishing her thought she leaped straight into his chest and knocked his head hard against the crate. His neck snapped but she didn't care because she was already drawing his weapon from its shoulder holster before his last heartbeat faded away.

The Hunters were all big men, mostly ex-military and ex-police, so they sat head and shoulders above the jet's seats, which made target acquisition so much easier for Takeko. She didn't stop to ask questions or shout a warning or a stupid martial arts kiai. Centuries ago she had learned to achieve the same results without warning the enemy the blow was coming. She fired five fast shots and hit four heads. The fifth man managed to duck behind his seat while likely drawing a weapon but Takeko pumped three more shots into the back of his chair, working down toward the floor. The non-shatter plastic frame and foam seat padding were no match for even the sub-sonic rounds.

Not giving him a chance to recover from the shock, Takeko charged his hiding spot, slamming two more rounds through the two seats. There was a chance he would shoot her feet out from under her so she kept moving until she was right on top of him. Her worry was unnecessary—one of her shots had taken out his throat chakra and another had violated his third eye chakra. A close look revealed that it was Demetri. Good riddance.

oOo

Liam felt a gentle touch on his mind and woke suddenly.

"Me, Coriander."

"Hi." He nudged Becca and she woke easily. Teagan stirred and sat up, then all three of them climbed out of the van.

"Hi. Ready?"

"Ready."

"Sure we do this?"

"Sure. War not won by waiting."

"So true. Coordinates here and ready."

Becca placed a bag of rags on the floor next to the workbench and helped Liam to sit down. "Might as well be comfortable."

"Not a luxury we get too often in the dying side of this life we lead."

"No, it isn't."

oOo

The smell of gunpowder in the small cabin was overwhelming and Takeko was amazed that none of her shots had punctured the fuselage. With her weapon still in firing position, ready to acquire a target, she turned and noticed two holes in the forward bulkhead at about the same time the door to the cockpit crashed open and a woman dressed in a crisp white blouse and uniform tie of flight crew stepped out with a massive piece of shining steel aimed at the Shield's chest. Takeko didn't hesitate, pulling the trigger twice more, aiming for the woman's unprotected centre mass. The crewmember went down without firing a shot and Takeko now saw that the woman was holding a Colt Python. A .357 Magnum calibre, the Python was probably the stupidest handgun to have on an aircraft. Takeko knew it was deadly accurate and had a smooth trigger pull, but one shot at this range would have cored a hole through her, the rear bulkhead, and anything else between the shooter and the night air. Stupid cow, bringing a cannon to a gunfight, she thought.

Through the open cockpit door she could see the back of the pilot's head and shoulders. The co-pilot was out of sight, which, considering the small size of the cockpit was quite an achievement.

"Pull the trigger and kill us both, Shield."

"Come out, come out, wherever you are."

"There's just the two of us."

"Bull. This jet uses a crew of three."

"My co-pilot was doubling as the stew. You just killed my back-up."

Takeko could only see one of his hands on the stick so she knew the other held a weapon. "Come on, Captain. This doesn't have to end this way. If you know I'm a Shield then you know I'm not afraid to die. But are *you* ready? Considering who you work for, are you ready to pay the price, fulfill whatever contract you signed?" She took two steps forward, trying to get an angle that would guarantee a kill without damaging the flight controls or blowing out the windshield. She couldn't get one.

"I don't plan on being the one to die up here, Light-trash bitch."

oOo

Teagan walked around the van solemnly and slowly, carrying Liam's sheathed Japanese tanto. Razor sharp, it would make it as quick and clean as possible. Liam held his hands out for the tanto but Teagan shook her head.

Whistle.

"Thank you, but no one does this but me. I'll not have either of you living with the fact that you had to kill me. So what if I get reborn a moment later, the weight is there, and only I will bear it." In silence Teagan reluctantly handed the Shield his weapon. He accepted it and nodded his thanks. "This isn't going to be sepuku, girls. I'm going for one quick thrust up under the rib cage and into the heart, not a ritualized Japanese suicide."

oOo

Takeko had run out of time. Through the windshield she could see a sprawling city. Somewhere in the United States, she suspected. It's been two lifetimes since I was last in America, she thought, just before she pulled the trigger and sent a round into the Captain's temple as he turned and poked his own weapon around the side of his seat.

Unlike his co-pilot who went down fast and silent, the captain's death-twitch pulled the trigger and a single round from a semi-automatic of some sort punched through Takeko's abdomen and severed her spine. She collapsed like a dropped doll, letting out her last breath as Takeko just as the autopilot lowered the landing gear and lifted the flying coffin's nose just enough to let the rear gear touch down first.

oOo

Liam nearly dropped the blade in shock. Into the link the four of them had formed he shouted. "What?!"

"Shield Death!" They all saw the flare of Light and in the tapestry and the following dark spot.

"Now?!"

"Now!" The unravelling was just as disturbing the second time around and darkening of that region was heartbreaking.

"Disaster?" The flare of a Shield's soul lit up a distant corner of the weave, off in a completely different direction.

"Coming. Have coordinates?"

"Have them. Ready to go."

"Where?"

"Santiago, Chile. I guide."

In their minds they all saw the spark that was Takeko leave her body and move on to be reborn.

"COMING!!" Coriander's mental shout through the blood link shattered their wandering thoughts about who it might have been and was their death quick.

"Earthquake! Massive! Power manifesting..." She was ready this time and so was able to focus faster on the pattern and the weave and the unnatural twisting of it. "Solomon Sea, beneath Misima Island, east-by-southeast Papua New Guinea! This it!"

Liam dropped the sword and Becca held him tight. Teagan joined in and they gave their power to Coriander. Becca could see the tapestry now and the building disturbance. "Grab! Wrap wills around and drag away, out to sea. Coriander, concentrate on coordinates, guide us. Lead us!"

Liam cried out, frustrated. "Can't see damned thing! You sure about this?"

Becca spoke aloud, in his ear. "This is it, Lover. Do you feel the power? The reverberating, low, soul-shaking sub-woofer of power? A Shield has just died, feel it, draw it in, and move with us."

He lowered his mental defences and... felt it! "Got it! Not a big one. Might fade away. Can we make it that far and still have power?"

Coriander was almost cheerful. "Halfway there! Zeroing on coordinates. Direct the blast? Restrict affected area? City nearby. Very close."

Liam couldn't see what the women saw but he could think. "Direct power down. Imagine large pipe straight down, over and around enemy. Push pipe down into ground, down deep into bedrock and hold. Hold as long as can keep shocks from spreading. Can't stop all but maybe minimize. Make sense?"

"Sense!"

"Perfect!"

"Got it!"

"Teagan?!"

"Me! In the head!"

"You have beautiful voice! Must hear—"

"NOW!"

With Coriander in the lead, focussing on the exact coordinates, the four of them took the force of the post-Shield-death disaster and directed it straight down into the ground beneath the DökktEfniTækni complex.

Chapter Nineteen: Good News/Bad News

The tension around the office was palatable but Rhianna did her best to tune it out while she analyzed what was happening to ShieldBreaker. Her screen was full of false positives, low percentages that only two days before were meaning confirmation, and Shield IDs that didn't even make sense. In only four hours there had been two repeats of the bad kill in Tasmania and Hunter Command had suspended the use of ShieldBreaker indefinitely.

She slammed her palm down on her desk when her tenth or eleventh attempt to break the problem down failed. "Damn it!!"

Heads prairie-dogged above the various cubicle walls.

"Doesn't anyone have a clue what the Hell is happening? Or even where Mr. Tabak is?"

"He got canned! They're meeting now to pick a replacement." A male voice piped up near the far wall, beside the supply room.

"Is that you, Cho? How do you...?" This was stupid, yelling back and forth. "Everybody, staff meeting. My desk. Now!"

The entire ShieldBreaker development team were on edge, worried about their jobs and even their lives, so they gathered quickly at Rhianna's desk. She did a head count and came up one short.

"Where's Pia?"

They all shrugged, except chubby Cho. "Bathroom. Monthly Mess."

J.J. slapped his arm. "Eres un cerdo... a pig!"

"You know you *love* it."

Before J.J. could rebutt the remark, the four-foot-long hanging fluorescent light fixtures started swaying above their heads on their chains. Then Rhianna's plastic LINUX penguin danced to the edge of the shelf of her cubicle and did a nose dive onto the desk and bounced to the floor. All over the office anything that wasn't nailed down commenced dancing to no discernable music.

"Quake!" Cho dove under a nearby desk, remembering his training from his childhood in Qinghai.

"Madre de dios!" J.J. crossed herself and dropped to her knees. "Dios en el cielo arriba, perdóname porque he pecado."

From under her own desk Rhianna glared at J.J. "*You're* the traitor, the Light spy! You're the one who told them about—." Pia's blood-curdling scream from the washroom cut off Rhianna's fury.

oOo

Mick Crowley dropped his weekender bag in the hall outside the conference room of the DET Santiago complex and charged into the board meeting, removing his Burberry overcoat as he searched for and found an open seat. There were twenty-one leather chairs around the massive tempered glass and walnut table and only three were empty. Two, now. Eighteen heads—ten men and eight women—turned to acknowledge Crowley's entrance, most nodding as much of a greeting as they dared.

Tau Drake stood at the head of the table, leaning on his fists. He stood in Wallace Tabak's place and although he stood a head shorter than Tabak, the fury he projected at this moment dwarfed his predecessor and everyone in the room.

"Crowley. About time."

Mick nodded. Power-wielders at this level didn't apologize or grovel. Obsequiousness was the domain of their assistants and aides.

"Two minutes to bring everyone up to speed and then we make the kind of decisions that make lesser men and women weep." His gaze cruised around the table, looking for anyone not entirely in the moment, anyone who would not leave the building alive.

"ShieldBreaker failed. Miserably. It was brilliant, it was genius incarnate, but someone at DET leaked it to Wei and they were able to create counter-measures before we could lock it in place and forge a protective firewall that didn't interfere with its capabilities. Tabak's team was brilliant but Wei's people were stellar. But they had help and we are going to cull every damned weak link in this organization to find any and all non-supporters." As he spoke he surveyed the leaders of the Dark for any guilty, downcast or avoiding eyes. There were none.

"Good. You understand me. Tabak is gone. *Terminated from the top.* He was a good man and ShieldBreaker had great potential, but this is not an organization known for its sentimentality and scrapbooking." He paused to drink from the Waterford crystal glass on the table in front of him and the others took advantage of the moment to drink, shift position, or just take a breath. A wrong move at the wrong moment in this room could mean death.

"I redirected three nearby Hunter Teams to Calgary to get this damned Shield. She's teamed up with another Shield and the searchers have detected *three* Loci between the two of them. I'm waiting to hear back from the Team Leaders. Due to the leaks here we did not receive the live feeds."

"*Three Loci?* Which ones?"

Drake smiled at Kristine Lazik, the first woman director of DET. "Charlemagne's Sword, Bunjil's Pipe, and Noah's Olive Pit. There's also the Pixie Princess that Oberon has a hate-on for."

"*And* the pixie?".

"Yes, I know. ShieldBreaker failed, but not before it brought us five more Loci."

"I heard we got the Grail." Crowley was the junior board member but never one to hesitate to face the issue at hand.

"Yes, we got the Grail again. We lost the Bracers in a blitz recovery attack in China but the Grail is in transit." He drank again and they all breathed. "We're here to achieve two goals. One: fill Wallace Tabak's vacant seat with a CEO. Two: commence a purge of all elements of Light from this organization. I have a team looking into ShieldBreaker and what, if anything, can be salvaged from the fiasco."

Axler Rhodes leaned forward to make eye contact with Drake. "Aren't we the ones who are supposed to infiltrate *them*?"

"Trust me, we have. That's how we've found out so quickly. Our people are moving up in Wei's organization slowly but surely."

"Can we not please just bomb the crap out of them?"

"They've moved their 'Campus of Light' twice in the last three years. We're close."

"I hear they took a Hunter in Australia."

"They did, but I'm not worried—he's trained to survive every measure of torture they can devise. Speaking of which, *we* caught another Shield, this one in Cape Town."

"Drake, you've avoided the little stock market 'problem'."

"It's been taken care. Fixed. We survived, thanks in fact to the techs on the ShieldBreaker team. Not only have we crushed the bug responsible, but the incoming Shield is his sister, so there *will* be a reckoning."

"How bad was the hit to the share price?"

"We lost 8.2% overall when the markets closed, but we expect a full recovery."

"What effect will this ShieldBreaker mess have?"

"Look, I understand everyone's concern but there's an emergency shareholders' meeting next Tuesday and we'll address financial issues there. Nominations for CEO?"

"I nom—". But Mick Crowley didn't finish his nomination because he got distracted by the dancing Waterford crystal as all of the glasses simultaneously shimmied across the tabletop. Then everything in the conference room jumped six inches in the air as if the building had belched. When it all came back down the table cracked in two and half of the board members were knocked to the floor.

"What the f—". Drake's last word went with him to his grave because the bottom fell out of the planet and everyone in the DökktEfniTækni complex went into free-fall just long enough to recognize the end of their world as they knew it

oOo

Brother Paul tapped lightly on the bamboo doorframe of Master

Wei's sanctuary and waited, Ozzy at his side.

"Paul. Please come in. Do you have word from Brother Eleazar?" Master Wei poured a second cup of tea and placed it before Paul. Ozzy found his water dish in the corner and curled up next to it.

"I do."

"And...?"

"Master, in however many centuries we have been doing our best to maintain Balance I have used the phrase 'Good News/Bad News' a great many times."

"And this would be another occasion for it?"

"This would be *the* occasion for it."

"Then because I like to end discussions on an upbeat note, hit me with the bad news first."

"Brother Eleazar—Liam—has..." He still wasn't sure exactly how to phrase the news, because it wasn't really all that bad. "Liam ambushed and killed approximately twenty-four Dark Hunters."

"That's a pretty serious achievement for a Shield whose very survival depends on staying below the radar."

"We knew a showdown was coming to him."

"How many casualties on our side?"

"None. We didn't really participate."

"He did all of this himself, in his condition?"

"Um, no. The Princess summoned forces from Faerie and there was a slaughter."

"*Faerie* did this?"

"A son of Oberon in fact *led* them."

"Fairies killed humans, here, in this realm?"

"Technically it was elves, dark elves, pixies, and a very hungry troll."

"In *this* realm?"

"Yes sir. I'm preparing a complete report for you."

"Are the two Shields still together?"

"Well, that's the next part of the bad news."

"Multi-part bad news... Paul, you've been busy."

"Not me. Liam has been; and Becca."

"The second part involves them as well? What more trouble could these two possibly have gotten themselves into?" He sipped his tea and offered Paul a cookie on a plate. "Fresh from the cafeteria. Quite good." Paul accepted and continued.

"We're still completely out of the loop as to how they managed to do this next thing, but apparently Liam killed one-hundred-and-twelve people in South America."

"All the way from Alberta? This isn't bad news, it's a miracle." He sipped, calm, half-smiling. "Brother Paul, who has fed you this interesting fiction?"

"I have confirmation from multiple sources world-wide."

"We'll rule out mass-hysteria for the time being. Go on."

"Sister Nura has died in a plane crash while being taken to a Dark facility for extended torture, we assume."

Master Wei placed his cup down and rang the small brass bell beside him. "I'm sorry to hear that. How many were lost in the follow-up disaster?"

"One-hundred-and-twelve."

"That's the same number that Liam is being given responsibility for."

"Exactly. It's the *same* event. Our Tracking Team in Italy determined that a small quake was about to strike off Papua New Guinea but a spell-spinning team in Utah watched as the force was redirected from the South Pacific to Santiago, Chile."

"Santiago?"

"Exactly."

"I'm going to take a wild guess and suggest that this is where the good news comes in, because right about now your report needs some."

"The quake hit on the *exact* coordinates of the suspected DökktEfniTækni headquarters."

"Well, it's about time someone did something about that building not being up to code."

"How do you want me to handle this, sir? This is pretty unShield-like behaviour even for this particular Shield."

"One of your thorough investigations would seem in order. Anyone we know die at DET?"

"The entire Board of Directors, sir."

"Hmm... that will set them back a few years. My first instinct is to throw a party because this is a monumental day. Our people work hard and sacrifice so much for the low pay we offer. But a party to celebrate an enemy's death would be crass in anyone's eyes."

"It most certainly would, sir."

"Then again, I haven't done anything crass since we celebrated the end of the abolition of slavery, so I think I'm about due." He took a last sip of his cooling tea and stood up, smiling. "Maybe a special service in the Peace Lounge for our fallen enemies... with music and dancing. I'm in the mood for a little ABBA."

oOo

It was early September, but it was a cool evening when Coriander pulled the Grand Caravan into the driveway of the bungalow. She touched a button on the dashboard and the small screen above the Blu-ray player showed no warm bodies outside the house within ten metres. She triggered the remote control to open the garage door and kept one eye on the screen to see if there was any quick movement indicating an attack or impending breach.

All was quiet so she slowly drove the Caravan into the garage, still not believing that there was enough room for the mirrors to clear the narrow arch. She pulled up until a scruffy tennis ball hanging on a string from the ceiling touched the windshield, indicating that she was far enough in. The overhead door closed behind her automatically and the connecting door to the house opened.

The official report from Brother Paul's investigation said that she was removed from the spell-spinning program because of her blatant disregard for Shield safety and for putting the entire complex at risk. Unofficially, her transfer was a welcome change. The stress was equal if not greater, but it was a labour of love she was glad to take on. She shut off the engine and got out of the vehicle. As she walked around to the rear of the van a voice spoke from the shadowed doorway into the house.

"Need a hand with the groceries?"

"No, sir, I do *not*. You're not getting out of your physiotherapy that easily. Get back in there and finish working that left shoulder."

"Daily physio creates a Pattern and I'm supposed to avoid Patterns, or did no one ever teach you that?" Liam held his cane in what had once been a nearly useless left hand. His grip was far from strong, but the improvement was clearly visible.

"Nice try. Taking a crap at 7 AM every morning creates a Pattern, too, but I don't see you changing that any time soon."

"Who put you in charge, anyway?"

Cor slid open the door and started transferring the four boxes of groceries from the van to the workbench behind her. "Well, it's a toss-up between Master Wei and Grandma. They both gave me strict instructions."

"You *know* she hates being called that. She's only four years older than you."

"She said was born the year Julius Caesar was assassinated! She's almost as old as you are!"

"Fine, if you don't need my help I'll put the kettle on. Little Princess Sunshine wants to go for a walk before dinner but I convinced her to at least wait until we've had a cup."

"Just so long as we're home in time to watch the Forty-Niners game."

"They've beaten the Packers three games in a row so what makes you think it'll be a game worth watching?"

"It's the Niners—nothing else matters." An answering hoarse bark came from within the house. Cor closed the van and picked up the first box, carrying it into the house. Liam stepped back inside and to one side to let her pass.

"I guess it's another Monday night dinner in front of the television with my two girls."

"You know you love it." She put the box on the kitchen counter and returned to the garage.

"Yah, I guess I do."

"Did you hear from Grandma today?"

"Just before you got home. She posted a coded message on her Wall saying all's well and she sends her love." He sat up on a kitchen stool, out of the way as Cor came in with the second box.

"Once we get the secured house network set-up I'll load Skype, and we can chat with her face-to-face, Grandpa."

"I'd like that. Thank you."

oOo

Becca sat on the back deck of the rented cottage and stared out over Southern Ontario's Georgian Bay. A sleeping, ten-week-old, Yorkshire terrier puppy lay on her lap. "This is the life, isn't it, Sedona?"

The leaves were just starting to change colour and all across the province, families were watching the setting sun light up the maples, oaks, elms, and poplars like it was their last autumn. She sipped her grapefruit juice and leaned back in the rocker, rubbing her belly. There was no bump, yet, but she was far too attuned to her body's rhythms to not know she was pregnant.

ooOoo

This is not about the objects themselves — the Grail, the Pebble, the Wand — but is rather about the people who originally imbued the objects with a portion of their hearts and souls, and it is about those who would protect that, even with their lives."

~Shield Master Wei (circa 879 CE, after penning his epic poem Beowulf.)

The Author's Note About Phoenix
(10-25-2014)

On October 23rd, 2014, at 12:43pm Mountain Time, Phoenix passed away peacefully in my arms, next to my heart—the only place she ever really wanted to be. Even though she was only ten years old, she was very sick and was not expected to live out the day. I chose to have a loving vet give Phoenix a calm, peaceful end, rather than one of fear and loneliness if she had died while I was away at work. She passed away feeling the sun on her face, and every ounce of love I have. That was two days ago, and the pain in my heart is indescribable. If you fell in love with her in this story, thank you. She really was so much more than just a dog—she saved my life.

Phoenix and me, in Bankhead, Alberta.
Rest in Peace, Princess P.

About the Author

"Canada's modern-day Aesop" (Barbara Budd, CBC Radio) is Timothy Reynolds—an internationally-published Canadian writer, photographer, a winner of *Kobo Writing Life's Jeffrey Archer Short Story Challenge*, a *2016 Baen Fantasy Adventure Award* finalist, and a Honorable Mention winner in both the *Writers of the Future* and the *Illustrators of the Future* Contests.

Tim thinks of himself as a 'twistorian', bending and twisting history into fictional shapes for sheer entertainment.

His popular humorous column in SEARCH Magazine (www.SEARCHMagazine.net) recounts some of the more bizarre G-Rated true tales from his life lived.

Originally from London, Ontario, he grew up in Toronto, but has called Calgary, Alberta home since 1999.

He can be found online at *www.tgmreynolds.com,*
www.TheTaoOfTim.com (blog)
@TGMReynolds (Twitter)
or Amazon's Author Central:
www.amazon.com/-/e/B003KCV338.

Thank you for reading **'The Broken Shield'**.
As a bit of a treat, check out the website for photos and the stories behind some of the Loci of Light:
www.tgmreynolds.com

Other Books by
Timothy Reynolds

· ***Waking Anastasia*** from Tyche Books. 2016.
      (Long-Listed for Alberta Readers' Choice Award)
· ***The Death of God and other Stories*** from
      Cometcatcher Press. 2015.
· ***the Cynglish Beat*** from Cometcatcher Press. 2010.
· ***Stand Up & Succeed*** from Cometcatcher Press. 2006.